Qiu Xiaolong

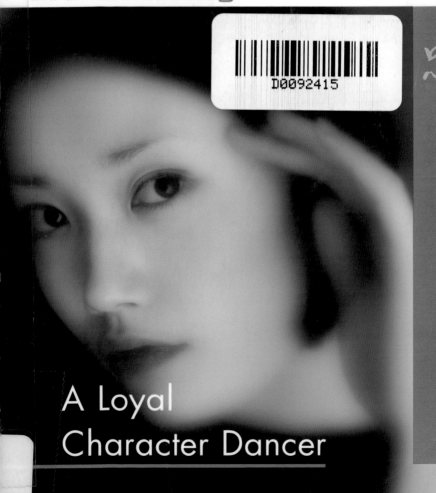

A Loyal Character Dancer

A
LOYAL
CHARACTER
DANCER

Qiu Xiaolong

SOHO

First published in the United States in 2002

by

Soho Press, Inc.
853 Broadway
New York, NY 10003

Library of Congress Cataloging-in-Publication Data

Qiu, Xiaolong, 1953–
    A loyal character dancer / Qiu Xiaolong.
        p. cm.
    ISBN 1-56947-341-2
    1. Police—China—Shanghai—Fiction. 2. Americans—China—
Fiction. 3. Shanghai (China)—Fiction. 4. Missing persons—Fiction.
I. Title.

    PS3553.H537 L69 2002
    813'.6—dc21

                                                                2002070580

10   9   8   7   6   5   4   3   2   1

For Julia

Acknowledgments

I want to thank my friends Marvin Reno, David Walsh, Brenda Seale, and Richard Newman for their help. I also want to thank my editor Laura Hruska, whose hard work has helped the characters dance on the pages.

A LOYAL CHARACTER DANCER

Chapter 1

Chief Inspector Chen Cao, of the Shanghai Police Bureau, found himself once again walking through the morning mist toward Bund Park.

In spite of its relatively small size, about fifteen acres, the location of the park made it one of the most popular places in Shanghai. At the Bund's northern end, the front gate of the park faced the Peace Hotel across the street, and its back gate connected with the Waibaidu Bridge, a name that remained unchanged since its completion in the colonial era, meaning literally *Foreign White Crossing Bridge*. The park was especially celebrated for its promenade of multicolored flagstones, a long curved walkway raised above the shimmering expanse of water which joined the Huangpu and Suzhou rivers. From its height, people could look out to view vessels coming and going against the distant Wusongkou, the East China Sea.

The front gatekeeper, a gray-haired, red-armbanded woman surnamed Zhu, yawned and nodded to Chen on that April morning as he tossed a green plastic token into the token box. Several of the people who worked there knew him well.

That morning, Chen was one of the earliest birds to arrive in the park. He walked to a clearing in the central area that was surrounded by poplar and willow trees. The white European-style pavilion with its spacious verandah stood out in pleasant relief against the newly painted green benches. The dewdrops clinging to the foliage glistened in the dawn light like a myriad of clear eyes.

The appeal of the park was enhanced for Chen by its associations. In his elementary-school years, he had read about the park's history. The official textbook of the time said that at the turn of the century the park had been open only to Western expatriates. There had been signs on the gates saying: *No Chinese or dogs allowed,* and red-turbaned Sikh guards stood there to bar the way. After 1949, the Communist government considered this a good example of Western powers' attitudes in pre-Communist China, and it was often cited in patriotism education. Had this actually happened? It was hard to establish the truth now, as the line between truth and fiction was always being constructed and deconstructed by those in power.

He mounted a flight of steps to the promenade, breathing in the fresh air of the waterfront. Petrels glided over the waves, their wings flashing in the gray light, as if flying out of a half-forgotten dream. The dividing line between the Huangpu River and Suzhou River became visible.

The park appealed to Chief Inspector Chen, however, for a more personal reason than its beauty or history.

In the early seventies, as a waiting-for-assignment high-school graduate, out of school, out of a job, he had come to practice tai chi in the park. Two or three months later, one mist-enveloped morning, after yet another halfhearted attempt at copying the ancient poses, he came upon a worn-out English textbook on a bench. How the book came to have been left there, he failed to discover. People sometimes placed old newspapers or magazines on the seats as protection from the dampness, but never a textbook. He carried the book to the park for several weeks, hoping someone might claim it. No one did. Then one morning, frustrated with an extremely difficult tai chi pose, he opened the book at random. From then on, he studied English instead of tai chi in the park.

His mother had worried about that change. It was not considered in good political taste to read any book except *Quotations from Chairman Mao*. However, his father, a neo-Confucian scholar, predicted that studying in the park might be propitious for him, in accordance with the ancient theory of *wuxing*: Among the five elements in Chen, water was lacking a little, so any place in association with water would benefit him. Years later, when he tried to look up that particular theory, Chen could not find it. Perhaps it had been made up for his benefit.

Those mornings in the park sustained him through the years of the Cultural Revolution. And in 1977, he entered Beijing Foreign Language University, having obtained a top English score on the newly restored college entrance examination. Four years later he was assigned, through another combination of circumstances, to a job at the Shanghai Police Bureau.

In retrospect, Chen's life seemed to be full of the ironic causalities of misplaced yin and yang, like that misplaced book in the park, or his misplaced youth of those years. One thing led to another, and to still another, so the result could hardly be recognized. The chain of causality was perhaps more intricate than Western mystery writers, whose works he translated in his spare time, would care to admit.

On the cool April breeze, a melody wafted over from the big clock atop the Shanghai Customs Building. Six thirty. It had played another tune during the Cultural Revolution: "The East Is Red." Time flowed away like water.

In the early nineties, under Deng Xiaoping's economic reform, Shanghai had been changing dramatically. Across Zhongshan Road, a long vista of magnificent buildings, which had once housed the most prestigious Western companies in the early part of the century and then Communist Party institutions after 1950, were now welcoming back those Western companies in an effort to reclaim the Bund's status as China's Wall Street. Bund Park, too, had been changing, though he did not like some of the changes. For example, the postmodern concrete River Pavilion stood like a monster beside him, slouching against the first gray of the morning, watching. So, too, had Chen changed from a penniless student to a prominent chief inspector of police.

Still, it remained his park. In spite of a heavy work load, he managed to come here once or twice a week. It was close to the bureau, a fifteen-minute walk.

Not too far away, a middle-aged man practiced tai chi, striking a series of poses: *grasping a bird's tail, spreading a white crane's wings, parting a wild horse's mane on both sides* . . . Chief Inspector Chen wondered what he might have become had he persisted in practicing. Perhaps he would now be like that tai chi devotee, wearing a white silk martial arts costume, loose-sleeved, red-silk-buttoned, with a peaceful expression on his face. Chen knew him. An accountant in an almost bankrupt state-run company, yet at that moment, a master moving in perfect harmony with the *qi* of the universe.

Chen took his customary seat, a green-painted bench which stood under a towering poplar tree. Carved on the back of the bench in small characters was a slogan that had been popular during the Cultural Revolution: *Long Live the Proletarian Dictatorship*. The bench had been repainted a couple of times, but the message showed through.

He took a collection of *ci* out of his briefcase and opened to a poem by Niu Xiji. *The mist disappearing / against the spring mountains, / the stars few, small / in the pale skies, / the sinking moon illuminates her face, / the dawn in her glistening tears / at parting.* . . . It was too sentimental for the morning. He skipped several lines to reach the last couplet: *With the green skirt of yours in my mind, everywhere, / everywhere I step over the grass so lightly.*

Another coincidence, he mused, tapping his fingers on the bench back. Not too long ago, in a riverfront café on the Bund, he had read this couplet for a friend, who now stepped over the green grass far, far away. Chief Inspector Chen had not come here, however, to indulge in nostalgia.

The successful completion of a major political case, involving Baoshen, the vice mayor of Beijing, had led to unexpected repercussions in his professional work, and in his personal life, too. He was still emotionally as well as physically drained. In a recent letter to his girlfriend Ling, he had written, "As our ancient sage says, 'Eight or nine out of ten times, things go wrong in this world of ours.' People are no more than the chance products of good or bad luck in spite of their intentional efforts." She had not replied, which did not surprise him. Their relationship was strained because of that case.

A gray-Mao-jacketed figure appeared behind him and addressed him in a serious, subdued voice, "Comrade Chief Inspector Chen."

He recognized Zhang Hongwei, a senior park security officer. In the seventies, Zhang had worn a Mao badge on his jacket, patrolling energetically as if steel springs had been installed under his feet, casting mistrustful glances at the English textbook in Chen's hand. Now a bald, wrinkled man in his fifties, Zhang walked with a shuffle, his gray Mao jacket unchanged, except for the missing Mao badge.

"Please come with me, Comrade Chief Inspector Chen."

He followed Zhang to a corner partially obscured by a cluster of evergreens level with the embankment, about fifteen feet away from the back gate. Lying on the ground, supine, was a mutilated body with multiple wounds, from which blood had spread in a surreal web. A line of red spots led from the bank to the place where the body lay.

Chief Inspector Chen had never dreamed that he would be called to examine a murder scene in Bund Park.

"I was making my morning round when I came upon it, Comrade Chief Inspector Chen. You often come here in the morning, we all know," Zhang said apologetically, "so—"

"When did you make your rounds this morning?"

"At about six. Immediately after the park opened."

"When did you make your rounds last night?"

"Eleven thirty. We checked several times before closing. No one was left here."

"So you're sure—"

Their conversation was interrupted by a peal of laughter ringing from the bank near the gate. There, a young woman posed with a Japanese umbrella for a young man's camera. Sitting on the embankment wall, she leaned her upper body out over the water. A dangerous pose. Her cheeks flushed, and the camera flashed. Possibly a young couple on a honeymoon trip. A romantic day starting with picture-taking in Bund Park.

"Vacate the park and close it for the morning," Chen ordered, frowning. He wrote a number on the back of a bookmark. "Dial this number from your office. Detective Yu Guangming's number. Ask him to come here as soon as possible."

As Zhang hurried away, Chen began to examine the body. A male in his early forties, of medium height and build, dressed in expensive-looking white silk pajamas. His face was blood-smeared and bore deep cuts, and the left side of his skull had been smashed by a heavy blow. It was hard to imagine what he might have looked like alive, but it did not take a medical examiner to see that he had been hacked more than a dozen times with some sharp and heavy weapon, heavier than a knife. The cuts on his shoulders were deep, to the bone. Considering the multiple wounds, there was surprisingly little blood on the ground.

There was only one pocket in the pajama top. Chen reached into it. Nothing there. Nor could he see any clothes label. Carefully, he touched the parts of the corpse's lower jaw and neck not covered in blood. Rigidity was noticeable, but the rest of the body was still relatively soft. There was some lividity in the legs. At the pressure of his finger, the discolored purplish spots blanched. So death had probably occurred four or five hours earlier.

He pulled up the dead man's eyelid—a bloodshot eye stared at the sky, which was dappled with clouds. The corneas were not yet opaque, reinforcing his estimate that death was recent.

How did such a body come to be found in Bund Park?

There was one thing Chief Inspector Chen knew about the park's security management. The security officers as well as the retired volunteer workers made their evening rounds diligently, looking in all directions, shouting over loudspeakers, "Hurry up! It's time!" and flashing their flashlights at lovers in shadowy corners before the gate was closed. They had once made a special report to the bureau about it, trying to justify extra funding for their night work. With the severe housing shortage in Shanghai, the park lent itself to the romantic yearning of young people who had no privacy at home and could easily forget the passage of time and the public nature of the space. Security did a thorough job here. Zhang had been adamant in ruling out the possibility of anybody hiding in the park before it closed, and Chen believed him.

Alternatively, people could have sneaked in after closing time; it would not have taken much effort to climb over the walls. One could have killed the other, then fled. However, traffic and pedestrians passed the area all night. Surely such an incident would have been seen and reported. The scene around the bushes did not support this hypothesis, either. There was no sign of a struggle. Two or three broken twigs were about all Chief Inspector Chen could discover. The fact that the body was dressed in pajamas further suggested that the murder had occurred earlier, in a room, from which the dead body had been moved into the park. Perhaps the body had been thrown from the river. The embankment was not high. At night's high tide, a body hurled from a boat could have landed on the embankment and rolled down into the bushes, which would also explain the line of the dark spots left on the bank.

But there was something puzzling Chen. No one would have tried to dispose of a body here without foreseeing its immediate discovery. The park was at the center of Shanghai, visited daily by thousands of people. Why transport the corpse here?

It was then that he saw the familiar figure of Detective Yu striding through the haze with a camera slung over his shoulder. A tall man of medium build, with a rugged face and deep-set eyes, Yu was his well-seasoned assistant, though Chen's senior by a couple of years. Yu was also his only colleague who did not grumble behind his back about the chief inspector's rapid rise, attributable to Deng Xiaoping's new cadre policy favoring those with a formal education. Yu had been a friend to him since they had solved the National Model Worker case.

"Here?" Yu said, without formally greeting his boss.

"Yes, here."

Yu started shooting pictures from different angles. He knelt by the body, zoomed in for close-ups, and examined the wounds carefully. Producing a ruler from his pants pockets, he measured the cuts on the front of the body before turning it over to check the wounds on the back. Yu then looked up at Chen over his shoulder.

"Any clue to his identity?" he asked.

"No."

"Triad killing, I am afraid," Yu said.

"Why do you think so?"

"Look at the wounds. Ax wounds. Seventeen or eighteen of them. There's no need for so many. The number may have a specific meaning. A common practice with gangsters. The blow to his skull would have been more than enough for the job." Yu stood up, putting the ruler back in his pocket. "An average wound length of two and a half to three inches. That bespeaks a steady hand with a lot of strength. Not amateur work."

"Good observations." Chen nodded. "Where do you think the killing took place?"

"Anywhere but here. The guy's still in his pajamas. The killer must have brought the body here. As a special warning. It's another sign of a triad killing. To send a message."

"To whom?"

"Perhaps to somebody in the park," Yu said. "Or somebody who will learn about it in no time. To spread the news fast and wide, there is no better place than the park."

"So you think the body has been left here to be found?"

"Yes, I think so."

"Then how shall we start?"

Yu asked a question instead. "Do we have to take the case, Chief? I'm not saying that the bureau should not take it, but as far as I remember, our special case squad takes only political cases."

Chen could understand his assistant's reservations. Normally their squad did not have to take a case until it was declared "special" by the bureau, for stated or unstated political reasons. "Special," in other words, was the label applied when the bureau had to adjust its focus to meet political needs.

"Well, there's been talk about setting up a new squad—a triad squad, but this might be classified as a special case. And we are not yet sure that it's a triad killing."

"But if it is, it will be a hot potato. A hand-burning one."

"You have a point," Chen said, aware of what Yu was driving at. Not too many cops would be interested in a case related to those gangs.

"My left eyelid kept twitching this morning. Not a good omen, Chief."

"Come on, Detective Yu." Chief Inspector Chen was not a superstitious man, not like some of his colleagues who would consult the *I Ching* before taking a case. If superstition did come into play, however, there was actually a reason he should take the case. It was in this park that his luck had taken a turn for the better.

"In grade school I learned that Chiang Kai-shek came to power with the help of the gangs in Shanghai. Several ministers in his government were members of the Blue triad." Yu paused, then went on, "After 1949, the gangsters were suppressed, but they staged a comeback in the eighties, you know."

"Yes, I know that." He was surprised at his assistant's unaccustomed eloquence. Yu usually spoke without book-quoting or history-citing.

"Those gangsters may be far more powerful than we imagine. They have branches in Hong Kong, Taiwan, Canada, the United States, and everywhere else in the world. Not to mention their connection to some of the top officials here."

"I have read reports about the situation," Chen said. "But after all, what are we cops for?"

"Well, a friend of mine got a job collecting debts for a state-run company in Anhui Province. According to him, he totally depends on the black way, the way of the triads. Not too many people believe in cops nowadays."

"Now that this has happened in the heart of Shanghai, in Bund Park, we cannot stand around with our arms folded," Chen said. "I happened to be in the park this morning. Just my luck. So let me talk to Party Secretary Li about it. At least we'll make a report and send out a notice with the victim's picture. We have to identify him."

When the body was finally taken away by the mortuary people, the chief inspector and his assistant walked back onto the embankment, standing with their elbows resting on the railing. The deserted park looked strange. Chen produced a pack of cigarettes—Kents. He lit one for Yu and another for himself.

" 'You know it cannot be done, but you have to do it anyway.' That's one of the Confucian maxims of my late father."

Yu shifted to a more conciliatory tone. "Whatever you decide, I'm with you."

Chen understood Yu's reasoning, but he did not want to discuss his own. The sentimental meaning Bund Park had for him was private. There was some political justification for his taking the case. If an organized gang killing was involved, as he suspected, it could affect the image of the city. In postcards, in movies, in textbooks, and in his own poems as well, Bund Park symbolized Shanghai. As a chief inspector, he was responsible for preserving the city's image. The bottom line was that the murder in the park had to be investigated, and he was here.

He replied, "Thanks, Detective Yu. I know I can depend on you."

As they left the park, they saw a group of people gathering in front of the gate, on which a notice had just been put, saying the park would be closed for the day due to redecoration.

When the truth was not to be told, one excuse was as good as another.

In the distance, a white gull glided over the slightly yellow water, silhouetted against the horizon, as if carrying the sun on its wings.

Chapter 2

"You have come a long way, Comrade Chief Inspector Chen."
Party Secretary Li Guohua of the Shanghai Police Bureau
smiled, leaning back in his maroon leather swivel chair by the
window. Party Secretary Li's spacious office overlooked the central area of Shanghai.

Chief Inspector Chen sat across the mahogany desk from
him, breathing into a cup of the new Dragon Well green tea, a
special treat few would have been offered in the powerful Party
Secretary's office.

As an emerging cadre with further promotion awaiting him,
Chen owed a lot to Li, his mentor in bureau politics. Li had
introduced Chen to the Party, spared no pains showing him the
ropes, and advanced him to his present position. An entry level
cop in the early fifties, Li had moved up steadily to the top of
the bureau, picking his way through the debris of political
movements, betting on the winners in inner–Party struggles. So
people saw Li's hand-picking of Chen as his potential successor
as another clever investment decision, especially after Chen's
relationship to Ling, a politburo member's daughter from Beijing, became known to the small inner circle. To be fair to Li,
however, he had not been aware of this relationship until after
Chen's promotion.

"Thank you, Party Secretary Li. As our sage has said, 'A man
is willing to lay down his life for the one who appreciates him,

and a woman makes herself beautiful for the one who appreciates her.' "

It was still not considered in good political taste to quote Confucius, but Chen guessed that Li would not be displeased.

"The Party has always thought highly of you," Li said in an official tone of voice. His Mao jacket was buttoned high to his chin in spite of the warm weather. "So this is a job for you, Chief Inspector Chen, for you alone."

"You have heard about it already." Chen was not surprised that somebody else had made a report to Li about the body discovered in Bund Park that morning.

"Look at this picture." Li produced a photo from a manila folder on the desk. "Inspector Catherine Rohn, a representative of the U.S. Marshals Service."

It was a photo of a young woman, perhaps in her late twenties, handsome, spirited, her large blue eyes sparkling in the sunlight.

"She is quite young." Chen studied the picture, thoroughly puzzled.

"Inspector Rohn has studied Chinese in college. She is sort of a sinologist in the Marshals Service. And you're the scholar on our force."

"Hold on—what job are you talking about, Party Secretary Li?"

Outside the office window, an occasional siren was heard in the distance.

"Inspector Rohn is going to escort Wen Liping to the United States. Your job is to help her accomplish this mission." Li cleared his throat before going on, "An important job. We know we can count on you, Chief Inspector Chen."

Chen realized that Li was talking about a totally different matter. "Who is Wen Liping? I do not have the slightest idea about this job, Party Secretary Li."

"Wen Liping is Feng Dexiang's wife."

"Who is Feng Dexiang?"

"A Fujian farmer, now a crucial witness in an illegal immigration case in Washington."

"What makes Feng so special?"

Li poured hot water into Chen's cup. "Have you heard of someone named Jia Xinzhi?"

"Jia Xinzhi—yes, I've heard of him, a notorious triad tycoon based in Taiwan."

"Jia has been involved in a number of international criminal activities. Jia is a heavyweight snake head. He's been arrested in New York in connection with these activities. To convict him, the American authorities need a witness who will testify to his involvement with an immigrant smuggling ship—*The Golden Hope.*"

"Oh, I remember reading about that disastrous operation a couple months ago. The ship, carrying more than three hundred Chinese, was stranded off the U.S. coast. When the Coast Guard arrived on the scene, there was only a sick pregnant woman remaining on board. She had been too weak to jump into one of the fishing boats that were supposed to transport them to shore. Later, several bodies were discovered in the sea—those who had failed to land in the boats."

"That's the ship," Li said. "So you are familiar with the background. Jia is the owner of *The Golden Hope.*"

"We have to do something about human smuggling," Chen said, putting down his cup, in which the tea leaves no longer appeared so green. "The situation has deteriorated in the last few years. Especially in the coastal areas. That's not the way we want China to open up to the world."

"Feng Dexiang was one of those on *The Golden Hope.* He managed to board a fishing boat. And he started in as a 'black man' in New York, working day and night to pay for his passage."

"I've heard that those people work like dogs. Most of them do not know what really awaits them there. We have to deal a crushing blow to the snake heads."

"Jia is as slippery as a rice paddy eel. The Americans have been after him for years. Now they finally have a good chance to nail him for the deaths of those from the ship who drowned," Li said. "Feng was caught in a gang fight in New York and arrested. Faced with criminal charges and deportation, he cut a deal in return for serving as a witness against Jia."

"Was Feng the only one from the ship who was found?"

"No, they caught several others."

"Why do they have to deal with Feng exclusively?"

"Well, once caught, illegal immigrants from China apply for political asylum on the basis of human rights issues, like the one-child-per-family policy and the threat of forced abortion. Political asylum is easily granted, and they do not have to make deals with the American government. Feng did not have a basis for such a claim. His only son died several years ago. So he chose to cooperate."

"What a shrewd bargainer!" Chen said. "But Jia is not only involved in illegal immigration, not just a snake head, but also a dragon head, an international triad leader. Once Feng's identity comes to light, ruthless retaliation may be expected."

"Since his testimony is indispensable at Jia's trial, the Americans have admitted Feng to their Witness Protection Program in cooperation with the U.S. Marshals. They have also granted his request for family reunification with Wen Liping, his wife, who is pregnant. They have asked for our help in this matter."

"If the trial helps to halt the flood of illegal emigration

from China, it will be a good thing for both countries." Chen searched for a pack of cigarettes in his pants pocket. "I hate to read Western propaganda depicting our government as the evil power behind it."

"It was not easy for our government to decide to grant this request."

"Why not?"

"Well, some of our old comrades do not like the way the Americans boss everyone else around." Li offered him a filter-tipped cigarette from a silver case—Panda, a brand available only to those of a Party cadre ranking much higher than Chen's. "Nor will it help our effort to stop the boat people by detaining their families. This has been one of our most effective measures against this smuggling of people out of China. It takes years for them to acquire legal status abroad. Then, when they arrange for their families to join them, we make things difficult. It takes several years more, at least."

"So they have to think about the consequences of such a long separation before setting out."

"Exactly. It may send a wrong message if Wen rejoins her husband so quickly. Nevertheless, the agreement to cooperate was reached after much discussion at high levels of our two governments."

"It is in the mutual interests of the two countries." Chen chose his words carefully. "If we do not cooperate, the Americans may think we are in favor of the continuance of illegal human smuggling."

"That's what I said in the ministry's teleconference this morning."

"Since the agreement has been reached, it's a matter of course to let Wen go to join her husband." Chen picked up the photo again. "Why should the U.S. Marshals send an officer all the way to Shanghai?"

"It has already taken some time for our local police to run through their procedures, to obtain all the documents and approvals needed. Feng swears he will not testify if Wen does not arrive before the trial date. The Americans have become worried. Inspector Rohn's trip has been proposed to help Wen get her visa, but it's really to put pressure on us."

"When will the trial begin?"

"April twenty-fourth. Today is April eighth."

"Then let's hurry up. In a special case, surely a passport and everything needed can be made ready in twenty-four hours. Why is this an assignment for me?"

"Feng's wife has disappeared. The Beijing ministry learned this last night, and Inspector Rohn is already on the way."

"How could she disappear?"

"We don't know. Whatever has happened, her disappearance has put us in an embarrassing situation. The Americans will suspect that we are trying to back out of our arrangement."

Chief Inspector Chen frowned. In normal circumstances, waiting for a passport application to be processed might take months for an ordinary Chinese citizen, but if the central government had given them the green light, the local police should have proceeded rapidly. Now, after an inexplicable delay, how could Wen have vanished? It did not make sense. Perhaps the whole thing constituted a cover-up? When national interests were involved, anything was possible. However, such a scenario did not seem too likely. Beijing could have refused to cooperate with the U.S. from the outset. To back out at this stage would mean a loss of face.

Instead of sharing these thoughts with Li, Chen asked, "So what are we supposed to do, Party Secretary Li?"

"We'll find Wen. The local police are already searching for her. You will take charge."

"Shall I accompany Inspector Rohn to Fujian?"

"No. This will be a joint investigation by the Shanghai and Fujian police. At present, your responsibility is for Inspector Rohn in Shanghai."

"How can I be in charge there if I am accompanying an American woman here?"

"She is our special guest—for the first Chinese-American joint action against illegal immigration," Li said. "What can she possibly do in Fujian? Things may be dangerous there. Her safety is a priority for us. To make her stay a safe and satisfactory one, you will keep her company in Shanghai. You will keep her informed and entertained."

"Is that a job for a Chinese chief inspector of police?" Chen stared at the pictures of Li on the office wall—the long, colorful career of a politician shaking hands with other politicians, delivering speeches at Party conferences, making presentations at the bureau, at different times, in different places. Li was the number-one Party officer in the bureau, and there was not a single picture showing Li engaged in policework.

"Of course it is. And a very important job too. The Chinese government is determined to keep the smuggling of humans under control. The Americans must not have any doubts about it. We must convince Inspector Rohn that we are doing our best. She may raise all kind of questions, and we'll let her know as much as we can. It takes an experienced officer like you to handle the situation. There is a line, needless to say, between the inside and the outside."

"What can that be—the line?" Chen interrupted, grinding out his cigarette in the crystal ashtray shaped like a swan.

"Inspector Rohn may be skeptical, for instance, about the passport process. A certain amount of bureaucracy may exist in our work, but it's like anywhere else in the world. No point making a big deal out of it. We must keep in mind the unsulliable image of the Chinese government. You will know what to say, Chief Inspector Chen."

He did not know what to say. It would not be an easy job to convince an American partner when he shared the same doubts. He would have to move as carefully as if he were treading on thin ice. Politics. Chief Inspector Chen had had enough. He put down his cup.

"I'm afraid I cannot take the case, Party Secretary Li. In fact, I came to discuss another investigation with you. A body was discovered in Bund Park this morning. The wounds on the body suggest it may be a triad killing."

"A triad killing in Bund Park?"

"Yes, both Detective Yu and I have reached the same conclusion, but we have no clue yet as to which gang is responsible. So I'll be focused on investigating this homicide case. It could damage the image of our new Shanghai—"

"That's true," Li cut him short. "It may well be a matter for your special squad, but Wen's case is far more urgent. The Bund Park case can wait until after Inspector Rohn leaves. That won't delay matters too long."

"I don't think I am a good candidate to take charge of Wen's case. Someone from Internal Security or the Foreign Liaison Ministry would be more suitable."

"Let me tell you something, Chief Inspector Chen. This is the decision of the ministry in Beijing. Minister Huang himself recommended you for the job during the teleconference."

"Why, Party Secretary Li?"

"Inspector Rohn can speak Chinese. So Minister Huang insisted that her Chinese counterpart must not only be politically reliable, but speak English as well. You are an English-speaking young cadre with experience in escorting Westerners."

"Since she speaks Chinese, I don't see why her partner here

has to be an English speaker. As for my experience, I have worked only as a representative of the Chinese Writers' Association. That was totally different—we discussed literature. For this job, an intelligence officer would be more qualified."

"Her command of Chinese is limited. Some of our people met her in Washington. She did a good job escorting them, but for the formal meetings, they had to hire a professional interpreter. We believe you will have to speak English most of the time."

"I'm honored that Minister Huang has thought of me," Chen said slowly, trying to come up with some other official-sounding excuses. "I'm just too young and inexperienced for such an assignment."

"Do you think it is a job for an old-timer like me?" Li sighed, his baggy eyes sagging in the morning light. "Don't let your years slip away without accomplishing something. Forty years ago, I liked poetry, too. Remember these lines by General Yue Fei? *Do not waste your youthful time doing nothing / until you're white-haired, / regretting in vain.*"

Chen was taken aback. Li had never before spoken of poetry with him, much less recited lines from memory.

"And there was another criterion discussed in the ministry meeting," Li continued. "The candidate should present a good image of our police force."

"What does that mean?"

"Isn't Inspector Rohn quite presentable?" Li took up the picture. "You will present a wonderful image of China's police force. A modernist poet and translator, with an intimate knowledge of Western literature."

This was becoming absurd. What was really expected of him? To be an actor, a tourist guide, a model, a public relations specialist—anything but a cop.

"That's the very reason that I should not take the job, Party

Secretary Li. People have already been talking about my exposure to Western culture. Bourgeois decadence or whatever. For me to accompany an American woman officer, dining, shopping, sightseeing—instead of doing real work. What will they think?"

"Oh, you will have work to do."

"What work, Party Secretary Li?"

"Wen Liping is from Shanghai originally. She was an educated youth in the early seventies. She could have come back to Shanghai. So you'll do some investigating here."

This sounded far from convincing. It did not take a chief inspector to interview Wen's possible contacts, unless he was supposed to put on a show to impress the American, Chen reflected.

Li stood up and put his hands on Chen's shoulders. "This is an assignment you cannot say no to, Comrade Chen Cao. It's in the interests of the Party."

"In the interests of the Party!" Chen also rose to his feet. Below him, traffic came to a bumper-to-bumper stop along Fuzhou Road. Further argument would be futile. "You always have the last word, Party Secretary Li."

"Minister Huang has it, actually. All these years, the Party has always trusted you. What was it you just quoted from Confucius?"

"I know, but—" He did not know how to continue.

"You take over the case at a critical moment, we understand. The ministry will provide you with a special fund. No limit to your budget. Take Inspector Rohn to the best restaurants, theaters, cruises—whatever you decide. Spend as much as you can. Don't let the Americans think we are all as poor as those boat people. This is foreign liaison work, too."

Most people would consider such an assignment desirable. First-class hotels, entertainment, and banquets. China must not lose face before Western visitors: one of the government foreign liaison regulations Chen had learned. There was another side, however, to such an assignment, the government's secret surveillance. Internal Security would lurk in the background.

"I'll do my best, I've just got a couple of requests, Party Secretary Li."

"Go ahead."

"I want to have Detective Yu Guangming as my partner on the case."

"Detective Yu is an experienced cop, but he does not speak English. If you need help, I would like to suggest someone else."

"I will send Detective Yu to Fujian. I don't know what the local police have done so far. We need to establish the cause of Wen's disappearance," Chen said, trying to catch any change of Li's expression, but seeing none. "Detective Yu can keep me informed about all the latest developments there."

"What will the Fujian police think?"

"I'm in charge, aren't I?"

"Of course, you have complete control over the whole operation. Your orders have already been cut."

"Then I will have him fly to Fujian this afternoon."

"Well, if you insist." Li agreed. "Do you need any help here? You'll be fully occupied with Inspector Rohn."

"That's true. I have some other work pending. And there's the body in the park, too."

"Do you really want to work on the Bund Park case? I don't think you have the time, Chief Inspector Chen."

"Some preliminary work has to be done. It cannot wait."

"What about Sergeant Qian Jun? He can serve as a temporary assistant for you."

Chen did not like Qian, a young graduate of the police academy with an old head for politics. It would be too much, however, to turn down Li's suggestion again. "Qian's fine. I will be out with Inspector Rohn most of the time. When Detective Yu calls in, Qian can relay messages."

"Qian can also help with the paperwork," Li added with a smile. "Oh, there's a clothing subsidy for this job. Don't forget to go see the bureau's accountant."

"Isn't that allowance only for people going abroad?"

"You will have to put on your best suit for people coming *from* abroad. Remember, present a worthy image of our police force. You can also have a room at the Peace Hotel. That's where Inspector Rohn will stay. It will be more convenient for you."

"Well—" The prospect of staying in that famous hotel was tempting. Staying in a room overlooking the Bund would not only be a treat for him. He had invited Detective Yu's family to come over to take a hot bath when he had stayed at the Jing River Hotel. Most Shanghai families did not have a bathroom, much less hot water. However, it would not necessarily be wise, Chen concluded, for him to stay in the same hotel as a female American officer. "That won't be necessary, Party Secretary Li. It's only ten minute's walk from here. We can save money for the bureau."

"Yes, we should always follow the time-honored tradition of the Party: Live simply and work hard."

As he left Li's office, Chen was disturbed by the elusive memory of what had happened to him, not too long ago, in another hotel.

What can be recaptured in memory / If it's lost there and then?

He pounded at the elevator button. The elevator was stuck again.

Chapter 3

The airplane was delayed.

Things were going wrong from the outset, Chen thought, as he waited at Shanghai Hongqiao International Airport. He stared at the information on the departure/arrival monitor, which seemed to stare back at him, reflecting his frustration.

It was a clear, crisp afternoon outside the windows, but local visibility at Tokyo's Narita airport, according to the information desk, was extremely poor. So passengers changing planes there, including Catherine Rohn flying via United Airlines, had to wait until the weather improved.

The closed gate looked inexplicably forbidding.

He did not like the assignment, though everyone else in the bureau might have agreed, for once, that he was the very candidate for it. Wearing a new suit, uncomfortable in a tightly knotted tie, carrying a leather briefcase, struggling to rehearse what he would say to Inspector Rohn upon her arrival, he waited.

Most of the people sitting around the airport, however, appeared to be in high spirits. A young man was so excited that he turned his cellular phone over and over, switching it from hand to hand. A group of five or six people, apparently of one family, kept sending one and then another, in turn, to the departure/arrival monitor. A middle-aged man tried to teach a middle-aged woman a few simple words in English, but finally gave up, shaking his head with a good-humored grin.

Sitting in a corner seat, musing about Wen's probable whereabouts, Chief Inspector Chen was inclined toward kidnapping by the local triad as the explanation for her disappearance. Of course, Wen might have met with an accident. In either case, the clues would be in Fujian. But his job was to keep Inspector Rohn safe and satisfied in Shanghai. Safe as she might be, how could she be satisfied? If the Fujian police did not succeed in finding Wen, how would he be able to convince her that the Chinese police had done their best?

As for the possibility of Wen having gone into hiding, it seemed unlikely. According to the initial information, she had been applying for a passport for months, and had made a couple of trips to Fuzhou for the purpose. Why should she voluntarily disappear at this stage? If she'd had an accident, by now she should have been discovered.

There was, of course, another possibility: The Beijing authorities wanted to back out. When national interests were involved, anything was possible. If so, his job would be pathetic at best, like a marble *go* piece placed on the game board to distract the opponent's attention.

He decided not to speculate further. There was no point. In a speech on China's economic reform, Comrade Deng Xiaoping had used the metaphor of wading across the river by stepping on one stone after another. When there's no foretelling the problems ahead, no planning can avoid them. That was the only course Chen could follow now.

Opening his briefcase, he reached for Inspector Rohn's picture for another look, but the photo he pulled out was of a Chinese woman—Wen Liping.

A haggard thin face, sallow, hair disheveled, with deep lines around her lusterless eyes, whose corners seemed weighed down by invisible burdens. This was the woman in the recent picture used in her passport application. So different from those in her high-school file, in which, Wen, looking forward to embracing her future, appeared young, pretty, spirited, her red armband flashing as she raised her arms to the skies during the Cultural Revolution. In high school, Wen had been a "queen," though that was not a term used in those years.

He was particularly impressed by a snapshot of her taken at the Shanghai Railway Station: Wen danced with a red paper heart bearing a Chinese character—*loyal*—in her hand. A long, graceful neck, terrific legs, strands of her black hair curled against her cheek, and a red armband on her green sleeve. She was in the center of a group of educated youths, her almond-shaped eyes squinting in the sunlight, with people beating drums and gongs in a sea of red banners in the background. Underneath the picture was a caption: *Educated Youth Wen Liping, graduate of the class of '70, the Great Leap Forward High School.* The picture had appeared in *Wenhui Daily* in the early seventies, when high-school graduates from cities, the "educated youths," were sent to the countryside in response to Chairman Mao's declaration: *It is necessary for the educated youths to receive re-education from the poor and lower-middle-class peasants.*

Wen went to Changle Village in Fujian Province, as a "relative-seeking" educated youth. Soon afterward—in less than a year—she had married Feng Dexiang, a man fifteen years her senior, the head of the Revolutionary Committee of the Changle People's Commune. There were different explanations for the marriage. Some described her as a too ardent believer in Mao, but others claimed pregnancy was the cause. She had a baby the following year. With her newborn infant bundled on her back, in sweat-soaked black homespun, laboring barefoot in the rice paddies, few would have recognized her as an educated youth from Shanghai. In the following years, she returned to Shanghai only once—on the occasion of her father's funeral. After the Cultural Revolution, Feng was removed from his position. In addition to her toil in the rice paddy and vegetable plots, Wen started working in a commune factory to support the family. Then their only son died in a tragic accident. Several months ago, Feng had left on board *The Golden Hope*.

Little wonder, Chen observed, that her passport picture looked so different from those in her high-school file.

The flower falls, the water flows, and the spring fades. / It's a changed world.

Twenty years gone in a snap of one's fingers, Wen had graduated from high school just two or three years earlier than he. Chief Inspector Chen thought now that he had comparatively little to complain about in his life, despite this absurd assignment.

He glanced at his watch. Still some time before the airplane arrived. At a phone booth, he dialed Qian Jun at the bureau. "Has Detective Yu called in?"

"No, not yet."

"The flight is delayed. I have to wait for the American and then accompany her to the hotel. I don't think I will make it back to the bureau this afternoon. If Yu calls, tell him to reach me at home. And see if you can also speed up the report on the autopsy of the body in the park."

"I will try my best, Chief Inspector Chen," Qian said. "So you're conducting that investigation now."

"Yes, a murder victim found in Bund Park is another political priority for us."

"Of course, Chief Inspector Chen."

Then he telephoned Peiqin, Detective Yu's wife.

"Peiqin, this is Chen Cao. I'm at the airport. Sorry about sending Yu away on such short notice."

"You don't have to apologize, Chief Inspector Chen."

"Has he called home?"

"No, not yet. He will call you first, I bet."

"He must have arrived safe and sound. Don't worry. I'll probably hear from him tonight."

"Thank you."

"Take care, Peiqin. Give my best to Qinqin and Old Hunter."

"I will. Take care of yourself."

He wished that he could be with Yu, discussing hypotheses with his usual partner, even though Yu was not enthusiastic about taking on the Wen case—even less so than he was about the Bund Park case. Though the two men differed in almost every way, they were friends. He had made several visits to Yu's home and enjoyed himself there, despite the fact that the entire apartment consisted of a room no more than ten or eleven square meters in size, where Yu, his wife and son, slept, ate and lived, next to the room which was his father's home. Yu was a warm host who played a good game of *go*, and Peiqin was a wonderful hostess, serving excellent food and discussing classical Chinese literature, too.

Regaining his seat in the corner, he decided to do some reading about human smuggling in Fujian. The material was in English, as this topic was banned from Chinese publications. He had read no more than two or three lines when a young mother pushing a stroller came to the seat beside him. She was an attractive woman in her mid-twenties, with thin, clear features and a touch of shadow under her large eyes.

"English?" she said, glancing at the material in his hand.

"Yes." He wondered whether she had taken the seat next to him because she had glimpsed his English reading matter.

She wore a white dress of light material, a caftan, which seemed to be floating around her long legs as she rocked the stroller with a sandaled foot. There was a blond baby sleeping in it.

"He has not seen his American daddy yet," she said in Chinese. "Look at his hair—the same golden color."

"He's cute."

"Blond," she said in English.

There were many stories about cross-cultural marriages nowadays. The sleeping baby looked adorable, but her emphasis on the color of his hair bothered the chief inspector. It sounded as if she thought anything associated with Westerners was something to be proud of.

He got up to make another phone call. Luckily, he discovered a booth that took coins for a long distance call. *Time is money.* That was a newly popular, politically correct slogan in the nineties. It was certainly correct here. The call was to Comrade Hong Liangxing, superintendent of the Fujian Police Bureau.

"Superintendent Hong, this is Chen Cao. Party Secretary Li has just assigned me to the Wen case, and I don't know anything about the investigation. You are really the one on top of the situation."

"Come, Chief Inspector Chen. We know the decision has been made by the ministry. We will do everything possible to help."

"You can start by filling me in on the general background, Superintendent Hong."

"Illegal emigration has been a problem for years in the district. After the mid-eighties, things took a turn for the worse. With the Open Door policy, people gained access to the propaganda of the West and began to dream of digging into the Gold Mountains overseas. Taiwan smuggling rings established themselves. With their large, modern ships, the journeys across the ocean became possible, and hugely profitable too."

"Yes, people like Jia Xinzhi became snake heads."

"And local gangs like the Flying Axes helped. Especially by

making sure people made timely payment to the smuggling rings."

"How much?"

"Thirty thousand U.S. dollars per person."

"Wow, so much. People could live comfortably on the interest of such a sum. Why should they take the risk?"

"They believe they can earn that much in one or two years there. And the risk is not that great because of changes in our legal system in recent years. If they're caught, they are no longer put into prison or labor camp. Just sent back home. Nor are there political pressures on them afterward. So they are not worried about the consequences."

"In the seventies, they would have received long prison sentences," Chen said. One of his teachers had been put into jail for the so-called crime of merely listening to the Voice of America.

"And one of the factors is—you won't believe it—American policy. When people are caught there, they should be sent back to China at once, right? No. They are allowed to stay for long periods and encouraged to apply for political asylum. So we have been overwhelmed. If the Americans can nail Jia this time, it will be a heavy blow to the smuggling rings."

"You are so familiar with all the factors involved, Superintendent Hong. Detective Yu and I really must depend on your help. I don't know if Yu has arrived in Fujian yet."

"I believe he did, but I haven't heard from him directly."

"I'm waiting for the American at the airport. My coins are running out. I have to finish now. I'll call you again tonight, Superintendent Hong."

"Call me any time, Chief Inspector Chen."

The discussion seemed to have gone more smoothly than he

had expected. Normally, local police would not be so cooperative with an outsider.

Putting down the phone, he turned to the arrival/departure monitor again. The time posted had changed. The airplane would arrive in twenty minutes.

Chapter 4

Detective Yu Guangming had left for Fujian by train instead of by air. There was hardly any difference in travel time, but his preference for the train was prompted by frugality. The police bureau had its regulations about travel expenses. The traveler could pocket half of the difference between the air fare and the train fare—a sizable amount when one went via "hard seat" instead of in a soft sleeper. More than one hundred fifty Yuan, with which he planned to buy an electric calculator for his wife, Peiqin. She was a restaurant accountant, but still used a wooden abacus at home, clicking and clacking the abacus pieces under her slender fingers late into the night.

So, sitting on a wooden bench, Detective Yu started reading material about Wen. There was not much in the folder. The part about Wen being an educated youth, however, gave him a sense of déjà vu. Both Peiqin and he had been educated youths in the early seventies.

Halfway through the dossier, he lit a cigarette and gazed thoughtfully at the spiraling smoke rings. The present always changed the past, but the past changed the present, too.

Classmates of the class of '70, Yu and Peiqin, no more than sixteen years old, had to leave Shanghai to "receive reeducation" on an army farm tucked away in remote Yunnan Province, on the southern China/Burma border. On the eve of their departure, the parents of the two young people had a long talk. The next morning, Peiqin came to his place, got into a truck, and sat with Yu, bashfully, unable to look up at him all the way to the Shanghai Railway Station. It was a sort of arranged engagement, Yu realized. Their families wanted them to take care of each other thousands of miles away. That they did, and more, though they did not get married there. Not because they had not grown affectionate, but because there might be a chance, with their status still listed as single, for them to move back to Shanghai. Under government policy, once married, educated youths had to settle down forever in the countryside.

The movement was discontinued, if not denounced, toward the end of the seventies, and they had come back to the city. Peiqin was assigned a job in Sihai Restaurant by the Office of Educated Youths. His father, Old Hunter, arranged to retire early so Yu could take his place as a cop in the Shanghai Police bureau. They got married. One year after the birth of their son Qinqin, their lives had slipped into a smooth yet ordinary routine—quite different from what they had dreamed of in Yunnan. A restaurant accountant, working in an oven of a *tingzhijian* cubicle over the kitchen, Peiqin's only indulgence was to read *The Dream of the Red Chamber*, which she did over and over during her half-hour lunch break. A low-level cop, Yu came to the realization that he would probably remain one. Still, he thought there was not much for him to complain about—Peiqin was a marvelous wife, and Qinqin was growing up to be a wonderful son.

He wondered why Wen had not returned to Shanghai like so many others. Many educated youths who had married got divorced so they could return home. In those years of absurd-ities, one had to do even more absurd things to survive. It would be difficult for people to comprehend nowadays, even for Chief Inspector Chen who, though only a few years younger, had not been to the countryside.

"Attention, it is the time for the night meal. Passengers who want to have a night snack please go to compartment six." A husky-voiced woman started reading an announcement over the train loudspeaker. "For tonight, there are fried rice cakes with pork, dumplings with Qicai stuffing, and noodles with mush-rooms. We also serve beer and wine."

He took out a package of instant noodles, poured water from the train thermos bottle into an enamel cup, and soaked the noodles in it. The water was not hot enough. It took several minutes for the noodles to soften. He also had a smoked carp head in a plastic bag, which Peiqin had prepared for him. But Detective Yu's mood did not improve. This assignment was practically a joke. It was as if the Shanghai police were going to try to cook in the kitchen of the Fujian police bureau. How could a Shanghai cop, single-handed, make a difference when the Fujian police had failed? Their having been given command of the Wen investigation did not make sense unless it was sim-ply a show for the Americans. He poked the staring eye out of the smoked carp head.

Around three in the morning, Yu dozed off, sitting up stiff and tight like a bamboo stick, his head bumping against the hard seat back.

When the sun glaring in his face woke him, the aisle was full of people waiting for their turn to wash up in the restroom. According to the announcement from the train loudspeaker, Fujian was close.

As a result of sitting up all night, his neck felt sore, his shoulders strained, and his legs numb. He shook his head at his reflection in the train window. A middle-aged man, his chin unshaven, his face etched with travel fatigue. No longer a tireless educated youth, sitting with Peiqin in the train to Yunnan.

Another result of traveling "hard seat" was that it took him five minutes at the Fujian railway station to locate a man holding a cardboard sign with his name on it. Sergeant Zhao Youli, of the Fujian Police, must have been looking for his Shanghai counterpart among the travelers stepping out of the soft sleeper compartments. Zhao had a chubby face, beady eyes, well-moussed hair, and wore an expensive white suit, a red silk tie, and well-shined dress shoes. His eyes narrowed into smiling slits at the sight of Yu.

"Welcome, Detective Yu. I'm assigned to work with you on the case."

"Thank you, Sergeant Zhao."

"I was looking for you over there," Zhao said.

"The sleeper tickets were sold out," Yu fibbed, growing self-conscious about his appearance. In his old Renli jacket, his pants all wrinkled after a night's travel, he looked like a body-guard rather than the partner of the well-groomed Zhao. "Are there any new developments, Sergeant Zhao?"

"No. We've been looking everywhere for Wen. No success. The case is a top priority for us. I'm so glad you've come all the way from Shanghai to help."

Yu caught the suggestion of sarcasm in Zhao's voice. "Come on, Sergeant Zhao. You don't have to say that. I don't know anything about the case. In fact, I don't know why I am here. It is by order of the Ministry."

The truth was that Yu did not expect to accomplish anything. Either his mission was simply political window-dressing or Wen had been kidnapped by Jia's Fujian accomplices. If the latter was the case, the search for Wen would be like fishing in the woods unless the local cops were determined to crack down on the gangsters.

"Well, 'The monk from a far-away temple can recite scripture more loudly'," Zhao said, smoothing his shining hair with his hand.

"If it is in Fujian dialect, I don't speak a single word of it. I cannot even ask for directions here," Yu said. "So you will have to take me to Changle Village."

"Why in such a hurry, Detective Yu? Let me take you to the hotel first—the Abundance Hotel. You've had a long night in the train. Take a break, have lunch with me, and then come to our county police bureau. There we will have a good discussion, and a reception dinner—"

"Well . . ." Yu was astonished at his local partner's lack of urgency. "I slept quite well on the train. Chief Inspector Chen will be waiting for my interview tapes."

They set out for Changle Village. Driving along a bumpy road, Zhao managed to make a brief report about the gang known as the Flying Axes.

This society had been founded in the late Qing dynasty in the Fujian area as a secret brotherhood, with a wide range of "business practices," including illegal salt distribution, drug trafficking, loan collection, protection, gambling and prostitution. These activities expanded in spite of the various governments' containment efforts, though the triad remained a local one. The gang was suppressed after 1949 under the communist government and some of the leading members were executed because of their connections to the Nationalists. In the last few years, however, the gang had staged a comeback. The human smuggling business was headed by Taiwan snake heads such as Jia Xinzhi, but the Fujian triad's role was essential. An illegal immigrant promised to pay the smugglers in installments. At first, the Flying Axes' role was to make sure that the payments were made on time. Then they became involved in the other aspects of the operation, such as recruiting people to go overseas.

Yu said, "Can you tell me more about Wen's disappearance?"

So Zhao went on to tell Yu about the work the Fujian police had done so far.

On the morning of April sixth, Zhao went to visit Wen for verification of her passport application. The Fujian police had been informed that an American officer was coming for Wen, so they were trying to speed things up. Wen was not at home. Nor was she at the commune factory. Zhao went there again in the afternoon, but still he had no luck. The next morning, he came to Changle with another policeman. The door to her house was locked. According to her neighbors, Wen had never before gone away for a whole day. She had to work in the commune factory, to take care of the family plot, and to feed the chickens and piglets. They looked into the pigsty, where the starving animals could hardly stand on their legs. So they decided to enter the house after checking for signs of forced entry. There were none, nor any sign of a struggle inside. They started canvassing the village, knocking at one door after another. Wen had last been seen there around 10:45 P.M. on April fifth, as she fetched water from the village well. By the afternoon of April seventh, they were sure that something had happened to her.

The local police had searched the neighboring villages, as well as hotels within the radius of a hundred miles. They also made inquiries at the bus depot. Only one bus had passed the village that night. So far, all their efforts had yielded nothing.

"It's beyond us," Zhao concluded. "Her disappearance is a mystery."

"What about the possibility of the Flying Axes kidnapping her?"

"That's not likely. Nothing unusual was noted in the village that night. She would have shouted or struggled, and someone would have heard. You will see for yourself in a minute."

It took them another fifteen minutes, however, before the village came in view. There was a striking discrepancy between the kinds of houses clustered there. Some were new, modern, substantial, like mansions in the best area of Shanghai, but others were old, shabby, and small.

"It's like two different worlds here," Yu observed.

"Exactly," Zhao said. "There's a huge gap between households with people abroad and those without. All these new houses have been built with money sent from overseas."

"It's amazing. These new houses would be worth millions in Shanghai."

"Let me give you some numbers, Detective Yu. A peasant's yearly income here is around three thousand Yuan, and that depends on the weather. Someone in New York can earn that sum in a week—living, eating, sleeping in a restaurant, and getting paid all in cash. One year's savings there is enough to pay for a two-story house here, full of new furniture and appliances, too. How can families without people abroad compete? They have to remain huddled in those ancient huts, in the shadow of the upstarts."

"Yes, you cannot do everything with money," Yu said, echoing the line from a new movie, "but you cannot do anything without it."

"The only way for the poor to turn the tables is to go abroad, too. Otherwise, they will be viewed as foolish, lazy, or incompetent. It's a vicious cycle. So more and more people leave."

"Did Feng leave for the same reason?"

"That must have been one of his reasons."

They came to Wen's house. An old one, probably built as early as the turn of century, though not small, with a front yard, a backyard, and a pigsty. It looked extremely shabby compared to the improved standard of the village housing. The door was locked from the outside with a brass padlock. Zhao opened it by inserting a small knife into the lock. In the deserted front yard, Yu saw two baskets of empty wine bottles in a corner.

"Feng drank a lot," Zhao said. "Wen collected the bottles to sell."

They examined the yard walls, the tops of which were covered in dust, but found no traces of anyone having climbed over.

"Have you found anything suspicious among the things she left behind?" Yu asked as they moved inside.

"Well, there's not much left behind."

Not much in the way of furniture anyway, Yu observed, taking out his notebook. The living room appeared inconsolably bare. A ramshackle table with two wooden benches were all he could see. There was, however, a basket of cans and plastic packages under the table. One of the packages bore a DANGER-INFLAMMABLE notice. Whatever it was, it did not appear to be something people would normally keep in the living room.

"What's that?"

"The material Wen used for her work," Zhao explained.

"What sort of work did she do at home?"

"What she did at the commune factory was simple. She worked with a sort of chemical abrasive. She dipped her fingers in it and rubbed the precision parts until they were smooth, like a human grinder. Folks here earn according to the number of products completed, piecework. To earn a few more Yuan in the evenings, she brought the chemicals and parts home."

They went into the bedroom. The bed was huge and old with

a carved design on the headboard. There was also a chest displaying the same craftsmanship. Most of the drawers contained rags, old clothes, and other useless stuff. One drawer was packed with a child's clothes and shoes, probably her dead son's. In another, Yu found a photo album with some pictures of Wen taken in high school.

One showed Wen at the Shanghai railway station, leaning out of the train window, waving her hand at the people on the platform who were undoubtedly singing and shouting revolutionary slogans. This was a familiar scene to Yu, who had seen Peiqin reaching out, waving to her family on the same platform. He put several pictures in his notebook. "Did Wen have any recent photos?"

"The only recent one is her passport picture."

"Not even a wedding picture?"

"No."

That was strange, Yu thought. In Yunnan, though they had not applied for their marriage certificate for fear of jeopardizing their chances of being allowed to return to Shanghai, Peiqin had made a point of having their picture taken in a standard bride-and-bridegroom pose. Now, years later, Peiqin would still refer to it as their wedding picture.

The bottom drawer of the chest contained a few children's books, a dictionary, a piece of old newspaper dated several months earlier, a copy of *The Dream of the Red Chamber* reprinted before the Cultural Revolution, an anthology of the best poems of 1988—

"A 1988 poetry collection," Yu said, turning toward Zhao. "Isn't this out of place here?"

"Oh, I thought so too," Zhao took it. "But do you see the paper embroidery designs kept between the pages? Village folks use books for that purpose."

"Yes, my mother used to do that too. So the designs would not get crumpled." Yu leafed through the volume. No signature. Nor was Wen's name mentioned in the table of contents.

"Do you want to send it to your poetic chief inspector?"

"No, I don't think he has time for poetry right now." Nevertheless, Yu made a note of it. "Oh, you mentioned her work in a commune factory. The commune system was abolished several years ago."

"That's true. People are just used to calling it the commune factory."

"Can we go there today?"

"The manager is away in Guangzhou. I will arrange a meeting for you as soon as he comes back."

After they finished examining Wen's house, they went to the village committee office. The village head was not in. An old woman in her eighties recognized Zhao and made tea for them. Yu telephoned the Shanghai Police Bureau but Chief Inspector Chen was not in either.

It was about lunchtime. Zhao did not refer to his reception plan again. They walked over to a noodles booth—a coal stove and several pots in front of a shabby house. While waiting for their fish ball noodles, Yu turned around to look at the rice paddy behind them.

Most of the farmers in the rice paddy were young or middle-aged women, working with their hair bundled up in white towels and their trouser bottoms rolled up high.

"This is another sign," Zhao said, as if reading Yu's thoughts. "This village is typical of the area. About two-thirds of the families have their men abroad. If not, it is like a stigma for that family. So there are practically no young or middle-aged men, and only their wives are left to work in the fields."

"But how long will those wives be left behind?"

"At least seven or eight years, until their husbands get legal status abroad."

After lunch, Zhao suggested a few families to start interviewing. Three hours later, however, Yu realized they would probably not get anything new or useful. Whenever they touched on the topics of human smuggling or gang activities, inevitably their questions were met with silence.

As for Wen, her neighbors shared an unexplained antipathy. According to them, Wen had kept to herself all those years. They still referred to her as the city woman or the educated youth, though she worked harder than most of the local wives. Normally Wen went to the commune factory in the morning, took care of the family plot in the late afternoon, and then finger-polished those parts she'd brought home at night. Always on the run, her head lowered, Wen had little time or desire to talk to others. As interpreted by Lou, her next-door neighbor, Wen must have been ashamed of Feng, the evil embodiment of the Cultural Revolution. Due to her lack of contacts with others, no one seemed to have noticed anything unusual about her on April fifth.

"That's my impression, too," Zhao said. "She seems to have remained an outsider here all these years."

Wen might have shut herself up right after her marriage, Yu thought, but twenty years was a long time. The fourth interviewee on their list was a woman surnamed Dong in the house opposite Wen's.

"Her only son left with Feng on the same ship, *The Golden Hope*, but he has not contacted home since," Zhao said before knocking at the door.

The person who opened the door for them was a small, white-haired woman with a weatherbeaten, deeply lined face. She stood in the doorway without inviting them in.

"Comrade Dong, we are conducting an investigation into Wen's disappearance," Yu said. "Do you have any information about her, specifically with respect to the night of April fifth?"

"Information about that woman? Let me tell you something. He's a white-eyed wolf, and she's a jade-faced bitch. Now they're both in trouble, aren't they? It serves them right." Dong drew her lips into a thin, angry line and shut the door in their faces.

Yu turned to Zhao in puzzlement.

"Let's move on," Zhao said. "Dong believes Feng influenced her son to leave home. He's only eighteen. That's why she calls him a white-eyed wolf—the most cruel one."

"Why should Dong call Wen a jade-faced bitch?"

"Feng divorced his first wife to marry Wen. She was a knockout when she first arrived. Locals tell all kinds of stories about the marriage."

"Another question. How could Dong have learned that Feng's in trouble?"

"I don't know." Zhao's eyes did not meet Yu's. "People here have relatives or friends in New York. Or they must have heard something after Wen's disappearance."

"I see." Yu did not really see, but he did not think it appropriate to push the matter further at the moment.

Yu tried to shake off the feeling that there might be something else behind Sergeant Zhao's vagueness. Sending a cop from Shanghai could be taken as a rebuke to the police in Fujian. That he found himself working with an unenthusiastic partner and unfriendly people was not much of a surprise to him, though. Most of his assignments with Chief Inspector Chen had been anything but pleasant.

He doubted whether Chen's work was going to be easier in Shanghai. It might appear so to others—the Peace Hotel, an unlimited budget, and an attractive American partner, but Yu knew better. Lighting another cigarette, he thought he would have said a definite no to Party Secretary Li. Because this job was not one for a cop. And that, perhaps, was why he would never become a chief inspector.

When they finished their interviews for the day, the village committee office had closed. There was no public phone service in the village. At Zhao's suggestion, they were about to set off for the hotel, a twenty-minute walk. As they reached the outskirts of the village, Yu approached an old man repairing a bicycle tire under a weatherbeaten sign. "Do you know anybody with a home phone here?"

"There're two phones in the village. One for the village committee, and the other at Mrs. Miao's. Her husband has been in the United States for five or six years. What a lucky woman—to have a phone at home!"

"Thanks. We'll use her phone."

"You have to pay for it. Other folks use her phone too. For their people overseas. When people call home from abroad, they speak to Miao first."

"Like the public phone service in Shanghai," Yu said. "Do you think Wen used Miao's phone too?"

"Yes, everybody in the village does."

Yu turned to Zhao with a question in his eyes.

"Sorry," Zhao said in embarrassment. "I did not know anything about it."

Chapter 5

The gate had finally opened.

A group of first-class passengers emerged, most of them foreigners. Among them Chief Inspector Chen saw a young woman wearing a cream-colored blazer and matching pants. She was tall, slender, her blond hair fell to her shoulders, and she had blue eyes. He recognized her at once, though she looked slightly different from the image in the photograph, taken perhaps a few years earlier. She carried herself with grace, like a senior executive of a Shanghai joint venture.

"Inspector Catherine Rohn?"

"Yes?"

"I'm Chen Cao, chief inspector of the Shanghai Police Bureau. I'm here to greet you on behalf of your Chinese colleagues. We will be working together."

"Chief Inspector Chen?" She added in Chinese, "*Chen Tongzhi?*"

"Oh yes, you speak Chinese."

"No, not much." She switched back into English. "I'm glad to have a partner who speaks English."

"Welcome to Shanghai."

"Thank you, Chief Inspector Chen."

"Let's get your luggage."

There was a long line of people queuing up at customs, holding passports, forms, documents, and pens in their hands. The airport suddenly appeared overcrowded.

"Don't worry about customs formalities," he said. "You're our distinguished American guest."

He led her through another passage, nodding at several uniformed officers by a side door. One of them took a quick look at her passport, scribbled a few words on it, and waved her through.

They walked out with her luggage on a cart and pushed it into the designated taxi area in front of a huge billboard advertising Coca-Cola in Chinese. There were not many people waiting there.

"Let's talk at your hotel, the Peace Hotel on the Bund. Sorry, we have to take a taxi instead of our bureau car. I sent it back because of the delay," he said.

"Great. Here comes one."

A small Xiali pulled up in front of them. He had intended to wait for a Dazhong, made by the joint venture of Shanghai Automobile and Volkswagen, which would be more roomy and comfortable, but she was already giving the hotel name in Chinese to the taxi driver.

There was practically no trunk space in a Xiali. With her suitcase in the front seat beside the driver, and a bag beside her in the backseat, he felt squeezed. She could hardly stretch her long legs. The air conditioning did not work. He rolled down the window, but it did not help much. Wiping the sweat from her brow, she slipped her jacket off. She was wearing a tank top. The bumpy ride brought her shoulder into occasional contact with his. Their proximity made him uncomfortable.

After they passed the Hongqiao area, traffic became congested. The taxi had to make frequent detours due to new construction underway. At the intersection of Yen'an and Jiangning roads, they came to a stop in heavy traffic.

"How long was your flight?" he asked, out of the need to say something.

"More than twenty-four hours."

"Oh, it's a long trip."

"I had to change planes. From St. Louis to San Francisco, then to Tokyo, and finally to Shanghai."

"China's Oriental Airline flies directly from San Francisco to Shanghai."

"Yes, it does, but my mother booked the ticket for me. Nothing but United Airlines for her. She insisted on it, for safety's sake."

"I see. Everything—" he left the sentence unfinished—*Everything American is preferable.* "Don't you work in Washington?"

"Our headquarters is in D.C. but I am stationed in the St. Louis regional office. My parents also live there."

"St. Louis—the city where T. S. Eliot was born. And Washington University was founded by his grandfather."

"Why, yes. There's an Eliot Hall at the university, too. You amaze me, Chief Inspector Chen."

"Well, I have translated some of Eliot's poems," he said, not too surprised at her surprise. "Not all Chinese cops are like those in American movies, good for nothing but martial arts, broken English, and Gongbao chicken."

"Those are just Hollywood stereotypes. I majored in Chinese studies, Chief Inspector Chen."

"I was joking." Why had he become so sensitive about the image of the Chinese police in her eyes, he wondered. Because of Party Secretary Li's emphasis? He shrugged his shoulders, touching hers again. "Off the record, I'm quite good at cooking Gongbao chicken, too."

"I would like to taste that."

He changed the topic. "So what do you think of Shanghai? It's your first time, right?"

"Yes, I've heard so much about this city. It's like a dream come true. The streets, the buildings, the people, and even the traffic, all seem strangely familiar. Look," she exclaimed as the car passed Xizhuang Road. "The Big World. I had a postcard of it."

"Yes, it's a well-known entertainment center. You can spend a day there, watching different local operas, not to mention karaoke, dance, acrobatics, and electronic games. And there's a variety of Chinese food available in Yunnan Gourmet Street beside it. The street is lined with snack bars and restaurants."

"Oh, I love Chinese food."

The taxi turned into the Bund. In the play of the neon lights, the color of her eyes seemed not to be exactly blue. He saw a greenish tinge. Azure, he thought. It was not just the color. He was reminded of an ancient line: *The change from the azure sea into the blue mulberry field*, a reference to the vicissitudes of the world, which came to have a melancholy connotation—about the experience of the irrecoverable.

To their left, concrete, granite, and marble buildings stretched along the Bund. Then the legendary Hong Kong–Shanghai Bank came into view, still guarded by the bronze lions which had witnessed numerous changes in its ownership. Next to it, the big clock on the top of the neoclassical Custom House chimed the hour.

"The building with the marble façade and pyramid-shaped tower at the corner of Nanjing Road is the Peace Hotel, originally the Cathay Hotel, whose owner made millions from the opium trade. After 1949, the city government changed its name. Despite its age, it maintains its rank as one of the finest hotels in Shanghai . . ."

The taxi pulled up in front of the hotel before he finished his speech. That might be as well. He had a feeling that she had been listening to him with tolerant amusement. A uniformed porter strode over, holding the door for the American. The red-capped-and-red-clad employee must have taken Chen for her interpreter and showered all his attention upon her. Chen observed this with wry humor as he helped to put the luggage on a hotel cart.

In the lobby, he heard fragments of jazz. A band composed of old men was playing in a bar at the end of the hall, pumping out old standards for a nostalgic audience. The band was so popular that it was mentioned in the newspapers as one of the Bund's attractions.

She asked about the dining room. The porter pointed to a glass door farther down the corridor, saying the dining room would remain open until three in the morning, and that there were bars nearby that stayed in business even later.

"We could have a meal now," he said.

"No, thanks. I ate on the plane. I'll probably stay awake until two or three o'clock tonight. Jet lag."

They took the elevator to the seventh floor. Her room was 708. As she slid in the plastic card, light flooded over a large room furnished with dark wood furniture inlaid with ivory. The room was decorated in Art Deco style; posters of actors and actresses of the twenties contributed to the period feeling. The only modern items were a color TV, a small refrigerator beside the dresser, and a coffee maker on the corner table.

"It's nine o'clock," Chen said, glancing at his watch. "After the long journey, you must be tired, Inspector Rohn."

"No, I'm not, but I would like to wash up a little."

"I'll smoke a cigarette in the lobby and return in twenty minutes."

"No, you don't have to leave. Just sit down for a minute," she said, gesturing toward the couch. As she headed to the bathroom with a bag, she handed a magazine to him. "I read it on the plane."

It was a copy of *Entertainment Weekly* with several American movie stars on the cover, but he did not open it. First, he checked the room for bugs. Then he moved to the window. Once he had wandered along the Bund with his schoolmates, wondering, looking up at the Peace Hotel. To look down from its windows had been beyond his wildest dreams.

But the view of Bund Park pulled him back to the present. He had not done anything about the homicide case yet. Farther to the north, buses and trolley buses rumbled across the bridge at frequent intervals. Nearby bars and restaurants displayed neon signs that flashed incessantly. Some stayed open all night. So there would have been hardly any possibility that people could climb into the park without being noticed, just as he had initially surmised.

He turned to make a pot of coffee. The talk he would have to have soon with this American partner would be difficult. He decided to call the bureau first. Qian was still there, dutifully waiting by the phone. Perhaps he had misjudged Qian.

"Detective Yu has just phoned in with an important lead."

"What is it?"

"According to one of Wen's neighbors, Wen received a phone call from her husband shortly before she disappeared on the night of April fifth."

"That's something," Chen said. "How did her neighbor know?"

"Wen did not have a phone at home. The conversation took place in her neighbor's home, but her neighbor knew nothing about the contents of that call."

"Anything else?"

"No. Detective Yu said he would try to call again."

"If he phones in soon, tell him to try me at the Peace Hotel. Room 708."

Now he had something concrete to discuss with Inspector Rohn, Chen thought with relief, putting down the receiver as she came out of the bathroom, drying her hair with a towel.

She was dressed now in blue jeans and a white cotton blouse.

"Would you like a cup of coffee?"

"No, thanks. Not tonight," she said. "Do you know when Wen will be ready to depart for the United States?"

"Well, I have some news for you, but it's not good, I'm afraid."

"Something wrong?"

"Wen Liping has disappeared."

"Disappeared! How is that possible, Chief Inspector Chen?" She stared at him for a second before she added sharply, "Killed or kidnapped?"

"I don't think she has been killed. That would have done nobody any good. We cannot rule out the kidnapping possibility. The local police have started their investigation but so far, there's no evidence supporting that hypothesis. All we know is that she got a phone call from her husband on the night of April fifth and disappeared shortly afterward. Her disappearance might have been caused by that phone call."

"Feng is allowed to call home once a week, but not to say anything that might jeopardize the case. A record is kept of the calls he makes; I hope his conversation was taped, but it may not have been. He's anxious for his wife to join him. Why would he say anything to cause her disappearance?"

"You had better check on his calls on April fifth. We would certainly like to know exactly what was said."

"I will find out what I can, but what are *you* going to do, Chief Inspector Chen?"

"The Fujian police are looking for her. Checking all the hotels and buses there. No leads yet. It is important to find her as soon as possible, we understand. A special group has been formed. I'm in charge of it. My partner, Detective Yu, went to Fujian last night. In fact, I got the tip about this phone call just five minutes ago. He will keep us informed with respect to developments there."

Catherine Rohn's response was quick. "For several months, Wen has been applying for a passport so she can join her husband. Suddenly, she disappears. A pregnant woman could not have gone far on foot, and you have no information about her taking a bus or a train, right? So she's still in Fujian, or someone has abducted her. You're the head of the special case group, yet you're here in Shanghai—with me. Why?"

"When more information reaches us, we will decide what steps to take. In the meantime, I'm going to conduct the investigation here. Wen is an educated youth from Shanghai who left for Fujian twenty years ago. She may have come back to this city."

"Do you have any other leads?"

"Not at present. I'll talk with Detective Yu and other people tonight," he said, trying to produce a reassuring smile. "Don't worry, Inspector Rohn. Wen wants to join her husband, so she will have to get in touch with him."

"You are assuming that she is able to do so. No, Feng cannot reveal his whereabouts. Not even his phone number. Or he will be kicked out of the witness protection program. That is the rule. There's no way she can get in touch with him directly. All she can do is telephone a bureau number and leak a message to be passed on."

"Feng may know where she is hiding. Or if she has been kidnapped, the kidnappers must contact Feng. So I have a suggestion for you. Call your office and put your people on the alert for any phone calls Feng gets or makes. Perhaps we can trace her that way."

"That's possible, but you know how crucial time is. We cannot be like that farmer in the Chinese proverb, who waits for a rabbit to knock itself out against the old tree."

"Your knowledge of Chinese culture is impressive, Inspector Rohn. Yes, we are pressed for time. Our government understands it well, or I would not be here with you today."

"If your government had cooperated effectively earlier, I would not be here with you, Chief Inspector Chen."

"What do you mean?"

"I cannot understand why it took so long for Wen to get her passport. She started the application process in January. Now it is mid-April. In fact, she should have been in the United States long since."

"January?" He did not have that date in mind. "I do not know too much about the process, Inspector Rohn. In fact, I did not get the assignment until yesterday afternoon. I'll look into it and give you an answer. Now I must leave so I can talk to Detective Yu when he calls me at my home."

"You can call him from here."

"He arrived in Fujian this morning and started working at once with the local police. He has not checked into a hotel yet. That's why I have to wait at home for his call." Chen stood up. "Oh, I have something else for you. Some information about the Fengs. Perhaps the part about Feng is not new to you, but Wen's dossier may be worth reading. I have translated some of it into English."

"Thank you, Chief Inspector Chen."

"I'll return tomorrow morning. I hope you sleep well your first night in Shanghai, Inspector Rohn."

In spite of the awkwardness of their conversation, which he had anticipated, she walked him down the crimson-carpeted corridor to the elevator.

"Don't stay up too late. We will have a lot to do tomorrow, Inspector Rohn."

She tucked a strand of her golden hair behind her ear. "Good night, Chief Inspector Chen."

Chapter 6

Catherine could not fall asleep despite her travel fatigue and the hands of a cloisonné clock on the nightstand indicating the beginning of a new day.

Finally, she threw off the sheet, got up, and walked to the window. The lights of the Bund surged up to greet her.

Shanghai. The Bund. The Huangpu River. The Peace Hotel . . . It was a pleasant surprise that the Shanghai Police Bureau had chosen this hotel for her. She was not in the mood, however, to marvel at the scene spread out beneath her. Her mission in China had totally changed.

Originally, it was to have been simple. To accompany Wen to the local offices for a passport, to fill out the visa forms at the American Consulate, and to escort her onto the airplane at her earliest convenience. According to Ed Spencer, her supervisor in Washington, all she was to do was to apply a touch of pressure when needed, to make the U.S. Marshals' presence felt, so the Chinese would expedite the matter. Ed joked about buying lunch for her in D.C. this weekend. Even allowing for minor delays, it should have taken her four or five days at most. Now she did not know how long she would have to stay in Shanghai.

Was the report of Wen's sudden disappearance simply a lie? It was possible. The Chinese had not been enthusiastic about Wen joining her husband in the United States. If Jia Xinzhi, the head of the smuggling ring, was convicted, that might make international headlines. The sordid details of this notorious business would not improve the image of the Chinese government abroad. Involvement of local law enforcement officials in the human smuggling trade had been suspected. In such a well-policed country, how could smugglers have succeeded in transporting thousands of people out of the country without the notice of the authorities? According to one report she had read on the plane, hundreds of illegal immigrants had traveled on military trucks from Fuzhou to a seaport for embarkation. To cover up their complicity, the Chinese authorities might be trying to prevent the witness's wife from leaving the country, so as to forestall the trial. First the inexplicable delay, now Wen's even more inexplicable disappearance. Was this a last-minute effort of the Chinese to wriggle out of the deal they had made? If this was the case, her mission would be impossible.

She scratched at a vicious mosquito bite on her arm.

Nor did she feel very compatible with Chief Inspector Chen, though his being assigned as her partner suggested that the Chinese were seriously trying to honor their commitment. Not merely because of his rank. There was something else about the man; he seemed sincere. But he could have been chosen to play a deceptive role. In fact, he might not even be a chief inspector. Maybe he was a secret agent with a special assignment: to string her along.

She called Washington. Ed Spencer was not in the office. She left a message, giving him the hotel phone number.

Putting down the phone, Catherine started to read the files Chen had left. There was not much about Feng that was new to her, but the information about Wen was fresh, plentiful, and well-organized.

It took her almost an hour to read it through. In spite of her background, she found several recurring Chinese terms hard to understand. She underlined them, hoping she might dig out definitions in a large dictionary the next day. Then she tried to frame her report to her supervisor.

What was there for her to do in China now?

She could simply wait, as Chief Inspector Chen suggested. Alternatively she might offer to join the investigation. It was an important case for them. Feng's testimony was needed and, to obtain it, they had to reunite him with his wife, if she was still alive. She decided it would be best for her to take part in the investigation. The Chinese had no reason to refuse the request unless there really was a cover-up effort on their side. Chen seemed certain that Wen was alive. But if she had been killed, no one could know how that would affect Feng's testimony.

Inspector Rohn had not been pleased with her special status as something of an expert on China in the Marshals Service, though it was that status that brought her here. Taking part in the investigation would be an opportunity to prove that her major in Chinese studies was not irrelevant to her position, and would also give her an opportunity to learn about the real Chinese people.

So she started writing a fax to Ed Spencer. After briefing him on the unexpected development, she requested that he look for a tape of Feng's phone call on April fifth, being especially alert to a possible coded message. She then asked his approval for her joining the investigation. At the end, she made a request for information about Chief Inspector Chen Cao.

Before she went down to the hotel's fax room, she added one sentence, asking Ed to send his reply to the hotel around 10 A.M. Shanghai time, so she could be waiting by the fax machine. She did not want anybody else to look at the contents, even if written in English.

After the fax went through, she had a quick meal in the dining room. Back in her own room, she took another shower. She was still not sleepy. Wrapped in a bath towel, she looked out again at the illuminated expanse of the river. She caught a glimpse of a ship bearing a striped flag. At that distance, she could not make out its name. It might be an American cruise ship anchored for the night in the Huangpu River.

Around four in the morning, she took two tablets of Dramamine, which she had brought with her in case of motion sickness. Its soporific side effect was what she needed. In addition, she took a bottle of Budweiser out of the refrigerator; its Chinese name was *Baiwei* meaning—"a hundred times more powerful." The Anheuser-Busch brewery had a joint venture in Wuhan.

As she turned from the window, she thought of a Song dynasty poem she had studied in a class. It was about a traveler's loneliness, in spite of the marvelous scenery. Trying to recall the lines, she fell asleep.

She was awakened by the bedside alarm clock. Rubbing her eyes, she jumped up, disoriented. It was 9:45. She had no time to take a shower. Pulling on a T-shirt and a pair of old jeans, she left her room wearing the hotel's disposable slippers which were almost paper thin, and seemed to be made of the same material as that used for transparent plastic raincoats. Hurrying down to the hotel fax room, she straightened her hair in the elevator with a pocket comb.

The fax for her came at the time she had specified. The feedback was more substantial than she had expected. First, the fact of Feng's phone call on April fifth was confirmed, and there was a tape. Ed was having its contents translated. As a potential witness, Feng was not allowed to disclose anything about his status in the program. Ed had no idea what he might have said to precipitate Wen's disappearance.

Second, her proposal to join the investigation was approved.

In response to her request for the background information on Chen, Ed wrote: "I've contacted the CIA. They will send us Chief Inspector Chen Cao's file. From what they told me, Chen is someone to watch. He is associated with the liberal reformers in the Party. He is also a member of the Chinese Writers' Association. He is described as an ambitious Party cadre, on the rise."

As she stepped out of the room with the fax in her hand, she saw Chen seated in the lobby browsing through an English magazine, a bouquet of flowers lying on a chair beside him.

"Good morning, Inspector Rohn." Chen stood up, and she realized he was taller than the other people in the lobby. He had a high forehead, penetrating black eyes, and his expression was intelligent. Dressed in a black suit, he looked more like a scholar than a policeman, an impression enhanced by the information she had just read.

"Good morning, Chief Inspector Chen."

"This is for you." Chen handed the flowers to her. "There were so many things happening at the bureau yesterday, I forgot to prepare a proper welcome bouquet for you in my rush to the airport. For your first morning in Shanghai."

"Thank you. It's beautiful."

"I called your room. No one answered. So I decided to wait for you here. I hope you don't mind."

She didn't mind. The flowers were a surprise, but as she stood beside him in her plastic slippers, with her hair in such a mess, she couldn't help a feeling of annoyance at his formal courtesy. This was not behavior she expected from a colleague, and she didn't quite care for the veiled reminder that she was "just" a woman.

"Let's go up to my room to talk," she said.

As they entered her room, she gestured for him to sit and picked up a vase from the corner table. "I'll put the flowers in water."

"Have you enjoyed a good night's sleep?" Chen asked, glancing around the room.

"Not really, but it should be enough," she said. She refused to be embarrassed by the disarray of the room. The bed was not made, her stockings were thrown down on the rug, pills were scattered on the night stand, and her rumpled suit had been tossed over the back of the chair. She made a curt excuse, "Sorry, I had to pick up a fax."

"I should have given you notice. My apologies."

"You are being very polite, Comrade Chief Inspector Chen," she said, trying to keep the sarcasm from her voice. "Last night you were up late too, I imagine."

"Last night, after I left you, I discussed the case with Superintendent Hong of the Fujian police. It was a long discussion. Early in the morning, my assistant, Detective Yu, phoned me. He explained that at his hotel, there's only one telephone at the front desk, and after eleven o'clock the night manager locks up the telephone and goes to bed."

"Why lock up the phone?"

"Well, a telephone is a rare commodity in the countryside," Chen explained. "It's not like in Shanghai."

"Is there new information this morning?"

"About your question concerning the delay in our passport approval process, I've got an answer."

"What is that, Chief Inspector Chen?"

"Wen would have received her passport several weeks ago, but she did not have her marriage certificate. No legal document to prove her relationship with Feng. She moved in with Feng in 1971. Government offices were all closed at the time."

"Why were the government offices closed?"

"Mao labeled a lot of cadres as 'capitalist roaders.' Liu Shaoqi, the head of the People's Republic, was thrown into jail without a trial. The offices were shut. The so-called revolutionary committees became the only power."

"I've read about the Cultural Revolution, but I did not realize that."

"So our passport people had to search the commune records. It took time. That's probably why the process has been so slow."

"Probably," she echoed, tilting her head slightly to one side. "So in China, every rule is to be strictly followed—even in a special case?"

"That's what I learned. Besides, Wen only initiated her application in mid-February, not in January."

"But Feng told us she applied in January—mid-January."

"That's my information. Even so, it has taken a long time, I have to admit. There may have been another factor. Wen does not have any *guanxi* in Fujian. This word may be translated as 'connections,' only *guanxi* means far more than that. It's not merely about the people you know, but about the people who can help you with what you want."

"The grease that keep the wheels turning, so to speak."

"If you like. Perhaps, like anywhere else in the world, the wheels of bureaucracy move slowly, unless there is some lubrication for the bureaucrats. That's where *guanxi* comes in. Wen has remained an outsider all these years, so she had no *guanxi* whatsoever."

She was astonished by Chen's frankness. He made no attempt to gloss over the way the system worked. This did not seem to be characteristic of an "emerging Party cadre."

"Oh, there is something else. According to one of Wen's neighbors, there was a stranger looking for Wen on the afternoon of April sixth."

"Who do you think that might have been?"

"His identity is still to be determined, but he was not local. Now, any news from your side, Inspector Rohn?"

"Feng did make a phone call to Wen on April fifth. We're having it translated and analyzed. I'll let you know as soon as I hear more."

"That may contain the answer to Wen's disappearance," Chen said, taking a look at his watch. "Tell me, what's your plan for the morning."

"I have no plan."

"Have you had your breakfast?"

"No, not yet."

"Excellent. My plan is to have a good breakfast," Chen said. "After my long discussion with Detective Yu this morning. I hurried over without having had a bite."

"We can have something downstairs," she proposed.

"Forget the hotel dining room. Let me take you to another place—genuine Chinese flavor, typical Shanghai atmosphere. Only a few minutes' walk away."

She looked for reasons for not going out with him, but came up with none. And it would be easier for her to ask to have a part in his investigation over a congenial breakfast. "You keep amazing me, Chief Inspector Chen, a cop, a poet, a translator, and now a gourmet," she said. "I'll change."

It took her a few minutes to shower, to don a white summer dress, and to comb her hair into obedience.

Before they left the room, Chen held out a cellular phone to her. "This is for your convenience."

"A Motorola!"

"You know what it is called here?" Chen said. "Big Brother. Big Sister if the owner is a woman. The symbols of upstarts in contemporary China."

"Interesting terms."

"In Kung Fu literature, this is what the head of a gang would sometimes be called. Rich people are called Mr. Big Bucks now-adays, and Big Brother and Sister carry the same connotation. I have a cell phone myself. It will make it easier for us to contact each other."

"So we're a Big Sister and a Big Brother, going out for a walk in Shanghai," she said with a smile.

Strolling along Nanjing Road, she saw the traffic was completely snarled. People and bikes kept cutting in and out of the smallest spaces imaginable between cars. The drivers had to keep braking all the time.

"Nanjing Road is like an extended shopping center. The city government has imposed restrictions on traffic here." Chen spoke like a tourist guide again. "It may become a pedestrian mall in the near future."

It took them no more than five minutes to reach the intersection of Nanjing Road and Sichuan Road. She saw a white Western-style restaurant on the corner. A number of young people were sipping coffee behind the tall, amber-colored windows.

"Deda Cafe," Chen said. "The coffee here is excellent, but we are going to a street market behind it."

She looked up to see a sign at the street entrance, THE CENTRAL MARKET. It marked a narrow street. Shabby, too. In addition to a variety of tiny stores with makeshift counters or tables displaying goods on the sidewalk, there was a cluster of snackbars and booths tucked into the corner.

"Formerly, it was a marketplace for cheap and secondhand goods, like a flea market in the United States." Chen continued plying her with information. "With so many people coming here, eating places appeared, convenient, inexpensive, but with a special flavor."

The snackbars, food carts, and small restaurants seemed to fill the air with a palpable energy. Most appeared to be cheap, low-class, in sharp contrast to those near the Peace Hotel. A curbside peddler spread out skewers of diced lamb on a makeshift grill, adding a pinch of spices from time to time. A gaunt herbalist measured out ancient medicinal remedies into a row of earthen pots boiling under a silk banner declaring in bold Chinese characters: MEDICAL MEAL.

This was where she wanted to be, at a clamorous, chaotic corner that told real stories about the city. Fish, squid, and turtles, were all displayed alive in wooden or plastic basins. Eels, quails, and frog legs were frying in the sizzling woks. Most of the bustling restaurants were full of customers.

They found a vacant table in a bar. Chen handed her a dog-eared menu. After looking at the strange names of the items listed, she gave up. "You decide. I've never heard of any of them."

So Chen ordered a portion of fried mini-buns with minced pork stuffing, shrimp dumplings with transparent skin, sticks of fermented tofu, rice porridge with a thousand-year-egg, pickled white squash, salted duck, and Guilin bean curd with chopped green scallions. All in small dishes.

"It's like a banquet," she said.

"It costs less than a continental breakfast in the hotel," he said.

The tofu came first, tiny pieces on bamboo sticks like shish kebabs. In spite of a wild, sharp flavor, she started to like it after the first few bites.

"Food has always been an important part of Chinese culture," Chen mumbled, busily eating. "As Confucius says, 'To enjoy food and sex is human nature.' "

"Really!" She had never come across that quotation. He could not have made it up, could he? She thought she caught a slight suggestion of humor in his tone.

Soon she became aware of curious glances from other customers—an American woman devouring common food in the company of a Chinese man. A pudgy customer even greeted her as he passed their table with an enormous rice ball in his hand.

"Now I have a couple of questions for you, Chief Inspector Chen. Do you think Wen married Feng, a peasant, because she believed so devoutly in Mao?"

"That's possible. But for things between a man and a woman, I don't think politics alone can be an explanation."

"Did many of the educated youths remain in the country-side?" she said, nibbling at the last piece of tofu.

"After the Cultural Revolution, most of them returned to the city. Detective Yu and his wife were educated youths in Yunnan, and they came back to Shanghai in the early eighties."

"You have an interesting division of labor, Chief Inspector Chen. Detective Yu is busy working in Fujian, and you stay in Shanghai to enjoy delicious snacks with an American guest."

"It is my responsibility as a chief inspector to welcome you on the occasion of your first trip to China, and of the first instance of anti-illegal-immigration cooperation between our two countries. Party Secretary Li made a special point of it. 'Make Inspector Rohn's stay in Shanghai a safe and satisfactory one' are my orders."

"Thank you," she said. His self-mockery was apparent now, which made their talk easier. "So when I go back home, I'm supposed to talk about the friendship between our two countries, and the politics in your newspapers."

"That is up to you, Inspector Rohn. It's the Chinese tradition to show hospitality to a guest from a faraway country."

"In addition to entertaining me, what else are you going to do?"

"I've made a list of Wen's possible contacts here. Qian Jun, my temporary assistant, is arranging for me to interview them this afternoon or tomorrow morning. In the meantime, I will keep exchanging information with you."

"So I am to sit in the hotel all day, waiting for phone calls, like a switchboard operator?"

"No, you don't have to do that. It's your first trip to China. Do some sightseeing. The Bund, Nanjing Road. I'll serve as your full-time tour escort over the weekend."

"I would rather join you in your work, Chief Inspector Chen."

"You mean take part in the interviews?"

"Yes." She looked him in the eye.

"I don't see any reason why not, except that most people speak the Shanghai dialect here."

His answer was a diplomatic one, she thought, but nonetheless an excuse.

"I had no problem talking with my fellow travelers in the airplane. They all spoke Mandarin to me. Can't we ask our interviewees to do the same? And you can help me out, if need be."

"I can try, but do you think people will talk freely in front of an American officer?"

"They will be more earnest," she said, "if they believe we mean business—an American officer plus a Chinese one."

"You have a point, Inspector Rohn. I'll consult Party Secretary Li."

"Is it part of your political culture never to give a straightforward reply?"

"No. I'll give you a straightforward answer, but I need to get his permission. Surely some procedures have to be followed, even in the U.S. Marshals Service."

"Granted, Chief Inspector Chen," she said. "So what do you want me to do now, while I await his permission?"

"If Wen's disappearance was caused by the phone call from

her husband, you'd better check for possible leaks in your department."

"I'll talk with my supervisor," she said, aware of the direction he was trying to lead her in, which she had anticipated.

"I've asked the hotel to set up a fax machine in your room. If there's anything else you need, do let me know."

"I appreciate your help. Now just one more question," she said on the spur of the moment. "Last night, looking out at the Bund, I thought of a classical Chinese poem. I studied an English version several years ago. About a poet's regret at being unable to share a transcendant scene with his friend. I cannot remember the exact lines. By any chance, do you know the poem?"

"Um—" He eyed her in surprise. "I think it is a poem by Liu Yong, a Song dynasty poet. The second stanza reads like this. *Where shall I find myself / Tonight, waking from a hangover—/ The riverbank lined with weeping willows, / The moon sinking, the dawn rising on a breeze. / Year after year, I will be far, / Far away from you. / All the beautiful scenes are unfolding, / But to no avail: / Oh, to whom can I speak / Of this ever enchanting landscape?*"

"That's it." She was amazed at his sudden metamorphosis. His face lit up when he recited those lines.

The CIA information was credible. He was a chief inspector and a poet too—at least he was familiar with both Eliot and Liu Yong. That intrigued her.

Chen said, "Liu's one of my favorites during the pre-Eliot period."

"What makes Eliot so special for you?"

"He cannot decide whether to declare himself to his love. At least not in 'The Love Song of J. Alfred Prufrock.'"

"Then Eliot should have learned from Liu."

"And I'd better go to Party Secretary Li now," he said, smiling as he arose.

On the corner of Sichuan Road they had to stand in the street as the sidewalk was filled by illegally parked bikes. They shook hands, ready to part, when she suddenly became aware of a motorcyclist dressed in black jeans and a black T-shirt, his face covered with a black helmet, on a powerful cycle heading straight at her at high speed. The rumbling monster would have crashed right onto her but for Chen's reaction. Still holding her hand, he yanked her onto the pavement and spun himself around to shield her. At the same time, his right leg kicked out backward, pivoting like in a Kung Fu movie. Missing Chen by a hair's breadth, the motorcycle dodged, swayed, but did not fall. With its tires screeching, it kicked up a cloud of dust and sped onto Nanjing Road.

The whole thing was over in a few seconds. The motorcycle disappeared in traffic. Several passersby gaped at them and moved on.

"I am so sorry, Inspector Rohn," he said, letting go of her hand. "Those reckless motorcyclists are dangerous."

"Thank you, Chief Inspector Chen," she said. They walked on.

Chapter 7

On his way to Party Secretary Li's office, Chen checked the bureau fax folder. There were several for him from the Fujian Police Bureau—additional information about the Flying Axes. He was pleased to find a cellular phone number for Detective Yu on the cover sheet as had been promised by Superintendent

Hong the previous night. He also found a page with a picture of a shabby house, beneath which ran a line in Yu's handwriting, "Wen's House in Changle Village."

Qian came over with a broad smile on his face and a large envelope in his hand. "I have had the information about Wen circulated, Chief Inspector Chen. Also, I've had a talk with Dr. Xia about the Bund Park case. The formal autopsy report will takes some time, but here is an informal summary."

"Good job, Qian," Chen said, going to his own small, Spartan office cubicle. The summary had been typed. Qian was proficient in Twinbridge, a Chinese software, but perhaps not as familiar with medical terms.

The Body in Bund Park

1) The time of death: Around one o'clock on the night of April eighth.

2) The cause of death: Head injury with fractures of the skull. Extensive damage to the lining of the brain. Bleeding from multiple wounds, eighteen of them. He could have received the fatal head blow before some of the wounds were inflicted. A general absence of bruises on his arms and legs shows he had not struggled before his death.

3) The body: The victim was in his mid-forties. Six feet tall, one hundred eighty pounds. He was strongly built with well-defined arm and leg muscles. His hands were well manicured. Good teeth, except for three gold ones. There was an old scar on his face.

4) He had had sexual intercourse shortly before death. There were still traces of semen and vaginal fluid on his sex organ. There was a deep cut two inches above his penis.

5) Needle tracks on his arms indicate he was a possible I.V. drug user. In addition, there were traces of some unknown drug in his body.

6) His silk pajamas are of excellent quality. There's no label; it had been removed, but its material seemed to be imported, with a V design woven into the material.

It was a clear report, which further pointed to the possibility of triad involvement, especially the evidence of the unknown drug in the body.

Something else caught his attention. If the victim had been murdered at home, having just had sex, there should have been two bodies in the park—his and his wife's. But if he had been with somebody else, and his sex partner—whoever that might have been—left immediately after the act, it suggested that the murder might have taken place in a hotel.

Chen made himself a cup of tea and dialed Qian's extension. "Send out a detailed description of the victim together with a picture, to hotels as well as neighborhood committees."

That was about all Qian could do at this stage.

However, Chief Inspector Chen wanted to do more. And to use somebody else for the job. There was no accounting for his mistrust of Qian. Perhaps it was merely a whim, a personal prejudice.

His cell phone started ringing. The LCD displayed Inspector Rohn's number. He pushed the button. "Is everything okay with you, Inspector Rohn?"

"I'm fine, thanks to your excellent kung fu this morning."

"Don't mention it. What's up?"

"The content of the phone conversation has been translated."

"What did Feng say?"

"It's a short conversation. According to our translator, Feng's message was: *Some people have got wind of it. Run for your life. Contact me when you're at a safe place.*"

"What did he mean?"

"Wen asked the same question. Feng just repeated the message," she said. "Now Feng tells my boss that he had gotten a warning on a slip of paper inserted in his grocery bag before he phoned his wife."

"What did it say?"

"Don't forget your pregnant wife in China."

"Your supervisor must look into it. If Feng's so well hidden, how did they get to him?"

"That's what he is investigating."

"Those secret societies are powerful," he added, "even in the United States."

"True," she agreed. "What about our investigation here?"

"I'm on my way to Party Secretary Li's office. I'll call you soon."

Chief Inspector Chen was not sure what Party Secretary Li's response would be. But he knew that interviewing potential contacts of Wen's would be monotonous. The company of an American partner would at least provide an opportunity for him to practice his English.

"How's everything, Chief Inspector Chen?" Li said, rising from his chair.

"Searching for this woman is like looking for a needle in a haystack."

"You are doing your best." Li poured a cup of jasmine tea for him. "How is Inspector Rohn getting along in Shanghai?"

"Fine. And she's quite cooperative too."

"You are the right person to handle her, Chief Inspector Chen. Any leads so far?"

"Detective Yu has found one. Wen got a phone call from Feng on April fifth and went into hiding because of the call."

"That's very important. In fact, that's great. I will pass the information to the leading comrades in Beijing today." Li did not attempt to conceal the excitement in his voice. "You have done an excellent job."

"How?" Chen was surprised. "I've not done anything yet."

"It's the Americans' carelessness that has caused Wen's disappearance. They should not have permitted anyone to get close enough to Feng to threaten him. They should not have allowed Feng to make that call," Li said, rubbing his hands. "The Americans' responsibility. That's it."

"Well, as for responsibility, I've not yet discussed it with Inspector Rohn. She said the U. S. Marshals would investigate."

"Yes, that's the way to go. The gang must have found out about Feng's witness status and whereabouts through some leak on the American side."

"That's possible," Chen said. He was thinking of what Yu had told him about the local Fujian cops' poor work. "But there could also be a leak on our side."

"Well, any other information from Inspector Rohn?"

"The Americans want to have the trial as scheduled. They are anxious about our progress."

"Any other news from Fujian?"

"No. Detective Yu has a difficult job there. The Flying Axes seem to be popular, and the local police are no match for them. They have no clue whatsoever. Nor are they eager to crack down on the gangsters. So what can Yu do—except knock on one unfriendly door after another?"

"The popularity of the triad tradition in the area, I understand. You did the right thing to send Detective Yu there."

"Now for my work here, I'm going to interview some of Wen's possible contacts. Inspector Rohn wants to join me," Chen said. "What do you think, Party Secretary Li?"

"I don't think that is part of her mission here."

"She said she got permission from her headquarters."

"Wen is a Chinese citizen," Li said deliberately. "It is up to the Chinese police to look for her. I don't see any necessity for an American officer to join our effort."

"I can tell her that, but the Americans may suspect that we are simply trying to cover up. It would add to the tension if we keep her out of our investigation."

"The Americans always look at others askance, as if they were the world's only police."

"That's true, but if she has nothing to occupy her here, Inspector Rohn will insist on going to Fujian."

"Um, you have a point. Can't you let Qian conduct the interviews while you keep her entertained with tourist activities?"

"She will insist on joining Qian then." He then added, "And Qian does not speak English."

"Well, I don't think it can do much harm for her to interview some ordinary Shanghainese with you. I don't have to repeat: the safety of Inspector Rohn has to be our top responsibility."

"So you think it is okay for her to work with me?"

"You have full authority, Chief Inspector Chen. How many times have I told you that?"

"Thank you, Party Secretary Li." Chen continued, after a pause, "Now about the other case. The body in Bund Park. I am planning to look into some potential triad connections here. They may also know something about whether Wen is in Shanghai."

"No, I don't think so. If you start asking questions, the Flying Axes will soon hear of it. Your efforts will only stir up a sleeping snake."

"We need to do something about the Bund Park murder case, too, Party Secretary Li."

"No hurry. Detective Yu will be back in a couple of days. It can be a job for him. At this moment, with Inspector Rohn staying here, you mustn't do anything foolish to bring a hornet's nest down about your ears."

Li's response did not really surprise him. The Party Secretary had never been enthusiastic about his investigating the Bund

Park case, and Li always had his reasons, political reasons, for doing or not doing something. His reaction to Feng's phone call was also understandable. To Li, it seemed to be much more important to place responsibility on the Americans than to find the missing woman. The Party Secretary was a politician, not a policeman.

After he finished his talk with Li, Chen hurried out of the bureau to a meeting with Old Hunter, Yu's father.

Earlier in the morning, the old man had phoned him, suggesting they have tea together. Not in the Mid-Lake Teahouse in the City God Temple Market where they had met on several occasions, but in another one called Moon Breeze, closer to the area where the old man performed his daily activities as an honorary advisor for the Traffic Control Office, wearing a red armband. The retired cop received little in pay, but he got a great kick out of the official-sounding title, imagining himself a staunch pillar of justice whenever he stopped a bike illegally carrying a baby on the back rack or a private taxi displaying an outdated license plate.

The Moon Breeze was a new teahouse. There seemed to be a revival of interest in tea among the Shanghainese. He saw a number of young people drinking with gestures made fashionable by the new movies, before he caught sight of Old Hunter slouching in a corner. Instead of southern bamboo music in the background, a waltz could be heard. Incongruously, strains of "The Blue Danube" rippled through the teahouse. Clearly this was a place for young customers who, though not yet adapted to Starbuck's coffee, needed some space in which to sit and talk. At a neighboring table, there was a mah-jongg battle going on in full swing, with the players as well as onlookers chattering and cursing.

"I have never been here before. It's so different from the Mid-Lake," Old Hunter said rather sadly.

A young waitress came over, light-footed, in a scarlet *cheong-sam* with high slits revealing her ivory thighs, bowing in Japanese fashion. "Do you need a private room, sir?"

Chen nodded. That was one of the advantages of visiting modern teahouses, in spite of the mixture of services.

"It's the bureau's expense," he said as they entered the room. It would be out of the question for the retired cop to pay for the room out of his meager pension. Being a chief inspector with a special budget had its advantages.

Most of the furniture in the private room was in classical style, but there were soft, comfortable cushions placed on the mahogany armchairs, and a dark purple leather sofa matching the color scheme of the room.

Putting the menu on the table, the waitress introduced the house special, "We have the special bubble tea."

"What kind of tea?"

"It's very popular in Hong Kong. You'll like it, sir," she said with a hint of mystery.

"Fine, bubble tea for me and Mountain Mist tea for him," Chen said. After she left, he asked, "How are things with you, Uncle Yu?"

"Like other old men. I'm just trying to make myself useful to society, like a piece of coal that still burns, giving off its last remaining heat."

Chen smiled. The simile was familiar; he remembered hearing it in a movie in the seventies. Times had changed, but not the old man's mind.

"Don't overwork, Uncle Yu."

Old Hunter started with one of his customary rhetorical questions. "You know why I wanted to meet you today, Chief Inspector Chen? I gave Yu a thorough dressing down before he left for Fujian."

"Why?" Chen was aware of the old man's other nickname,

Suzhou Opera Singer. It was a reference to a southern dialect opera known for its performers' tactics of producing drama out of the air, prolonging the tale through endless digressions, and pouring on classical references like black pepper.

"He had reservations about the job, and I said to him, 'In normal circumstances, I would advise you to avoid investigating those gangsters like the plague, but if Chief Inspector Chen wants to fight this battle, follow him through water and through fire. He has more to lose than you, hasn't he? It is a crying shame for us that a corpse killed by triad gangsters has turned up in Bund Park. With a few more honest Party cadres like him, things would not have gotten into such a mess.' "

"Yu and I are good friends. He is the more practical, down-to-earth one. I really depend on him. Now that he's in Fujian, I have a hard time doing my job alone."

"Things are falling apart! The beast of corruption is moving in all over the country. Good people lack conviction. To accomplish anything in today's society, they have to go about in two ways—the black way and the white way. I used to patrol the markets, but now it's the black way—those gangsters—in control. Remember Jiao, the dumpling vendor who carried a miniature kitchen on her shoulders?"

"Yes, the woman selling dumplings close to the Qinghe Lane. She helped us. What happened to her?"

"That's a good location for business. Some people wanted to drive her away from that corner. Her kitchen was smashed one night. The neighborhood police could do nothing. There's no clue as to who did it, they told me. In some new businesses, the gangsters are even bolder. For instance, those karaoke girls and private rooms. A really lucrative business. Five hundred Yuan for one hour in the late evening, the golden time period. Not to mention the tip and extra money. The club owners maintain a good relationship with us because we can make things difficult for them, but they have better relationships with the gangs because they can make things impossible. The girls may be stabbed, the rooms may be damaged, and the owners may be kidnapped—"

Old Hunter's lecture was interrupted as the waitress came back into the room bearing a lacquer tray with an exquisite white china teapot and a single cup. The bubble tea came in a long paper cup with an extra thick straw sticking out of a plastic lid.

The Mountain Mist tea looked good. Chen could tell by the green tea color in the white cup. He took a sip of the bubble tea through his straw. A tiny sticky ball rolled on his tongue. The size of a small marble, but with the rich taste of milk, soft, slippery, almost sensual. But was this really tea?

Perhaps he, too, was antiquated, like Old Hunter, who spit a tiny tea leaf into the cup before continuing. "How can things get into such a mess? Pure and simple. Some of our high-ranking cadres are black-hearted. They take money from the gangsters, and cover up for them in return. Have you heard a story about Party Secretary Li's brother-in-law?"

"No, I haven't."

"Well, that brother-in-law had a bar on Henshan Road. The diamond area of the city. A swell business. How he got the license and lease, people never knew or asked. One day, someone got drunk, smashed a table, and slapped him. The next day, the drunkard came back, knelt on the floor, and slapped his own face hundreds of times. Why? The Blue is behind it. That triad has more power in this city than the government. If the drunkard had not done that, his whole family would have been killed. After this, no one has dared to make any trouble in the bar."

"It could be a gesture to Li," Chen said reluctantly, as he was aware of Old Hunter's grudge against Li. The two had joined the force at about the same time. One did nothing but police work, and the other did nothing but politics. After thirty years, the gap between the two had grown huge. "Yet Li himself might have nothing to do with it."

"Possibly," Old Hunter said, "but you never know. Things are really out of control." The old man continued in indignation, chewing at a tea leaf with his tea-stained teeth, "Now about the dead body in Bund Park. It's unusual. If it happened in those coastal areas close to Hong Kong, or in Yunnan Province where the drug traffic moves across the borders, I would not be so surprised. Since President Jiang was formerly the Mayor of Shanghai, the gangsters keep a low profile here. They do not want to twist the tiger's whiskers. Before this, I cannot remember having heard of any blatant triad killing in Shanghai."

"It may have been the work of organizations from outside Shanghai." Chen nodded, taking another long sip of his tea. "Perhaps to send a message to people here."

"So I suggest you have another story placed in the newspaper. Give vivid details concerning the ax wounds to the body. See if a snake will crawl out of the cave."

"That's a good idea."

"If you're going to deal with those gangsters, Chief Inspector Chen, you cannot do it in your white way only. You have to be very flexible. It is necessary for you to get whatever help you can. Say, from someone familiar with both the black and white ways, and with street connections, too."

It was the old man's way of offering help, Chen realized. The retired cop was an old hand, with contacts of his own. "I cannot agree more. In fact, I was thinking of asking for your help, Uncle Yu."

"Whatever I can do, Chief Inspector Chen."

"I have two cases on my hands. They are not related, but each may have something to do with the black as well as the white way. I doubt that Qian Jun is experienced enough to do a good job, and Party Secretary Li, as you know, won't want to become involved for his always politically correct reasons."

"Give me all the details. Forget about Party Secretary Li."

"First, with respect to the victim in Bund Park, we have not identified him yet, but the initial report from Dr. Xia supports our hypothesis." He handed a copy of the report to Old Hunter. "He was killed shortly after having had sex with someone, still in his pajamas. So possibly he was killed at home or in a hotel. If in a hotel, I don't think it could have happened in a state-run five-star one, which would have had to report, but there are so many private places, massage parlors and the like."

"And underground brothels, too, Chief Inspector Chen. You will not find anything about these places in the bureau's data files."

"Second, there is Wen Liping's case. Yu is working on it in Fujian. A former educated youth from Shanghai, Wen may have come back to the city." He produced a picture of Wen. "If she's not staying with a relative, those cheap private hotels without a business license would also be her choice."

"Good, I will check all the possible places. I'm old, but I can still do something." Then the old man added seriously, "Don't ever underestimate these thugs. They can haunt you like demons lurking in the dark, striking at a moment you can never anticipate. Last year, an old colleague of mine disappeared in the middle of a gang investigation. His body has never been found."

"I'm sorry to drag you into it, Uncle Yu."

"Don't say that, Chief Inspector Chen. I'm glad to be useful. I have nothing to worry about, a bag of old bones. Whatever comes, it's not a bad bargain at my age. You are young, and you still have a long way to go. You cannot be too careful with the triads."

"Thanks. I will be very careful."

After he parted with Old Hunter outside the Moon Breeze, Chen called Inspector Rohn. "We are going to interview Wen Liping's elder brother, Wen Lihua, tomorrow morning."

"So the answer is a straightforward yes?"

"According to Confucius, 'A man is not fit to stand if incapable of keeping his word.' "

" 'So you start panting for breath,' " she said, laughing, " 'the moment people say you're fat.' "

"Oh, you know that Chinese expression too!" It was an idiomatic one he had heard only once among old Beijingese. Inspector Rohn had an exceptional command of Chinese proverbs.

"When do we start?" she said. "I'll wait for you in front of the hotel."

"No, you don't have to do that. Traffic can be terrible. Around eight, but I'll call your room."

"Fine, I'll be waiting."

As he turned off the phone, something he had just said flashed across his mind.

Traffic.

Because of the terrible traffic in the area around the Peace Hotel and strict speed limits, vehicles literally crawled. And it was there, that morning, as they stood on the corner of Nanjing and Sichuan Road, that the motorcycle had come out of nowhere, racing right at her. Sichuan Road was not a street frequented by motorcyclists. He seemed to remember having heard a sputtering sound as they stood talking there on the street corner. The motorcycle had nearly run her down. It must have started up nearby, which made the incident even more suspicious. If the rider had just started his engine, why else would he have accelerated like that?

Inspector Rohn had just arrived in Shanghai. Only three people were aware of her mission. Could the Fujian triad have struck so fast? What was he confronting in his search for Wen? For the first time, he had an ominous feeling about this investigation.

Was it because of Party Secretary Li's emphasis on Inspector Rohn's safety?

Or because of Old Hunter's lecture on the black way?

He was disturbed by the memory of clutching Inspector Rohn, to keep her out of the reach of a crazy motorcyclist. If it was no accident, what further threats to Inspector Rohn's life might there be?

Chapter 8

Standing by a Mercedes, Chen saw Catherine Rohn stepping out of the hotel's revolving door wearing a white dress, like an apple tree blossoming in the April sunlight of Shanghai. She looked refreshed and she broke into a smile at the sight of him.

"This is Comrade Zhou Jing, our bureau's driver," Chen introduced her. "He will be with us for the day."

"Nice to meet you, Comrade Zhou," she said in Chinese.

"Welcome, Inspector Rohn," Zhou said, looking over his shoulder with a broad grin. "People call me Little Zhou."

"They call me Catherine."

"Little Zhou is the best driver in our bureau." Chen took his seat beside her.

"This is the best car," Zhou said. "And we are doing our best, Inspector Rohn, or Chief Inspector Chen would not be with you today."

"Really!"

"He's our ace inspector, the rising star in the bureau, you know."

"I know," she said.

"Don't exaggerate like that, Little Zhou." Chen said. "Keep your eyes on the road."

"Don't worry. I'm familiar with the area. So I'm taking a short cut."

Chen started speaking in English to her. "Any new information on your side?"

"Ed Spencer, my boss, checked the grocery store where Feng did his shopping. Feng does not drive. Nor has he any friends in D.C. Going to a couple of Chinese stores within walking distance is about all he does there. It is an old store, with no recorded connection to the secret societies. The receipt showed that Feng had visited the store on the day he phoned the warning. He bought noodles and rented several Chinese videotapes. On the way home, he also stepped into a Chinese gift and herb store, and a Chinese barbershop. So the warning could have been put into his grocery bag in these places too."

"I've discussed the new development with Party Secretary Li. It is important, we believe, to find out how the gangsters discovered his whereabouts."

"Beats me. Our special group consists only of Ed and me. Our translator, Shao, is an old CIA hand," she said. "I don't think there was a leak on our side."

"The decision to let Wen go to the United States was made at a very high level of our government. Neither Party Secretary Li nor I had heard anything about Feng or Wen until the day before your arrival," Chen countered.

"It was a blow to Feng's confidence in our program. He called his wife without telling us first. Ed is about to relocate him."

"I would like to make a suggestion, Inspector Rohn. Keep him where he is. Put more men around him for his protection. The gang may try to contact him again."

"It may be dangerous for him."

"If they had intended to take his life, they would have done so instead of warning him first. I believe they just want to prevent him from speaking out against Jia. They will make no attempt on his life unless they have no other choice."

"You have a point, Chief Inspector Chen. I will discuss it with my boss."

Due to Little Zhou's short cut, they soon reached Shandong Road, where Wen Lihua, Wen Liping's brother, lived with his family. It was a small street lined with old rundown houses from the turn of the century. The street in the Huangpu District had been part of the French concession but, in recent years, as it was surrounded with new buildings, it had become an eyesore. The street entrance was crammed with illegally parked bikes, cars, and illegally stored rusty steel and iron parts from a neighborhood factory. Little Zhou had a hard time maneuvering the car to a stop in front of a two-story house. On the discolored, cracked front door the faded number hardly showed.

The staircase was dark, steep, narrow, dust-covered, dim even during the day. The boards creaked under their feet, suggesting several steps were in bad repair. Most of the paint on the banister had long since peeled off. Catherine climbed up cautiously in her heels, and almost stumbled.

"Sorry," Chen said, grasping her elbow.

"No, it's not your fault, Chief Inspector Chen."

He noticed her wiping her hands on a handkerchief as they reached the second floor. There they saw an oblong room packed with odds and ends: broken wicker chairs, discarded coal stoves, a table with a leg missing, and an antique cabinet that might have served as a cupboard. There was a dining table with several stools in a corner.

"Is this a storage area?" she asked.

"No. It was originally a living room, but now it's a common room—for three or four families living on the same floor, each getting a portion of the space."

There were several doors along one side of the common room. Chen knocked on the first one. It was answered by an old woman who shuffled out on bound feet.

"You're looking for Lihua? He's in the room at the end."

The door at the end was opened by someone who had heard their footsteps. A man in his mid-forties, tall, lanky, bald, with thick eyebrows and a mustache, wearing a white T-shirt, khaki shorts, rubber-soled sandals, and a tiny bandage on his forehead. He was Wen Lihua.

They entered a room of fifteen or sixteen square meters. Its furnishing bespoke poverty. An old-fashioned bed sported a blue-painted iron headboard still displaying a plastic poster of Chairman Mao waving his hand on top of Tiananmen Gate; the original design on the headboard was no longer recognizable. In the middle of the room was a red-painted table, which bore a plastic pen holder and a bamboo chopsticks container—an indication of the table's multiple uses. There were a couple of threadbare armchairs. The only thing relatively new was a silver-plated frame holding a picture of a man, a woman, and a couple of kids huddled together behind a collective smile. The picture must have been taken years earlier when Lihua had still had hair combed over his forehead in a rakish way.

"You know why we are here today, Comrade Wen Lihua?" Chen held out his card.

"Yes. It's about my sister, but that's all I know. My boss told me to take the day off to help you." Lihua gestured them to be seated on the chairs around the table and brought over cups of tea. "What has she done?"

"Your sister has not done anything wrong. She has applied for a passport to join her husband in the United States," Catherine said in Chinese, holding out her identity card.

"Feng's in the United States?" Lihua scratched his bald head, then added, "Oh, you speak Chinese."

"My Chinese is not good," she said. "Chief Inspector Chen will conduct the interview. Don't worry about me."

"Inspector Rohn has come here to help," Chen said. "Your sister has disappeared. We wonder whether she has contacted you."

"Disappeared! No, she has not contacted me. This is the first time I've heard that Feng is there or that she plans to join him."

"You may not have heard from her recently," Chen said. "But anything you know about her will help us."

Catherine took out a mini tape recorder.

"Believe it or not, I have not talked to her for several years," Lihua sighed deep into his cup. "And she is my only sister."

Chen offered him a cigarette. "Please go ahead."

"Where shall I start?"

"Wherever you please."

"Well, our parents had only the two of us, me and my sister. My mother passed away early. Father brought us up—in this very room. I'm ordinary. Nothing worth talking about. Not now, not then. But she was so different. So pretty, and gifted too. All her elementary-school teachers predicted a bright future for her in socialist China. She sang like a lark, danced like a cloud. People used to say she must have been born under a peach tree."

"Born under a peach tree?" Catherine asked.

Chen explained, "We describe a girl as beautiful as a peach

blossom. There is also a superstitious belief that someone born under a peach tree will grow up to be a beauty."

"Whether born under a peach tree or not," Lihua continued with another sigh wreathed in cigarette smoke, "she was born in the wrong year. The Cultural Revolution broke out when she was in sixth grade. She became a Red Guard cadre as well as a leading member of the district song-and-dance ensemble. Schools and companies invited her to appear and sing the revolutionary songs and dance the loyal character dance."

"Loyal character dance?" she asked once again. "Please excuse my interruption."

"During those years, dancing was not allowed in China," Chen said, "except in one particular form—dancing with a paper cut-out of the Chinese character for Loyalty or with a red paper heart bearing the character, while making every imaginable gesture of loyalty to Chairman Mao."

"Then came the movement of the educated youths going to the countryside," Lihua went on. "Like others, she responded to Mao's call whole-heartedly. She was only sixteen. Father was concerned. At his insistence, instead of leaving with her schoolmates, she went to a village in Fujian Province, Changle Village, where we had a relative who would look after her, we hoped. Things seemed not to be too bad at first. She wrote back regularly, talking about the necessity of reforming herself through hard labor, planting seeds in the rice paddy, cutting firewood on the hill, plowing with an ox in the rain . . . In those years, a lot of young people believed in Mao as if he were a god."

"Then what happened?"

"She suddenly stopped writing. It was impossible for us to call her. We wrote to the relative, and he said vaguely that she was fine. After a lapse of several months, we got a short letter from her, saying that she was married to Feng Dexiang, and expecting a baby. Father went there. It was a long, difficult trip. When he came back, he was a changed man, totally broken, white-haired, devastated. He did not tell me much. He had cherished high hopes for her.

"We hardly heard from her at all then." Lihua rubbed his forehead forcefully with one hand, as if in an effort to ignite his memory. "Father blamed himself. Had she remained together with her schoolmates, she, too, might have eventually returned home. This notion sent him to an early grave. And that's the only time she came back to Shanghai. To attend Father's funeral."

"Did she talk to you when she came back?"

"Only a few meaningless words. She was totally changed. I wondered whether Father could have recognized her in her black homespun and white towel hood. How could Heaven have been so unfair to her? She cried her heart out, but talked little to anybody. Not to me. Nor even to somebody like Zhu Xiaoying, her best friend in high school. Zhu came to the funeral and gave us a quilt."

Chen saw Catherine taking notes.

"Afterwards, she wrote back even less," Lihua continued in a flat tone. "We learned that she got a job in a commune factory, but that was no iron rice bowl. Then her son died in an accident. Another devastating blow. We got the last letter from her about two years ago."

"Are there others in Shanghai still in contact with her?"

"No, I don't think so."

"How can you be sure?"

"Well, her classmates had a reunion last year. A grand party in the Jin River Hotel, organized and paid for by an upstart who had an invitation card mailed to each classmate, saying that anyone unable to attend could send a family member instead. Wen did not come back for the reunion. So Zhu insisted on my going. I had never been to a five-star hotel before, so I agreed. During the meal, several of her former classmates approached me for information about her. I was not surprised. You should have seen her in high school. So many boys were infatuated with her."

"Did she have a boyfriend in school?" she asked.

"No, that was unthinkable in those years. As a Red Guard cadre, she was too busy with her revolutionary activities." Lihua added, "Secret admirers, perhaps, but not boyfriends."

"Let's say secret admirers," Chen said. "Can you name any of them?"

"There were quite a few of them. Some were present at the reunion, too. Some of her schoolmates are down and out. Like Su Shengyi, totally broke. But he was a Red Guard cadre then, and came to our home a lot. He went to the reunion for a free meal, just like me. After a few drinks, he told me how he had admired Wen, his eyes brimming with tears. And Qiao Xiaodong was there too—he's already in a waiting-for-retirement program, gray-haired, broken-spirited. Qiao had played Li Yuhe in *The Story of the Red Lantern*. They were in the same district song-and-dance ensemble. How things change."

"What about the upstart who paid for the reunion?"

"Liu Qing. He entered a university in 1978, became a *Wenhui Daily* reporter, a published poet, and then started his own business. Now he's a millionaire with companies in Shanghai and Suzhou."

"Was Liu also a secret admirer of hers?"

"No, I don't think so. He did not talk to me, too busy making toasts to other classmates. Zhu told me that Liu was a nobody in high school. A bookish boy with a black family background. He wouldn't have presumed to be Wen's admirer. It would have been like an ugly toad's mouth watering at the sight of a white swan. Indeed, the wheel of fortune turns quickly. It does not have to take sixty years."

"Another Chinese proverb," Chen explained. " 'The wheel of fortune turns every sixty years.' "

Catherine nodded.

"My poor sister was practically finished when she was only sixteen. She was too proud to come to the reunion."

"She has suffered too much. Some people close up after a traumatic experience, but where there's life, there is always hope." Catherine said, "Is there no one your sister might contact in Shanghai?"

"No one except Zhu Xiaoying."

"Do you have Zhu's address?" Chen said. "And the addresses of some of her schoolmates too, like Su Shenyi and Qiao Xiaodong?"

Lihua took out an address book and scribbled a few words on a scrap of paper. "Five of them are in here. Among them, I'm not sure about Bai Bing's. It's a temporary one. He moves a lot, selling fake stuff in Shanghai and elsewhere. I don't have Liu Qing's, but you can find his easily enough."

"One more question. Why didn't she try to come back to Shanghai after the Cultural Revolution?"

"She never wrote to me about it." There was a slight catch in Lihua's voice. This time he rubbed his hand across his mouth. "Zhu may be able to tell you more. She also came back in the early eighties."

As they stood up, Lihua said hesitantly, "I'm still confused, Chief Inspector Chen."

"Yes. What do you want to know?"

"Nowadays so many people go abroad—legally or illegally. Particularly the Fujianese. I've heard quite a lot about them. What is so important about my sister?"

"The situation is complicated," Chen said, adding his cell phone number to his card. "Let me say this. Her safe arrival there is in the interests of the United States and China. A Fujian triad also may be looking for her. If they get hold of her, you can imagine what they will do. So if she contacts you, let us know immediately."

"I will, Chief Inspector Chen."

Chapter 9

It was Detective Yu's third day in Fujian.

There had been hardly any progress, but he had had second thoughts. The discovery of Feng's phone call seemed to lead in a new direction. Interviews with Wen's neighbors, however, had diminished the probability that she was hiding in the area. Wen had no local friends or relatives, and Feng's had long since cut themselves off. Some villagers showed undisguised hostility by refusing to talk about the Fengs. It was hard to conceive that Wen Liping could have lain low there for days.

As for the possibility of her having left the area, that also appeared unlikely. She had not boarded the only bus passing through the village on that particular night, nor any of the buses passing within a radius of fifty miles. Yu had conducted careful research at the Transportation Bureau. There was no possibility of a taxi coming anywhere near the village unless it was requested several hours beforehand. And there was no record of such an order.

Another idea suggested itself. Wen might have left the village, but been abducted before she boarded a bus. If so, unless the local police took direct action against the gangsters, she would never be found in time, or at all.

So Detective Yu had talked to Superintendent Hong about possible moves against the local triad. In response, Hong gave him a list of the leading local gangsters, but the list indicated that none of them was available—all were either in hiding or out of the district. Yu suggested that they make arrests of low-level members. Hong maintained that the ringleaders alone would have the information they sought, and he also declared that it was up to the Fujian police to decide how to cope with the gangsters. In terms of cadre rank, Superintendent Hong's was higher than Chief Inspector Chen's. So Detective Yu was left with the useless list, as well as an impression that the local police were not pulling their weight—at least not on behalf of a Shanghai cop. And he suspected, gloomily, there might be something else involved.

Whatever his suspicions, Yu had to keep on doing what he now considered futile—interviewing people who had no relevant information, just as Chief Inspector Chen was doing in Shanghai.

On the interview list for that particular day, there was an appointment with the commune factory manager Pan in the late afternoon, but Yu got a call from Pan around nine in the morning.

"I have a business meeting this afternoon. Can we move our appointment up?"

"When would you like it?"

"What about between eleven thirty and twelve?" Pan said. "I'll come to your hotel as soon as I have finished things here."

"That will be fine."

Yu contemplated informing Sergeant Zhao of the change, but he thought better of it. For the past few days, Zhao had been of little help. Sometimes Yu even had a feeling that interviewees chose not to talk because of Zhao. So he phoned Zhao, saying that Pan could not come in the afternoon, and that he himself would stay in the hotel for the day, writing a letter home, doing some laundry, and drafting a report to the bureau. Zhao readily agreed. Yu had heard a rumor that Zhao had a profitable business sideline; perhaps he was glad of some time free of police-work to devote to it.

Yu considered it too wasteful to have his laundry done by the hotel when he could save two Yuan a day by doing it himself. Kneading the dirty clothes on a wooden washboard in a concrete sink, he thought of his years like the foaming water dripping away through his fingers.

In his childhood, he had nurtured dreams about a career in the police force, listening to his father's stories about solving cases. A few years after he himself became a cop, however, he had few illusions left about his career.

His father, Old Hunter, though an experienced officer and loyal Party member for so many years, had ended up a sergeant at retirement, with too meager a pension to indulge in a pot of Dragon Well Tea. Detective Yu had to be realistic. With his lack of education and social connections, he was in no position to dream of a great career in the force. Just one of the insignificant cops at the bottom, making the minimum wage, having little say in the bureau, forever at the end of the waiting list of the housing committee—

And that was another reason he had not been keen on this assignment. There would be a housing committee meeting late this month in the bureau. Yu was on the waiting list. If he stayed in Shanghai, he might be able to push the committee members a little, perhaps in imitation of a recent movie, by sleeping on his bureau desk as a gesture of protest. He believed he had every reason to complain. He'd had to stay under his father's roof for over ten years after his marriage. It was a crying shame for a man approaching forty not to have a home of his own. Even Peiqin occasionally complained about it.

The housing shortage had a long history in Shanghai, which he understood. It became a burning issue for people's work units—factories, companies, schools, or governmental bureaus—which got an annual housing quota from the city authorities and made assignments based on an employee's years in service as well as other factors. It was especially difficult at the Shanghai Police Bureau, where so many cops had worked all their lives.

Nevertheless, Detective Yu took his job seriously, believing he could make a difference in other people's lives. He had developed a theory about being a good cop in China now. It depended on one's ability to tell what could and what could not be done effectively. It was because there were many cases not worthy of hard work as the conclusion was predetermined by the Party authorities. For instance, the outcome of those anti-government-corruption cases, in spite of all the propaganda fanfare, would be only to swat a mosquito but not to slap a tiger. They were symbolic, only for show. So, too, this investigation, though not part of a political campaign, seemed to be merely a matter of form. And that was perhaps true of the Bund Park case, too. The only effective action would be to uproot the triads, but the authorities were not ready to do so.

But Wen's case had started to interest him. He had never imagined that an ex-educated youth could have led such a wretched life. And what had happened to Wen, he shuddered to think, could have happened to Peiqin. As an ex-educated youth himself, he felt obliged to do something for the poor woman, though he did not know what or how.

Shortly after he finished his laundry, Pan arrived at the hotel. A man in his early forties, extraordinarily tall and thin, like a bamboo stick, Pan had an intelligent face, adorned by a pair of frameless glasses. He talked intelligently, too. Always to the point, specific, not losing his way in details.

The interview did not provide any new information, but it gave a clear picture of Wen's life during her factory years. Wen had been one of the best workers. There, too, she made a point of keeping to herself. As it seemed to Pan, however, it was not because she was an outsider, or because the other workers were prejudiced against her. She had been too proud.

"That's interesting," Yu said. The difficulty of reconciling the past to the present. Sometimes people retreat into a shell. "Did she try to better her circumstances?"

"She had no luck. She was so young when she fell into Feng's hands, and then it was too late by the time Feng met his downfall," Pan said, stroking his chin. " 'Heaven is too high, and the emperor is too far away.' Who cared for an ex-educated youth in a backward village? But you should have seen her when she first arrived here. What a knockout!"

"You liked her."

"No, not I. My father had been a landlord. In the early seventies, I would not have dreamed of it."

"Yes, I know all about the family background policy during the Cultural Revolution," Yu said, nodding contemplatively.

Yu knew that perhaps he alone had reasons to be grateful for that notorious policy. He had always been ordinary—an ordinary student, an ordinary educated youth, and an ordinary cop, but Peiqin was different. Gifted, pretty, like those characters in *The Dream of the Red Chamber*, she might never have crossed his path but for her black family background, which had pulled her down, so to speak, to his level. He had once broached the topic to her, but she cut him short, declaring she could not have asked for a better husband.

"When I became factory manager in 1979," Pan went on,

"Wen was literally a poor lower-middle-class peasant. Not only in her class status, but in her appearance. No one took pity on Feng. I took pity on her. I suggested that she come to work here."

"So you alone did something for her. That's good. Did she talk to you about her life?"

"Not if she could help it. Some people like to talk about their misfortunes all the time, like Sister Qiangling in Lu Xun's story 'Blessing.' Not Wen. She preferred to lick her wounds in secret."

"Did you try to do anything else for her?"

"I don't know what you are driving at, Detective Yu."

"I'm not driving at anything. What about the work she took home?"

"Theoretically, the parts and chemicals are not allowed to be taken home, but she was so poor. A few extra Yuan made a difference to her. Since she was the best in the workshop, I made an exception for her."

"When did you learn about her plan to join her husband in the United States."

"About a month ago. She wanted me to write a statement about her marital status for her passport application. When I asked about her plans for the future, she broke down. Only then did I learn about her pregnancy." Pan said after a pause, "I was curious about Feng's efficiency. It normally takes years before people can begin the process of getting their families out. So I asked some other villagers. And I learned he had a deal there—"

There was a light tap on the door.

Detective Yu rose to open it. There was no one outside. He saw a tray of covered dishes on the ground, with a card saying, "Enjoy our special."

"What great timing! This hotel is not bad. Have lunch with me here, Manager Pan. We can continue our talk over the meal."

"Well, I owe you one then," Pan said. "Let me buy you Fujian wok noodles before you leave."

Yu took away the covering paper disclosing a large bowl of stir-fried rice, fresh and colorful, with scrambled egg and Chinese barbecued pork, a covered urn, and two side dishes, one of salted peanuts, one of tofu mixed with sesame oil and green onion. He was surprised to smell something like liquor as he pulled the paper lid off the urn.

"Crab marinated in wine," Pan said.

There was only one pair of plastic chopsticks on the tray. Luckily, Peiqin had packed several pair of disposable chopsticks in his bag, so Yu handed a pair to Pan.

Pan picked up a loose crab leg with his fingers.

"I love crabs," Yu shrugged his shoulders, "but I do not eat them raw."

"Don't worry. There won't be any problem. Soaking the crab in the strong liquor takes care of it."

"I just can't eat uncooked crab." It was not exactly true. In his childhood, a bowl of watery rice with a piece of salted crab had been his favorite breakfast. Peiqin had made him give up raw seafood. Maybe that was the price of having a virtuous wife. "You have all the crab, Manager Pan," Yu reluctantly offered.

The rice smelled pleasant, the pork had a special texture, and the small side dishes were palatable. Yu did not really miss the crab. They talked more about Wen.

"Wen did not even have an account in the bank," Pan said. "All her earnings were taken by Feng. I suggested that she keep some money at the factory. She did."

"Did she take it out before she disappeared?"

"No. I was not in the factory the day she disappeared, but she took none of her money," Pan said, finishing the golden digestive glands of the crab with relish. "It must have been a decision made on the spur of the moment."

"During all these years, has anyone come to visit Wen here?"

"No, I don't think so. Feng's insanely jealous. He wouldn't have encouraged visitors." Turning the crab's entrails inside out, Pan had something like a small old monk sitting on his palm. "The evil guy, you know."

"I know. In the White Snake legend, the meddlesome monk had to hide in the crab entrails—" Yu left the sentence unfinished as he heard a faint moan from Pan.

Pan was already doubled over in pain, pressing a hand to his stomach. "Damn. It feels like a knife piercing me here." His face was beaded with perspiration and had turned a livid color. He began to moan.

"I'll call for an ambulance," Yu said, jumping up.

"No. Take the factory pickup," Pan managed to say.

The pickup was parked in front of the hotel. Yu and a hotel janitor lost no time carrying Pan on to the truck. The county hospital was several miles away. Yu had the janitor sit beside him to give directions. Before he started the engine, however, Yu ran back to his room and picked up the urn of wine-soaked crab to take with them.

Three hours later, Yu was ready to head back to the hotel, alone.

Pan had to stay in the hospital, though he was pronounced out of danger. The doctor's diagnosis was food poisoning.

"In an hour," the doctor said, "it would have been too late for us to do anything."

The result of the tests of the contents of the crab urn were highly suspicious. The crab contained bacteria—many times more than was allowable. The crab used must have been dead for days.

"It's strange," the nurse said. "People here never eat dead crab."

It was more than strange, Detective Yu reflected, as he plodded along the country road. There was an owl hooting somewhere in the woods behind him. He spat a couple of times on the ground, a subconscious effort to ward off the evil spirits of the day.

The moment he got back to the hotel, he checked at the hotel kitchen.

"No, we didn't send that food to you," the chef said nervously. "We don't have that kind of room service."

Yu dug out a hotel brochure. Room service was not mentioned. The chef suggested that the lunch might have been delivered by a nearby village restaurant.

"No, we never got such an order," the restaurant owner whined over the phone.

They could have made the delivery by mistake, and were now trying to deny responsibility. But that was unlikely: the delivery man would have asked for payment.

Detective Yu was sure that he had been the target. If he had stayed alone in the hotel and eaten all the food himself, he would have ended up in the hospital, or the morgue. No one would have bothered to test the leftovers in an urn. The gang would not have had to worry. Food poisoning accidents happened everyday. The local police wouldn't even have been called in. The schemer could not have known that Yu did not eat raw crab.

So he was getting on someone's nerves. Someone wanted to put him out of the way. This was now a battle for Detective Yu. He was determined to fight, though his enemy had the advantage of prowling in the dark, watching and waiting, striking out at any opportunity. Like the lunch—.

Suddenly, he detected an alarming hole in his theory. The gangsters should have seen Manager Pan come into his room. They should not have made the attempt. Had they received incorrect information that Detective Yu was alone in his hotel room?

Nobody but Sergeant Zhao had known his plans for the day. He had told Zhao he would be alone. And the lunch tray was meant for one, with only one pair of chopsticks.

Chapter 10

Leaving Zhu Xiaoying's place, Inspector Rohn started to grope her way down the stairs with Chief Inspector Chen in the lead.

Following Lihua's list, they had interviewed several of Wen's schoolmates: Qiao Xiaodong at Jingling High School, Yang Hui at the Red Flag Grocery, and finally Zhu Xiaoying at her home. None of them provided any relevant information. People might have been emotional at their class reunion, but they were too busy with their daily lives to really care for a schoolmate with whom they had long lost contact. Zhu was the only one who had kept sending New Year's cards to Wen, but she, too, had not heard anything from her for years. If there was anything new, it was about why Wen had failed to come back to Shanghai after the Cultural Revolution. Zhu attributed it to her brother Lihua, who had balked at the prospect of Wen having to squeeze in with his family in that same single room.

Moving down the ancient staircase, Catherine raised one foot when a step suddenly caved in under her. She stumbled, lost her balance, and pitched forward. Before she could stop herself, she bumped into Chief Inspector Chen. He reacted by positioning himself in front of her, his hand grasping the rail. Pressed against him, she tried to steady herself as he turned back so that he was holding her in his arms.

"Are you all right, Inspector Rohn?" he said.

"I'm fine," she said, disengaging herself. "Maybe I'm suffering from jet lag."

Zhu rushed down holding a flashlight. "Oh, those ancient steps are totally rotten."

One of the treads was broken. Whether Inspector Rohn had stumbled first, or that step had inexplicably crumbled, was not clear.

Chen was about to say something, but checked himself. He ended up apologizing mechanically, "I'm sorry, Inspector Rohn."

"For what, Chief Inspector Chen?" she said, seeing his embarrassment. "But for your intervention again, I could have hurt myself."

She took a step and swayed. He put his arm around her waist. Leaning heavily against him, she let him help her down the stairs. At the foot of the stairs, as she tried to lift her damaged foot for a closer look, she winced at a sharp pain in her ankle.

"You need to see a doctor."

"No, it's nothing."

"I should not have taken you out today, Inspector Rohn."

"I insisted on it, Chief Inspector Chen," she said a little testily.

"I've an idea," Chen said with a determined expression. "Let's go to a herbal drug store. Mr. Ma's. Chinese medicine will help."

* * *

The herbal drug store in question was located in the old town of Shanghai. A golden sign above the door frame displayed two big Chinese characters in bold strokes: "Old Ma," which could also mean "Old Horse."

"Interesting name for a herbal drug store," she said.

"There is a Chinese proverb: 'An old horse knows the way.' Old, experienced, Mr. Ma knows what he's doing, though he's not a doctor or pharmacist in the conventional sense."

An elderly woman in a long white uniform came toward them and broke into a smile. "How are you, Comrade Chief Inspector Chen?"

"I'm fine, Mrs. Ma. This is Catherine Rohn, my American friend." Chen introduced them to each other as they moved into a spacious room furnished as an office. Its white walls were lined with large oak cabinets sporting numerous tiny drawers, each of which had a small label on it.

"What wind has brought you here, Chen?" Mr. Ma, a white-haired, white-bearded man wearing silver-rimmed spectacles and a long string of carved beads, rose from his armchair.

"Today's wind is my friend Catherine, a wind from across the oceans. How is your business, Mr. Ma?"

"Not bad, thanks to you. How is your friend?"

"She has sprained her ankle," Chen said.

"Let me take a look."

Catherine slipped off her shoes and had her ankle examined. It ached under his touch. She doubted whether the old man could tell anything without an x-ray.

"Nothing on the surface, but you never know. Let me apply a paste to your foot. Better remove it after two or three hours. If the inner injury comes to the surface, you don't have to worry."

It was a sticky yellow paste. Mr. Ma spread it around the

injured part. It felt cool on her skin. Mrs. Ma helped to wrap her ankle in a roll of white gauze.

"She also feels a little giddy," Chen said. "She has had a long trip. And she's been busy since her arrival. An herbal drink may boost her energy level."

"Let me take a look at your tongue." Mr. Ma examined her tongue and felt her pulse for a couple of minutes with his eyes closed, as if lost in meditation. "Nothing seriously wrong. The yang is slightly high. Maybe you have too much on your mind. I'm writing you a prescription. Some herbs for balance, and some for blood circulation."

"That'll be great," Chen said.

Mr. Ma flourished a skunk-tail-brush pen over a piece of bamboo paper and handed the prescription to Mrs. Ma. "Choose the freshest herbs for her."

"You don't have to tell me that, old man. Chief Inspector Chen's friend is our friend." Mrs. Ma started measuring out a variety of herbs from the small drawers—one pinch of white stuff like frost, another of a different color, almost like dried petals, and also a pinch of purple grains like raisins. "Where are you staying, Catherine?"

"The Peace Hotel."

"It's not easy to prepare traditional Chinese medicine in a hotel. You need to have a special earthen pot and to watch over the process. Let us prepare the medicine and send it to you by messenger."

"Yes, that's better, old woman." Mr. Ma stroked his beard approvingly.

"Thank you," Catherine said. "It is so thoughtful of you."

"Thank you so much, Mr. Ma," Chen said. "By the way, do you have any books about triads or secret societies in China?"

"Let me check." Mr. Ma stood up, went into a back room,

and came out presently with a thick volume. "I happen to have one. You can keep it. I no longer run a bookstore here."

"No, I'll return it. You have saved me a trip to the Shanghai Library."

"I'm glad my dust-covered books can still be of some use, Chief Inspector Chen. Anything we can do for you, you know, after—"

"Don't say that, Mr. Ma," Chen cut the old man short. "Or I dare not come here again."

"You have so many books—not just medical books, Mr. Ma." Catherine was interested in the curtailed conversation between the two men.

"Well, we used to run a used bookstore. Thanks to the Shanghai Police Bureau," Mr. Ma said with undisguised sarcasm, twisting his beard between his fingers, "we're running this herbal drugstore instead."

"Oh, our business is pretty good," Mrs. Ma intervened in a hurry. "Sometimes more than fifty patients a day. From all walks of life. We have nothing to complain about."

"Fifty patients a day? That's a lot for a herbal drugstore that does not accept state-issued medical insurance." Chen turned to Mr. Ma with a renewed interest. "What kind of patients are they?"

"People come here for various reasons. For some, because the state-run hospital cannot do anything about their problems, for some, because they cannot go there for their problems. For instance, injuries in a gang fight. The state-run hospital will immediately report it to the police. So I've helped a few of them." Mr. Ma looked up at Chen before going on with a hint of defiance. "It's your job to catch them, Chief Inspector Chen, if they are criminals. They come to me as patients, so I treat them as a doctor."

"I see, Doctor Zhivago."

"Don't call me that." Mr. Ma waved his hands hurriedly, as if trying to chase away an invisible fly. 'Once bitten by a snake, forever nervous at the sight of a coiled cord.' "

"Some of these people must be grateful to you," Chen said.

"You can never tell with them, but like in kung fu novels, they always talk about paying their debts of gratitude." Mr. Ma added after touching the beads for a few seconds, "Nowadays, they are capable of anything. Their long arms reach to the skies. I have to do something for them, or my practice will be in big trouble."

"I understand, Mr. Ma. You don't have to explain it to me, but I have to ask you another favor."

"Anything."

"We're looking for a woman, a pregnant woman from Fujian. A Fujian triad called the Flying Axes may be looking for her, too—she was an educated youth from Shanghai years ago. If you happen to hear anything about her, please let me know."

"The Flying Axes—I don't think I have met any of its members. This is Blue territory, you know. But I can ask around."

"Your help will be invaluable to us, Mr. Ma, or shall I say, Doctor Zhivago?" Chen stood up to leave.

"Then you'll have to be the general." Mr. Ma smiled.

Catherine was intrigued with their talk, particularly the part about Doctor Zhivago. Years earlier, her mother had bought her a music box that played "Lara's Song." The novel had since become one of her favorites. The tragedy of an honest intellectual's life in an authoritarian society. Now the Soviet Union was practically finished, but not China. There was something fascinating about the background of the conversation, almost like a scroll of a traditional Chinese painting, in which the blank space suggested more than what was presented on the paper.

When they got back to the hotel, it was near six. She heard

him telling Little Zhou to leave. "Don't wait for me. I'll take a taxi home."

In her room, the chambermaid had prepared everything for the night. The bed was turned down, the window closed, and the curtain drawn. There was a pack of Virginia Slims by a crystal ashtray on the nightstand, an imported luxury that suited her status here. Everything had been prepared for a distinguished guest. As he helped her seat herself on the couch, she said, "Thank you, Chief Inspector Chen, for all you have done for me."

"Don't mention it. How do you feel now?"

"I feel much better now. Mr. Ma is a good doctor." She motioned him to sit in the sofa. "Why did you call him Dr. Zhivago?"

"It's a long story."

"We are finished for the day, aren't we? So please tell me the story."

"You will probably not be interested in it."

"I majored in Chinese studies. There's nothing more interesting to me than a story about Doctor Zhivago in China."

"You should have a good rest, Inspector Rohn."

"According to your Party Secretary Li, you are supposed to make my stay a satisfactory one, Chief Inspector Chen."

"But if you call in sick tomorrow, Party Secretary Li will hold me responsible."

"I cannot take my evening walk along the Bund," she pleaded in mock seriousness, but she felt a bit vulnerable, too, as she spoke. "I am alone, in this hotel room. Surely you could humor me."

Perhaps he realized how she felt, her ankle sprained, her yin-yang system out of balance, in a solitary hotel room, in a strange city, where she had no one to talk to—except him. He said, "Fine, but you have to lie down, and make yourself comfortable."

So she slipped off her shoes, reclined on the couch, and laid her feet on a cushion he placed for her. Her posture was modest enough, she thought, her dress pulled down over her knees.

"Oh, I've forgotten all about Mr. Ma's instructions," he said. "Let me take a look at your ankle."

"It's better now."

"You have to take off the paste."

When the gauze was removed, she was astonished to see her ankle had turned black and blue. "The bruise did not show in Mr. Ma's office."

"This yellowish paste is called Huangzhizhi. It is capable of bringing the inner injury to the surface, so you can heal more quickly."

He went into the bathroom and came back with a couple of wet towels.

"The paste is no longer useful now." He knelt down by the couch to wipe off the remainder and to rub her ankle. "Does it still hurt?"

"No." She shook her head, watching Chen examine the bruise, making sure there was no paste left.

"Tomorrow you will be able to run like an antelope again."

"Thank you," she said. "So, it's time for the story."

"Would you like a drink first?"

"A glass of white wine would be perfect. What about you?"

"The same."

She watched him open the refrigerator, take out a bottle, and come back with the glasses.

"You are making it a special evening." She raised herself slightly on one elbow, sipping the wine.

"The story goes back to the early sixties," Chen started, sitting in the chair drawn close to the couch, gazing down at the wine, "when I was still an elementary-school student . . ."

In the early sixties, the Mas had owned a used-book store, a husband-and-wife business. As a kid, Chen had bought comic books there. Out of the blue, the local government declared the bookstore "a black center of antisocialist activity." The charge was made on the evidence of an English copy of *Doctor Zhivago* on its shelves. Mr. Ma was put in jail, where he was allowed to take with him, out of all his books, only a medical dictionary. Toward the end of the eighties, he was released and rehabilitated. The old couple did not want to reopen the bookstore. Mr. Ma thought of running a herbal drugstore with the knowledge he had acquired in prison. His business license application traveled from one bureaucratic desk to another, however, without making any progress.

Chen had been an entry level cop then, not the one in charge of "rectification of wrong cases." When he heard about Mr. Ma's situation, however, he managed to put in a word through Party Secretary Li and obtained the license for the old man.

Afterwards, Chen happened to talk to a *Wenhui* reporter, dwelling on the irony of Mr. Ma becoming a doctor because of *Dr. Zhivago*. To his surprise, she wrote for the newspaper an essay entitled "Because of *Dr. Zhivago*." The publication added to the popularity of Mr. Ma's practice.

"That's why the old couple are grateful to you," she said.

"I did little, considering what they went through in those years."

"Do you feel more responsible now that you are a chief inspector?"

"Well, people complain about the problems with our system, but it is important to do something—for people like the Mas."

"With your connections—" she paused to take a sip of her

wine, "which include a woman reporter writing for the *Wenhui Daily.*"

"Included," he said, draining his glass in one gulp. "She is in Japan now."

"Oh."

His cell phone rang.

"Oh, Old Hunter! What's up?" He listened for several minutes without speaking and then said, "So it must be someone important, I see. I'll call you later, Uncle Yu."

Turning off the phone, he said, "It's Old Hunter, Detective Yu's father."

"Does his father work for you too?"

"No, he's retired. He's helping me with another case," he said, standing. "Well, it's time for me to leave."

He could not stay longer. She did not know about his other case. And he would not tell her about it. It was not her business.

As she tried to rise, he put a hand lightly on her shoulders. "Relax, Inspector Rohn. We have a lot of work to do tomorrow. Good night."

He closed the door after him.

The echo of his footsteps faded along the corridor.

There was a sound of the elevator bobbing to a stop and then starting to descend slowly.

Whatever reservations Inspector Rohn might have about her Chinese partner, and his possible involvement in a cover-up, she was grateful for this evening.

Chapter 11

Chen failed to reach Old Hunter. He had forgotten to ask where the old man had called from. He had been too preoccupied with telling the story of Dr. Zhivago in China to an attentive American audience of one. So he decided to walk home. Perhaps before he got there, his phone would start ringing again.

It rang at the corner of Sichuan Road, but it was Detective Yu.

"We're in for it, Chief."

"What?"

Yu told him about the food poisoning incident at the hotel and concluded, "The gang is connected to the Fujian police."

"You may be right," Chen said, not adding his own comment: *not only with the Fujian police.* "This investigation is a joint operation, but we don't have to report to the local cops all the time. Whatever action you're going to take, go ahead on your own. Don't worry about their reaction. I will be responsible."

"I see, Chief Inspector Chen."

"From now on, call me at my home or on my cell phone. Send faxes to my home. In an emergency, contact Little Zhou. You cannot be too careful."

"Take care of yourself, too."

The food poisoning incident made him think of Inspector Rohn. First the motorcycle, and then the accident on the staircase.

They might have been followed. While they were talking with

Zhu upstairs, something could have been done to the steps. Under normal circumstances, Chief Inspector Chen would have treated such an idea like a tall tale from *Liaozhai*, but they were dealing with a triad.

Anything was possible.

The triad might be proceeding on two fronts, in Shanghai and in Fujian. They were more resourceful than he had anticipated. And more calculating, too. The attempts, if that is what they were, had been made to seem like accidents, orchestrated so that there was no way to trace them to the perpetrators.

He thought about warning Inspector Rohn, but refrained. What would he tell her? The omnipresence of gangsters would not contribute to a positive image of contemporary China. Whatever the circumstances, he had to keep it in mind that he was working in the national interest. It was not desirable for her to think of the Chinese police or China in a negative way.

Looking at his watch, he decided to phone Party Secretary Li at home. Li invited him to come over to talk.

Li's residence was located on Wuxing Road, in a high cadre residential complex behind walls. There was an armed soldier standing at the entrance gate and he made a stiff salute to Chen.

Party Secretary Li waited in the spacious living room of a three-bedroom apartment. The room was modestly furnished, but larger than Lihua's entire home. Chen seated himself on a chair beside a pot of exquisite orchids swaying lightly in the breeze that came through the window, breathing elegance into the room.

There was a long silk scroll on the wall, bearing two lines in *kai* calligraphy: *An old horse resting in the stable still aspires / to gallop thousands and thousands of miles*. It was a couplet from Chao Cao's "Looking out to the Sea," a subtle reference to Li's own situation. Prior to the mid-eighties, Chinese high-ranking cadres never retired, hanging on to their positions to the end, but with the changes Deng Xiaoping had introduced into the system, they, too, had to step down at retirement age. In a couple of years, Li would have to leave his office. Chen recognized the red seal of a well-known calligrapher imprinted under the lines. A scroll of his was worth a fortune at an international auction.

"Sorry to come to your home so late, Party Secretary Li," Chen said.

"That's okay. I'm alone this evening. My wife is at our son's place."

"Your son has moved out?"

Li had a daughter and a son, both in their mid-twenties. Early last year, the daughter got an apartment from the bureau by virtue of Li's cadre rank. A high-ranking cadre was entitled to additional housing because he needed more space in which to work in the interests of the socialist country. People grumbled behind his back, but no one dared to raise it as an issue in the housing committee meeting. It was surprising that Li's son, a recent college graduate, had also received his own apartment.

"He moved last month. She is with him tonight, decorating his new home."

"Congratulations, Party Secretary Li! That's something worth celebrating."

"Well, his uncle made a down payment on a small apartment and let him move in," Li said. "Economic reform has brought about a lot of change in our city."

"I see," Chen said. So this was the result of housing reform. The government had started to encourage people to buy their own housing to supplement their work units' assignments, but few could afford the price—except the newly rich. "His uncle must have done well in his business."

"He has a small bar."

Chen was reminded of Old Hunter's story about Li's untouchable brother-in-law. Those upstarts were successful not because of their business acumen, but because of their *guanxi*.

"Tea or coffee?" Li asked with a smile.

"Coffee."

"Well, I only have instant."

Then Chen started by briefing Li about the food poisoning incident in Fujian.

Li responded, "Don't be too suspicious. Some of our Fujian colleagues may not be too pleased with Detective Yu's presence. It's their domain, I can understand that. But it goes way too far to accuse them of being connected with a gang. You don't have any evidence, Chief Inspector Chen."

"I'm not saying all of them are tied to the triad, but one insider can do a lot of damage."

"Take a break, Comrade. Both Yu and you are overwrought. There's no need to imagine yourself fighting in the Bagong Mountains, with every tree and weed an enemy soldier."

Li referred to a battle during the Jin dynasty, when a panic-stricken general's imagination turned everything into the enemy chasing him into the mountains. But Chen suspected that it was Li who had lost sight of the enemy. This was no time to take a break. Perceiving a slight change in Li's attitude toward the investigation, he wondered whether he had done something more than his Party boss had expected.

He shifted his focus to Inspector Rohn's cooperation, one of Li's main concerns.

"The Americans are pursuing the investigation in their interests," Li commented. "It is a matter of course for her to cooperate. As long as they know we are doing our best, we don't have to worry. That's all we need to do."

"That's all we need to do," Chen echoed.

"We'll try to find Wen, certainly, but it may not be easy to accomplish this within the time frame—their time frame. We don't have to go out of our way for them."

"I've not worked on such a sensitive international case before. Please give me more of your specific instructions, Party Secretary Li."

"You've been doing a great job. The Americans must see that we are trying our best. That's very important."

"Thank you," Chen said, familiar with Li's way of saying something positive to soften what would follow.

"As an old-timer, I would just like to make a few suggestions. Your visit to Old Ma, for example, may not have been an excellent choice. Ma is a good doctor. No question about it. I still remember your effort to help him."

"Why not, Party Secretary Li?"

"The Mas have their reasons to complain about our system," Li said, frowning. "Have you told Inspector Rohn the story of Dr. Zhivago in China?"

"Yes, she asked me about it."

"You see, the Cultural Revolution was a national disaster. A lot of people suffered. Such a story is nothing new here, but may be sensational to an American."

"But that happened even before the Cultural Revolution."

"Well, that's like what happens in an investigation," Li said. "You are not doing anything now, but it's still what you have already done."

Chen was astonished by Li's reproof, which was not totally irrelevant.

"Also, I'm concerned by the accident in Zhu's place. Those old houses with dark, rotten staircases. Fortunately, nothing serious has happened, or the American might really get suspicious."

"Well—" *I really am suspicious,* Chen did not say.

"That's why I want to reemphasize that you must provide a

safe and satisfactory stay for Inspector Rohn. Think of something else to do. You have served as an escort for Westerners. A cruise on the river is a must for a tourist. And a visit to the Old City." Li said, "I'm going to invite her to a Beijing Opera. I'll let you know as soon as I have made arrangements."

So Party Secretary Li actually wanted him to stop the investigation, though he did not say so explicitly.

Why? Chen was perplexed. There were so many possible points for him to ponder over. As he had suspected, he'd been given this assignment more for the appearance of carrying out an investigation than to obtain a result. If he was going to do a real job, it would have to be done without the bureau's knowledge.

He tried to clear his mind on the way home, but he was still exasperated when his apartment building came in sight.

Turning on the light in his apartment, he compared his strikingly plain room with Li's. No exquisite orchids breathing the owner's elegant taste. No silk scrolls sporting the calligraphy of renowned scholars. A room is like a woman, incapable of standing comparison, he reflected.

He took out the cassette tape of Yu's interview in the village. It had been express-mailed to his home. The information provided by Wen's neighbors was not really new. The apathy shared by them was also understandable, considering what Feng had done during the Cultural Revolution.

To some extent, the chief inspector thought he could understand the isolation Wen had inflicted upon herself. During his first few years in the police bureau, he had also alienated himself from his former friends who had started teaching in colleges or interpreting at the Foreign Ministry. A cop's career had not been his expectation for himself, nor his friends'. Ironically, that was one of the reasons that he had thrown himself into translating and writing in those days.

Wen must have been a proud woman.

The tape rolled slowly on to the interview with Miao, the owner of the only private phone in the village, about how the village folks paid her for their calls to people overseas. When people called home from abroad, they also used her phone. Miao explained, "When someone calls from overseas, there may be a long wait before his family comes to the phone. As international calls can be very expensive, some of them make a point of calling at a scheduled time. For Feng, it was always Tuesday evening, around eight o'clock. But for the first two or three weeks, he called more frequently. Once Wen was not at home, and another time she did not want to come to pick up the phone. They did not get along so well, you know. With such a husband, I do not blame her. A fresh flower stuck in a heap of ox dung. It's surprising that he calls every week. I don't think he has made much money. He has been there for only a few months . . ."

He pushed the stop button, rewound the tape, listened to it again, stopped it, made a note, and pushed the play button again.

"Anyway, before eight o'clock on Tuesday, Wen would come to wait by the phone. The last call was an exception. It came on a Friday. I remember. Feng said that it was urgent. So I had to run to get her. I do not know anything about the contents of their talk. I thought she looked upset afterwards. That's about all I can tell you, Detective Yu."

As the tape came to an end, Chief Inspector Chen lit a cigarette, trying to do some thinking.

Normally, for the first couple of days, there were a number of directions to pursue in search of a missing person, but once they were covered, and no clue discovered, the search came to a dead end. Still, some details were worth exploring. For one thing, why would Wen have refused to answer an expensive international call? Even if their relationship was terrible, wouldn't she still want to join her husband in America?

He slipped off his shoes, lay down on the sofa, picked up a copy of *Wenhui Daily*. There was a column discussing doctors and nurses taking "red envelopes" or petty graft from patients. Maybe that was another reason why Mr. Ma enjoyed such good business. Visits to a state-run hospitals were covered by insurance, but the amount in the "red envelopes" could be staggering. Some called it a form of corruption; others attributed it to unreasonable distribution of wealth in the society. He put aside the newspaper, intending only to rest his eyes for a few minutes. He dozed off in spite of himself.

The insistent clanging of the phone intruded into his fading dream. It was Old Hunter.

"Sorry to call you so late," Old Hunter said.

"No, I've been waiting for your call," he said. "I was with Inspector Rohn in the hotel. So please go on with your report, in detail."

"First, about the victim's pajamas. Some part I have told you already. No label in the pajamas, but there is a fine design woven into the material, shaped like a V connected with an elliptical circle. I spoke with Tang Kaiyuan, a fashion designer. According to Tang, the design stands for Valentino, an international brand. Very expensive. There's no store selling it in Shanghai. So the victim must have been a rich man. Possibly from another province. Maybe from Hong Kong."

"It may be a fake, a knockoff," Chen commented.

"I thought about that, too. Tang said that it's not likely. He has never seen fake Valentino pajamas here. Knockoffs come in large quantities. No one will try to make just one or two pieces. A month ago, there was a raid on a warehouse and more than three hundred thousand cheap Polo logo T-shirts were found.

If they had been put on the market, the real, high-priced Polo brand shirts would have been unsaleable."

"Tang has a good point."

"I also had a discussion with Dr. Xia. That's why I did not have time to call you. The good doctor's willing to go out of his way for you. Remember the unidentified drug he found in the body of the ax-murder corpse? When we discussed the fact the victim had had sex shortly before he was killed, the doctor got an idea that the mysterious drug might be a sort of aphrodisiac, and he took out a thick reference volume there and then. Sure enough, he found a drug with similar molecular structure. At the time when the book was published, this drug was available only in Southeast Asia. It can be very expensive."

"The victim must have been able to afford expensive luxuries, with such a brand of pajamas, and such a drug, but he doesn't sound like one of those new capitalists to me."

"I agree," Old Hunter said. "I will do further research tomorrow."

"Thanks, Uncle Yu. Not a single word about your discovery to the people in the bureau."

"I understand, Chief Inspector Chen."

It was almost twelve as Chen put down the phone. All in all, the day had not ended too badly, though his dream had been broken into by the phone call.

Of that dream, only one fragmented scene remained in his mind. He was walking to an ancient bridge over a Qing dynasty moat, alone, crunching over a blanket of golden leaves, somewhere in the Forbidden City. A poem by Zhang Bi, a Tang dynasty poet, came to mind.

The dream comes lingering back to the old place:
The winding verandah, the circling balustrade.

There is nothing like the moon, still shining on the petals
Fallen in the spring court, for the lonely visitor.

Chief Inspector Chen made himself another cup of black coffee, trying to cleanse his palate and his mind of the dream. This was not a night for recollecting poems. He had to think.

Chapter 12

The phone began ringing before her alarm went off. Rubbing her eyes, Catherine snatched up the receiver. It was her boss's voice on the line, clear, familiar, though thousands of miles away. "Sorry to wake you, Catherine."

"It's okay."

"How are things?"

"Lousy," she said. "The Fujian police have made no progress. Here in Shanghai, we've not gotten any leads by interviewing Wen's possible contacts."

"You know the trial date. The INS has been driving us crazy."

"Is it possible to postpone the trial?"

"Not a popular idea, I'm afraid."

"Politics. Here, too. Is there any information about the gang that threatened Feng?"

"Feng has not heard from them again. We have taken your suggestion and are keeping him in the same place. If the gang has Wen, they will send another more explicit message to him."

"The Chinese believe that the triad is looking for her but may not have her yet."

"What's your opinion of the Chinese?"

"The Shanghai Police Bureau or Chief Inspector Chen?"

"Well, both," Spencer said.

"The bureau has made a point of treating me as a distinguished guest. Party Secretary Li Guohua, the bureau's top official, is going to meet me today or tomorrow. A courtesy, I guess. As for Chief Inspector Chen, I would say he works conscientiously."

"I'm glad to hear they treat you well, and your Chinese partner is a decent guy. Now about Chen, the CIA would like you to gather some information on him."

"They want me to spy on him?"

"That is too strong a word, Catherine. Just pass on the information you happen to have about him. What people is he associated with? What cases does he handle? What books does he read and write? That kind of thing. The CIA has its own sources, but you are someone they can trust."

She agreed but she did not like it.

Then the phone rang again. It was Chen.

"How are you this morning, Inspector Rohn?"

"Much better."

"Your ankle?"

"The paste has worked. No problem today," she said, rubbing her ankle, which still felt slightly tender.

"You scared me yesterday." There was relief in his voice. "Are you up for another interview today?"

"Sure. When?"

"I have a meeting this morning. What about this afternoon?"

"Then I'll do a little research in the Shanghai Library in the morning."

"About Chinese secret societies?"

"Right." In addition, she was going to collect some information about Chen. Not merely for the CIA.

"The library is also on Nanjing Road. A taxi will take you there in less than five minutes."

"I'll walk if it is so close."

"That's up to you. I'll meet you at twelve in a restaurant opposite the library, across the street. The Verdant Willow Village. That's the name of the restaurant."

"See you then."

After a quick shower, she left the hotel. She strolled along Nanjing Road, an extended shopping center, not only lined with shops on both sides, but also with rows of peddlers in front of the shops. She crisscrossed the street several times, lured by the interesting window displays. She had not done any shopping since her arrival.

At the intersection of Zhejiang Road, she had to resist the temptation to enter a vermilion restaurant with engraved pillars sustaining a yellow-glazed tile roof—an imitation of the ancient Chinese architectural style. A waitress dressed in the Qing dynasty costume bowed enticingly to the people passing by. Instead, Catherine bought a piece of sticky rice cake from one of curbside peddlers, nibbling it like the Shanghai girls walking in front of her. It was rather fashionable to talk about the Chinese people as natural capitalists, born wheelers and dealers, and to explain the economic boom in that way, but she believed it was their collective energy released after so many years of state economic control, being given the opportunity to do something for themselves for the first time, that had led to the transformation she saw around her.

And she encountered no more curious glances than she would have in St. Louis. Nor did she meet with any accident except shoulder-bumping and elbow-pushing as she squeezed past a crowded department store. She had been disturbed by the accidents in the last two days, but perhaps she had been clumsy from jet lag. She was well rested that morning. Soon she came in view of the library. She gave small change to beggars on the steps as she would have done in St. Louis.

As she entered the Shanghai Library, an English-speaking librarian came over to help. She had two subjects, the Flying Axes and Chen. To her surprise, Catherine found practically nothing on triads in their literature. Perhaps writing about those criminal activities was forbidden in contemporary China.

She found several magazines containing Chen's poems and translations. And a few translations of mysteries under Chen's name, too. Some of them she had read in English. What fascinated her was the stereotyped "translator preface" for each of the books. It consisted of an introduction giving the author's background, a brief analysis of the story, and an invariable conclusion using political clichés—*due to the author's ideological background, the decadent values of the Western capitalist society cannot but be reflected in the text, and Chinese readers should be alert against such influence* . . .

Absurd, and hypocritical too, but such hypocrisy might have accounted for his rapid rise.

The librarian stepped into the reading room with a new magazine. "Here is a recent interview with Chen Cao."

There was a color picture of him in a black suit with a conservative tie, looking like an academic. In the interview, using T. S. Eliot as an example, Chen claimed that poetry should be written without the pressure of having to be a poet. He mentioned Louis MacNeice, who had to earn a living at another job. Chen acknowledged their influence on his poetry and mentioned the title of a poem suffused with melancholy. She found "The Sunlight on the Garden," read it, and made copies. The CIA's purpose was political, but Chen's essay might throw more light on her Chinese partner as a human being. Eliot and Mac-Neice, Chen used their stories to justify his own career. She returned the material to the librarian.

As she left the library, she saw Chen waiting in front of the restaurant. Less scholarly-looking than in the magazine picture, he wore a black blazer with khaki pants. He took several steps across the street, met her halfway at the safety island, and led her into the restaurant. There, a hostess ushered them into a private room on the second floor.

She examined the bilingual menu. After reading a few lines, she pushed it over to him. She understood each of the characters, but not their combination. The English translation, or rather the transliteration, did not help much.

A waiter carried over a long-billed brass kettle and poured a graceful arc of water into her cup. In addition to the green tea leaves, there were also tiny pieces of red and yellow herbs at the bottom of the cup.

"Eight Treasure Tea," Chen said. "Supposed to be potent for boosting your energy."

She listened in amusement as he discussed the house specials with the waiter. He turned to ask her approval at intervals. A perfect escort, this chosen representative of the Shanghai Police Bureau.

"The name of the restaurant comes from a line of a Song dynasty poem, *There's a home deep in the verdant willows.* I've forgotten the author."

"But you remember the name of the restaurant."

"Yes, that's more important. As Confucius tells us, 'You cannot be too fastidious in choosing your food.' That's the first lesson for a sinologist."

"I guess you are a regular customer here," she said.

"I've been here two or three times." He ordered a South Sea bird's nest soup with tree ears, oysters fried in spiced egg batter, a duck stuffed with a mixture of sticky rice, dates, and lotus seeds, a fish steamed live with fresh ginger, green onions, and dried pepper, and an exotic-sounding special whose name she did not catch.

After the waiter had withdrawn, she rested her eyes on him. "I'm just wondering—"

"Yes?"

"Oh, nothing. Forget it." Several cold dishes appeared on the table, which gave her an excuse not to continue. She was curious as to how he had acquired all his epicurean knowledge. An ordinary Chinese chief inspector could not have afforded it. She realized she was already carrying out the CIA's task, yet this did not spoil her appetite.

"I'm just wondering," she said, "if our interviews here can lead anywhere. Wen seems to have totally cut herself off from her past. I can hardly see any possibility of her coming back to Shanghai after so many years."

"We have just started. In the meantime, my temporary assistant Qian has been checking hotels as well as neighborhood committees." He picked up a piece of chicken with his chopsticks. "We may hear something soon."

"Do you think Wen could have afforded to stay in a hotel?"

"No. I think you're right, Inspector Rohn. Feng has not sent any money home. His wife does not even have a bank account. So I have had Old Hunter look into cheap, unlicensed hotels as well."

"Isn't Old Hunter engaged with another case?"

"Yes, but I asked him to help with this case, too."

"Any breakthrough in the other case?"

"Not much progress there either. It involves a body found in the park. Old Hunter has just identified the dead man's pajama brand by the V pattern woven into the fabric."

"Mmm, Valentino." she said. "Now in our case, there's

another thing that troubles me. As far as we can tell, Wen has not yet made any effort to contact her husband. This does not make sense. Feng wanted her to run for her life, but not out of his life. She knows about the trial date, so if she didn't know how to contact him she should have gotten in touch with the police. With each passing day, the possibility of her rejoining Feng before the trial becomes fainter. It's the seventh day that she's been missing."

"That's true. Things may be more complicated than we originally imagined."

"What else can we do here?"

"This afternoon, we are going to interview another schoolmate of Wen's, Su Shengyi."

"The secret admirer in high school. A red guard cadre, now down and out, right?" She could not help being suspicious. This seemed a total waste of time.

"Yes, you're right. One never forgets his first love. Su may know something."

"After the visit, what? Am I supposed to remain at the hotel as a distinguished guest, shopping, sightseeing, and sharing these fantastic meals with you?"

"I'll discuss it with Party Secretary Li."

"Another straightforward answer?"

"Cheers." He raised his teacup in a toast.

"Cheers," Catherine said, raising her teacup. The tiny dried fruit, Chinese wolfberry, rose to the surface like a scarlet period. There was not much she could do with this Chinese partner, who responded to her sarcasm with an unruffled air. It amused her to toast with tea, though.

Another course arrived, bubbling in an earthenware pot. It looked different from American Chinatown specials. Its creamy gravy tasted like chicken broth, but the meat was unlike chicken. It had a jellied texture.

"What's that?"

"Soft shell turtle."

"I'm glad I didn't ask first." She caught the spark of amusement in his eyes. "Not bad."

"Not bad? It's the most expensive item on the menu."

"And is a turtle also a fabled aphrodisiac in China?"

"That depends." Chen helped himself to a substantial portion.

"Chief Inspector Chen!" She feigned shock.

"Today's special." The waiter was back with a white bowl containing what seemed to be large snails immersed in brownish juice, and a glass bowl of water.

Chen put his fingers into the bowl of water, wiped them with a napkin, and picked up one of the shells. She watched him sucking the meat out with an effort.

"It is luscious," he said. "River spiral shells. Often translated as river snail. You eat it like a snail."

"I have never had snails."

"Really!" He took a bamboo toothpick, picked the meat out, and offered it to her on the end of the toothpick.

She should have refused. Instead, she leaned over the table and let him put it into her mouth. It tasted good, but the experience was slightly disquieting.

The Chinese cop was turning into a challenge. He seemed to fancy himself as a charmer.

"It tastes better if you suck the meat out yourself," he said.

So she did. The meat came out together with the juice. It did taste better that way.

When the bill came, she tried to pay it, or at least her share. He refused. She protested, "I cannot let the Shanghai Police Bureau pay all the time."

"Don't worry about that." He crumpled the receipt. "Can't I buy a lunch for an attractive American partner?"

He seemed to be a man to whom compliments came easily. Perhaps it was cultural. Perhaps he had his orders.

He was pulling out the chair for her when his phone started to ring. He turned it on, and his face became serious as he listened. At the end of the call, he said, "I'll be there."

"What's up?"

"We have a change in plans," he said. "The call was from Qian Jun at the bureau. We've had a response to the missing person notice. A pregnant provincial woman has been reported working in a restaurant in Qingpu County, Shanghai. Apparently she's from the south, speaking with a strong southern accent."

"Could it be Wen?"

"If Wen boarded a train for Shanghai, it's possible she changed her mind and got off there, one or two stops before Shanghai. Perhaps she did not want to bring trouble down on her people. So she found a job there instead of moving into a local hotel."

"That makes sense to me."

"I'm going to Qingpu," Chen said. "It's a long shot. Many people are pouring into Shanghai for jobs—even into the counties. So quite possibly it's a false lead. There may be a lot of things that would be more interesting for you to do here, Inspector Rohn."

"I wish I had something more interesting to do." She put down her chopsticks. "Let's go."

"I'll get a car at the bureau. Do you mind waiting for me here?"

"Not at all." Still, she wondered: was he trying to keep her away from his office for some reason? She wished she could trust him, but knew she'd be a fool to do so.

*   *   *

She was surprised when Chen pulled up in a medium-size Shanghai. "So you're driving today?"

"Little Zhou was not on the bureau car service rota. The other drivers were busy."

"A high-ranking cadre like you," she said, stepping into the car, "I thought you would always have a chauffeur at your service."

"I'm not a high-ranking cadre. But thanks for the compliment."

Chapter 13

Chen had not told Catherine Rohn the real reason why he had chosen to drive. He trusted Little Zhou but others could easily learn his movements through the bureau car service. So he had taken the car without telling anybody.

It was a long drive to Qingpu County. A pleasant breeze came through the windows. As if by a tacit understanding, they did not talk about their work. Looking at the varying countryside, she started questioning him about language exchange programs at Chinese universities.

"Universities such as Fudan, East China Normal, and Shanghai Foreign Language may offer some teaching positions to native English speakers in exchange for their tuition in Chinese studies," Chen said. "Preferably to those with English degrees."

"I have a double major. One's in English."

"The exchange programs do not pay much. Not bad according to the Chinese standards, but you would not be able to afford to stay at the Peace Hotel."

"I don't have to stay at a luxurious hotel." She pushed a strand of hair off her forehead. "Don't worry, Chief Inspector Chen. I'm just curious."

Soon the scene changed to a more rural one: rice paddies, vegetable plots, with some new, colorful houses here and there. Under Deng Xiaoping's policy of "Letting some people get rich first," prosperous peasant entrepreneurs were springing up like mushrooms. As they drove past a small lush green field, he exclaimed, "Qicai. Spring has made a late start here!"

"What?"

"Qicai. Called shepherd's purse in English. I don't know why it was given such a name. It is delicious."

"Interesting. You're a botanist too."

"No, I am not. But once I tried to translate a Song dynasty poem, in which the poet finds himself gathered, deliciously, together with this greenish blossom on his lover's tongue, and then on his tongue."

"What a pity! You don't have the time to gather any today."

It was about two o'clock when they reached the site in Qingpu County where their quarry had been reported. It was a shabby restaurant in a village market. The door was ajar, and a wooden bench stood in the doorway. There were no customers at this time of the day.

Chen raised his voice. "Anybody here?"

A woman came out of the kitchen in the rear, wiping her hands on an oily apron. She had a thin face with deep-set eyes, high cheekbones, and wore her gray-streaked hair in a bun at the nape of her neck. She appeared to be in her late thirties. The roundness of her belly was slightly visible.

She looked very different from the woman in the passport picture. The disappointment in Catherine's eyes mirrored his.

He handed his card to the woman mechanically. "We need to ask you a few questions."

"Me?" She looked frightened. "I've done nothing wrong."

"If you've done nothing wrong, you don't have to worry. What's your name?"

"Qiao Guozhen."

"Do you have your I.D.?"

"Yes, here it is."

Chen examined it closely. It had been issued in Guangxi Province. The picture on the I.D. card was of this woman. "So your family is still there?"

"Yes, my husband and my daughters are there."

"Why are you here by yourself—in your pregnancy? They must be worried about you."

"No, they are not worried. They know I'm here."

"Do you have some family problem?"

"No, no problem at all."

"You'd better tell me the truth," he bluffed. It was not really his business, but he felt the need to do something in front of Inspector Rohn. "Or you will get into serious trouble."

"Don't send me back home, Comrade Chief Inspector. They will force me to have an abortion!"

Catherine cut in for the first time. "What? Who will do that to you?"

"The village cadres. They have birth control quotas to meet."

"Tell us everything," Catherine said. "We won't get you into any trouble."

Chief Inspector Chen looked at the two women, Qiao sobbing, Catherine fuming, himself standing by helplessly like an idiot. "What is the story, Comrade Qiao?"

"We have two daughters. My husband wanted to have a son. Now I'm pregnant again. We were fined heavily for the birth of our second daughter. The village committee said a heavy fine would not be enough this time, I would have to have an abortion. So I ran away."

"You're from Guangxi," Chen said, aware of Catherine's close attention. "Why have you come all the way here?"

"My husband wanted me to stay here with his cousin, but she had moved away. Fortunately, I met Mrs. Yang, the owner of the restaurant. She hired me."

"So you work for your room and board?"

"Yang also gives me two hundred Yuan a month, in addition to tips," Qiao said, putting a hand on her belly. "Soon I will not be able to work out front. I have to earn as much as I can."

"What's your plan?" Catherine asked.

"I'll give birth to my baby here. When my son is two or three months old, I'll go back."

"What will your village cadres do to you?"

"After a baby has been born, they cannot really do anything. A heavy fine, probably. We're not worried about that." She turned to Chen, pleading in a trembling voice. "So you're not going to send me back home?"

"No. Your problem is with your village cadres, not with me. I just don't think it's a good idea for a pregnant woman like you to be so far from home."

"Do you have a better idea?" Catherine said sarcastically.

A man entered the restaurant, but at the sight of the chief inspector and his American partner, he left immediately without saying a single word.

"You have my card. Take good care of yourself," Chen said, standing up. "If you need help, let me know."

They walked out of the restaurant in silence. The tension between them did not improve as they got into the car. He started the engine with a screeching sound.

The air inside the car felt stuffy.

It was a shame, he admitted to himself, that the local cadres had put so much pressure on Qiao, and that Inspector Rohn happened to be a witness. It was not the first time that he had heard stories about pregnant women going into hiding until after their deliveries. It was nonetheless unpleasant to hear it from somebody's own mouth.

His American partner must have been thinking about China's violation of human rights. The world in a drop of water. She did not say a single word. His hand accidentally hit the horn.

"Well, the local cadres may have overdone it," he tried to break the silence, "but our government has no choice. The population control policy is a necessary one."

"Whatever problem your government may have, a woman must be able to choose to have her baby—and at her own home."

"You can hardly imagine how serious the problem is here, Inspector Rohn. Take Qiao's family for example. They already have two daughters, and they will go on having more—until they finally have a son. The continuation of the family name, as you probably know from your Chinese studies, is the most important thing to these people."

"It's their choice."

"But in what context?" he retorted. Last night Li had warned him not to go out of his way for the American. And here he was, being lectured to by an American about China's human rights problem. "China does not have a lot of arable land. Less than ninety million hectares, to be exact. Do you think poor farmers like the Qiaos can afford to take good care of five or six kids in an impoverished province like Guangxi?"

"You're using the numbers from the *People's Daily*."

"Those are facts. If you had lived as an ordinary Chinese for more than thirty years, you might view the situation from a different perspective."

"How, Comrade Chief Inspector Chen?" For the first time since they had returned to the car she looked up at him.

"You would have seen a few things for yourself. Three generations squeezed under one roof, and that a single room, buses packed with people like sardines in a can, and newly married couples obliged to sleep on their office desks as a protest to the housing committee. Detective Yu, for example, does not have a room of his own—the one his family now lives in used to be Old Hunter's dining room. Yu's nine-year-old son, Qinqin, still sleeps in the same room as his parents. Why? Because of overpopulation. Not enough housing or even space for the people. How can the government afford not to do something about it?"

"Whatever excuses you may have, basic human rights cannot be denied."

"Such as the right of people to pursue happiness?" He found himself getting heated.

"Yes," she said. "If you don't acknowledge that, there's nothing we can discuss."

"Fine, then what about illegal immigration? According to your Constitution, there's nothing wrong with people seeking a better life. America should welcome all immigrants with open arms. Then why are you pursuing this investigation? Why must people pay to be smuggled into your country?"

"That's different. There must be international law and order."

"That's exactly my point. There are no absolute principles. They are always being modified by time and circumstances. Two or three hundred years ago, no one was complaining about illegal immigration to North America."

"When did you become an historian?"

"I'm not." He tried to control himself as he turned onto a road lined with new industrial buildings.

She did not try to conceal the sarcasm in her voice. "Perhaps that's what you want to be, a celebrated mouthpiece for the *People's Daily*. Still, you cannot deny the fact that poor women are deprived of their right to have babies."

"I'm not saying that the local cadres should have gone that far, but China must do something about overpopulation."

"I'm not surprised to hear this brilliant defense from you. In your position, Chief Inspector Chen, you must identify with the system."

"Maybe you're right," he said, somberly. "I cannot help it, just as you cannot help seeing things here from a perspective formed by your system."

"Whatever. I've had enough of your political lectures." Her blue eyes were ocean-deep, unfathomable, antagonistic.

It bothered Chen, who was still aware of her attractiveness despite her being so critical of China.

A couplet from an anonymous Western Han dynasty poem came to his mind.

The Tartar horse rejoices in the north wind.
The bird of Yueh nestles on the south branch.

Different attachments. Different places. Perhaps Party Secretary Li was right. There was no point in his going out of his way to pursue this investigation.

Two thousand years ago, what was now the United States of America might have been called the Land of Tartars.

Chapter 14

It never rains but it pours.

Chief Inspector Chen's phone started ringing.

It was Mr. Ma. "Where are you, Chief Inspector Chen?"

"On the road back from Qingpu."

"Are you alone?"

"No, with Catherine Rohn."

"How is she?"

"Much better. Your paste is miraculous. Thank you."

"I'm calling about the information you wanted yesterday."

"Go ahead, Mr. Ma."

"I've got a man for you. He may know something about the woman you are looking for."

"Who is it?"

"I have one request, Chief Inspector Chen."

"Yes?"

"If you get what you need, will you leave him alone?"

"I give you my word. And I'll never mention your name."

"I do not want to be a stool pigeon. It's against my principles to provide information to the government," Mr. Ma said earnestly. "His name is Gu Haiguang, a Mr. Big Bucks, the owner of the Dynasty Karaoke Club on Shanxi Road. He has his connections in the triad world, but I don't think he is a member. In his business, he has to be on good terms with the black way."

"You've taken a lot of trouble for me. I appreciate it, Mr. Ma."

He turned off the phone. Chen didn't want to discuss Ma's information with Catherine immediately though he knew she must have overheard some of the conversation. He took a deep breath. "Let's stop here, Inspector Rohn. I'm thirsty. What about you?"

She said, "A fruit juice would be fine."

He pulled up at a convenience store, where he bought some drinks, together with a paper bag of fried mini buns. As he entered, another car drove by slowly, then reversed and pulled into the lot.

"Please help yourself," he said when he returned, holding out the buns covered with minced green onion, colorful, but greasy.

She took only the drink.

"The call was from Mr. Ma." He opened his cola can with a pop. "He asked about you."

"It's very kind of him. I heard you thank him a couple of times."

"Not just that. He has found someone connected with the gang who will speak to us."

"A Flying Axes member?"

"No, probably not, but we should interview him, if you're no longer mad."

"Of course we will interview him. It's our job."

"That's the spirit, Inspector Rohn. Please eat some buns. I don't know long it will take. Afterward, I will buy you a better meal—one fit for a distinguished American guest."

"There you go again." She picked up a bun with a paper napkin.

"Whatever I say during the interview, Inspector Rohn, please don't jump to conclusions."

"What do you mean?"

"For one thing, the tip came from Mr. Ma. I do not want to bring any trouble down on him."

"I see. You must protect your source." She stuffed a bun into her mouth. "I've no objection to that. I owe him a favor. Who is this mysterious man we are going to see?" She added, "And what will my role be?"

"He is the owner of the Dynasty Karaoke Club. It's a hot place for young people. To sing along, to dance along. You won't need to do anything. Just relax and enjoy the place as our American guest."

They pulled onto the road. He checked his rearview mirror from time to time. A half hour later, they reached the intersection of Shanxi and Julu Roads. There, he made a right turn and pulled up by the half-open gate to a wall-enclosed mansion. A vertical white sign read: SHANGHAI WRITERS' ASSOCIATION. The doorman recognized Chen and opened the gate wide.

"You're bringing an American guest today?"

"Yes, for a visit."

She looked at him in puzzlement as the car rolled along the driveway to a stop alongside of a parked car. "Did you want to show me around the Writers' Association first?"

"There's no place to park near the Dynasty. We'll leave the car here and take a shortcut through the back. It's only a two or three minutes' walk."

It was only one of the reasons for leaving the car at the Association. Chen did not want to park a car with a bureau plate at the club. It might be recognized. And he could not shake off the feeling that they had been followed, though he wondered how a Fujian gang could have been so resourceful so far from their home territory. As they drove, he had been checking in the rearview mirror, but with such heavy traffic, it was difficult for him to be sure.

He let her through a hallway, and then out of a back door.

The new five-story building of the Dynasty Karaoke Club came in sight. Entering the spacious lobby, they found themselves standing on a vast marble floor that shone like a mirror. At one end of the main room, there was a stage with a band sitting underneath a huge TV screen, which showed singers performing along with the captions. In front of the stage were about thirty tables. Some people were sitting, drinking, while others were dancing in the space between the stage and tables. At the other end a marble staircase led to the second floor. This was different from the arrangement of the other clubs Chen had visited.

A young man in a white T-shirt and black jeans appeared on stage and made a gesture toward the band. The band started playing a jazz piece adapted from the modern Beijing Opera *Taking Tiger Mountain by Surprise*. It had been extremely popular during the early seventies, and told of a small detachment of the People's Liberation Army fighting the Nationalist troops. Never had Chen imagined that a melody about PLA soldiers chasing tigers and bandits in snowstorms could be adapted so successfully into a piece to dance to.

"Chairman Mao's words warm my heart,/ bringing spring to melt the snow away . . ."

How many times had he heard this refrain, sitting with his high-school friends in the movies? For a second, the past and the present were fused into one swirling scene. The fashionably dressed dancers, but also the soldiers in uniforms, pranced frenziedly before his eyes—trendy young people doing wild, exotic steps.

Then a stout, unshaven man glided to the center of the floor, clicking his fingers, drawing a great roar from the bystanders. The dancer's features were oddly similar to Comrade Yang Zi-rong, the hero of the original Beijing Opera.

Chen gestured toward a young hostess in a purple velvet

dress, who came over, bowing. "What can I do for you?" she inquired.

"We need a private room. The best."

"The best, of course. There's only one left."

They were led upstairs, and along a curving corridor lined with private chambers, into a lavishly decorated room, with a flat Panasonic TV screen set into the wall. A high capacity Kenwood stereo system with several speakers stood beside it. A remote control and two microphones lay on a marble coffee table in front of a black leather sectional sofa.

The hostess unfolded a menu for them.

"Bring us a fruit platter. A coffee for me and a green tea for her." He turned to Catherine. "The food here is okay, but we'll dine later at the Jing River Hotel, a five-star hotel."

"Whatever you say," she said, intrigued by this proclamation of extravagance. And how did he know if the food was good or not?

The room was decorated like a rendezvous for lovers. A crystal vase on the corner table held a bouquet of carnations. The floor was thickly carpeted. There was also a liquor cabinet on the wall, whose glass shelves displayed bottles of Napoleon brandy and Mao Tai. The light was lambent, adjustable to different intensities. The floral-papered walls had been specially soundproofed. With the door closed, they could not hear any noise from outside, though all the other rooms must have been occupied by karaoke singers.

Little wonder business was thriving, even at a price of two hundred Yuan an hour, Chen thought. And this was not the peak time-period price. From seven P.M. to two in the morning it could be as high as five hundred Yuan an hour, according to Old Hunter.

The hostess brought them another sort of menu—a list of

song titles in both English and Chinese. Underneath each name was a number.

"You may choose any song you like, Catherine," he said. "All you have to do is push the number on the remote control, and sing along with the captions on the screen."

"I did not realize that karaoke was so popular here," she said.

Karaoke had been imported from Japan in the mid-eighties. Originally, it had been confined to a few large restaurants. Then entrepreneurs saw an opportunity. They converted restaurants into karaoke halls, open twenty-four hours a day. Next, the private room came into vogue. The hall was partitioned into many small chambers, each nicely furnished to give a sense of privacy. Some entrepreneurs went so far as to have a whole building redesigned for the purpose. Soon, people came not just for the karaoke, but for something else in the guise of karaoke.

With hotels still requiring I.D. and marriage certificates before people could check in, these private karaoke rooms, with their locked doors, met the understood yet unstated needs of the city suffering from a housing shortage. People did not have to feel awkward here. Ostensibly, they were only attending a karaoke party.

Karaoke girls, often abbreviated as K girls, also appeared. Nominally, they were supposed to sing with a customer who did not have a female companion. When the door was locked, however, the other services the K girls provided could well be imagined.

Chen did not see a single K girl that afternoon. Perhaps this was due to the time of the day. Or perhaps it was because he was with someone already.

He did not explain any of this to Inspector Rohn.

When the hostess came back with their order, he said. "Who is your boss?"

"General Manager Gu."

"Tell him to come here."

The hostess asked in astonishment, "What shall I say to him?"

He cast a glance at Catherine. "I have some international business opportunities to discuss with him."

Almost immediately, a middle-aged man appeared, wearing a pair of black-rimmed glasses, sporting a beer belly as well as a diamond ring on his finger. He held out his business card to Chen. It read: Gu Haiguang.

Chen handed over his card in return. Gu seemed shocked, but he controlled himself, quickly waving the hostess out of the room.

"I'm here to introduce myself to you, General Manager Gu. This is my friend Catherine. I wanted to show her the best karaoke club in Shanghai." Chen continued, "There's a lot we can do for each other. As the old saying goes, 'The mountain is high, and the river is long.' "

"Indeed, there are many possibilities in the future. I'm so honored to meet you today, and your beautiful American girlfriend. I have heard about you, Chief Inspector Chen. Your name has been in newspapers headlines. Your honorable presence lights up our humble place. Today is our treat."

This would not be a small sum. Chen believed. For a couple of hours in a private room, plus the food, the bill could run to a month's salary for him. Most of the clients must be newly rich or officials spending government money.

"You are most kind, but that's not why I wanted to meet you, General Manager Gu."

"Sergeant Cai is also a regular client of ours. He patrols the area."

Chen had heard about cops accepting graft in the form of free entertainment from karaoke clubs. After all, a cop deserved to sing a few songs, too. One problem with graft was, however, that it snowballed.

"As a chief inspector, I want to do a good job." Chen took a leisurely sip of his coffee. "But that will be difficult without people's help."

"It's the same in our business. As one of our old sayings goes, 'At home, you depend on your parents, and out in the world, you rely on your friends.' I am so pleased that we have become acquainted today. Your help will be invaluable to us."

"Now that we're friends, General Manager Gu, I would like to ask you a couple of questions."

"Gladly, I will tell you anything I know." Gu was all smiles.

"Has a gang called the Flying Axes contacted you?"

"Flying Axes? No, Chief Inspector Chen," Gu said, his eyes suddenly alert. "I'm a decent business man. But a karaoke club has visitors from all walks of life. Occasionally from those secret societies as well. They come here like other customers. To sing, to dance, to have a good time."

"Oh yes, there are a lot of private rooms here. Private services, too." Chen stirred his coffee spoon deliberately. "You are a clever man, General Manager Gu. We can talk plainly. Whatever you pass on to me as a friend will be kept confidential."

"I'm so honored that you consider me a friend." Gu seemed to be stalling for time. "Really. I'm overwhelmed."

"Let me tell you something, General Manager Gu. Lu Tonghao, the owner of Moscow Suburb, is an old pal of mine. When he first started his business, I managed to get a loan for him."

"Moscow Suburb! Yes, I've been there. To get along in today's society, people really have to rely on their friends. Especially a friend like you. No wonder the restaurant enjoys such success."

Chief Inspector Chen was aware of the close attention Inspector Rohn was paying to the conversation. Still, he went on.

"Lu has a bevy of Russian girls walking around in their mini slips. No one gives him any trouble. It's so easy for people to find problems, you know, with a restaurant or a karaoke business."

"That's true. Fortunately, we do not have any problems with ours—" Gu said more slowly. "Well, except for the parking lot behind our building."

"Parking lot?"

"There's a space behind our building. For our location, this is really a godsend. So convenient for customers to park their cars there. The Shanghai Metropolitan Traffic Control people have come to us several times, saying that the space has not been zoned as a parking lot for the club."

"If it's a matter of a zoning problem, I can give them a call. Perhaps you may not know that I served as the acting director of Traffic Control last year."

"Really, Director Chen!"

"Now about the gang—from Fujian." Chen put down the cup and looked Gu in the eyes. "Does that ring a bell?"

"A Fujian triad. I don't know. Oh, now I remember something else. Someone came to me yesterday. Not from Fujian, but from Hong Kong. A certain Mr. Diao. And he asked me if I had hired anyone from Fujian. A woman in her mid-thirties, three or four months pregnant. That's so unlikely. Most of the girls working here are under twenty-five, and we have more good-looking young women applying than we can hire, let alone a pregnant one."

"Did Mr. Diao give you any description of the woman he was looking for?"

"Let me think." Gu said. "Not particularly nice looking.

Sallow, wrinkled, a lot of sadness in her eyes. A woman who looked like a Fujian farmer."

"Are you sure that Mr. Diao's not a gangster?"

"I don't think so. He would have stated his organization and rank when he introduced himself." Gu added, belatedly, "And he would not have come to me if he were a gangster."

"Your club is not a likely place to find such a woman. Mr. Diao must have known better." Chen said. "Why did he come here?"

"I don't know. He must have been desperate, bumping everywhere like a headless fly."

"Do you know where he is staying?"

"He did not leave his address or phone number. He said he might check back."

"If he does, find out where he can be found and give me a call." Chen had written his cellular phone number on the back of his card. "Any time."

"I'll do that, Chief Inspector Chen. Anything else?"

"Well, another thing," Chen said. Gu seemed to be quite cooperative now that he had played the bargaining chip of the parking lot. The chief inspector decided to push his luck a little further. "A body was discovered in Bund Park a few days ago. Possibly a triad killing. There were many ax wounds to the body. Have you heard anything about it?"

"I think I read about it in the *Xinming Evening Newspaper*."

"The victim could have been murdered in a hotel room, or in a place like yours."

"You cannot be serious, Chief Inspector Chen."

"I'm not saying it happened here, General Manager Gu. I make no accusation. But you are well-informed and move in the right circles. The Dynasty is the number-one karaoke club in Shanghai," Chen said, patting Gu's shoulder. "Some clubs or other places stay open all night, and they do not do a proper business like yours. The victim was in his pajamas, having just had sex. You see, I'm giving you all the details, in confidence."

"I appreciate your trust, Chief Inspector Chen. I will try my best to find out for you."

"Thank you, General Manager Gu. As it is said, 'Some people can never understand each other all their lives, not even when they are white-haired, but some do the moment they take off their hats.' " Chen rose to his feet. "I'm glad that we have met today. Now I have to leave. Please give me the bill."

"If you consider me a friend, don't talk about payment. I cannot bear to lose face like that."

"Oh no, you cannot let him lose face, Chief Inspector Chen," Catherine said.

"Here are two VIP cards," Gu said. "One for you, one for your beautiful American girlfriend. You must come back again."

"Of course we will." Catherine smiled, taking Chen's arm as they walked out.

This was a carefully calculated message for Gu: Chief Inspector Chen had his weaknesses. She did not let go of his arm until they lost themselves in the crowd. They did not start talking until they got back to the car.

The Flying Axes were looking for Wen, not only in the Fujian area, but elsewhere, desperately, "Bumping everywhere like a headless fly—" just as they were. By April twenty-fourth, however, failure to locate Wen would be a success for the gangsters.

Chapter 15

It was not until they came in sight of the hotel that he remembered, "Oh, the dinner I promised you. I've forgotten all about it, Inspector Rohn."

"It's just five o'clock. I'm not hungry yet."

"What about Deda? It is close to the hotel. We can talk there."

Deda was a two-story restaurant on the corner of Nanjing and Sichuan Road. Its European-style front formed a sharp contrast to the Central Market beside it.

"During the Cultural Revolution, it was called Workers, Peasants, and Soldiers Restaurant," Chief Inspector Chen said. "Now it has changed back to the original name, Deda, meaning 'Great German'."

There were quite a number of young people on the first floor, smoking, talking, stirring desires or memories into their coffee cups. He led her to the second floor, where food was served. They chose a table by a window overlooking Nanjing Road. She ordered a glass of white wine, and he, coffee and a wedge of lemon pie. At his recommendation, she also had a Deda special, a piece of chestnut cream cake.

"You have a reason for everything, Chief Inspector Chen. You were like a fish swimming in triad waters—at the Dynasty."

"It takes time to crack a hard nut like Gu. Time is what we cannot afford. So I tried a different approach."

"Your performance was impressive, making friends, and exchanging favors."

"I'll let you in on a secret. One of my favorite genres is the kung fu novel."

"Like the Western in American literature. People know it's a fantasy, but they still enjoy it."

"You might say that the present-day triad world is a poor imitation of the more glamorized one in the kung fu novels. Of course there are differences but they share values. For one, *yiqi*. An ethical code of brotherhood, of loyalty, with emphasis on the obligation to reciprocate favors."

"Is *yiqi* so important in China because the legal system is flawed?"

"You could say that," he said, impressed by her acute observation. "But *yiqi* is not necessarily negative. My father was a Confucian scholar. And I still remember an old saying he taught me. 'If somebody helps you with a drop of water, you should repay him by digging a spring for him'."

"You have made a special study," she said, taking another small sip of wine.

"Gu is a shrewd businessman. *Yiqi* does not come out of nowhere. If he sees some future benefit, he is more likely to cooperate. It would not hurt him to talk a little—in a private room—to a chief inspector. That little is all I need."

"Oh, Gu has more than that I think," she said. "Mr. Diao, the Hong Kong visitor, may have not left his phone number, but Gu can find him. It really depends on how much he wants his parking lot."

"You are right. I'll have a talk with my former secretary at Traffic Control."

"The visitor could be a Flying Ax. They may have a branch in Hong Kong."

"As far as I know, the gang does not have a branch in Hong Kong. And a Fujian accent would be hard to cover up. Besides, I don't see why a visitor should try to conceal his identity from Gu."

"Why not, Chief Inspector Chen?"

"There's a gang rule—'declaring the mountain door.' One has to make clear his organization background and rank so others will deal with him."

"That's a point," she said, nodding. "But if he's not a Flying Ax, who is he?"

"I don't have the answer."

"You mentioned the other case to Gu, the body in Bund Park, with all the ax wounds. Could there be some connection between that killing and Wen's disappearance?"

"It's probably a coincidence. A lot of gangs use axes."

"Don't the triads use guns at all?"

"Some do, but in gang fights, they prefer knives and axes. There is very strict gun control in China."

"Yes, your government refused my request to carry a gun."

The waiter came to their table with a dessert cart.

"In the tradition of kung fu novels," he resumed as soon as they were left alone, "it is necessary to apologize by making a banquet. This is no banquet, but I am sincere in making my apologies."

"What are you apologizing for?" She was surprised.

"Inspector Rohn, I want you to know that I'm sorry about my overreaction in Qingpu. I should not have associated my defense of my government's birth-control policy with the issue of illegal immigration to the U.S. I didn't mean to offend you."

"Let's put it behind us. You pushed your defense too far, and I went overboard, too. We're both to blame," she said. The fact was that after their argument she trusted him more. He had lost his composure; he had not been acting. "But you did a great job with Gu this afternoon. This may be important."

"Well, but for your strained ankle, we would not have visited Mr. Ma, and then we would not have learned of Gu. It's really serendipitous, a chain of coincidences."

"And if Mr. Ma hadn't had a copy of *Dr. Zhivago* on his shelf years ago, and become a doctor because of it, or even earlier, if you hadn't wandered into his bookstore for your comic book . . . it may be a very long chain indeed," she said.

In spite of their reconciliation, she did not invite him to her hotel. They shook hands outside the café, standing on the sidewalk, still filled with illegally parked bikes.

He remained there for a minute, watching her walk across traffic-jammed Sichuan Road. Her black purse swung against her side, her long hair brushed her shoulders. As her slender figure reemerged from the waves of bikes, she appeared to be far away.

There was no accident this time.

He heaved a sigh of relief.

He phoned Meiling at the Shanghai Metropolitan Traffic Control Office.

"What's up, Director Chen."

"Don't call me that, Meiling. I only served as acting director when Director Wei was in hospital."

Director Wei had returned, but he remained in unstable health. People had been talking about Chen's moving back to the position. It was a suggestion he meant to resist.

"I still think of you as my boss," Meiling insisted. "What can I do for you today?"

"There is a karaoke club called Dynasty, on Shanxi Road. Our traffic control people have approached its owner, Gu Haiguang, about a zoning issue with respect to the parking lot there. If it is a borderline case, can we make a special study of it?"

"No problem, if that's what you want."

"There's no hurry. Before we do anything, I want you to contact Gu, telling him I have talked to you, and that Traffic Control will be giving the matter special consideration. Don't promise immediate approval or anything else."

"I see. I will ask Director Wei to give him a call. He has a high opinion of you."

"No, don't go out of your way, Meiling. If you can phone him tomorrow, that should be more than enough."

"I will do it the first thing tomorrow morning. Whatever you want us to decide, that's what Mr. Gu will get."

"I'll also need the help of Old Hunter for a few days." He added, "I'm working on an important case. I have to depend on the people I can trust, like you and Old Hunter."

"I'm glad you put me together with him. As our advisor, he does not have to report here every day. He may choose to conduct a special field study somewhere for a week. I'll tell Director Wei."

"Thank you, Meiling. I really owe you. When I've finished the job on my hands I'll take you to the Dynasty for a karaoke evening. I've got a VIP card."

"Whenever you have time, Director Chen. Take care."

Chen's next phone call was to Old Hunter. "I have to ask another favor of you, Uncle Yu. I need you to keep a close watch on the Dynasty Karaoke Club on Shanxi Road. The owner's name is Gu Haiguang. Tap his telephone twenty-four hours a day. Dig into his background. But try to get it done without the bureau's knowledge."

"You never know what connections a Mr. Big Bucks may

have inside the bureau," Old Hunter said. "You are right to be careful. This is a job for an old hunter. I still have a good nose, and ears too. But what about my traffic control responsibility?"

"I've talked to Meiling. You do not have to report there next week."

"Great. I will station myself in front of the club all day and send someone in as a customer—hold on, I have a better idea. I can get in myself. Some old people go there to kill time listening to old songs. No need for a private room or anything. I'll have someone else, Yang Guozhuang, another retired cop, do the telephone line tapping. He worked for many years in Tibet before his retirement. I helped him get his residence permit so he could move back into the city. As a rightist in 1957, he really suffered a lot. And you know what—just because of an entry in his diary."

"Thank you, Uncle Yu." Chen knew he'd better cut the old man short, or he would digress into a long tale about Yang's suffering during the antirightist movement. "If you need to have a private room, pay for it. Don't worry about the expense. We can draw on the special fund."

"Is Gu connected with the secret societies?"

"Connected, yes. You will have to watch out."

"So, is this about the body in the park or the other case?"

"Both, perhaps," Chen said, ending the call. Catherine Rohn might be right. Before he was able to do some more thinking along these lines, the phone rang again.

This time, it was Party Secretary Li.

Chapter 16

Catherine returned to her hotel alone.

Slipping off her shoes, she rubbed her ankle for several seconds before she walked to the window. Along the river, vessels moved against the eastern shore, shining under the inflamed clouds. Below her, people hurried along the Bund, in one direction or another, looking straight ahead. Chief Inspector Chen might be among them, walking toward the hotel with his briefcase.

Turning from the window, she stared at the thick dossier on her desk. That she looked forward to his company, she assured herself, was entirely professional. She wanted to discuss the new direction for the investigation after their visit to the Dynasty Karaoke Club. There was something else suspicious about the Hong Kong visitor.

She also wanted to show Chen that her attitude was free from Western prejudices and that, in spite of their differences, they had their common goal. Stories of forced abortion were not new to her, unfortunately. She knew he was a Chinese cop, working within the system.

Wen was probably no longer in Fujian. The Flying Axes must have reached a similar conclusion. So what could she do in Shanghai, working with Chief Inspector Chen? He had invoked *yiqi* with Gu. She hoped this approach would succeed, and quickly.

She started to dash off a few words on a pad, crossed them

out, and was thinking hard, when the fax machine began to emit a roll of paper. It was from Washington.

The cover page bore only one line: Information about Chen, from the CIA.

Chief Inspector Chen Cao is an emerging Party cadre, touted as a successor to Superintendent Zhao or Party Secretary Li of the Shanghai Police Bureau. It is said that last year Chen was on the top candidate list for the position of Shanghai Propaganda Minister. He also served as the acting director of Shanghai Traffic Control and attended the Seminar of the Central Party Institute. The last event is seen as an unmistakable sign of his further promotion within the Party system. As one of the "liberal reformists" within the Party, Chen enjoys a connection with powerful people at a higher level.

As for his professional performance, he has recently been in charge of several politically important cases, including the national model worker investigation last year, and a recent one concerning the vice mayor of Beijing.

Chen majored in English literature in college in the late seventies, but for some unknown reason, he was assigned to the police. Chen is on the invitation list of the U.S. News Agency as a writer.

In his mid-thirties, Chen remains a bachelor. He has his own apartment in a good location. Like other emerging cadres, he keeps a low profile in his personal life, but it is alleged that the father of his (ex?) girlfriend, Ling, is a leading politburo member.

Catherine put the fax into her file. She made a cup of coffee for herself.

An enigmatic man. She was intrigued by the part about his relationship with a politburo member's daughter. One of the High Cadres' Children. She had read about that prestigious group, privileged by their family connections, corrupt, power-ful. Were they still seeing each other? The CIA data was vague. She wondered whether a spoiled HCC would make a good wife for him. If he married an HCC, would he turn into one?

Catherine caught herself. Chief Inspector Chen was just a temporary partner in China. It was the CIA's business to be concerned with his life, not hers. The information about Chen was irrelevant now; what she needed was a clue to Wen's whereabouts, which she did not have.

She was jolted by the ringing of her phone. It was Chen. There was traffic noise in the background.

"Where are you, Chief Inspector Chen?"

"On my way home. I had a call from Party Secretary Li. He invites you to a Beijing Opera performance this evening."

"Does Mr. Li want to discuss the Wen case with me?"

"I'm not sure about that. The invitation is to demonstrate our bureau's attention to the case, and to you, our distinguished American guest."

"Isn't it enough to assign you to me?" she said.

"Well, in China, Li's invitation gives more face."

"Giving face—I've heard only about losing face."

"If you are a somebody, you give face by making a friendly gesture."

"I see, like your visit to Gu. So I have no choice?"

"Well, if you say no, Party Secretary Li will lose face. The bureau will, too—including me."

"Oh no! Yours is one face I have to save." She laughed. "What shall I wear to the Beijing Opera?"

"Beijing Opera is not like Western opera. You don't have to dress formally, but if you do—"

"Then I'm giving face, too."

"Exactly. Shall I pick you up at the hotel?"

"Where is the theater?"

"Not far from your hotel. On the corner of Fuzhou and Henan Roads. The City Government Auditorium."

"You don't have to pick me up. I'll take a taxi there. See you."

"Oh, by the way, I have not discussed this afternoon's visit with Party Secretary Li."

She understood this last remark was a deliberate warning.

She started to dress and reached for her suit, but after such an eventful day, especially after their argument in Qingpu, she felt tempted to appear more feminine. She decided on a black dress with a low neckline.

In front of the City Government Auditorium, she saw the surprise on Chen's face before she noticed somebody standing by him, Party Secretary Li, a stout man in his early sixties, his wrinkled face dominated by the heavy bags under his eyes.

They were ushered into an elegant reception room where there was an impressive array of pictures on the walls showing high-ranking officials shaking hands with distinguished foreign guests or with the actors and actresses.

"I welcome you on behalf of the Shanghai Police Bureau, Inspector Catherine Rohn." Li spoke in a rather stiff official tone, despite the smile on his face.

"Thank you, Mr. Party Secretary Li. It is a great honor to meet you today."

"It is the first time that our two countries are cooperating on an illegal immigration case. It is a top priority for our bureau, and for our Party authorities and government."

"I appreciate the cooperation of the Shanghai Police Bureau, but there has been no progress so far."

"Don't worry, Inspector Rohn. We've been doing our best, both in Shanghai and Fujian. You will escort Wen Liping to the United States in time." Li changed the subject abruptly. "Now, this is your first trip to Shanghai, I've heard. What is your impression of this city?"

"Fantastic. Shanghai is more marvelous than I imagined."

"What about the hotel?"

"Fabulous. Chief Inspector Chen has told the hotel people to treat me as a 'distinguished guest.' "

"That's what he should have done." Li nodded vigorously. "So how is your Chinese partner?"

"I could not ask for a better colleague."

"Yes, he is our ace inspector. A romantic poet to boot. That's why we have assigned him to you."

"You call him a romantic poet," she said, jokingly, "but he calls himself a modernist."

"You see, modernism is no good. Inspector Rohn says so too," Li said to Chen. "Be romantic. Revolutionary romantic, Chief Inspector Chen."

"Romantic, revolutionary romantic," Chen echoed. "Chairman Mao used this phrase in 1944 in the Yen'an Forum Talk."

It was obvious to her that Party Secretary Li did not know much about literary terms. Chen seemed to be good-humored, even a bit offhand, toward his boss. Was it because of his special connections within the Party system?

They were ushered to their reserved seats; she sat between Li and Chen. The lights grew dim. An orchestra of traditional Chinese musical instruments started playing and the audience burst out cheering.

"Why are they cheering now?" Catherine asked.

"Beijing Opera is an art of many facets," Chen said. "Singing, posing, performing martial arts, and playing music. A master of a traditional Chinese musical instrument like the *erhu* can make a huge difference. The audience is applauding the music."

"No, that's not why they are clapping now," Li interjected. "Our chief inspector knows a lot about literature, but Beijing Opera is different. A well-known actress will soon appear on the stage. So people are applauding in advance. It's the convention."

"Yes, our Party Secretary is an expert on Beijing Opera," Chen said. "I've only read about it in a tourist guide book."

With the rise of the curtain, cymbals preceded the singsong voices of the actors and actresses. An episode of *The White Snake* unfolded on the stage, a romantic story about a white snake spirit who changes into a beautiful woman in love. The White Snake summoned the turtle soldiers, crab warriors, carp knights, and other animal spirits from the river to overwhelm a temple. In spite of her heroic fight to rescue her lover, detained by a meddlesome monk in the Gold Mountain Temple, she was defeated.

Catherine enjoyed the performance, impressed by the spectacular display of martial arts, glittering costumes, and traditional music. There was no need to understand a single word of the play to appreciate it. Then the White Snake Lady started a series of somersaults across the stage.

"This is symbolic of inner as well as outer intensity," Chen said. "The banners in her hands outline the waves of the battle. Everything is suggested by her hand gestures and body movements."

The curtain finally fell amid the thunderous applause of the audience.

Afterward, Party Secretary Li offered to drive Inspector Rohn to her hotel, but she declined, saying that she preferred to walk back along the Bund.

"Splendid, you already know your way around." Li turned to Chen. "Chief Inspector Chen, you may escort Inspector Rohn."

Chapter 17

The Bund stretched out along the river like an unfurled scarf.

Catherine was still immersed in the Beijing Opera. "So what's the moral of the story?"

"It's ambiguous," Chen said. "From the orthodox perspective, romantic passion between animal spirits and human beings must be forbidden. In fact, with the institution of arranged marriage dominant in traditional Chinese society, any prenuptial romantic passion was forbidden. Even so, this love story has always been popular."

She nodded. "So the White Snake is a metaphor. You don't have to believe in ghosts to enjoy *Hamlet*."

"No, and the love story does not have to be between animal spirits and human beings. Look at the lovers on the Bund. They stand for hours, as if fixed there. In my high modernist period, I once came up with an image—comparing those lovers to snails stuck on the wall. The poem has never been published." He changed the topic. "My high school's not far away, on the corner of Sichuan and Yen'an Roads. As a student, I used to wander along the Bund frequently."

"The Bund must be one of your favorite places."

"Yes. The bureau is also close. I enjoy coming here before or after a day's work."

They slowed to a stop beside Bund Park. The water lapped against the bank. They watched the moonlight flecking the waves, gulls hovering around the vessels, and the luminous eastern shore.

"I know a place with a better view," he said, pointing.

"You're the guide."

He led the way into the park, climbing a spiral wrought-iron staircase to a large cedar deck that jutted out over the water. They chose a white cloth-covered table. He had a cup of coffee, and she had a bottle of orange juice. The view was spectacular.

It was close to the murder scene he had examined the day he had been assigned to Wen's case. From where he sat, he could see that corner, partially covered by shrubbery, the top of which seemed to be trembling in a fitful breeze. It was strange, for the leaves on other trees remained motionless. He cast another glance at it. The bush remained eerily alive.

He took a sip of his coffee, turning to her. She drank from the bottle. A candle in a bowl on the table shed a yellowish light on her face.

"You're like a fashionable Shanghai girl tonight. No one would imagine that you're a U.S. Marshal."

"Is that a compliment?"

"A great many people must have asked questions about your choice of career."

"Not many that I'd care to answer," she said wistfully. "It's simple. I was unable to find a job utilizing my Chinese."

"I'm surprised. There're so many American joint ventures here. Your command of Chinese would be an invaluable asset to them."

"A lot of companies send people to China, but only those with business backgrounds. It is cheaper for them to hire a translator locally. A micro-brewery did offer me a position as a bar manager. An American girl wearing their special bar costume for Chinese customers—sleeveless and backless top and mini shorts."

"So you applied for the Marshals Service?"

"I had an uncle who is a Marshal. *Guanxi*—I suppose. He sort of introduced me. I had to attend training seminars, of course."

"How did you become an inspector?"

"After a few years, I was promoted. There is plenty to do in the St. Louis office, and I go to D.C. or New York occasionally to deal with things related to China. From day one, my supervisor promised I would have an opportunity to come to China. At last here I am."

"Chinese people are not unfamiliar with the image of American policewomen—Lily McCall in *Hunter*, if I remember her name, was one. That was one of the few American TV series available to us in the early eighties. Officer McCall was a huge hit here. In the window of the Shanghai First Department Store, I once saw a sleeveless silk pajama top called the McCall Top. It was because the female detective wore such a seductive top in one episode."

"Really! An American policewoman inspiring a Chinese fashion?"

"In one episode, McCall decides to marry someone. She quits her job. Some Chinese fans got so frustrated that they wrote to the newspapers to say she should go on being a cop, and a wife, too, though some doubted her ability to do so. They saw an insoluble contradiction."

She put down her juice. "Maybe Chinese and Americans are not that different."

"What do you mean, Inspector Rohn?"

"When you are a woman and also a cop, it is difficult to maintain a relationship with a man unless he's also a cop. Women often quit their jobs. Now, what about you?"

"Me?"

"Yes. Enough about my career. It's only fair for you to tell me about yours, Chief Inspector Chen."

"I majored in English and American literature," he said, with a trace of reluctance. "One month before graduation, I was told that the Ministry of Foreign Affairs had requested my file. In the early eighties, the government was responsible for college graduates' job assignments. A diplomatic career was considered great for an English major, but at the last minute, during the routine family background check, one of my uncles was found to have been a 'counterrevolutionary,' executed in the early fifties. He was an uncle I had never seen. This connection nonetheless disqualified me for the foreign service. Instead, I was assigned to the Shanghai Police Bureau.

"I had no preparation for police work but I had to be given a job—the so-called benefits of the socialist system at the time. No college student had to worry about finding a job. So I reported to the bureau. Existentialists talk about making choices for yourself, but choices are more often made for you rather than by you."

"Still, you have had an excellent career. Chief Inspector Chen."

"Well, that's another story. I'd better spare you the sordid details of bureau politics. Suffice to say that I've been lucky so far."

"It's interesting to think about a parallel between us. Two cops in Bund Park, neither one of us having set out to become one. As you said, life is like a chain of unpredictable events— seemingly irrelevant links."

"One more example. The very day I took over Wen's case, just a few hours earlier, I had been shown the body in the park. The way it came to my attention was coincidence. I happened to have received a *ci* collection from a friend of mine. So I went to the park that morning to read a few pages." With the coffee cup in his hand, he began to tell her about the Bund Park case.

At the end of his account, she said, "Maybe the victim was connected to Wen in some way."

"I don't see how. Besides, if the Flying Axes had killed the man, they would not have left so many ax wounds on the body. It's like putting their signature on it."

"I don't have an answer to that," she said, "but it reminds me of something I read about the Italian Mafia. They killed in imitation of another organization, in order to muddy the water, to confuse the police."

He put down his coffee to consider this. It was possible, he conceded, that the park victim had been killed by somebody purposely copying the methods of the Flying Axes.

"If so, there must be a reason for it."

"A third party who would benefit?"

"A third party—" He had not yet considered a third party in connection with the Bund Park corpse.

What would a third party gain by transporting a body with multiple ax wounds to the park and leaving it there?

He was disturbed by elusive yet confusing ideas, like the sparkle of the candlelight, which could not be caught before it dissolved in the darkness.

The candle on the table before them was burning low, flickering. Draining her drink, she sighed. "I wish I were here on vacation."

But she was not and they had work to do. There were so many unanswered questions.

They rose slowly, descended the stairs and left the café.

Walking toward the corner, he found one answer. Behind the bush that had seemed to move, a young couple sat on a yellow plastic sheet, their arms locked around each other, shutting out the world. They had no idea that a body had been discovered on the spot a few days earlier.

So his thought about one aspect of the case was reconfirmed. The body could not have been left there before the closing time. Park security would have easily noticed anyone hiding behind the bushes, even at night.

"A romantic image?" she asked, noticing his abstraction.

"Oh no, I'm not thinking about poetry." He did not want her to associate this romantic scene with a corpse.

Chapter 18

They left the park.

People stood in a line along the bank, shoulder to shoulder, talking to each other without regard for those standing next to them. After a few steps, Catherine noticed a young couple vacating a small space by the embankment wall.

"I would like to stand here for a while." She added, mischievously, "Stuck on the wall like a snail, to use your simile."

"Whatever our distinguished guest prefers," Chen said. "Perhaps more like a brick in the wall. A brick in the socialist wall. As a metaphor, that was more popular during the socialist education movement."

They stood there, leaning on the railing. To their left, the park gleamed like a "night-brightening pearl," a phrase she had read in a Chinese legend.

"How do you find time for literary pursuits in your present job?" she asked.

"Politics aside, I like my job because, in a way, it helps my writing. It gives me a different perspective."

"What perspective?"

"In my college days, to write a poem meant such a lot to me, it seemed there was nothing else worth doing. Now I doubt that. In China's transitional period, there are many things more important to the people, at least of more immediate, practical value."

"You put it defensively, as if you had to keep on convincing yourself," she said.

"You may be right," he said. He took a white paper fan out of his pants pocket. "How much I've changed since then."

"Changed into a chief inspector. A rising star in the Shanghai Police Bureau, I believe." She saw that there were lines in brush calligraphy on the folding fan. "Can I have a look?"

"Sure."

She took the fan. There was a couplet on it. The writing was difficult to read in the flickering illumination provided by the ever-changing neon lights.

Drunk. I whipped a precious horse; / I do not want to weigh down a beauty with passion.

"Your lines, Chief Inspector Chen?"

"No, Daifu's. A confessional Chinese poet, like Robert Lowell."

"Why the parallel between a horse and a beauty?"

"A friend of mine copied the couplet for me."

"Why those two lines?" She waved the fan lightly.

"His favorite couplet, perhaps."

"Or a message for you."

He laughed.

The ringing of his phone took them by surprise.

"What's up, Uncle Yu?" he said, one hand cupped over the phone. He then took her by the elbow, and they began to walk as he listened.

She understood why he had to resume their stroll. Wedged between people along the wall, confidential conversation was out of the question. And the use of a cell phone was still rare and attracted attention. They encountered covetous glances from the milling crowd.

There was no change of expression as he listened. He spoke little. At the end of the conversation, he said. "Thank you. It is very important, Uncle Yu."

"What's up?" she said.

"It was Old Hunter. Something about Gu," he said, turning off the phone. "I asked him to keep an eye on the karaoke owner. He has been tapping Gu's telephone lines. It seems Gu is an honorary member of the Blue. He made several phone calls after we left the Dynasty. A couple of them were about a missing Fujianese. A man. Gu used a nickname."

"A missing Fujianese," she repeated. "Did he mention Wen?"

"No. The Fujianese seemed to have a mission, but they were speaking in triad code. Old Hunter needs to do some research tonight."

"Gu knew something he didn't tell us," she said.

"Gu spoke of a visitor from Hong Kong, not from Fujian. So why look for a missing Fujianese—"

For the first time, they were talking like partners, without guarding their words or thoughts from one another, when a white-haired peddler approached them, displaying something in his hand.

"A family heirloom. It brings good fortune to young couples. Believe me. I'm seventy years old. The state-run factory I used to work for went bankrupt last month. I cannot get a single penny of my pension, or I would not sell it for anything."

It was a Qilin-shaped green jade charm on a red silk string.

"In Chinese culture," she said, looking up at Chen, "jade is supposed to bring luck to its owner, isn't it?"

"Yes, I've heard that, but it doesn't seem to have brought luck to him."

"The red silk string is very pretty."

In the moonlight, the jade shone deep green against her white palm.

"How much?" Chen asked the peddler.

"Five hundred Yuan."

"Not too expensive," she whispered to him in English.

"Fifty Yuan." Chen took the charm from her hand and put it back in the peddler's.

"Come on, young man. Nothing is too expensive for your beautiful American girlfriend."

"Take it or leave it," Chen said, taking Catherine's hand as if to walk away. "It looks like plastic."

"Take a close look, young man," the old man said with an air of indignation. "Feel it. You can tell the difference. So cool to your touch, right?"

"Fine, eighty."

"One hundred fifty. I can give you a five-hundred-Yuan receipt from a state-run store."

"One hundred. Forget about the receipt."

"Deal!"

He handed over a bill to the peddler.

She listened to their bargaining with interest. 'Ask for a price as high as the sky, but bargain it down to the earth,' she thought, recalling another old Chinese saying. In an increasingly materialistic society, bargaining existed everywhere.

"I cannot help marveling at you, Chief Inspector Chen," she said as the old man started shuffling away with the money in his hand. "You haggled like—like anything but a romantic poet."

"I don't think it's plastic," he said. "Maybe it's some sort of hard stone without real value."

"Jade, I'm positive."

"For you." He put the charm in her hand, imitating the old man's tone. "For a beautiful American friend."

"Thank you so much."

They walked through the night breeze.

The Peace Hotel came in sight, sooner than she had expected.

She turned to him by the gate. "Let me buy you a drink in the hotel."

"Thanks, but I cannot come in. I have to call Detective Yu."

"It's been a lovely night. Thank you."

"The pleasure has been mine."

She took the jade charm out of her pocket. "Would you put it on for me?"

She swung around, without waiting for an answer from him.

They were in front of the hotel, with the red-capped-and-clad doorman standing at the gate, smiling respectfully as always.

She could feel the soft tendrils of her hair stirring with his breath as his fingers clasped the red string round her neck, lingering for a second at her nape.

Chapter 19

Waking in the early morning with a slight suggestion of headache, Chen rubbed his eyes as he read the latest news about the *go* tournament between China and Japan reported in the previous evening's newspaper. This was an escapist indulgence he had not permitted himself for several days.

That morning, he thought he had an excuse. This was the final round between the two countries' champions. The Japanese was said to be a Zen master as well—capable of remaining detached in an intense game. Paradoxical. A *go* player, by definition, must be intent on winning a game, just as a cop must solve a case. And the outcome of the game was represented as politically symbolic, like the case on his hands. The ringing of the telephone, however, interrupted any further thought about the battle on the game board. It was Party Secretary Li.

"Come to my office, Chief Inspector Chen."

"Anything new about Wen's case?"

"We'll talk when you get here."

"I'll come as soon as I have breakfast."

It was early, not yet seven thirty. It must be urgent. Normally, Li would not arrive at his office until after nine thirty.

Chen opened his small refrigerator. There was only half a steamed bun from the bureau canteen, two or three days old, and hard as a rock. He put it in a bowl of hot water. There was little left of his month's salary. Not all the expenses he incurred in Inspector Rohn's company could be reimbursed. Like the purchase of the jade trinket. To maintain the image of a Chinese policeman, he had to pay a price.

The telephone rang again. This time, it was Minister Huang in Beijing. The minister, who had never before called him at home, seemed very concerned about the progress of the Wen case.

"It is a special case," Huang said, "important to the relationship between the two countries. A successful cooperation with the Americans will help to lessen tension, you know, after the Tiananmen incident."

"I understand, Minister Huang. We're doing our best, but it is difficult to find someone within such a short time frame."

"The Americans understand you're doing a conscientious job. They are just anxious for a breakthrough. They have called us several times."

Chen hesitated as to whether he should share his suspicions with the minister, especially about the gang's ties to the Fujian police. He decided not to. Not directly at least. The politics behind this connection might be complicated. It would make the investigation more difficult if the minister chose to back the local police.

"Detective Yu is having a hard time in Fujian. The local police have given him no leads at all. They seem to have too many things on their hands. Yu cannot deal with those gangsters single-handedly. And I cannot dictate orders from thousands of miles away."

"Of course you can. You have full authority, Chief Inspector Chen. I myself will give Superintendent Hong a call. Whatever political decisions you have to make, the ministry is firmly behind you."

"Thank you, Minister Huang." So far he had not had to make any political decisions. Nor did he know what the minister meant by this phrase.

"Police work entails a hell of a lot of problems. It takes a most capable man to do the job well. There are not many young officers like you nowadays." Huang concluded emphatically, "The Party counts on you, Comrade Chief Inspector Chen."

"I understand. Whatever the Party wants me to do, I will do, even if I have to go through mountains of knives and seas of fire." He thought of two Tang dynasty lines. *Beholden to your making a general of me on the stage of gold, / flourishing the Jade Dragon sword, I'll fight for you to the end.* The old minister had not only recommended him for the job, but also called him at home, personally, to discuss the case. "I won't let you down, Minister Huang."

As he put down the receiver, however, Chief Inspector Chen felt far from flourishing the Jade Dragon sword.

Minister Huang should have called Party Secretary Li. The phrase "a hell of a lot of problems" did not sound reassuring at all. The old minister had left something unsaid. Chen had an ominous feeling. If Minister Huang had purposely left Li out of the loop, what implication did that have for his own career?

Twenty minutes late, he stepped into Party Secretary Li's office, not at all detached, unlike the Japanese *go* player described in the *Xinming* newspaper.

"I will be having meetings all day," Li said, breathing over a cup of hot soybean soup. "I want to have a talk with you now."

Chief Inspector Chen started by briefing him on their interview with Qiao, the pregnant woman from Guangxi.

"You have put in a lot of hard work, Chief Inspector Chen, but the subjects of your interviews were not that well chosen."

"Why do you say that, Party Secretary Li?"

"It's okay to let Inspector Rohn come along as you interview some of Wen's relatives, but taking her with you to see Qiao, the pregnant Guangxi woman, was not a good decision. The

Americans always raise a hue and cry about our birth control policy."

Chen decided not to mention their meeting with Gu for the time being. Indecent business, triad connections, police protection—all this would not present an ideal picture of socialist China.

"I did not know it would turn out like that," he said. "I argued with Inspector Rohn about our birth control policy."

"You stood up for our principles, I have no doubt about that," Li said slowly, taking up the glass swan ashtray, which shone like a crystal ball in a fortuneteller's hand. "Do you know what happened after your visit to the Guangxi woman?"

"What?"

"She was abducted by a group of unknown men. Two or three hours after your visit. She was later found lying unconscious in a wood not too far away. No one knew who had left her there. Though not beaten or abused, she suffered a miscarriage. She was rushed to the local hospital."

"Is her life in danger?"

"No, but she bled too much, so the doctor had to operate on her. She won't be able to have another child."

Chen cursed under his breath. "Is there any clue to the kidnappers?"

"They were not locals. They came in a jeep, claiming the woman was a fugitive from the south. So no one tried to stop them."

"They must have mistaken her for Wen and let her go when they found out the truth."

"That's possible."

"That's outrageous! Kidnapping a pregnant woman in broad daylight, and in Qingpu, Shanghai." Chen's thoughts moved in a frantic swirl. They must have been followed from the start and all the way to Qingpu. There was no question about it now.

The motorcycle accident. The broken stair step. The food poisoning. And now the abduction of Qiao. "Only two or three hours after our visit! Those gangsters must have gotten a tip from some insider here. There is a leak at the bureau."

"Well, I don't think it will hurt to be careful."

"They have declared war on us. And then there is the body in Bund Park. For the Shanghai Police Bureau it's a big slap in our face! We have to do something, Party Secretary Li."

"We will do something. It's a matter of time. It's also a matter of priorities. At this moment, the safety of Inspector Rohn has to be our top concern. If we try to crack down on the triads now, they may retaliate."

"So are we to do nothing but wait until they strike again?"

Li did not answer his question. "In the course of this investigation, some accidental encounter with those gangsters is possible. They are capable of anything. If something happens to Inspector Rohn, it will be a hell of a responsibility for us."

"A hell of a responsibility," he muttered, thinking of "a hell of a lot of problems" mentioned earlier by Minister Huang. "We are cops, aren't we?"

"You don't have to look at it that way, Chief Inspector Chen."

"In what way then, Party Secretary Li?"

"Detective Yu has been conducting the investigation in Fujian. If you think it necessary, you can decide someone else is needed there, too." Li said. "As for your interviews here, I wonder whether they can really lead to anything. Inspector Rohn does not have to participate in them. All you need to do is to keep her informed of any new developments. I don't think those gangsters will attempt anything against her if she takes a leisurely walk along the Bund."

"But they must believe Wen may be hiding here. Or they would not have abducted Qiao in Qingpu."

"If any new leads turn up here, Qian can take care of them. You don't have to go out of your way. As long as she knows our people are doing their best, it will be good enough—politically."

"I have done some thinking about the case—politically— Party Secretary Li. For one thing, the relationship between China and America has been strained since the summer of 1989. If we succeed in delivering Wen to the U.S. Marshals, it will be a meaningful gesture."

That line of argument might work with Party Secretary Li. He would not mention Minister Huang's phone call.

"That may be true," Li said, taking the last sip of his soybean soup. "So you are all for continuing the investigation with Inspector Rohn's participation?"

"When you first talked me into taking the case, you quoted from Yue Fei," Chen said, crushing out his cigarette. "His last two lines are my favorites, *When I set the mountains and rivers in order, / I bow to Heaven.*"

"I understand, but not everyone does." Li tapped his finger on the table for a minute before he went on, "Some people are talking about your giving a gift to Inspector Rohn, and putting it on for her in front of the hotel."

"That's absurd," Chen protested, trying to grasp the significance of the information. Some people. It must be Internal Security—the police of the police. A small trinket meant nothing, but in the report made by Internal Security, it could mean anything—*Chief Inspector Chen has lost his Party spirit, flirting with an American secret agent.* "Internal Security? Why?"

"Don't worry about who made the report, Chief Inspector Chen. If you haven't done anything wrong, you don't have to be nervous about the devil knocking at your door in the depth of the night."

"It was after the Beijing Opera. Following your suggestion, I walked Inspector Rohn back to the hotel. A peddler on the Bund tried to sell her a trinket. Some peddlers make a point of ripping off foreign tourists, according to the newspapers. So I bargained for her for a necklace. And she asked me to put it on for her."

He didn't mention that he had paid for it. Since he did not expect to seek reimbursement from the bureau, it made no difference as far as his expense report went.

"Yes, the Americans can be so . . . different."

"As a representative of the Chinese police, I believe it's proper to show hospitality. It's beyond me who the devil—" He had a lot more he wanted to say, but he saw the expression pass across Li's face. It was not the moment to blow off steam since Internal Security was involved.

It was not the first time for Chief Inspector Chen.

The involvement of Internal Security might have been understandable in the National Model case, in which the ever-glorious Party image was at stake. But in this investigation, Chief Inspector Chen had not been doing anything that could possibly jeopardize the Party's interests.

Unless someone wanted to put an end to his investigation. Not in the interests of the Party, but in that of the triads.

"Don't think too much about it," Li said. "I have made it clear to the informer: This is a very special case. Whatever Comrade Chief Inspector Chen does is done in the interests of the country."

"I appreciate it, Party Secretary Li."

"Don't mention it. You're not an ordinary cadre. You've got a long, long way to go." Li stood up. "It's not an easy job for you. A lot of stress, I understand. I have talked with Superintendent Zhao. We'll arrange a vacation for you next month.

Take a week off, and go to Beijing—see the Great Wall, the Forbidden City, and the Summer Palace. The bureau will cover the expense."

"That would be great," Chen said, rising. "I have to go back to work now. By the way, how did you learn about the abduction in Qingpu, Party Secretary Li?"

"Your man Qian Jun called me late last night with this information."

"I see."

Li walked Chen to the door and said, with his hand resting on the door frame, "About a week ago, I dialed your old phone number by mistake. So I had a long talk with your mother. We old people share common concerns."

"Really! She has not spoken to me about it." Chen marveled at Li's capacity occasionally to add a human touch to Party politics.

"She believes it is the time for you to settle down. A family for yourself, you know what she means. It is up to you to make the decision, but I think she's right."

"Thank you, Party Secretary Li." Chen saw what Li was driving at. The proposed Beijing vacation was part of it. With Ling in the background. Party Secretary Li's remarks may have been well meant, but his timing was portentous.

Why should Li have brought this up today?

After leaving Li's office, Chen took out a cigarette. But he put it back into his pocket. There was a water cooler at the a corner of the corridor. He drank some water, then crushed the paper cup into a wad and dropped it into a wastebasket.

Chapter 20

The moment he got back in his office, Chen dialed Qian Jun.

"Oh, I called you several times last night, Chief Inspector Chen, but I could not reach you. I lost your cell phone number. I'm really sorry about it. So I called Party Secretary Li."

"You lost my cell phone number!" He did not believe Qian's explanation. He could have left a message at his home. It was understandable that a young ambitious cop might try to please the number-one Party boss—but by circumventing his immediate superior? He began to wonder why Li had insisted on assigning Qian to him.

"You know what happened to the Guangxi woman, Chief Inspector Chen?"

"Yes, Party Secretary Li has told me. How did you learn of it?"

"After I talked to you, I got in touch with the Qingpu police. They called me in the evening."

"Any new developments today?"

"No. The Qingpu police are still trying to find the jeep the men rode in. It had an army license plate."

"Tell them to contact me as soon as they have any leads. They are responsible for what happened in their area," Chen said. "Anything new about the body in Bund Park?"

"No. Nothing but the official autopsy report from Dr. Xia. There's nothing new in it. No response from hotels and neighborhood committees, either. I've interviewed a number of hotel managers. More than twenty of them. None of them provided any clue."

"I doubt that they have the guts to speak. The gangsters would never leave them in peace if they did."

"That's true. Several months ago, a café reported a drug dealer to the police, and it was totally smashed the next week."

"What else are you going to do?"

"I'll keep calling the hotels and neighborhood committees. Please tell me what else I can do, Chief Inspector Chen."

"There is one thing you can do," Chen said testily. "Go to the hospital. Ask the doctors to do their best for Qiao. If money is an issue, draw on our special budget."

"I'll go there, Chief, but the special budget—"

"Don't give me any *buts*! That's the least we can do," Chen snapped, slamming down the receiver.

He was perhaps too upset to be fair to the young cop. He felt enormously responsible for what had happened to Qiao, who had gone through all that for her baby, and still lost it in the end. What was worse, she could never become pregnant again. A devastating blow to the poor woman.

Chen broke a pencil in two, like an ancient soldier breaking an arrow in a pledge. He must find Wen, and soon. That would be his way to retaliate against human smuggling. Against Jia Xinzhi. And against all the evil of the triads.

He brooded over Qiao's bad luck in finding the job in Qingpu. "Fortune begets misfortune, and misfortune begets fortune," as Lao-tse had said thousands of years earlier. So many provincial people had poured into Shanghai, they could not find jobs even with the help of a new institution in the market economy—the Shanghai Metropolitan Employment Agency. Qiao had succeeded, but that success had led to disaster for her.

There was another office for him to call, he realized. Wen

might have turned to the job agency for a temporary position, such as a live-in waitress or nanny.

The answer he got was not encouraging. Their records did not show anyone matching Wen's description, nor was a pregnant woman considered a likely candidate in the present day job market. The agency manager promised, however, to call if any relevant information turned up.

Then Chen phoned the Peace Hotel. It was still his responsibility to keep Catherine Rohn company, whatever criticism this might lead to. She was not in. He left a message. This was not the moment for him to go to the hotel, holding a bouquet of flowers. Not after Internal Security had reported his putting a trinket around her neck, and Party Secretary Li had chosen to bring up the subject.

He had worked with her for only a couple of days. A partner assigned to him temporarily. It could have been, however, one of the unstated reasons for Party Secretary Li's proposing the vacation in Beijing. A timely reminder. Everything was politics, and everything would be grist for Li's mill.

He decided to go to his mother's place during the lunch break.

It was not far away, but he had Little Zhou drive him there in the Mercedes. On the way, he stopped by a food market, where he bargained with a fruit peddler for several minutes before he bought a small bamboo basket of dried Longyan pulp. He recalled Inspector Rohn's gibe about his bargaining skills.

The sight of the familiar old building in Jiujiang Road seemed to promise the brief respite he needed from politics. Some of his former neighbors greeted him as he stepped out of the Mercedes which he was using for his mother's benefit. She had never approved of his career choice, but in an increasingly materialistic neighborhood, his cadre status, with a chauffeur holding the door for him, might help hers.

The common cement sink by the front door was still damp. He spotted deep-green moss sprouting abundantly, like a large map, near the tap. The cracked walls needed extensive repairs. Several holes at the foot of the side wall, from which the crickets of his childhood had jumped out, were still there. The stairway was musty and dark, and the landings were piled with broken cardboard boxes and wicker baskets.

He had not visited his mother since he had taken over the Wen case. There, in the same small plain attic room, he was amazed to see a colorful array of breads, sausages, and exotic-looking dishes in disposable plastic containers on the table.

"All from Moscow Suburb," his mother said.

"That Overseas Chinese Lu! He can be overwhelming."

"He calls me 'Mom,' and refers to you as his real brother in need."

"He's been harping on the same story all this time."

" 'A friend in need is a friend indeed.' I've been reading Buddhist scripture. It's not for nothing you do good deeds in this world. Whatever you do leads to something, either what you expect or what you don't expect. Some people call it luck, but it's really karma. Another friend of yours, Mr. Ma, has also visited me."

"When?"

"This morning. A regular medical checkup, that's what the old man calls it."

"It's very thoughtful of him," he said. "Any problems, Mother?"

"My stomach has not been so comfortable of late. Mr. Ma insisted on coming over. It's not easy for an old man to climb the stairs here."

"What did he say?"

"Nothing serious. The imbalance of yin and yang, so on and so forth. He had the medicine delivered here," she said. "Like Lu, Mr. Ma is anxious to pay you back, or he won't be at ease. A man of *yiqi*."

"The old man has suffered so much. Ten years for a copy of *Dr. Zhivago*. What I did was nothing."

"Wang Feng wrote the article about him, didn't she?"

"Yes, that was her idea."

"How is she doing in Japan?"

"I haven't heard from her for a long time."

"Any news from Beijing?"

"Well, Party Secretary Li talks about arranging a Beijing vacation for me," he said evasively.

His mother did not really approve of his relationship with Ling, he knew. The old woman was concerned that *High above, in the jade palace of the moon, / it could be too cold*. What had worried Su Dongpo thousands of years earlier worried her, but what worried her more was the reality of his approaching thirty-five, still a bachelor. As the saying went, "Anything in a vegetable basket has to be counted as a vegetable now."

"That's good," she said with a smile.

"I'm not sure if I can make it."

"So, you're not sure—" His mother left the sentence unfinished, "Well, Mr. Ma told me you brought an American girl to his place."

"She is my partner temporarily."

"You seemed to think a lot of her, Mr. Ma said."

"Come on, Mother. I have to take good care of her. If anything happens to her, I will be held responsible."

"Whatever you say, Son. I'm old, and I hope you will settle down, just like everybody else."

"I'm too busy with my work, Mother."

"I do not know anything about your work. The world has changed too much. But I don't think entanglement with an American will do you any good."

"Don't worry, Mother. It's totally out of the question."

He was disturbed, though. Normally, his mother refrained from interfering—except for quoting the same Confucian maxim, "There are three unfilial things in the world; to be without offspring is the worst." Now she seemed to agree with what Party Secretary Li had tacitly suggested.

People cannot see the mountains clearly when they are in the mountains, Su Dongpo had written on a Buddhist temple wall in the Lu Mountains. But Chief Inspector Chen was not in the mountains, he believed.

He did not talk much as he helped his mother prepare lunch. Before he finished warming up the dishes from Moscow Suburb, however, his cell phone rang.

"Chief Inspector Chen, this is Gu Haiguang speaking."

"General Manager Gu. What's up?"

"I've got something for you. There was someone from Fujian here a couple of days ago. I am not sure if he's a Flying Ax. He got in touch with some organization people here and then disappeared."

"So he was not Diao, the Hong Kong visitor to the club you mentioned?"

"No, definitely not."

"What was he doing in Shanghai?"

"He was looking for someone."

"For the woman I described to you?"

"I have not yet got any details, but I will try my best to find out, Chief Inspector Chen."

"When was that Fujianese last seen?"

"On the afternoon of April seventh. Some people saw him

having dumplings in a snack bar on Fuzhou Road. There was a car waiting for him. A silver Acura."

The date matched. The development seemed to be encouraging. Possibly it related to the park case, or to Wen's case. Or maybe both.

"Great job, General Manager Gu. What's the name of the restaurant?"

"I don't know. It sells a special kind of Fuzhou dumplings. *Yanpi*. It's close to the Foreign Language Bookstore." Gu added, "And please call me Gu, Chief Inspector Chen."

"Thank you, Gu. There're not too many silver Acuras in the city. It will be easy to check through the Traffic Control Office. I really appreciate your tip."

"Don't mention it. Meiling, your secretary, called me this morning. She may come over to take a look at the Dynasty. For a club like ours, she said a parking lot would be essential."

"I'm glad she thinks so."

"She also told me a lot about you, Chief Inspector Chen."

"Really!"

"Everybody knows you will soon be the director of the Traffic Control Office. Indeed, with your connections at the highest level, that position means nothing to you."

Chen frowned though he understood why Meiling had said those things to Gu. It had worked. And Gu had made several calls to obtain information for him. Gu finished the conversation with a warm invitation.

"You have to come again, Chief Inspector Chen. Your stay was too short yesterday. We have to drink to our friendship."

"I will," he promised.

His mother must have noticed something. "Is everything all right?"

"Everything is fine, Mother. I just need to make another phone call."

He dialed Meiling, asking her to check into the registrations of silver Acuras. She promised to do so immediately. Then she discussed the parking lot issue with him. It happened to be a borderline case. If the land was not zoned as the parking lot for the club, the city might realize sizable extra income. She needed to do some additional research. Toward the end of their conversation, she heard his mother coughing in the background and insisted on saying a hello to "Aunt Chen."

When they finished speaking, a resigned smile appeared on his mother's face. She began to rewarm the dishes. The small attic was filled with a strong gas smell from the coal briquette stove. It was a bit too heavy for her to carry in and out. In the days before he had gotten his own apartment, it had been his job to carry the stove onto the stair landing and bring it back in the evening. The staircase was so narrow that kids were always bumping into the stove in the dark. His mother did not want to move into his one-bedroom apartment, though he had asked her.

His father, his broad forehead lined with worries, seemed to be looking at him with a melancholy expression from the black-framed picture on the wall.

He dug into a small dish of tofu seasoned with sesame oil and green onions and finished a bowl of watery rice absent-mindedly.

To his dismay, his cell phone started ringing again as he was ready to leave. When he turned it on, he got a fax signal. The signal repeated. He turned the phone off in frustration.

"I know you are doing well, Son, with your cellular phone, bureau car, secretary girl, and a general manager calling you during lunch," his mother said, walking him downstairs to the door. "You are part of the system now, I understand that."

"No, I don't think I'm part of it. But it is necessary for people to work within the system."

"Do something good then." she said. "As Buddhist scripture says, 'Something as small as a bird's peck is preordained and has consequences'."

"I will keep it in mind, Mother," he said.

He thought he understood why his mother had kept talking about doing good things in the Buddhist spirit. Worried about his prolonged bachelorhood, she had been burning incense to Guanyin every day, praying that retribution for any wrongdoing by the family would befall her instead.

"Oh, Aunt Chen!" Little Zhou sprang out of the car with half of a steamed bun in his hand. "Whenever you need the use of a car, give me a call. I'm Chief Inspector Chen's man."

His mother shook her head slightly as the car pulled away, noting her neighbors' envious looks.

Little Zhou started playing a CD of *The Internationale* in a rock version. Those heroic words failed to uplift his spirits. He told Little Zhou to pull up at the corner of Fuzhou and Shandong Roads. "I want to browse in a bookstore. Don't wait for me. I'll walk back."

Several bookstores were located there, both state-run and private. He felt tempted to go into the one where he had bought his father's book on the contingency of history. He had forgotten the arguments in the book, except for the fable about how a pampered palace goat contributed to the overthrow of the Jing dynasty. He also remembered the colorful poster of the bikini-clad girl that had been offered to him, which he had not accepted. Indeed, he was an unfilial son; he had strayed so far from his father's expectations.

Instead, he walked over to a dumplings bar across the street. Like that private bookstore, the small bar had been converted from a residence. A simple sign declared in bold characters: YANPI DUMPLING SOUP. In the front, a middle-aged man was dropping the dumplings into a large wok. There were only three tables in the bar. Before a cloth curtain at the back, a young girl stood kneading the cream-colored dough, mixing the rice wine and minced eel meat into it.

On the wall was a red poster explaining the origin of Yanpi, the dumpling skin made of wheat flour, egg, and fish meal. Chen ordered a bowl, which tasted delicious, though it had a singular fishy smell. It became acceptable after he added vinegar and chopped green onion to the soup. He wondered what other non-Fujian customers would think of it. As he finished, he suddenly realized something else.

The restaurant was close to Wen Lihua's residence, the home in which the missing woman, Wen, had grown up. It was no more than a five-minute walk.

He approached the owner, who was busy ladling dumplings out of the wok. "Do you remember someone who came to your place in a luxurious car a few days ago?"

"This is the only place selling genuine Yanpi in the whole city. It's not uncommon for people to drive halfway across Shanghai for a bowl of Yanpi. Sorry, but I cannot remember a particular customer because of his car."

Chen then handed him a card together with a picture of the victim found in the park. "Do you remember this man?"

The owner shook his head in bewilderment. The young girl walked over, took a look at the picture, and said she remembered seeing a customer with a long scar on his face, but she was not sure if this was the same man.

Chen thanked her. He decided to walk back to the bureau. Sometimes he thought more clearly while walking, but not this afternoon. On the contrary, he felt more confused than ever by the time he reached the bureau.

There was only one message in his office from the state job agency, providing him with the names and numbers of several private employment agencies. After spending an hour making one phone call after another, he concluded that the information from the private sector was practically the same. It was out of the question for a middle-aged, pregnant woman like Wen to find a job in Shanghai.

Gu's metaphor came buzzing back to him, as the stack of papers piled up on his desk, the phone rang incessantly and the pressure on him increased. He stood up to practice tai chi in his cubicle. The effort did not relieve his tension. It actually served as another subconscious reminder of the unsolved case in the park. Perhaps he should have practiced tai chi all these years, like the elderly former accountant, who at least enjoyed inner peace, moving in harmony with the *qi* of the world.

What might have been was like the flower in the mirror, or the moon in the water. So vividly alive, he could almost touch it, but it was not real.

And what was he going to do about the proposed "vacation" in Beijing? It was not a matter of making or not making a decision in his personal life, not as Party Secretary Li had supposed. In China, the personal could hardly be separated from the political. He could have tried harder to court Ling, but his awareness of her HCC status prevented him from making any further effort.

Was it really so hard for him to be a bit more courageous, to disregard others criticizing him as a political climber?

On a moment's impulse, Chen picked up the phone, thinking of the number in Beijing, but he ended up calling Inspector Rohn instead.

"I've been trying to reach you all afternoon, Chief Inspector Chen!"

"Really, Inspector Rohn!"

"You must have turned off your cell phone."

"Oh yes, it rang several times with a fax signal. I turned it off, and forgot about it."

"Because I could not reach you, I called Detective Yu."

"What is his news?"

"Wen was actually seen leaving the village the night of April fifth! Instead of taking a bus, she hitchhiked and got a ride on a truck heading to the Fujian railway station. The truck turned off a few miles before it reached the station and Wen got out. The truck driver contacted the local police bureau this morning. The description matched, except that he was not sure if the woman was pregnant."

"That's possible. Wen's only in her fourth month. Did she mention to him where she was going?"

"No. She may still be in Fujian Province, but it is more likely that she has left."

He seemed to hear a train whistle in her background. "Where are you, Inspector Rohn?"

"The Shanghai Railway Station. Can you meet me here? According to Detective Yu, a train left Fujian for Shanghai at 2 A.M. on April sixth. Tickets were sold out long before that date. The ticket seller remembered one of the people approaching him for an emergency ticket was a woman. Yu suggested we make inquiry at the Shanghai Railway Bureau. That's why I am here, but I don't have authority to ask questions."

"I'm on my way," Chen said.

The visit turned out to be a prolonged one. The Fujian train did not arrive at the station until after late afternoon. They had to wait for hours before they could obtain the conductor's records. Three ticketless passengers had boarded the train at the Fujian station in the early hours of April sixth. Judging by the amount they paid, Shanghai was the destination of two of them. The third got off before Shanghai. The attendant remembered one was a woman because the other two were businessmen who chatted all the way. The woman had squatted silently near the door. The attendant had not noticed where she left the train.

So the "lead" led nowhere. No one knew where the woman got off, nor whether she was, indeed, Wen.

Chapter 21

Later, Chief Inspector Chen entered the Dynasty Karaoke Club with Meiling, his former secretary in the Shanghai Metropolitan Traffic Control Bureau. Their visit to the club was prompted by a phone conversation with Mr. Ma, the old herbal doctor..

Ma had given him additional background information about Gu. Gu had been born into a middle-ranking Party member's family. His father had served as a manager of a large state-run tire company for more than twenty years. The outbreak of the Cultural Revolution turned the veteran manager into a "capitalist roader," wearing a huge placard around his neck, on which his name was crossed out in red. He was sent to a special cadre school to reform himself through hard labor, and he did not return home until after the Cultural Revolution, a shrunken shadow of the former Bolshevik, with a crippled leg, a total stranger to Gu, who had grown up on the streets, determined to take a different road. Gu went to Japan via a language program in the mid-eighties, where, instead of studying, he worked at all kinds of jobs. After three years, he came back with some capital, and in the new market economy, he soon became a successful entrepreneur, the class his father had spent his life fighting against. Gu then expanded into the karaoke business, and through a large donation to the Blue, the triad that controlled such activities in Shanghai; bought an honorary membership as security for his business. He rubbed elbows with various triad heads at the Dynasty.

Gu had initially gotten in touch with Mr. Ma because of his K girls, who would be reported to the city authorities if they went to state-run hospitals for treatment of their venereal diseases. Mr. Ma agreed to help, provided Gu would not allow those sick girls to give any private service until they had recovered.

"Gu is not a totally rotten egg. At least he cares about his girls. Yesterday he asked me several questions about you. I don't know why. These people can be unpredictable and dangerous. I don't want anything to happen to you," Mr. Ma concluded gloomily. "Personally, I don't believe in meeting force with force. The soft is stronger than the hard. There are not too many decent cops left today."

Chen believed that Gu had withheld information. If he squeezed harder, more might be extracted. Meiling's position in the Traffic Control Office might make a difference. She agreed to accompany him without asking a single question, a truly understanding secretary. So at the shadowy back door of the Shanghai Writers' Association, he met Meiling and walked with her to the splendidly lit club.

He was pleased to see her wearing contacts for the evening. Without her silver-rimmed glasses, she appeared more feminine. She also wore a new dress, sharply nipped in at the waist, accentuating her fine figure. The old saying was right. 'A clay Buddha image must be magnificently gilded, and a woman must be beautifully dressed.' She merged into the fashionable crowd effortlessly, unlike the ordinary business-first secretary, but she carried her business cards, handing one to Gu when they were introduced.

"Oh, you overwhelm me," Gu exclaimed. "I never guessed both of you would come tonight."

"Meiling is always so busy," Chen explained. It was not the moment for him to worry about what Gu might think of him, first bringing an American girl, and now his Chinese former secretary, to the club. Actually, this might help to convince Gu that the chief inspector was someone he could make a friend of. "She happened to have some time tonight, so I brought her over to meet you."

"Director Chen is giving his personal attention to your parking lot," Meiling said.

"I really appreciate it, Chief Inspector Chen."

As they arrived at a sumptuous room on the fifth floor, a line of K girls in black slips and black slippers appeared, welcoming Chen like the imperial maids at a palace entrance. Their white shoulders flashed against the saffron walls.

Apparently, Gu no longer minded Chen's seeing the other side of his business. The large karaoke room was furnished more elegantly than the one Chen had visited the previous day, and there was a master bedroom adjoining it.

"The suite is not for business, but for my friends," Gu said. "Give me a call any time, and this suite will be reserved for you. Come with your friend or by yourself."

It was a hint. Chen noticed a sly smile playing over Meiling's lips. She understood, though she sat demurely on the huge sectional sofa.

At Gu's nod, a slim girl came into the room. "Let's start with an appetizer," Gu said. "Her name is White Cloud. The best singer in our club. And a Fudan University student. She performs only for the most special guests here. Choose any song you would like to hear, Chief Inspector Chen."

White Cloud had a piece of *dudou*-like red silk, no larger than a handkerchief, wrapped around her breasts, tied with the thinnest straps at her back. Her gauzy pants were semi-transparent. With the microphone in her hand, she bowed to Chen.

Chen chose a song entitled "Sea Rhythm."

White Cloud had a beautiful voice enriched by a singular nasal effect. Kicking off her slippers, she began to dance to the song, swaying voluptuously to the ebbing and flowing of the music. At the beginning of the second song, "Weeping Sand," she extended her hands to Chen. When he hesitated, she leaned over to pull him up. "Won't you dance with me?"

"Oh, I'm honored—"

She took his hand, propelling him toward the center of the room. He had taken the required dancing lessons at the bureau, but he had had little time to practice. He was amazed at how easily he could be guided around by her. She danced with a sensual, effortless grace, her bare feet gliding along the hard-wood floor.

"Your clothes are like clouds, and your face is like a flower." He tried to pay her a compliment, but he regretted it as soon as he uttered it. His hand was on her bare back—*"jade-smooth"*—another quotation, but any reference to her clothes sounded like a joke.

"Thank you for comparing me with Imperial Concubine Yang."

So she knew the origin of the lines. Indeed, a Fudan university student. He tried to hold her at some distance, but she pressed her body against him, melting into his arms. She made no effort to conceal her ardor. He felt her pointed breasts through the light material.

He did not know when the microphone had come into Mei-ling's hand. She was singing as captions appeared on the screen. It was a sentimental piece:

"You like to say you are a grain of sand, / occasionally fallen into my eyes, in mischief. / You would rather have me weep by myself / than to have me love you, / and then you disappear in the wind / like the grain of sand . . ."

White Cloud also quoted a couplet from Li Shangyin, the bard of star-crossed lovers, whispering in his ear, *"It is difficult to meet, and to part, too. / The east wind languid, and the flowers fallen . . ."* She said it to evocative effect as the song was coming to a stop, her hand lingering in his.

He chose to comment on the poem, "A brilliant juxtaposition of an image with a statement, creating a third dimension of poetic association."

"Isn't that called *Xing* in the *Book of Songs*?"

"Yes. *Xing* does not specify the relationship between the image and the statement, leaving more room for a reader's imagination," he expounded. He had no problem talking to her about poetry.

"Thank you. You're really special."

"Thank you. You're marvelous," he echoed in his best dancing-school manner, bowing before he moved back to the sofa.

At Gu's insistence, a bottle of mao tai was opened. Several cold dishes appeared on the coffee table. The liquor was strong, suffusing Chen with a new warmth.

Between sips, Meiling started to talk about the zoning issue with regard to the parking lot.

She was clearly conveying that it was in the power of her office to decide the future of the parking lot. She left a form on the table for Gu to sign as the first step.

In the middle of their talk, White Cloud came back with a large black plastic bag. Carefully, she untied the string around the neck of the bag, reached her hand in as fast as a lightning, and came out with a snake twitching in her grasp, hissing, its scarlet tongue protruding.

A monstrous snake weighing perhaps five or six pounds.

"The heaviest big king snake available," Gu said proudly.

"It's the custom," White Cloud explained, "for our customers to see the living snake before it's cooked. In some restaurants, the chef will kill the snake in front of the customers."

"We don't have to do that today," Gu said, waving the girl out. "Tell the chef to do his best."

"Is she really a Fudan student?" Meiling asked.

"Oh yes. She's majoring in Chinese literature. A clever girl. And practical too," Gu said. "In one month here, she can earn about one year's salary as a high-school teacher."

"She works to support her studies," Chen concluded rather uncomfortably.

White Cloud came back carrying a large tray with several small bowls and cups on it. One bowl contained snake blood, another held something like a small greenish ball immersed in liquor. At Gu's request, she started listing the wonderful effects of the snake as medicine.

"Snake blood is good for blood circulation. It is useful in treating anemia, rheumatism, arthritis, and asthenia. Snake gall bladder proves especially effective in dissolving phlegm and improving vision—"

"You have to have the gall, Chief Inspector Chen," Gu insisted. "The gall is associated with *yin* and has a special effect on human health."

This medical theory did not appeal to Chen. He knew it was customary to save the gall for a distinguished guest. Kneeling, White Cloud held the cup out to him in both hands, respectfully. The gall looked a ghastly greenish color in the clear liquor. It was hard to imagine what it would taste like.

With one determined gulp, he swallowed without tasting, as he used to swallow an oversized pill in his childhood. He did not know whether it was the effect of his imagination, or whether the snake gall was really that potent. It produced in his stomach an instant chill that contrasted with a burning sensation in his throat. *Yin*, in traditional Chinese medical theory.

"Now you must have the blood. That's *yang*," Gu urged.

In kung fu fiction, drinking wine mixed with rooster blood was part of the triad initiation ceremony, like a blood oath: to share weal and woe. Gu had a bowl in his hand too, perhaps in a gesture with a similar connotation. Chief Inspector Chen had no choice but to drain the bowl, trying his best to ignore the strange smell.

Then a platter of fried slices of snake meat was set on the table. White Cloud fed him a slice with her fingers. Tender, under a golden crispy surface, it tasted like chicken with an unusual texture.

He tried to lead the conversation in the direction he wanted.

"We did not have enough time yesterday, Gu. There's a lot more we could have talked about."

"Exactly, Chief Inspector Chen. As for what you wanted me to find out yesterday, I have done some legwork—"

"Excuse me, General Manager Gu," Meiling said, rising. "I think I need to take a close look at the parking lot. White Cloud may accompany me there."

"That's a good idea," Chen said gratefully.

When they were left alone, however, Gu did not provide much new information. Gu discussed what he thought suspicious about the way Mr. Diao, that Hong Kong visitor, had appeared. A Flying Ax would not have come to Gu, since he was not really a Blue member. Diao should have gone to the

Eldest Brother of the Blue. Gu was out of his element when trying to play detective, but he had learned that Diao had also visited the Red Capital Bathhouse.

Apparently, Gu had really tried hard to get information. Chen nodded, sipping his wine. If that Fujianese was a Flying Ax looking for Wen, Diao might be from a rival organization. A third party, as Inspector Rohn had suggested.

"Thank you, Gu. You have done great work."

"Come on, Chief Inspector Chen. You have taken me as a friend," Gu declared, "and for a friend, I'm willing to have my ribs pierced with knives." Gu had turned red in the face, beating his chest with a fist, not a gesture Chen had expected to see in a private karaoke room.

When Meiling returned with White Cloud, another bottle of Mao Tai was opened.

Gu kept toasting "Chief Inspector Chen's great achievement and prosperous future." Meiling joined in the toasts. Kneeling by the table, White Cloud busily added wine to his cup.

Chen could not remember how much he'd had to drink. Warmed with gratification at such recognition, he was coming to terms with his status here.

Seizing the opportunity when Meiling excused herself, he posed a question to Gu, "Has Li Guohua been here?"

"Li Guohua, the Party Secretary of your bureau? No, not here. But one of his relatives has a bar in a very good location. It was the Eldest Brother of the Blue who told me this."

"Really!" That his brother-in-law had a bar was not news, but Gu had specifically mentioned the Eldest Brother of the Blue as his source. This was disturbing. Heretofore Party Secretary Li had been a prototype of Party correctness for Chen as well as a political mentor.

Was this why Li had been so reluctant to have him pursue

an investigation dealing with the triads? Perhaps why Li had insisted on assigning Qian to him as a temporary assistant?

"I can find out more for you, Chief Inspector."

"Thank you, Gu," he said.

Meiling came back into the room. A new piece of music played. It was a tango. White Cloud, kneeling with a cup for him in her hand, looked up at him. There was a small blood-stain on her bare sole. Maybe it was blood from the big king snake. He felt tempted to have another dance with her.

He was not drunk—not as drunk as Li Bai, beneath the Tang dynasty moon, who had written about dancing with his own shadow. In a lonely moment, Li Bai must have enjoyed his intoxicated departure from humdrum existence. Escape, though no more than momentary, seemed to be desirable tonight at the Dynasty.

At the sight of Meiling checking her watch, Chief Inspector Chen thought about asking her to go home now, on her own. However, he rose to leave instead.

Chapter 22

Detective Yu was wakened by a hoarse, long-drawn-out sound.

As he roused himself from the dream, blinking in the half-light of the room, the sound was repeated several times in the distance. Still disoriented, he had a feeling that the eerie sound came from another world. Was it the cry of a white owl? It was probably not unusual in this area. He reached for his watch.

Twenty to six. Gray daylight was starting to filter through the plastic blinds.

An owl's hoot was supposed to be ominous, according to folklore, especially when it was heard first thing in the morning.

In Yunnan, he and Peiqin had sometimes awakened amid nameless birds' twittering. Different days. Different birds, too. After a night's wind and rain, the slope outside their window would be covered with fallen petals. He was missing Peiqin again.

Rubbing his eyes, he made an effort to shake off the feeling the owl's cry had induced. There was no reason to suspect that it was going to be a bad day.

Chief Inspector Chen had discussed with him the likelihood that the Flying Axes would take desperate measures. It was alarming, but understandable. Considering the huge profit in human smuggling, the gang would make every attempt to get hold of Wen, on its own or through connections, to prevent her husband from testifying.

His phone started ringing. The number on the LCD display was a local one. The call came from Manager Pan, the first time they'd spoken since the food poisoning accident.

"Is everything all right, Pan?"

"I'm fine. I entertained a customer last night in a bathhouse in Tingjiang Village. And I saw Zheng Shiming playing mahjongg there with several good-for-nothing guys."

"Who is Zheng Shiming?"

"A Flying Ax. He did some business with Wen's husband Feng two or three years ago."

"That's a piece of news. You should have called me last night."

"I'm not a cop. I did not associate Zheng with your investigation there and then," Pan said. "But it may not be too late. A mah-jongg game can last all the night. If you go over right now, I bet you'll still find him there. He has a red motorcycle. A Honda."

"I'm on my way," Yu said. "Anything else about Zheng?"

"Last year Zheng was in jail for gambling. He's just out on probation for medical treatment. Playing mah-jongg is way out of line." Pan added after a short pause, "Oh, I have also heard stories about Zheng and Merry Widow Shou, the owner of the bathhouse. She loves to have her legs entwined with Zheng's."

"I see." That was why Pan called him so early in the morning. A sly dog. After a night of mah-jongg, a six-thirty visit was well-calculated to catch them off guard.

"Oh, you didn't hear anything from me, Detective Yu."

"Of course not. Thanks."

"Thanks to you. If you hadn't saved me, I would have died of food poisoning at your hotel."

Detective Yu was past the stage of feeling disappointed with the local police for withholding information from him. A person like Zheng could not have been overlooked. He decided to go to Tingjiang Village without notifying Sergeant Zhao. After a second's thought, Yu also took his pistol with him.

The village was no more than fifteen minutes' walk away. It was difficult to believe that there was a public bathhouse there. Indeed, the wheel of change turned nonstop in the world of red dust—that of the common people—both forward and backward. The renewed prosperity of the bathhouse business in the nineties owed less to old people's nostalgia than to its new service. For the newly rich, it was a place where they were able to buy the satisfaction of being served from head to foot, and sometimes served in other parts as well. Detective Yu had received reports about those indecent services. There must be some wealthy customers in this area as money poured in from abroad.

When he reached the village, the first thing he saw was a bright red motorcycle standing by a white-painted house that displayed the image of an enormous bathtub. Apparently this bathhouse had been converted from a residence. Through the partially open door, he saw a small stone courtyard littered with coal, wood, and stack upon stack of bath towels. He walked in. A huge white tile tub occupied the space of the original living room and dining room. Deck chairs were lined up against the wall. There was another room with a bamboo-beaded door curtain and a sign saying, LONG HAPPINESS ROOM. The private room for wealthy customers.

He pushed aside the curtain and saw a folding table with several chairs. The table was littered with pieces of a mah-jongg set, teacups, and ashtrays. Judging by the lingering traces of smoke in the air, the game could not have finished too long ago. Then he heard a man's voice coming from a room upstairs. "Who's there?"

Whipping out his gun, Yu ran upstairs and kicked open the door. He saw what Pan had led him to expect: a naked man entangled with a naked woman on a rumpled bed. Their clothes lay on the floor. The woman tried to cover herself up with the sheet, and the man reached for something on the nightstand.

"Don't move. I will shoot."

At the sight of the gun, the man withdrew his hand. The woman frantically attempted to cover her groin, forgetting about her slack breasts with dark, hard tips and the other parts of her angular body. A mole under her rib cage produced a weird three-nippled effect.

"Cover yourself." Yu threw a shirt to the woman.

"Who are you?" The man, a muscular hunk with a long scar above his left eyebrows, pulled on his pants. "The axes fly down from the sky, I'm third-story high."

"You must be Zheng Shiming. I am a cop. Drop your gang jargon."

"You're a cop? I've never seen you before."

"Take a close look." Yu produced his badge. "Zhao Youli is my local assistant. I'm here on a special case."

"What do you want with me?"

"Let's talk—in another room."

"Fine," Zheng said with recovered composure, casting a glance at the woman as he was ready to step out. "Don't worry, Shou."

As soon as they moved down into the private room, Zheng said, "I don't know what you want to talk to me about, Officer Yu. I have done nothing wrong."

"Oh, really? You gambled last night, and you were in jail for that same reason."

"Gambling? No. We played for fun."

"You can explain that to the local police. In addition, I am an eyewitness to your fornication."

"Come on. Shou and I have been seeing each other for several years. I'm going to marry her," Zheng said. "What do you really want?"

"I want you to tell me what you know about Feng Dexiang and the Flying Axes."

"Feng is in the United States. That's all I know. As for the Flying Axes, I have just gotten out of prison. I have nothing to do with them."

"You did some business with Feng a couple of years ago. Start by telling me about that. Tell me how you met him—when and where?"

"Well, it was about two years ago. We met in a small hotel in the city of Fuzhou. We were in a deal for some American cigarettes shipped in from Taiwan."

"Smuggled in from Taiwan? So you were his partner in illegal business."

"Only for a few weeks. After that, I never worked with him again."

"What kind of man is Feng?"

"A stinking rat. Rotten from head to foot. He would betray you for a bread crumb."

"A stinking rat?" That was the description used by several other villagers, Yu remembered. "Did you meet his wife while you were partners?"

"No, but Feng showed her picture to me several times. Fifteen years younger. Really gorgeous."

"So he carried Wen's picture around with him. He must have cared a lot for her."

"No, I don't think so. He wanted to brag about what a beauty he had deflowered. The way he talked about her was so dirty. He described in detail how she struggled, screaming, bleeding like a pig when he forced himself on her the first time—"

"What a bastard, to boast of such things to others!" Yu cut Zheng short.

"He also slept around. With half a dozen girls. I happened to know one of them, Tong Jiaqing. What a nymphomaniac! Once several guys had a go at her all together, Feng, Blind Ma, and Shorty Yin—"

"Did he talk to you about his plans to go to the United States?

"That's common knowledge here. Most of the men in his village are gone. Like everybody else, Feng talked about becoming a millionaire in the United States. Anyway, he's politically finished here."

"You're both Flying Axes," Yu said. "He must have talked to you about his travel racket."

"I have had nothing to do with those arrangements. Feng once boasted to me about his close relationship to some of the big bugs, that's about all I know."

"Including Jia Xinzhi?"

"Jia is not a member of our organization. He's more like a business partner, responsible for the ship. I do not remember Feng mentioning Jia. I'm telling you the truth, Officer Yu."

What Zheng had so far said could be true, Yu judged; he had revealed nothing crucial to the organization. As for a notorious scum like Feng, knowledge of some further evils in his personal life would not change anything. "I know you've just come out, Zheng, but I can easily put you back in if you refuse to cooperate. I need more than what you've told me."

"I'm a dead pig anyway. It makes no difference if you throw me into the boiling water," Zheng said stonily. "Put me back in prison if you can."

Detective Yu had heard of gang *yiqi*. Still, few would be a boiled pig rather than a betraying rat. Perhaps Zheng thought Yu was merely bluffing. A Shanghai badge might mean little to a local gangster, but Yu was not anxious to call in Sergeant Zhao.

The deadlock was broken by Shou's entrance, her wooden slippers clicking on the hardwood floor. Dressed in blue-striped pajama tops and pants, she carried a tea pot and two cups on a black lacquer tray.

"Comrade Officer, please have some Oolong tea."

That Shou would chose to come into the room was unexpected. Another woman would have remained sobbing upstairs, too ashamed to reappear before the cop who had just seen her naked. Now with her body concealed by her pajamas, she appeared presentable, decent, not the lascivious woman Pan had suggested. She had fine features, though worries had etched lines around her eyes. She might have been eavesdropping.

"Thanks." Taking a cup, Yu pushed on. "Let me put it this

way, Zheng. Have you heard anything about what the gang may do to Feng or his wife?"

"No, I've heard nothing. Since I came out, I've been living with my tail tucked in."

"With your tail tucked in? What you did last night with your tail sticking out was enough to put you back inside for years. Playing mah-jongg is a serious parole violation. Use those dead pig brains of yours, Zheng."

"Zheng has done nothing wrong," Shou cut in. "I wanted him to stay overnight."

"Leave us alone, Shou," Zheng said. "It has nothing to do with you. Go back to your room."

As Shou left the room, looking back at them, Yu said deliberately, "A nice woman. Do you want to drag her into trouble on your account?"

"It has nothing to do with her."

"I'm afraid it has. I will not only put you back inside, but also have the bathhouse closed on the grounds that it is a house of gambling and prostitution. She will be put behind bars, too, but not in the same cell with you, I will make sure of that. The local cops will do what I tell them."

"You are bluffing, Officer Yu." Zheng stared at him defiantly. "I know Sergeant Zhao."

"You don't believe me? Superintendent Hong is in charge of the province. You must know him, too." Yu said, taking out his phone. "I am calling him right now."

He dialed the number, showed Zheng the LCD display, and pressed the speaker phone button so the conversation could be heard by both of them.

"Comrade Superintendent Hong, this is Detective Yu Guangming speaking."

"How is everything, Detective Yu?"

"No progress, and Chief Inspector Chen calls every day. Remember, this case is of serious concern to the Beijing ministry."

"Yes, we understand. It is top priority for us too."

"We have to exert more pressure on the Flying Axes."

"I agree, but as I told you, the leaders are not here."

"Any of their members will do. I've discussed it with Chief Inspector Chen. Lock them up, as well as the people connected with them. If we use enough pressure, they will cave in."

"I'll work out a plan with Zhao and call you again."

"Now we can talk." Detective Yu looked Zheng in the eyes. "Let me make one thing clear to you. At this moment, the local police don't know I'm here. Why? My investigation is highly confidential. So if you cooperate, no one will talk—not you, not Shou, and not me. What you did last night is not my concern."

"It was really nothing—last night," Zheng said in a suddenly husky voice. "But now I remember one thing. One of the mahjongg players, a guy named Ding, asked me about Feng."

"Is Ding a Flying Ax?"

"I think so. I had never met him before."

"What did he say?"

"He asked if I heard anything about Feng. I hadn't. In fact, it was from Ding that I first learned about Feng's deal with the Americans. And about Wen's disappearance, too. The organization is very upset."

"Did he tell you why?"

"Not in detail, but I can guess. If Jia is convicted, it will be a huge loss to our smuggling operation."

"There are enough Taiwan smuggling rings to take up the slack. I don't think the Flying Axes have to worry about that."

"The reputation of the organization is at stake. 'A grain of rat dung may spoil a whole pot of white porridge.' " Zheng added after a pause, "Perhaps it's more than that. Feng's role in the operation is another factor."

"Now that's something. What do you know about his role?"

"Once the departure time of a ship is arranged, snake heads like Jia want to sign up as many passengers as possible. They'll lose profits if the ship is half full, so it is our responsibility to get the word around. Feng was engaged in recruiting. He developed a network and made himself useful to the village folks. They would consult him to learn, for example, which snake heads are reliable, whether the price is negotiable, what captains are experienced. So Feng has in his head a list of the people involved—on both the supply and demand sides. If he turns that over, it will be a terrible blow to the whole business."

"He may have turned it over already." Yu had not heard about this. Perhaps the Americans had focused on Feng only as a witness against Jia. "Did Ding tell you what the gang plans to do with his wife?"

"He cursed like mad. Something like, 'The bitch changed her mind. She won't get away so easily!'"

"What does that mean—changed her mind?"

"She was waiting for her passport, but she ran away at the last minute. I believe that's what he meant."

"So what are they going to do?"

"Feng is worried about the baby in her belly. If they get hold of her, Feng will not squeak. So they are hunting her down."

"Almost ten days have passed, they must be really anxious now."

"You bet. They have sent gold axes out."

"Gold axes?"

"The founder of the Flying Axes had five small gold axes made with the inscription, 'When you see the gold ax, you see me.' If another organization fulfills a request made with a gold ax, they are entitled to any favor in return."

"So other gangs are involved in the search for Wen, outside Fujian?"

"Ding mentioned some people in Shanghai. They will do whatever they can to beat the cops to Wen."

Detective Yu was alarmed—as much on behalf of Chief Inspector Chen and his American companion as for Wen. "What else did he tell you?"

"I think that's all. I've told you everything I know. Every word is absolutely true, Officer Yu."

"Well, we will find out," Yu said, believing that Zheng had revealed all he knew. "One more thing. Give me the address of this prostitute, Tong."

Zheng wrote a few words on a piece of paper. "No one knows about your visit here?"

"No one. Don't worry about that." Yu rose from the mahjongg table, adding his cell phone number to the card. "If you hear anything more, contact me."

He left the bathhouse like a satisfied customer, with his hosts accompanying him to the door.

Turning to look back at the end of village, he saw Zheng still standing with Shou in the doorway, his arm grasping her waist, like a couple of crabs tied together with a straw in the market. Perhaps they did care for each other.

Chapter 23

Chief Inspector Chen had a terrible hangover on Sunday morning, thanks to the karaoke party the night before.

Vaguely he remembered one scene in his quick-fading dream. He had been traveling in an express train, going somewhere, though his destination did not appear on his punched ticket. It was a long, boring trip. There was hardly anything to do but stare at the unchanging aisle where changing feet were passing— in straw sandals, shining boots, leather loafers, fashionable mules . . . Then turning toward his own reflection in the window, he noticed a fly circling around a spot near the frame. The moment he raised his hand in annoyance, it buzzed away. But immediately it returned, buzzing, to the same old place. He did not see anything there to attract it. The train was still moving yet not moving . . .

And he wondered as the light streamed through the blinds: *Is it Chief Inspector Chen that dreams of being a fly, or is it the fly that dreams of being a cop?*

Some details of the party the previous night came back to him. How was he different from those depraved officials in Baoshen's case? Of course he had visited the club for his work, he rationalized.

He had sworn that he would do everything in his power to deliver a crushing blow to the gangsters, yet he had not supposed then that he, too, would have had to descend to such deviousness, toasting to friendship with an honorary Blue.

And there was Li's connection. Li might not have told him everything about the investigation. In fact, Minister Huang's recommendation of him for the job and call to him at his home was suggestive. Chief Inspector Chen might well need to have a card to play against the powerful Party Secretary.

It was then, at eight thirty, that Party Secretary Li's phone call came, which did not provide much hope of relief for his headache.

"It's Sunday, Chief Inspector Chen. Entertain Inspector Rohn the best you can, so she won't make troublesome demands."

Chen shook his head. There was no arguing with Li, especially when Internal Security lurked in the background. People's grumbled about the possibility of his succeeding Party Secretary Li, but he wondered now whether it was such a desirable position.

Inspector Rohn did not sound too disappointed at his proposal for the day. Perhaps she also realized that further interviews in Shanghai were futile. He suggested that they meet for lunch at Moscow Suburb.

"A Russian restaurant?"

"I want to show you the rapid changes taking place in Shanghai," he said. He also wanted to bring his friend Lu some business.

He had planned to have a meeting with Old Hunter before lunch, but he did not make it. As he put down the phone, he received an express delivery. Detective Yu's cassette tape bore a label that read: *Interview with Manager Pan*. Listening to it took priority. After applying a wet towel to his forehead, he sat on the sofa and played the tape. At the end, he rewound it to replay the part where Manager Pan told of learning about Feng's deal in the United States. As he listened one more time, he made a quick note, wondering whether Yu had noticed the point.

Glancing at his watch, he realized he had no time to ask Yu this question. He had to hurry.

Restaurant owner Lu, expansive in the three-piece charcoal gray suit, wearing a scarlet tie fixed with a diamond pin, was waiting for them outside Moscow Suburb.

"Buddy, you've not been here for ages. What good wind's brought you today?"

"Meet Catherine Rohn, my American friend. Catherine, this is Overseas Chinese Lu."

"Nice to meet you, Mr. Lu," she said in Chinese.

"Welcome. Chief Inspector Chen's friend is my friend," Lu declared. "A private room is reserved for you."

They needed the special treatment. The dining hall was packed. A number of foreigners who spoke English were dining there. A Russian hostess led them into an exquisitely decorated room, her slender waist swaying like the poplar tree in a breeze. The tablecloth gleamed snow white, glasses shone under highly polished chandeliers, and the exquisite silverware could have come from the Winter Palace. The waitress planted herself behind their table, motionless.

Lu waved her away. "Come back later, Anna. I haven't talked to my buddy for a long time."

"How is business?" Chen asked.

"Not bad at all," Lu beamed. "We've got a reputation for genuine Russian cuisine, and genuine Russian girls."

"Well known for both!"

"Exactly. That's why people come pouring in."

"So you're really a successful Overseas Chinese now," Chen said. "I appreciate what you have done for my mother."

"Come on. She is like my mother, too. She's a bit lonely by herself, you know."

"Yes, I want her to move in with me, but she says she's used to that old attic."

"She wants you to have the one-bedroom apartment for yourself."

Chen knew what Lu was driving at. There was no point in bringing it up in the presence of Inspector Rohn. So he said, "I consider myself lucky to have a one-bedroom apartment just for myself."

"You know what Ruru says? 'Chief Inspector Chen belongs to an endangered species.' Why? A shining key to a three-bedroom apartment would have been long since delivered by one of those upstarts to someone in your position," Lu said with a low chuckle. "No offense, buddy. She cooks a good soup but does not understand how upright a cop you are. Oh, Gu Haiguang, of the Dynasty Club, came here yesterday, and he mentioned you."

"Really! Do you think he dropped in by chance?"

"I don't know. He has been here before, but yesterday he asked questions about you. I told him you helped me get started. It was like sending a poor friend charcoal in the depth of the winter."

"You don't have to tell people that, Lu."

"Why not? Ruru and I are proud to have a friend like you. Come here every week. Let Little Zhou drive you. It's only fifteen minutes. Your bureau canteen is an insult. Are you on an expense account today?"

"No, I'm not on bureau business today. Catherine is a friend of mine. So I want her to have dinner at the best Russian restaurant in Shanghai."

"Thank you," Lu said. "It's a pity Ruru's not here, or she would entertain you like at home. It is our treat today."

"No, I have to pay. You don't want me to lose face in front of my American friend, do you?"

"Don't worry, buddy. You'll have your face. And our best food."

Anna brought them a bilingual menu. Chen ordered a broiled veal chop. Catherine chose smoked trout with borscht. Standing between them, Lu kept suggesting the house specials like someone in a TV commercial.

When they were finally left alone, Catherine asked Chen, "Is he an overseas Chinese?"

"No, it's his nickname."

"Does an overseas Chinese talk like he does?"

"I don't know. In some of our movies, overseas Chinese are shown as very excited to be coming back home, exaggerating a lot. Lu talks like that on the topic of food, but he got his nickname in a different way. During the Cultural Revolution, "Overseas Chinese" was a negative term, used to depict people as politically unreliable in connection with the Western world, or in association with an extravagant bourgeois life style. In high school, Lu took obstinate pride in cultivating his "decadent" tastes—brewing coffee, baking apple pie, tossing fruit salad, and of course, wearing a Western-style suit to dinner. So he got the nickname."

"Have you acquired all your epicurean knowledge from him?" she asked.

"You could say that. Nowadays, 'Overseas Chinese' is a positive term, carrying the connotation of someone rich, successful in business, connected with the Western world. Lu has turned into a successful entrepreneur with his own restaurant. So now the name fits the reality."

She took a small sip of water, the ice cubes clinking pleasantly in the glass. "He asked you who was going to pay. Why?"

"If I'm here on bureau business, on an expense account, he will charge me two or three times more. A common practice. Not just for our bureau, but for all state-run companies. The 'socialist expense.' "

"But how come—I mean two or three times more?"

"In China, most people work for state-run companies. The system calls for a sort of averaging. Theoretically, a general manager and a janitor should earn about the same salary. So the former uses company money for his own benefit—for dining and entertaining: 'socialist expense,' even if they are treating their families or friends."

The waitress brought in a bottle of wine in a basket and two small dishes of caviar on a silver tray. "Compliments of the house."

They watched the waitress go through the ceremony of uncorking the bottle, pouring a bit into Chen's glass, and waiting expectantly. He handed it over to Catherine.

She sampled it. "Good."

As the waitress withdrew, they raised their glasses in a toast.

"I'm glad you told him that I'm your friend," she said. "But let's split the check."

"No. It's on the bureau. I told him I was paying because I did not want to incur too much expense. It would be a serious matter of loss of face for a Chinese not to pay in the company of his girlfriend—let alone a beautiful American girlfriend."

"A beautiful American *girlfriend!*"

"No, I did not tell him that, but that's probably what he imagines."

"Life here is so complicated—'socialist expense' and 'face loss.' " She raised her cup again. "Do you think Gu came here on purpose?"

"Gu did not mention his visit to me last night, but I think you are right."

"Oh, did you see him again last night?"

"Yes, for a karaoke party. I took Meiling, the secretary of the Traffic Control Office."

"So you took another girl there!" She feigned shock.

"To show how serious I am about the parking lot, Inspector Rohn."

"In exchange for information, I understand. Did you get anything new, Chief Inspector Chen?"

"Not about Wen, but he promised he would try." He drained his wine, remembering the Mao Tai mixed with the snake blood, choosing not to talk about the karaoke party in detail. "The party did not finish until two, with all the exotic foods you can imagine, plus two bottles of Mao Tai, and a splitting headache for me this morning."

"Oh, poor Comrade Chief Inspector Chen."

Their main course arrived. The food was excellent, the wine mellow, and his companion charming, Chen's hangover almost vanished. The afternoon sunlight streamed through the window. A Russian folk song entitled "The Red Berry Blossom" played in the background.

For a moment, he reflected that his assignment for the day was not that bad. He took another sip. Fragments of lines came to his mind.

> *The sunlight burning gold,*
> *We cannot collect the day*
> *From the ancient garden*
> *Into an album of old,*
> *Let's pick our play,*
> *Or time will not pardon—*

He was momentarily confused. These were not exactly his lines. Was he still drunk? Li Bai claimed that he wrote best when intoxicated. Chen had never experienced this.

"What are you thinking about?" she said, carving into her fish.

"Some lines. Not mine. Not all of them."

"Come on, you're a well-known poet. The librarian in the Shanghai Library knows about you. How about reciting one of your poems?"

"Well—" He felt tempted. Party Secretary Li had told him to keep her entertained. "Last year, I wrote a poem about Daifu, a modern Chinese poet. Remember the two lines on my folding fan?"

"About whipping the horse and the beauty alike, right?" she said with a smile.

"In the early forties, Daifu was caught in a tabloid typhoon over his divorce. He left for a Philippine island, where he started a new life, living anonymously. Like someone in your witness protection program. He changed his name, grew a big beard, opened a rice shop, and bought an 'untouched' native girl, about thirty years younger, who did not speak a single word of Chinese."

"Gauguin did something like that," she said. "Sorry, please continue."

"It was during the war against Japan. The poet was involved in resistance activities. Allegedly he was killed by the Japanese. A myth has since evolved. Critics claim that he did everything— the girl, the rice shop, and his beard—as a cover for his anti-Japanese activities. My poem was a reaction to those claims. The first stanza is about the background. I'm skipping it. The second and third stanzas are about the poet's life as a rice merchant in the company of the native girl.

"*A gigantic ledger opened him | in the morning, figures | moved him up and down | along a mahogany abacus | all day, until the curfew | closed him in her bare arms, | in a peaceful sack of darkness: | time was a handful of rice streaming out | through his fingers. A chewed betel nut | stuck on the counter. He quit | holding himself like a balloon | forsaken against a horizon blazing | with cigarette butts.*

"One midnight he awoke with the leaves / shivering, inexplicably, at the window. / She grasped at the mosquito net / in her sleep. A gold fish jumped out, / dancing furiously on the ground. / Wordless, a young woman's capacity / for feeling jealousy and / the incorrigibly plural correspondence / of the world illuminated him. / It must have been another man, dead / long before, who had said:/"The limits of his poetry / are the limits of his possibility."

"Is that all?" She gazed at him over the rim of her glass.

"No, there's one more stanza, but I cannot remember all the lines. It tells that years later, critics came like pilgrims to that native woman who, in her sixties, could bring nothing back, except the memory of Daifu making love to her."

"It's so sad," she said, twisting in her slender fingers the stem of the glass. "And so unfair to her."

"Unfair to feminist critics?"

"No, not just that. It's way too cynical. Not that I do not like your poem, I do." She continued after taking another small sip. "Let me ask you a different question. When you wrote the poem, what kind of a mood were you in?"

"I cannot remember. It was such a long time ago."

"A lousy mood, I bet. Things were going wrong. Messages did not get through. Disillusionment hit home. And you became cynical—" She added, "Sorry if I'm intruding."

"No, it's okay," he said, taken aback. "You're right in a general sense. According to our Tang dynasty poet Du Fu, people do not write well when they are happy. If you are content with life, you simply want to enjoy it."

"Antiromantic cynicism can be a disguise for the poet's personal disappointment. The poem reveals another side of you."

"Well—" He was at a loss. "You're entitled to your reading. Inspector Rohn. In deconstruction, every reading can be a misreading."

Their talk was interrupted by a phone call from his deputy, Qian.

"Where are you, Chief Inspector Chen?"

"Moscow Suburb," Chen said. "Party Secretary Li wants me to entertain our American guest. What do you have to report?"

"Nothing particular. I'm in the bureau today. Detective Yu may call in at any time, and I'm still making phone calls to hotels. If anything comes up, you can reach me here."

"So you're working on Sunday, too. Good for you, Qian. Goodbye."

Chen felt slightly disturbed, however. It was possible that Qian had intended to show how hard working he was, especially after the Qingpu incident. But why did he want to know where Chen was? Perhaps he should not have disclosed his whereabouts.

Anna came to offer desserts from a cart.

"Thank you." Chen said. "Leave it here. We'll choose for ourselves."

"Another linguistic question," Catherine said, selecting chocolate mousse.

"Yes?"

"Lu calls Anna and other waitresses his little sisters. Why?"

"They're younger, but there is another reason. We used to call Russians our 'elder brothers,' believing they were more advanced and we were only in the early stage of Communism. Now Russia is viewed as poorer than China. Young Russian girls come here, seeking jobs in our restaurants and nightclubs, just as Chinese go to the United States. Lu is so proud of this."

She dug her spoon into her mousse. "I need to ask you a favor—as your American girlfriend—as your buddy imagines."

"Whatever I can do, Inspector Rohn." He was conscious of a subtle change in her. Her tone lacked the edge of the previous day.

"I have heard of a 'knockoff' street in Shanghai. I would like to ask you to accompany me there."

"A knockoff street?"

"Huating Road, that's the name of it. People sell all kinds of fake brands there. Like Louis Vuitton, Gucci, or Rolex."

"Huating Road—I have never been there myself."

"I can go myself, with a Shanghai map in hand. Only the peddlers will charge me a much higher price. I don't think my Chinese is good enough for bargaining."

"Your Chinese is more than adequate." Chen put down his wineglass. This was not an activity the authorities would recommend. Such a street market reflected no credit on China. If she chose to tell someone, it could be an embarrassment to the city government. But she would be able to do so even if he did not go with her. "Is it a good idea to go there, Inspector Rohn?" he said.

"Why do you ask?"

"You can buy such things at home. Why spend your time looking for fakes here?"

"You know how much a Gucci shoulder bag costs?" She put hers on the table. "Mine is an off brand. Don't think all Americans are millionaires."

"No, I don't," Chen said.

"One of Wen's classmates, Bai—I think that's his name— sells fake stuff. No one knows where he is. So we can ask about him. These knockoff peddlers must have a network."

"We don't have to go there to find him." He did not think interviewing one more classmate of Wen's could make much difference. "We deserve a break today."

"There's also a possibility that we will spot an imitation Valentino. The victim in the park wore that brand of pajama, didn't he?"

"Yes," he said, admitting to himself that she had a tenacious memory for detail. He had mentioned the pajama brand to her only once in passing. "As a chief inspector, I should not go there, but you are my responsibility. Party Secretary Li repeated this to me this morning. So, I'm your tour guide."

When they were ready to leave, Overseas Chinese Lu made another red-faced effort to decline Chen's payment.

"Tell you what," Chen said, "next time I'll come in alone, order the most expensive dish in the house, and let you be the host. Okay?"

"Sure. Don't let me wait too long." Lu accompanied them to the door, holding a camera.

"Thank you so much, Mr. Lu," she said.

"Call me Overseas Chinese Lu," he said to Catherine, bending to kiss her hand courteously, in a gesture appropriate to an overseas Chinese in the movies. "We're privileged to have a beautiful American guest like you. Come again. Next time, Ruru and I will prepare something special for you."

Several customers leaving the restaurant looked at them curiously. Lu stopped a young man with a crew cut and a light green cell phone in his hand.

"Please take a picture of the three of us. I'll frame it. The most distinguished guests of Moscow Suburb."

Chapter 24

It took them less than ten minutes by subway to reach Huating Road. Chief Inspector Chen was surprised at the crowd at the street market. There were also a number of foreigners, with small calculators, bargaining or gesticulating with their fingers. They had probably read the same tourist guide book as Catherine Rohn.

"You see, your Chinese is more than enough," he said.

"I was afraid I would be the only foreign devil here," she said.

The narrow street was lined on both sides with booths, kiosks, stands, barrows, and stores. Some specialized in a particular product line, like purses and shoulder bags, T-shirts, or jeans; some displayed an eclectic mixture. Armies of small vendors had created a marketplace out of a former residential area in the last few years. This had been happening throughout the city. A lot of stores were makeshift extensions, or conversions, of the original residences. Some peddlers did business on tables under awnings and umbrellas with brand logos, or simply on the pavements, giving the street the appearance of a fair.

They asked about Bai, the peddler, but no one volunteered information. It was not surprising. There might be more than one knockoff market. She did not seem too disappointed. Nor did they find Valentino pajamas there. Old Hunter's information had been reliable.

She stopped at a booth to examine a leather purse. She slung it over her shoulder and appeared satisfied, but instead of bargaining for it, she left it saying, "Let me comparison shop at a few other stores first."

Entering a tiny shop, they saw various familiar-looking, inexpensive products on shelves at the entrance, most of them bearing "made in China" labels. The goods were the same as those in state-run stores. Further inside, however, appeared all sorts of copies of high-style goods. The owner, a broad-shouldered woman in her late forties, greeted them with a grin.

Catherine took his arm, whispering, "For the benefit of the owner, so she won't take me for an American sucker."

While the gesture made sense, it made him oddly pleased. She started to browse just like other customers with an intensity he had not expected.

Another store displayed traditional Chinese costumes. The street, frequented by foreign tourists equally interested in exotic Oriental products, was home to a couple of specialized boutiques. She lit upon a scarlet silk robe embroidered with a golden dragon. As she stroked the smooth material, the owner of the store, a gray-haired woman wearing a pair of gray-rimmed glasses, said affably, "You can try it on here, American lady."

"How?" Catherine looked around. There was no fitting room.

"It's easy," the owner said, pointing at a piece of cloth folded back and hooked on the wall. "Pull it out, hook it onto the other wall, and it is a fitting room curtain. You can put on the robe behind it."

"Ingenious," Chen said. What stretched out across the corner of the room was, however, not exactly a curtain. The material was too thin, too short. It was more like a fashionable apron.

Beneath the curtain, he saw Catherine's dress falling in a heap at her feet. Looking up, he caught a glimpse of her white shoulders before she wrapped herself in the scarlet robe.

"Take your time, Catherine. I'll smoke a cigarette outside."

As he lit a cigarette outside the store, he saw a young man in front of another store across the street dialing a cell phone and casting a long glance in their direction. A Chinese onlooker would be intrigued by the sight of an American woman changing her clothes behind the makeshift curtain. Chen did not feel comfortable in his temporary role, standing there like a bodyguard, a "flower protector" in classical Chinese literature.

Something else was bothering him, too. He was not sure what. He dropped the cigarette before he finished, stamping it out under his heel, and went back into the store. She pulled aside the curtain and emerged holding the robe wrapped in a plastic bag.

"I bought it."

"The American lady speaks Chinese so well," the owner said with an obliging smile. "I'm giving her the price for a regular Chinese client."

They resumed their shopping, bargaining, comparing, making small purchases here and there. As they squeezed their way through the market, it started to rain. They hurried into a garagelike store, where a young salesgirl was perched on a high chair behind the counter. Probably in her early twenties, she was cute in a clean-cut way, and she wore a black DKNY top that showed her belly button, and a pair of shorts with a Tommy Hilfiger logo on the hip. She dangled her Prada slippers and smoked a brown More cigarette. She stood up to meet them, a collective image of contemporary fashion.

"Welcome to our store, Big Brother."

It was a strange greeting, he thought. The young salesgirl appeared to focus her attention on him.

"It's raining," he said. "So we'll look around."

"Take your time, Big Brother. Your girlfriend deserves the best."

"Yes, she does," he said.

"Thank you," Catherine said in Chinese.

The salesgirl introduced herself. "My name is Huang Ying. It means Oriole in Chinese."

"What a lovely name!"

"Our products are no low-quality fakes. The companies themselves sell to us through an unofficial channel."

"How?" Catherine asked, taking up a black handbag bearing the label of an exclusive Italian designer.

"Well, most of them have joint ventures in Hong Kong or Taiwan. This handbag, for example. They ordered two thousand. The Taiwan factory produced three thousand. The same quality, needless to say. And we get one thousand directly from the factory. For less than twenty dollars."

"It's genuine," Catherine said, after taking a closer look.

Chen could not see anything special about it—except for the price tag. It seemed enormously expensive to him. Handing the bag back to her, he noticed a row of colorful fashionable clothes hanging on a stainless-steel rack in a corner. The price tags seemed staggering.

There was also a length of scarlet velvet—a fitting room curtain partially hiding a cushioned stool by the back door. This store was of better quality—at least in that respect. When people changed, they would feel more secure.

"Take a look at this watch." Oriole took out a display case. "The company is not well known for its watch line. So why bother? It's because they are manufactured in Taiwan, and sold here."

"Hasn't the government tried to close this market?" Catherine said to him.

"The market patrollers come here from time to time, but things can be worked out," Oriole said glibly. "Say he takes away ten T-shirts and says, 'I've confiscated five of your T-shirts, right?' And you say, 'Five, that's correct.' So instead of hauling you in, he turns in five, pockets five, and lets you off."

"Nothing else has been done here?" Chief Inspector Chen felt embarrassed.

"Occasionally the cops come by. They raided Bald Zhang's at the end of the street last month, and sentenced him to two years. It can be dangerous."

"If it's so dangerous, why do you still do it?"

"What choice do I have?" Oriole said bitterly. "My parents worked all their lives at Shanghai Number 6 Textile Mill. Laid off last year. Broken iron rice bowls. No benefit of the socialist system anymore. I have to support the family."

"Your store must make a good profit," Chen said.

"It's not my store, but with the money I'm earning, I cannot complain."

"Still, it's not a job—" he did not finish the sentence. He was in no position to be condescending or compassionate. Oriole might earn more than a chief inspector. In the early nineties, there was nothing like the opportunity to make money. Still, it was not a decent job for a young girl—

Catherine was busy comparing watches, trying their effect, one by one, on her wrist. It might take her some time to make up her mind. How long, he wondered. Rain beat on the partially rolled-down aluminum door.

As he looked out, his glance swept over a man across the street dialing his cell phone, staring in their direction.

The same light green cellular phone.

It was the man who had taken pictures for them in front of Moscow Suburb earlier in the afternoon, and also the man who had looked into the Oriental clothes store fifteen minutes earlier.

He turned and asked Oriole, "Can you draw the fitting room

curtain? I like the black slip, the Christian Dior." He took it from the clothes stand and put it into Catherine's hand. "Would you try it on?"

"What?" She stared at Chen, aware of the pressure of his hand.

"Let me pay you the tag price, Oriole," he said, handing several bills over to the salesgirl, "I'd like to see the effect on her. It may take a short while."

"Sure, take as much time as you want," Oriole took the money, grinned eloquently, and pulled the curtain for them. "When you have finished, let me know."

Another customer entered the store. Oriole stepped toward him, repeating over her shoulder, "Take your time, Big Brother."

There was hardly enough space for two behind the curtain. Catherine looked up at Chen with the slip in her hands and questions in her eyes.

"Leave through the back," he whispered in English and opened the door, which led to a narrow alley. It was still raining, with thunder rumbling in the distance and lightning streaking across the distant horizon.

Closing the door after them, he led Catherine to the end of the lane, which merged into Huating Road. Turning back, he saw the flashing neon sign of Huating Café on the second floor of a pinkish building on the corner between Huating and Huaihai roads. On the first floor was another clothing store. A gray wrought-iron staircase at the back of the building led up to the café.

"Let's have a cup of coffee there," he said.

They mounted the slippery staircase, entered an oblong room furnished in European style, and seated themselves at a table by the window.

"What's up, Chief Inspector Chen?"

"Let's wait here, Inspector Rohn. Maybe I am wrong." He did not go on as a waitress approached, bringing them hot towels. "I must have a cup of hot coffee."

"I could do with the same."

After the waitress brought the coffee, Catherine said, "Let me ask you a question first. This street must be an open secret. Why does the city government allow its existence?"

"Where there is demand, there is supply—even for fakes. No matter what measures the city government may take, people will continue their business. According to Karl Marx, for a three-hundred-percent profit, a lot of people are willing to sell their souls."

"I'm not entitled to be a critic today, not after I made my purchases." She stirred ripples in her coffee with a silver spoon. "Still, something must be done."

"Yes, not just about the market, but also about the ideas behind it, the excessive exaltation of the material. With Deng Xiaoping saying that 'to get rich is glorious,' capitalistic consumerism has grown out of control."

"Do you think what people practice here in reality is capitalism rather than communism?"

"You have to find the answer to this question for yourself," he replied evasively. "Deng's openness to capitalist innovation is well-known. There's a saying of his: 'It doesn't matter whether it's a white or a black cat, as long as it catches a rat.' "

"Cat and rat, rhyme and reason."

"Few Chinese keep cats as pets, you know. For us, cats exist for the sole purpose of catching rats."

The rain had ceased. Looking out the window, he could see into Oriole's store. The velvet curtain was still drawn. He was not sure if Oriole knew they had left. His prepayment of the price as marked must have been suspicious enough. He caught Catherine glancing in the same direction.

"Fifteen years ago, those brands were never heard of here. Chinese people were content to wear one style of clothes: Mao jackets, blue or black. Things are so different now. They want to catch up with the newest world fashions. From an historical perspective, you have to say that it's progress."

"You are capable of lecturing on a lot of things, Comrade Chief Inspector Chen."

"For a lot of things in this transitional period, I do not have an answer, let alone a lecture. I'm just trying to come to terms with them myself." Without conscious thought, he had built a tiny edifice of sugar cubes, which was now crumbling by his coffee mug. Why had he been so willing—even eager to discuss all these things with her?

It was then he heard a commotion sweeping down on the street like thunder rolling in from a distance, and people shouting and screaming in chorus: "They are coming!"

He saw street peddlers gathering up their displays in a frenzy, store owners closing their doors helter-skelter, several people running with big plastic bags on their backs. In Oriole's store, the girl jumped out from behind the counter, plunged the store into semi-darkness by turning off a switch, and tried to pull down the aluminum door. But it was too late. Plainclothes police were already rushing in.

What he had suspected was confirmed.

They had been followed. By someone with inside contacts. Otherwise, the police would not have come so quickly, nor rushed directly to that store. A tip had been given, perhaps via that light green cell phone. The informer must have supposed that Chen and his American companion were inside. But for his wariness, they would have been apprehended, together with Oriole. Catherine's status as a U.S. Marshal would have caused serious complications. As for Chen, he had committed a serious violation of the foreign liaison regulations. The existence of such a street market was a political disgrace. He should not have brought an American here, let alone an American officer in the middle of a sensitive investigation. He would have been suspended, at the least.

Had the Flying Axes orchestrated all this—in addition to other "accidents"? He wondered how a Fujian gang, which had never before made its impact felt out of its province, could be so resourceful in Shanghai.

Another possibility suggested itself to him. Some people within the system had long planned to get rid of him. Internal Security's report about his fastening Inspector Rohn's necklace, for instance, must have found its way into his dossier because of this. This very assignment might have been a trap, set so he would commit a blunder in the company of an attractive American woman officer. It could backfire, however, if it was discovered that the attempt to entrap him was being made at the expense of an internationally important case. He was not without his ally at the highest level—

Catherine touched his hand lightly. "Look."

Oriole was being marched out of the store. She was a changed girl, her hands handcuffed behind her back, her hair disheveled, and her face scratched, no longer young and vivacious. Her top was wrinkled, one strap dangled from her shoulder, and she must have lost her slippers in the scuffle, so she walked barefoot into the street.

"Did you know the police would come?" Catherine asked.

"No, but while you were examining the watches, I saw a plainclothes man outside."

"Did they come for us?"

"It's possible. If an American were caught here with a heap of purchases, it might be played as a political card."

He was in no position to tell her what else he suspected, though he saw the clouds of suspicion gathering in her eyes.

"But we could have left the store in a normal way," she said skeptically. "Why all the drama—moving behind the fitting curtain, leaving through the back door, and running across the alley in the rain."

"I wanted them to believe we were still behind the curtain."

"For such a long time," she said, blushing slightly in spite of herself.

Suddenly, he thought he saw a familiar figure in the crowd, a short cop with a walkie-talkie in his hand. Then he found that it was not Qian. Yet the man with the light green cell phone had appeared outside Moscow Suburb after Qian's call.

A middle-aged customer at the next table, pointing his fingers at the salesgirl, burst out, "What a worn-out shoe!"

Oriole must have stepped into a puddle. She left a line of wet footprints behind her.

"What does he mean?" Catherine appeared puzzled. "She is barefoot."

"It's slang, meaning 'hussy' or 'prostitute.' A worn-out shoe in the sense that it has been worn by so many people, and so many times."

"Is she engaged in prostitution?"

"I don't know. The business of this street is not legitimate. So people imagine things."

"Will she get into serious trouble?"

"A few months or a few years. It depends on the political climate. If our government finds it politically necessary to highlight the action taken against those fakes, she will suffer. Perhaps it's the same with your government's emphasis on Feng's case?"

"There's nothing you can do about it?" she said.

"Nothing," he echoed, though he was sorry for Oriole. The raid had been intended to catch them, he was sure of it. The girl had been caught instead. She should be punished for her business practices, but not like this.

A war had been declared, and there were casualties already. First Qiao, now Oriole. The chief inspector was still in the dark, however, with no certainty as to whom he was fighting.

Oriole was already near the end of the street.

Behind her, the line of her wet footprints was already disappearing.

In the eleventh century, Su Dongpo had come up with the famous image: *Life is like the footprint left by a solitary crane in the snow, visible for one moment, and then gone.*

Lines sometimes came to Chen in the most difficult situations. He did not know how he was able to feel poetic when gangsters were closing in on him. At that instant something else flashed through his mind.

"Let's go, Catherine." He stood up, took her hand, and dragged her downstairs.

"Where?"

"I have to hurry back to the bureau. Something urgent. I've had an idea. Sorry, I'll call you later."

Chapter 25

Several hours later, Chen tried to reach Catherine by phone without success. Nevertheless, he went up to her room hoping to find her.

At his first knock, the door opened. She was wearing the scarlet silk robe embroidered with the golden dragon, bare-legged and barefoot. She was drying her hair with a towel.

He was at a loss for words. "I'm sorry, Inspector Rohn."

"Come on in."

"Sorry to arrive so late," he said. "I called you several times. I wasn't sure you were in."

"Don't keep on apologizing. I was taking a shower. You are a welcome guest here, just as I am a distinguished guest of your bureau," she said, motioning him to sit on the couch. "What would you like to drink?"

"Water, please."

She went to the small refrigerator and came back with a bottle of spring water for him. "Something important has come up, I guess?"

"Yes." He produced a sheet of paper from his briefcase.

"What's that?" She took a quick look at the first few lines.

"A poem from Wen's past." He took a gulp from the bottle. "Sorry, it's difficult to read my handwriting. I did not have the time to type it."

She seated herself beside him on the couch. "Could you read it for me."

As she leaned over to look at the poem, he thought he smelled the scent of the soap on her skin, still wet from the shower. Taking a breath, he started to read, in English:

"Fingertip Touching

We are talking in a jammed workshop
picking our way, and our words.
amid all the prizes, gold-plated statuettes
staring at the circling flies. 'The stuff
for your newspaper report: miracles made
by Chinese workers,' the manager says.
'In Europe, special grinders alone
can do the job, but our workers' finger-
polish the precision parts.'
Beside us, women bending over the work,
their fingers
shuttling under the fluorescent light,
My camera focusing on a middle-aged one,
pallid in her black homespun blouse
soaked in sweat. Summer heat overwhelms.
Zooming in, I'm shocked to see myself
galvanized into the steel part
touched by Lili's fingertips,
soft yet solid
as an exotic grinder.

"Who is the reporter in the first stanza?" she asked with a puzzled expression.

"Let me explain after I finish.

Not that
Lili really touched me. Not she, the prettiest

忠

leftist at the station, July, 1970.
We were leaving, the first group
of 'educated youths,'
leaving for the countryside,
'Oh, to be re-re-re-educated by
the po-or and lo-lo-wer middle class peasants!'
Chairman Mao's voice screeched
from a scratched record at the station.
By the locomotive Lili
burst into a dance, flourishing
a red paper heart she had cut, a miracle
in the design of a girl and a boy
holding the Chinese character—'loyal'
to Chairman Mao. Spring
of the Cultural Revolution wafted
through her fingers. Her hair streamed
into the dark eye of the sun.
A leap, her skirt
like a blossom, and the heart
jumped out of her hand, fluttering
like a flushed pheasant. A slip—
I rushed to its rescue, when she
caught it—a finishing touch
to her performance. The people
roared. I froze. She took my hand,
waving, our fingers branching
into each other, as if my blunder
were a much rehearsed act, as if
the curtain fell on the world
in a piece of white paper
to set off the red heart, in which
I was the boy, she, the girl.

'The best fingers,'
the manager keeps me nodding. It's she.
No mistake. But what can I say,
I say, of course, the convenient thing
to myself, that things change, as
a Chinese saying goes, as dramatically
as azure seas into mulberry fields,
or that all these years vanish—in a flick of your cigar.
Here she is, changed
and unchanged, her fingers
lathered in the greenish abrasive,
new bamboo shoots long immersed
in icy water, peeling, but
perfecting. She raises her hand, only
once, to wipe the sweat
from her forehead, leaving
a phosphorescent trail. She
does not know me—not even
with the Wenhui Daily's reporter
name label on my bosom

'No story,'
the manager says.
'One of the millions
of educated youths, she has become
"a poor-lower-middle class peasant" herself,
her fingers—tough as a grinder,
but a revolutionary one, polishing up
the spirit of our society, speaking
volumes for our socialism's superiority.'
So came a central metaphor
for my report.

An emerald snail
crawls along the white wall.

"A sad poem," she murmured.

"A good poem, but the translation fails to do justice to the original."

"The language is clear, and the story is poignant. I don't see anything wrong with the English. It's very touching indeed."

" 'Touching' is the very word. I had a hard time finding English equivalents. It is Liu Qing's poem."

"Who? Liu Qing?"

"That classmate of Wen's—her brother Lihua mentioned him—the upstart who sponsored the reunion?"

"Yes. 'The wheel of fortune turns so quickly.' Zhu also mentioned him, saying he was a nobody in high school. Why is his poem suddenly so important to us?"

"Well, a poetry anthology was found in Wen's house. I think I mentioned it to you."

"It is mentioned in the file. Hold on, the revolutionary grinder, the commune factory, the workers polishing the parts with their fingers, and Lili—"

"Now you see. That's why I want to discuss the poem with you tonight," he said. "After parting with you, I called Yu. Liu Qing's poem is in that anthology, and Yu faxed me a copy of it. The poem was first published five years ago in a magazine called *Stars*. Liu worked as a reporter for *Wenhui Daily* then. Like the speaker in the poem, he wrote about a model commune factory in Changle County, Fujian Province. Here is a copy of the newspaper report." He produced a newspaper out of his briefcase. "Propaganda stuff. I had no time to translate it.

"Few bookstores—except in large cities—sell poetry now. It's unimaginable that a poor peasant woman would go all the way from her village to buy a poetry collection."

"Do you believe the poem tells a true story?"

"It's difficult to say how much is true. The visit to Wen's factory, as described in the poem, was coincidental. But Liu used the same metaphor in his newspaper story—*a revolutionary grinder polishing up the spirit of the socialist society*. It could have been part of the reason he quit his job."

"Why? Liu did nothing wrong."

"He should not have written such political baloney, but he did not have the guts to refuse. In addition, he must have felt guilty for having done nothing to help her."

"I think I see your point now." She perched on the edge of the bed, facing him. "If the story in the poem is a true one, Liu did not reveal his identity to her at the time, let alone offer help to her. That's the meaning of the image of the emerald snail crawling at the end. It's Liu's guilt, a symbol of Liu's regret."

"Yes, a snail carries a burden forever. So the moment I finished translating the poem I hurried over."

"What do you intend to do now?" she said.

"We must interview Liu. He may not have spoken to Wen then, but later he must have sent her a copy of the anthology, which she kept. And possibly there were other contacts between them, too."

"Yes, possibly."

"I've talked to people at the *Wenhui Daily*," Chen said. "When Liu quit his job about five years ago and started a construction material company in Shanghai, he got several contracts from the Singapore government for the Suzhou New Industry Zone. Now he has two construction material factories and a timber yard in Suzhou, in addition to his company in Shanghai. I called Liu's home this afternoon. His wife said that he was in Beijing negotiating a deal and would return to Suzhou tomorrow."

"Are we going to Suzhou?"

"Yes. It's a long shot. Party Secretary Li will have the train tickets delivered to the hotel tomorrow morning."

"Party Secretary Li can be so efficient," she said. "How early do we leave?"

"The train leaves at eight. We arrive in Suzhou about nine thirty. Li suggests that we spend a day or two there."

He proposed vacationing as camouflage for their investigation. Li had readily approved of the plan.

"So we will be tourists," she said. "Now, how did it occur to you to connect the poem with our investigation? I'll make you a cup of coffee if you'll tell me. Special coffee beans, from Brazil. A treat."

"You're learning the Chinese way fast. To exchange favors. The very essence of *guanxi*. But it's late. We are leaving early tomorrow."

"Don't worry. We can nap on the train." She took a coffee grinder with a small bag of coffee beans from the closet, and looked for an outlet. "I know you like strong coffee."

"Did you bring this coffee from America?"

"No, I bought it in the hotel. They provide every convenience. Look at the grinder. Krups."

"Things are expensive in the hotel."

"I'll let you in on a secret of mine," she said "We have a traveling allowance, the amount of which depends on the location. For Shanghai, I get ninety dollars a day. I do not consider myself extravagant if I use half a day's allowance to entertain my host."

She found an outlet behind the sofa. The cord was not long enough. She put the grinder on the carpet, plugged it in, and poured the beans into the grinder. Kneeling, she ground the coffee, revealing her shapely legs and feet.

Soon, the room was full of a pleasant fragrance. She poured a cup for him, put a small spoon for sugar, and milk, on the coffee table, and produced a piece of cake out of the refrigerator.

"What about yourself?" he said.

"I don't drink coffee in the evening. I'll have a glass of wine."

She poured white wine for herself. Instead of sitting beside him on the couch, she returned to her position on the carpet.

Sipping at his coffee, he wondered if he should have declined her offer. It was late. They were alone in her room. But the events of the day had been too much for him. He needed to talk. Not just as a police officer, but as a man—with a woman whose company he enjoyed.

He had conducted a thorough search of her hotel room. There had been no secret audio or video or taping equipment hidden. They should be safe. He was not so sure about this, however, after the day's events, after Party Secretary Li's information about Internal Security.

"The best coffee I've ever had," he said.

She raised her glass. "To our success."

"I'll drink to that," he said, clinking his mug against her glass. "About the poem. Oriole's wet footprints disappearing along the street reminded me of a Song dynasty poem."

"A Song dynasty poem?"

"It's about the transience of one's existence in this world— like the footprints left by a crane in the snow, visible only for one moment. Looking at her footprints, I tried to work out some lines. Then I thought of Wen. Among the people in her life, there is also a poet, Liu Qing."

"It might be an important lead," she said.

"At the moment we haven't any others."

"A fresh pot of coffee?"

"I'd rather have a glass of wine," he said.

"Yes. You should not drink too much coffee in the evening."

The fax machine in the room abruptly started emitting a long roll of paper, four or five pages. She took a look at the slightly tacky scroll without tearing it out of the machine.

"Just background information about the smuggling of immigrants. Ed Spencer did some research for me."

"Oh, I learned something from Detective Yu," he said. "The Flying Axes have requested assistance from other triads. One of them may be active in Shanghai."

"No wonder," she said simply.

That might account for the accidents here, perhaps even the raid on the market, but there was still a lot left unanswered.

She took a long drink, emptying her glass. His still remained half full. As she bent to pour herself more wine, he thought he glimpsed the swell of her breasts through the opening of her robe.

"We're leaving early. It is such a long way for you to go back home—"

"Yes, we're leaving early tomorrow morning." He got to his feet.

Instead of moving to the door, he took a couple of steps toward the window. The night breeze was sweet. The reflection of the neon signs lining the Bund rippled on the river. The scene seemed to lie before them like the world in a dream.

"It's so beautiful," she said, coming to his side at the window.

A short spell of silence ensued. Neither said anything. It was enough for him to feel her closeness, looking out to the Bund.

And then he caught sight of the park and the darkling riverfront—*swept with confused alarms of struggle and flight / where ignorant armies clash by night*—a scene experienced by another poet, at another time, in another place, with someone standing by him.

The thought of the unsolved case of the park victim sobered him.

He had not talked to Gu, or to Old Hunter that day.

"I really have to go," he said.

Chapter 26

The train arrived on time. At nine thirty it pulled into Suzhou.

In a side street a few blocks from the railway station, Inspector Rohn took a fancy to a small hotel. With its latticed windows, vermilion-painted verandah, and a pair of stone lions guarding the gate, it gave the appearance of antiquity.

"I do not want to stay in a Hilton here," she said.

Chen agreed. He did not want to notify the Suzhou Police Bureau of their arrival. For a stay of a couple of days, one place was as good as another. And a hotel tucked away in the old section of the city would be a less likely destination for them, should anyone try to trace them. He had exchanged tickets for Hangzhou provided by Party Secretary Li at the station without telling anyone that they were headed for Suzhou.

The hotel was originally a large Shiku-style house, whose façade was covered with old-fashioned designs. A short line of flat colored stones were laid across the minuscule front yard as a walkway. The manager hemmed and hawed, showing no eagerness for their company, and finally admitted, shamefacedly, that the hotel was not meant for foreigners.

"Why?" Catherine asked.

"In accordance with the city tourism regulations, only hotels with three stars can accommodate foreigners."

"Don't worry." Chen produced his I.D. "It's a special situation."

Still, there was only one "high-class room" available, which was assigned to Catherine. Chen had to stay in an ordinary room.

The manager kept apologizing as he led them upstairs to Chen's room first. It had space only for a single hard-board bed. There was nothing else in it. Outside, along the corridor, the manager showed them a couple of public bathrooms: one for men, one for women. Chen would have to make his phone calls from the front desk in the lobby downstairs. Catherine's room was equipped with air-conditioning, telephone, and an adjoining bathroom. There was also a desk with a chair, but both were so small that they looked like they had come from an elementary school. The room was carpeted though.

After the manager excused himself amid profuse apologies, they seated themselves, Chen on the only chair, and Catherine on the bed.

"Sorry about my choice, Chief Inspector Chen," she said, "but you can use this phone."

Chen dialed Liu's home.

A woman answered the phone, speaking with a distinct Shanghai accent. "Liu's still in Beijing. He will be back tomorrow. The airplane arrives at eight thirty in the morning. Would you like to leave a message?"

"I'll call back tomorrow."

Catherine had unpacked. "So what are we going to do?"

"As that Chinese proverb says, we will enjoy ourselves in this earthly paradise. There are many gardens here. Suzhou is known for its garden architecture—pavilions, ponds, grottoes, bridges, all laid out to create a leisurely and comfortable ambiance, which reflected the taste of the scholarly and official class during the Qing and Ming dynasties." Chen produced a Suzhou map. "The gardens are very poetic, with meandering bridges, moss-covered trails, gurgling brooks, fantastic-shaped rocks, ancient messages hanging from the eaves of the vermilion pavilions, all contributing to an organic whole."

"I can no longer wait, Chief Inspector Chen. Choose a destination for me. You're the designated guide."

"We'll visit the gardens, but can you first give your humble guide half a day's leave?"

"Of course. Why?"

"My father's grave is in Gaofeng County. It's not far away, about one hour by bus. I have not visited it for the last few years. So I would like to go there this morning. It's just after the Qingming festival."

"Qingming festival?"

"The Qingming festival comes on April fifth, a day traditionally reserved for worshipping at ancestral graves," he explained. "There are a couple of gardens near here. The well-known Yi Garden is within walking distance. You could visit it this morning. I'll return before noon. Then we can have a Suzhou-style lunch at the Xuanmiao Temple Bazaar. I'll be at your service for the whole afternoon."

"You should go there. Don't worry about me." She then added, "Why is your father's grave in Suzhou—I'm just curious."

"Shanghai's overcrowded. So cemeteries were developed in Suzhou. Some old people believe in Feng Shui—they want a gravesite with a view of mountains and rivers. My father chose the site himself. Then we moved his casket here. I've visited it only two or three times."

"We'll go to the temple in the afternoon, but I don't want to walk by myself in the morning. Such a beautiful city," she said with an impish glint in her blue eyes. *"To whom shall I speak / of this ever enchanting landscape?"*

"Oh, you still remember Liu Yong's lines!" Chen refrained from explaining that the Song dynasty poet had composed those lines to his lover.

"So, can I go with you?"

"You mean to the cemetery?"

"Yes."

"No, I cannot ask you to do that. It is too much of a favor to ask of you."

"Is it against the Chinese custom for me to go there?"

"No, not necessarily," Chen said, deciding not to tell her that one took only his wife or fiancée to a parent's grave.

"Then let's go there. I'll just be a moment." She went to wash and change.

While waiting, he dialed Yu, but got only Yu's voice mail. He left a message and his cell phone number.

She emerged, wearing a white shirt, light gray blazer, and a slim matching skirt. Her hair was pinned back.

He suggested they take a taxi to the cemetery. She wanted to take the bus. "I would like to spend a day like an ordinary Chinese person."

He did not think she could really succeed. Nor did he like the idea of having her bumped about in an overcrowded bus. Luckily, a few blocks from the hotel, they saw a bus with a sign saying CEMETERY EXPRESS. The fare was twice as much, but they got on without any trouble. The bus was not so much packed with passengers, as with what they carried—wicker baskets of cooked dishes, plastic bags of instant food, bamboo briefcases probably laden with paper "ghost" money, and half-broken cardboard boxes bound around with strings and ropes to keep their contents from spilling out. They squeezed into the seat just behind the driver, which afforded them the small space underneath the driver's seat in which to stretch their legs. She handed the driver a pack of cigarettes—a souvenir of her status as a "distinguished guest" at the Peace Hotel. The driver grinned back at them.

Despite the open windows, the air in the bus was stuffy, and the seat's imitation leather covering felt hot. There was a mixed smell of sweating human bodies, salted fish, meat soaked in wine, and every other offering imaginable. Nevertheless, Catherine appeared to be in high spirits, chatting with a middle-aged woman across the aisle, examining other passengers' offerings with great interest. Above the cacophony of voices, a song was broadcast via invisible speakers. The singer, popular in Hong Kong, warbled in a high-pitched voice. Chen recognized the lyrics: a ci poem written by Su Dongpo. It was an elegy for Su's wife, but it could be read in a more general way. Why had the cemetery bus driver chosen that particular ci for the trip? The market economy worked everywhere. Poetry, too, had become a product.

Chief Inspector Chen did not believe in an afterlife but, under the influence of the music, he wished there were one. Would his father recognize him, he wondered. So many years—

Soon they were in sight of the cemetery. Several old women were coming toward them from the foot of the hill. Wearing white towel hoods, they were clothed in dark homespun, even darker somehow than the ravens in the distance. This was a scene he had witnessed during his last visit.

He grabbed her hand. "Let's go quickly."

But it was difficult for her to do so. His father's grave was somewhere halfway up the hill. The path was overgrown with weeds. The paint on the direction signs had faded. Several steps were in bad repair. He had to slow down, pushing his way through the overhanging pines and rambling briars. She nearly stumbled.

"Why are some characters on the tombstones red, and some black?" she asked, as she picked her way carefully among the stones.

"The names in black indicate those already dead, and the names in red indicate those still alive."

"Isn't this bad luck for the living?"

"In China, husband and wife are supposed to be buried together under the same tombstone. So after one's death, the other will have the tombstone erected with the couple's names both engraved on it—one in black, and one in red. When both of them pass away, their children will put their coffins—or cinerary urns—together and repaint all the characters in black."

"This must be a time-honored custom."

"Also a disappearing one. The family structure is no longer so stable here. People get divorced or remarried. Only a handful of old people still follow this tradition."

Their talk was interrupted as the black-attired old women reached them. They must have been in their seventies or even older, though they shuffled their bound feet steadily forward. He was amazed—such old people, moving with such difficulty, on such a hazardous mountain path. They were carrying candles, incense, paper ghost money, flowers, as well as cleaning implements.

One of them wobbled over on her bound feet, pushing a paper model of a "ghost" house at him. "May your ancestors protect you!"

"Oh, what a beautiful American wife!" another exclaimed. "Your ancestors underground are grinning from ear to ear."

"Your ancestors bless you!" the third prayed. "You two have a wonderful future together!"

"You'll make tons of money abroad!" the fourth predicted.

"No." He kept shaking his head at the chorus in Suzhou dialect, which Catherine did not understand, fortunately.

"What are they saying?" she asked.

"Well, lucky words to please us, so we will buy their offerings or give them money." He bought a bouquet of flowers from an old woman. The flowers did not look so fresh. Possibly they had been taken from somebody else's grave. He did not say anything. Catherine bought a bunch of incense.

As he finally located his father's grave, the old women carrying brooms and mops rushed over to clean the tombstone. One of them produced a brush pen and two small cans of paint, and started repainting the characters with red and black paint. This was done as a service, for which he had to pay. It was partially because of Catherine, he thought. Those old women must have assumed he was immensely rich, with an American wife.

He brushed away the remaining dust from the tombstone. She took several pictures. It was thoughtful of her. He would show those pictures to his mother. After sticking the incense in the ground and lighting it, she came to stand beside him, imitating his gesture, with her palms pressed in front of her heart.

What would be the late Neo-Confucian professor's reaction to this sight—his son, a Chinese cop, with an American woman cop?

Closing his eyes, he tried to have a moment of silent communion with the dead. He had let the old man down terribly, at least in one aspect. The continuation of the family tree had been one of his father's highest concerns. Standing by the grave, still a bachelor, the only defense Chief Inspector Chen could make for himself was that in Confucianism, one's responsibility to the country was considered more important than anything else.

This was not, however, the meditative interlude he had expected. The old women started their chorus again. To make things worse, a swarm of mosquitoes buzzed around them, huge, black, monstrous mosquitoes that intensified their bloodthirsty assault to the chorus of the white-haired ones' blessings.

In a short while, he suffered a couple of vicious bites, and noticed Catherine scratching her neck.

She produced a bottle from her handbag and sprayed it on his arms and hands, then rubbed some on his neck. The mosquito spray, an American product, did not discourage the Suzhou mosquitoes. They lingered, buzzing.

Several other old women loomed up from another direction.

They had to leave, he concluded. "Let's go."

"Why in such a hurry?"

"The atmosphere is ruined. I don't think I will have a moment's peace here."

When they reached the bottom of the hill, they ran into another problem. According to the cemetery bus schedule, they would have to wait there for another hour.

"There are several bus stops on Mudu Road, but it would take us at least twenty minutes to reach the nearest one."

A truck pulled up beside them. The driver stuck his head out the window. "Need a lift?"

"Yes. Are you going to Mudu?"

"Come on. Twenty Yuan for you both," the driver said, "but only one can sit inside with me."

"You go ahead, Catherine," he said. "I'll sit in the back."

"No. We'll both sit in the back."

Stepping onto the tire, he swung himself over into the back

of the truck and pulled her up. There were several used cardboard boxes in the flatbed. He turned one inside out and offered it to her as a seat.

"It's the first time for me," she said, cheerfully, stretching out her legs. "When I was a kid, I wanted to sit in the back of a truck just like this. My parents never allowed it."

She slipped off her shoes and rubbed her ankle.

"Still hurts? I'm so sorry, Inspector Rohn."

"Here you go again. Why?"

"The mosquitoes, these old women, the trail, and now the truck ride."

"No, this is the real China. What's wrong?"

"These old women must have cost you a small fortune."

"Don't be too hard on them. There are poor people everywhere. The homeless in New York, for instance. So many of them. I'm not rich, but giving away my change won't bankrupt me."

Her clothes were all rumpled, sweat-soaked, and her shoes were off. Looking at her, seated on a cardboard box, he realized how much more she was than merely vivacious and attractive. She had a radiance.

"It's so kind of you," he said. Still, it was not appropriate for him, as a Party member, to show an American the poverty of China's rural areas, even though she had told him about the homeless in New York. He was anxious to resume his role as a guide. "Look, the Liuhe Pagoda!"

The truck pulled up a few blocks ahead of Guanqian Road, where the Xuanmiao Temple was located. Sticking his head out of the window, the driver said, "I can't go any farther. We're at the center of the city now. The police will stop me for letting people sit in back. Don't worry about catching a bus. You can walk from here to Guanqian Road."

Chen jumped out of the truck first. Bikes were racing by him.

Seeing the hesitation in her eyes, he reached out his arms. She let him lift her down.

The magnificent Taoist temple on Guanqian Road soon came in view. In front of it, they saw a bazaar consisting of food vendors as well as a variety of other booths selling local products, knickknacks, paintings, paper cutouts, and small things not readily available in general stores.

"It's more commercialized than I expected." She gladly accepted a bottle of Sprite he bought for her. "I suppose it's inevitable."

"It's too close to Shanghai to be much different. All the tourists don't help," he said.

They had to purchase entrance tickets to the temple. Through the brass-trimmed red gate, they could see a corner of the flagstone-paved courtyard, packed with pilgrims and wreathed in incense smoke.

She was surprised at the turnout. "Is Taoism so popular in China?"

"If you talk about the number of Taoist temples in China, it is not. It is more influential as a life philosophy. For instance, those performing tai chi in Bund Park are Taoist followers in a secular sense, following the principle of the soft conquering the strong, and the slow beating the fast."

"Yes, yin turning into yang, yang into yin, everything in the process of changing into something else. A chief inspector turning into a tour guide, as well as a postmodernist poet."

"And a U.S. Marshal into a sinologist," he said. "In terms of its religious followers' practice, Taoism may not be that different from Buddhism. Candles and incense are burned in both."

"If you build a temple, worshippers will come."

"You can put it that way. In an increasingly materialistic society, some Chinese people are turning to Buddhism, Taoism, or Christianity for spiritual answers."

"What about Communism?"

"Party members believe in it, but in this transition period, things can be difficult. People don't know what will happen to them the next day. So it may not be too bad to have something to believe in."

"What about you?"

"I believe that China is making progress in the right direction—"

The arrival of a yellow-satin-robed Taoist priest cut short any further statement by Chen.

"Welcome, our reverend benefactors. Would you like to draw a piece?" The Taoist held out a bamboo container, in which were several bamboo sticks, each bearing a number.

"What's this?" she asked.

"A form of fortune telling," Chen said. "Choose a stick. It can tell you what you want to know."

"Really!" She pulled one out. The bamboo stick bore a number: 157

The Taoist led them to a large book on a wooden stand, and turned to the page with the matching number. There was a four-line poem on the page.

Hills upon hills, there seems to be no way out;
The willows shady and flowers bright, another village appears.
Under the heart-breaking bridge, green is the spring water,
Which once reflected a wild-goose-flushing beauty.

"What does the poem mean?" she asked.

"Interesting, but it is beyond me," Chen said. "The Taoist will interpret it for a fee."

"How much?"

"Ten Yuan," the Taoist said. "It will make a difference for you."

"Fine."

"What time period do you want to inquire about—the present or the future?"

"The present."

"What do you want to know?"

"About a person."

"In that case, the answer is obvious." The Taoist broke into an obliging smile. "What you are looking for is right there for you. The first couplet suggests a sudden change at a time when things seem to be beyond help."

"What else does the poem tell?"

"It may pertain to a romantic relationship. The second couplet makes it clear."

"I'm confused," she said, turning to Chen. "You're the one right here for me."

"It is intentionally ambiguous." Chen was amused. "I'm right here, so who do you have to look for? Or it could be about Wen, for all we know."

They started to walk around in the temple, examining the clay idols on cushion-shaped stones—the deities of the Taoist religion. When they were out of the Taoist's hearing, she resumed her questioning. "You are a poet, Chen. Please explain these lines to me."

"What a poem means and what a fortunetelling piece means can be totally different. You've paid for the fortunetelling, so you have to be content with his interpretation."

"What is wild-goose-flushing beauty?"

"In ancient China, there were four legendary beauties, so beautiful that everything else reacted in shame: the bird flushed, the fish dived, the moon hid, and the flower closed up. Later, people used this metaphor to describe a beauty."

They then moved on, strolling into the temple courtyard. She started taking pictures, like an American tourist, he thought. She seemed to be enjoying every minute of it, shooting from many different angles.

She stopped a middle-aged woman. "Could you take a picture for us?" she asked. She stood close to him. Her hair gleaming against his shoulder, she gazed into the camera with the ancient temple in the background.

The bazaar in front of the temple was swarming with people. She spent several minutes looking for exotic but inexpensive souvenirs. Besides several baskets of herbs, which filled the air with a pleasant aroma, she bargained with an old peasant woman displaying tiny bird's eggs, plastic bags of Suzhou tea leaves, and packages of dried mushrooms. At a folk toy booth, he rattled a slithery paper snake on a bamboo stick, a reminder of his childhood.

They chose a table shaded by a large umbrella. He ordered Suzhou-style dumplings, peeled shrimp with tender tea leaves, and chicken and duck blood soup. Between bites, she resumed her questions about the fortunetelling poem.

"The first and the second couplet are both by Lu You, a Song dynasty poet, but from two different poems," he said. "The first is often quoted to describe a sudden change. As for the second, there's a tragic story behind it. In his seventies, when Lu revisited the place where he had first seen Shen, a woman he loved all his life, he wrote the lines, gazing into the green water under the bridge."

"A romantic story," she said, swallowing a spoonful of the chicken and duck blood soup.

Chapter 27

They reached the hotel in the growing dusk.

From her room, Chief Inspector Chen made a phone call to Detective Yu. Aware of Inspector Rohn's presence, Yu did not say much on the phone, except that there would be a new interview tape delivered to Chen.

Then she said she wanted to phone her supervisor.

He excused himself to smoke a cigarette in the corridor.

It was a short conversation. She came out before he finished the cigarette. Looking out at the ancient city in the dusk, she said that her boss suggested she return home. She did not seem eager to comply.

"We may make some progress tomorrow," she said.

"Let's hope so. Maybe the fortunetelling poem will do the trick. I'll take a rest in my room. Tomorrow will be a long day."

"If anything happens, call me." She remembered there was no phone in his room. "Or knock at my door."

"I will." He added, "Maybe we can take a walk this evening."

He went to his room. When he turned on the light, to his surprise, he saw a man sitting there—to be more exact, taking a nap with his back resting against the headboard.

Little Zhou looked up with a start. "I've been waiting for you. Sorry I fell asleep in your room, Chief Inspector Chen."

"You must have waited for a long time. What has brought you here, Little Zhou?"

"Something from Detective Yu. Marked to be delivered to you, ASAP."

Since Qiao's abduction, Chen had made a point of contacting Yu by cell phone, and in an emergency, through Little Zhou, whom Chen trusted.

"You didn't have to come all this way," Chen said. "I will be back at the bureau tomorrow. Nobody knows of your trip to Suzhou?" Chen asked.

"Nobody. Not even Party Secretary Li."

"Thank you so much, Little Zhou. You are taking a great risk for me."

"Don't mention it, Chief Inspector Chen. I'm your man. Everybody knows that in the bureau. Let me drive you back tonight. It's safer in Shanghai."

"No, don't worry. We have something to do here," Chen said. "Let me talk to the hotel manager. There should be another room available. You can return to Shanghai tomorrow morning."

"No, you don't have to. If there's nothing for me to do here, I'm leaving. But first I'll go to the night market for some local products."

"Good idea. Live river shrimps are a must. And Suzhou braised tofu too." He wrote his cell phone number on a card for Little Zhou. "Both you and Lu can call me at this number."

He walked out to the door with Little Zhou. "It's a long drive back to Shanghai. Take care, Little Zhou."

"Two hours. No sweat."

Back in his room, he opened the envelope. It contained a cassette tape with a short introduction from Yu.

Chief Inspector Chen:

Following the interview with Zheng, I found Tong Jiaqing in a hair salon. Tong is a girl in her early twenties, charged with indecent practices on several occasions, though discharged soon afterward each time. The following is the interview with her in one of those private rooms. As you did in the national model worker case, I made an appointment at the salon.

Yu: So you are Tong Jiaqing.

Tong: That's correct. Why do you ask that?

Yu: I am from the Shanghai Police Bureau. Take a look at my card.

Tong: What! A cop. I've done nothing wrong, Officer Yu. Since the beginning of the new year, I've been working here as a law-abiding hairdresser.

Yu: I know what you do. That's not my business. As long as you cooperate by answering my questions, I will not bring any trouble down on you.

Tong: What questions?

Yu: Questions about Feng Dexiang.

Tong: Feng Dexiang? Um, he used to be one of my clients.

Yu: At this hair salon?

Tong: No, at the massage salon in the city of Fuzhou.

Yu: That's where the police charged you several times. So did you see him a lot there?

Tong: That was more than a year ago. He had some sort of small business, trading fake jade bracelets or selling mud-covered crabs. So for a while, about four or five months, he came to the salon once or twice a week.

Yu: Give me the details of his visits.

Tong: Well, you can guess. Do I need to tell you the details? You're recording my statement. It will be used as evidence against me.

Yu: Not if you cooperate. You know Zheng Shiming, don't you? He gave me your address. I'm on a special assignment here.

With your past record, you know how easy it would be to put you back in jail. No one will be able to procure your release this time.

Tong: Don't scare me. I was just one of the massage girls. At a massage salon, you know, there's basic service and full service. A client pays fifty Yuan for basic, but four or five hundred Yuan for full, not including the tip.

Yu: Now at the price of four or five hundred Yuan, Feng came once or twice a week for half a year. That was a lot of money. You must have some expertise. Feng had a small business, as you said. How could he have afforded this?

Tong: I don't know. Those people never tell you what they really do. They only tell you what they want you to do. And then they do whatever they like with their stinking money.

Yu: Did you know that Feng was married?

Tong: A massage girl does not ask such questions. But he told me about it the first night.

Yu: What did he say about his marriage?

Tong: He said he had lost all interest in Wen. A piece of dead meat in bed. No fresh taste or smell. No response. He got those dirty videotapes from Taiwan, for her to do the same hot stuff as in the tapes. She was unwilling, and he punished her.

Yu: A perverted bastard. What kind of punishment?

Tong: He bound her hands and feet, burned her breasts with a candle, struck her body with a piece of firewood, and fucked her like an animal. It's the punishment she deserved, he said—

Yu: Why did he want to tell you all that?

Tong: Because he wanted to do the same things with me. You know what? He used to be a butcher before he became the commune head in the Cultural Revolution. When she bled and screamed like a pig, that turned him on.

Yu: What had she done to deserve punishment?

Tong: He believed that she ruined his career. But for the scandal with her, he could have stayed in power.

Yu: He raped her. How could he have blamed her?

Tong: That's not the way he saw it. He called her the white tiger star in his life.

Yu: Then why didn't he divorce her?

Tong: I think I can guess. Whenever he made some money, he squandered it in places like where I worked. So he wanted to keep something in reserve. A home to go back to, a purse to snatch, a body to abuse.

Yu: I see. You understand him well. When did you last see Feng?

Tong: About a year ago.

Yu: Did he tell you about his plans to go to the United States?

Tong: That's no secret in Fujian. He promised to bring me over when he got there.

Yu: What about his wife?

Tong: He called her trash. Good riddance. I did not believe him. He made me that promise in exchange for free service.

Yu: So there was no change in his feeling toward his wife before his departure?

Tong: No. None at all. It's just because of her pregnancy—

Yu: Now wait a minute, Tong. You just said you have not seen him for a year. How did you know that?

Tong: Well—I heard what other people say.

Yu: Who? Most of the men in his village are gone. You are not telling me the truth, Tong. You are still in contact with Feng, aren't you?

Tong: No, I swear I have nothing to do with him now.

Yu: Let me tell you something. Zheng's a much harder nut to crack, but he cracked when he heard Superintendent Hong's promise to do whatever I wanted. So Zheng told me a lot, and about you too. How once several people had a go at you together, Zheng said, Feng, Blind Ma, Shorty Yin.

Tong: What! Zheng told you that, the thousand-ax-hacked rascal. He was the fourth beast that night.

Yu: That alone would be enough to put you back behind the bars. Group sex is forbidden absolutely. Now I'll tell you what. I'm here in plainclothes. No one knows anything about my visit. Why? I'm working on a case directly under the central government.

Tong: No one knows anything about our talk?

Yu: No one. That's why I arranged to have this talk in a private room. I'll pay you for the full service in front of other people. No one will suspect anything.

Tong: Um, I'll take your word, Officer Yu. I may have something for you, but I did not know anything about Feng's current situation until last week. A gangster came to me.

Yu: A Flying Ax came to you! For what, Tong?

Tong: He asked me the same questions you have just asked.

Yu: What is his name?

Tong: Zhang Shan. He said he's from Hong Kong, but he did not fool me that easily. From Hong Kong indeed, like I'm from Japan. That bastard had a face as thick as a rock wall.

Yu: How did you know? He did not have his residence permit printed on his face.

Tong: I could not give him any information, so he demanded free full service or he would cut my face. Do you think a Hong Kong man would stoop so low? A totally rotten thousand-year-egg.

Yu: Did he tell you anything about Feng?

Tong: In bed, he gave me no rest for half a night. Afterward, he mumbled something about Feng and his wife.

Yu: That may be important. What did he say?

Tong: The organization is really pissed off. They are leaving no stone unturned to dig up his wife.

Yu: What if they find her?

Tong: That depends on Feng.

Yu: What does that mean?

Tong: He did not explain. They will probably hold her hostage. Imprison her in a dungeon. Torture her. Anything you can imagine. If Feng does not cooperate, they will impose the Eighteen Axes, I guess.

Yu: Eighteen Axes?

Tong: Hack her with eighteen blows of an ax. The worst form of the triad's punishment. As a warning to others.

Yu: Now there are only two weeks before the trial. What will they do if they do not find her by then?

Tong: I don't know, but I think they are really worried about something. I have no idea what it is. They won't stop until they get hold of her. At any cost, Zhang said.

Yu: At any cost. I see. Anything else?

Tong: That's all, Officer Yu. A bastard like him does not want to talk much when he is satiated. I did not want to appear interested in Feng. I did not know you would come today.

Yu: Well, if what you have told me is true, you probably won't hear from me again. But if it is not, and I find out, you know what will happen.

Tong: It's nothing but the truth.

Chief Inspector Chen pushed the off button and lit a cigarette.

He was depressed. He had been involved with more sordid cases, but something troubled him about this one. Sitting, resting his head against the hard headboard, he seemed to see exotic patterns of light and shadow dancing on the opposite wall, like a devil-mask dancer in a movie.

He did not like his job.

It more than shocked him that Wen's life had been so horrible. Now he saw why she had not applied for the passport in January. Why should she want to join such a husband? That immediately led to another question. What had brought about her change of mind? For a once-high-spirited girl, "the prettiest leftist," wearing the proud armband of the Red Guard, how could she have chosen to live the rest of her life like a piece of stale meat on a cutting stump, to be carved and cut by a butcher of a husband?

The tape presented a more disturbing question. Again, here was a Hong Kong visitor, rather than a local thug. Tong's judgment was questionable. There's nothing too low for a gangster, whether from Hong Kong or Fujian. But why should the Flying Axes have sent a Hong Kong gangster to approach Tong, a salon girl in Fujian?

What's more, what was the "something" that would bother the gangsters, and make them stop at nothing to find Wen.

Tong might not be a reliable informant. Nevertheless, Chen was struck with an ominous premonition.

Something might be terribly wrong with his earlier hypothesis. He only knew that he was at a critical juncture. One move amiss, and the whole game would be irrecoverably lost.

In a game of *go*, he would change his position by leaving that battle for the time being, to focus on another, or to start a new one. *Tactical repositioning.* After all, he might stage a comeback when the situation changed. So one possible option was for him to close the investigation. Give up.

From Party Secretary Li's point of view, Chief Inspector Chen had already done his job well enough. And Catherine Rohn's supervisor also wanted her to return.

As for Wen Liping, ironic as it might appear, he had to acknowledge that wherever she was, it would probably not be much worse than in Feng's company.

Party Secretary Li was right about one thing. Inspector Rohn's safety was a matter of top priority, for which Chen felt immensely responsible. The gangster had said *at any cost*—that made him shudder. If anything happened to her, he would never be able to forgive himself.

Not merely because of politics.

He had sensed her sympathy earlier in the day. Particularly by his father's grave. No one else had ever accompanied him there. The gesture had a meaning for him. He realized that despite their differences Inspector Rohn had come to mean more to him than a temporary partner.

But it was absurd of him to be contemplating such things with his investigation bogged down in a mire of unanswered questions, inexplicable complications, unpredictable hazards, and with Wen Liping still missing.

Could he really quit now, with what he saw as the national interest at stake, and risk Feng failing to testify against Jia? With the possibility of "eighteen axes" looming for Wen—a pregnant woman, helpless, with no money or job?

The cigarette burned his fingers.

He was seized with an urge. To forget those contradictory thoughts, about Wen, about politics, about himself. He longed for an evening at the Cold Mountains Temple, by the Maple River, with the moon rising, the crow calling, the frosty sky enfolding, the riverside maples swaying, the fishing lights glittering, and the arrival of a guest boat at the stroke of midnight. . . . To lose himself in the world of Tang poetry, for however brief a moment.

As he stepped out of his room, he saw the light still on in Catherine's. But he continued down the stairs to the front desk. There he picked up the phone, then hesitated. Several people were standing around idly. Not far away, another group of people sat in front of a color TV. He put down the receiver and walked into the street.

The city of Suzhou seemed not to have changed much in spite of China's Open Door Policy. Here and there, new apartment buildings appeared amidst old-styled houses, but he failed to find a public phone booth. Walking, he came to the arch of an ancient white stone bridge. He crossed, coming unexpectedly into a brightly lit thoroughfare with a variety of shops. It was like a juxtaposition of different times.

At one corner of the thoroughfare, he saw a post office open. In its spacious hall several people waited by a row of phone booths with glass doors, above each of which a strip showed the relevant city name and phone number. A middle-aged woman looked up, pushed open the door, and picked up the phone inside.

He started to fill out a request form to call Gu. Once more he hesitated. He'd better not reveal his whereabouts to someone like Gu. So he put down Mr. Ma's phone number. Gu might have contacted the old doctor.

After ten minutes, the number he had requested showed up on the screen. He stepped into the booth, closed the door behind him, and picked up the phone.

"It's me, Chen Cao, Mr. Ma. Has Gu contacted you?"

"Yes, he did. I called the bureau. They told me you were in Hangzhou."

"What did Gu tell you?"

"Gu seemed to be really concerned about you, saying that some people, powerful people, are opposing you."

"Who are they?"

"I asked him, but he did not tell me. Instead he asked me

whether I had heard anything about a Hong Kong triad called Green Bamboo."

"Green Bamboo?"

"Yes. I asked several people about them this afternoon. It's an international organization with its headquarters in Hong Kong."

"Anything about its activity in Shanghai?"

"No, nothing so far. I will keep asking. You take care, Chief Inspector Chen."

"I will. You too, Mr. Ma."

As he left the post office, his steps were dragging. Various things appeared to be entangled like bamboo roots under the ground. The Green Bamboo. Chief Inspector Chen had not even heard of them until now.

And he lost his way in the unfamiliar city. After having made a few wrong turns, he came to the Bausu Pagoda Garden. He bought an entrance ticket, though it was too late for him to go into the pagoda.

Strolling aimlessly in the garden, in the hope that some ideas might come to him, he saw a young girl reading on a wooden bench. No more than eighteen or nineteen, she sat quietly with a book in one hand, a pen in the other, and a newspaper spread on the bench. Her lips touched the shining top of the pen, and the bow on her pony tail fluttered like a butterfly on a breath of air. This scene reminded him of his days in Bund Park, years earlier.

What could she be reading there? A poetry collection? He took a step toward the bench before he realized how deluded he was. He saw the title of book: *Market Strategy*. For years, the stock markets had been closed, but now "stock madness" was sweeping the country, even this corner of the ancient garden.

He climbed a small hill and stood on top of it for several

minutes. Not far away, he seemed to hear the murmur of a cascade. He glimpsed, in the distance, a faint flickering light. On this April night, the stars appeared high, bright, whispering to him through memories . . .

Such stars, but not that night, long ago, lost,
For whom I stand tonight, against the wind and frost.

But tonight it was not as bad as in Huang Chongzhe's lines, not as cold. He whistled, trying to pull himself out of his mood. He was not meant to be a poet. Nor was he cut out to be an overseas Chinese making a "grave-sweeping" trip with an American girlfriend—as those old women had imagined. Nor a tourist, wandering about in the city of Suzhou at leisure.

He was a police officer, incognito, conducting an investigation, unable to make a decision until after the next day's interview.

Chapter 28

Early the next morning, they arrived at Liu's residence in a suburb of Suzhou.

Inspector Rohn was amazed at its Western-style grandeur. Liu lived in a magnificent mansion behind substantial walls, forming a sharp contrast to the general image of the city. The iron gate was not locked, so they walked in. The lawn looked as well-kept as a golf course. Beside the driveway stood a marble sculpture of a girl, sitting after a bath, bending her head in thought, her long hair cascading like a waterfall over her breasts.

Chief Inspector Chen pressed the bell; a middle-aged woman came to the door.

Catherine took her to be in the late thirties or early forties, judging by the lines at the corners of her eyes, though they did not detract from her fine features. She was dressed in a purple silk tunic and matching pants, over which she had tied a white embroidered apron. She wore her hair in an old-fashioned bun, but she could still be considered attractive.

It was difficult for Catherine to guess the woman's status in the house. Not a maid, nor the hostess. Liu's wife was in Shanghai.

Ambiguity also appeared in the way she treated her guests. "Please take a seat. General Manager Liu will be back in half an hour. He's just called me from his car. Did you telephone him yesterday?"

"Yes, I did. I'm Chen Cao. Catherine is my American friend."

"Would you like something to drink, tea or coffee?"

"Tea will be fine. Here is my card. Liu and I are both members of the Chinese Writers' Association."

What was up his sleeve, Catherine wondered.

Anything was possible from the enigmatic chief inspector. She decided to let him talk, and she would provide a little echo, as an American friend of his might.

"You have a distinct Shanghai accent," Chen said.

"I was born in Shanghai. I have only come to Suzhou recently."

"You are Comrade Wen Liping, aren't you?" Chen stood up, holding out his hand. "Nice to meet you."

The woman stepped back in alarm.

Catherine was stunned.

This was not the Wen in the photo—a broken woman with a listless expression, but a good-looking, cheerful person with alert eyes.

"How do you know my name? Who are you?"

"I am Chief Inspector Chen of the Shanghai Police. This is Catherine Rohn, an inspector in the United States Marshals Service."

"Did you come here to find me?"

"Yes, we have been looking for you everywhere."

"I'm here to accompany you to the United States," Catherine said.

"No, I am sorry. I'm not going," Wen exclaimed, flustered but determined.

"Don't worry, Wen. Nothing will happen to you. The American police are going to place you in a witness protection program," Chen said. "The snake heads will be put in jail. The gangsters will never be able to find you. The safety of your family is guaranteed."

"Yes, we'll take care of everything," Catherine said.

"I do not know anything about such a program," Wen said in a panic-stricken voice, her hands covering her belly instinctively.

"When you arrive in the United States, our government will help you in a number of ways, providing you with a cash allowance, medical insurance, housing, a car, furniture—"

"How can that possibly be?" Wen cut Catherine short.

"All this is arranged in exchange for your husband's cooperation, his testimony in court against Jia. It's a promise made by our government."

"No. Whatever you promise, I am not going."

"You have been applying for your passport for months," Chen said. "Now both the Chinese and American governments are concerned with your situation. So we have not only taken care of the passport, but your visa is ready, too. Why have you changed your mind?"

"Why am I so important?"

"Your husband has insisted on your going to the United States as the condition of his cooperation. So you see, he is concerned for you."

"Concerned for me?" Wen said. "No, for his son in my belly."

"If you refuse to go," Catherine said, "do you know what will happen to your husband?"

"He is working for your government. I'm not."

"So, now you are staying with another man, a rich upstart, is that it?" Catherine said, "You are condemning your husband to spend his life in prison!"

"Don't say that, Inspector Rohn," Chen intervened in a hurry. "Things may be more complicated. Liu—"

"No."

Lowering her head, Wen sat still, like a plant withered by frost. She spoke, murmuring with trembling lips, "You can say whatever you want about an ill-fated woman like me. But don't say anything against Liu."

"Liu's a good man. We understand," Chen said. "Inspector Rohn is just anxious about your safety."

"I have said I will not go, Chief Inspector Chen," Wen said resolutely. "I will not say anything more."

Several minutes of awkward silence followed. Wen merely hung her head, in spite of Chen's repeated effort to renew the conversation. Only once did she look up at the clock on the wall, her eyes brimming with tears.

The silence was broken by hurried footsteps outside the door, a key turning in the lock, and a sob from Wen.

In came a middle-aged man. He was dark-haired, slim, austere-looking, perhaps in his early forties. He had an air of prosperous distinction and wore an expensive suit. The only thing that did not fit his image was a gigantic live carp dangling from his hand, about two feet long, its mouth pierced with a piece of wire, still twitching, its tail almost touching the carpet.

"What's happening here?" he said.

Wen stood up, took the carp to carry it to the kitchen sink, and returned to his side. "They want me to go to the United States. The American officer insists that I leave with her."

"So you are Mr. Liu Qing?" Catherine handed him her card. "I am Catherine Rohn, Inspector, U.S. Marshals Service. This is Chief Inspector Chen Cao of the Shanghai Police Bureau."

"Why should she go with you?" Liu demanded.

"Wen's husband is there," Chen said. "At his request, Inspector Rohn has come here to escort her to him. Wen will be put in a witness protection program there. She will be safe. You should persuade her to leave with Inspector Rohn."

"Witness protection program?"

"Yes, she may not know how the program works," Chen said. "The program has been arranged for her family's protection."

Liu did not respond at once. Instead, he turned to Wen, who met his gaze without saying a word. Liu nodded, as if having read the answer in her eyes.

"Comrade Wen Liping is my guest. Whether she wants to leave or stay, is really up to her to decide," Liu said. "No one can force her to go anywhere. Not anymore."

"You have to let her go, Mr. Liu," Catherine said. "Her husband has made the request to the U.S. government. The Chinese government has agreed to cooperate."

"I am not preventing her from leaving, absolutely not," Liu retorted. "Go ahead and ask her."

"No, nobody is keeping me here," Wen said. "I want to stay."

"Have you heard her, Inspector Rohn?" Liu said. "If her husband broke your law, he should be punished. No one has any objection to that, but how can the U.S. government determine a Chinese citizen's fate against her own will?"

Catherine was not prepared for such hostility from Liu. "She can start a new life in the United States. A better life."

"Don't think each and every Chinese wants to crawl to the United States," Liu snapped.

"I have to inform the Chinese authorities of your attitude. You are obstructing justice," she said.

"Go ahead. You Americans are always talking about human rights. She has the right to stay where she wants. Gone are the days when you could order Chinese people around. Here is my attorney's number." Liu stood up, giving her a card, then gesturing toward the door. "Now please leave, both of you."

"Chief Inspector Chen, your government has promised full cooperation." Catherine also rose to her feet. "The local police bureau has to act."

"Calm down, both of you," Chen said, turning to Liu. "Inspector Rohn has a point, and you have one, too. It's understandable that people look at things from their own perspectives. Can we have a talk, just you and I?"

"There's nothing to talk about, Chief Inspector Chen." Liu thought for a moment. "How did you find her?"

"Through your poem. 'The Fingertip Touching.' I, too, belong to the Writers' Association."

"So you are Chen Cao." Liu said. "I thought the name was familiar, but it does not change anything."

"Have you heard of Wu Xiaoming's case?" Chen asked.

"Yes, it was in the headlines last year. That HCC bastard."

"I was in charge of it. It was a difficult case. I pledged that justice would be served. And I kept my word. As a poet as well as police officer, I give you my word. I will not force you or Wen to do anything. Let's have a talk, and then you can judge whether she should discuss her options with me."

"Chief Inspector Chen," Catherine protested.

"Hasn't she made herself clear enough?" Liu said. "Why waste any more time?"

"Wen should decide for herself, but it will not be a sound decision unless she has a good grasp of the situation. Otherwise she will make a decision you are both going to regret. Some of the factors involved are serious, I assure you, and neither of you are aware of them. You won't let her run headlong into danger, will you?"

"Then talk to her," Liu said.

"Do you think she will listen to me right now?" Chen said. "You are the only one she'll listen to."

"Are you going to keep your word, Chief Inspector Chen?"

"Yes, I will write a report to the bureau to explain her decision, whatever it may be."

Catherine wondered at his approach. The Chinese authorities had never seemed enthusiastic. They had found Wen, but now Chen did not appear very anxious to make her leave China. Why had Chen brought her with him then?

"Fine, let's talk in my study upstairs," Liu said to Chen before he turned to Wen Liping. "Don't worry. Have lunch with the American. No one will force you to do anything."

Chapter 29

Liu's office was far more spacious than Chen's at the Shanghai Police Bureau. More luxuriously furnished, too: a huge U-shaped steel desk, a swiveling leather recliner, several leather armchairs, and shelves filled with hardcover books. There was a mini-tower computer with a laser printer on the desk. Liu seated himself in an armchair and asked Chen to sit in another.

Chen noticed several miniature gilded Buddhist statues on the shelves. Each of them was clothed in a colorful silk robe. It reminded him of a scene he had witnessed years earlier in his mother's company, in an ivy-mantled temple in Hangzhou, of a gilded clay image of Buddha sitting high in the hall, while pilgrims in miserable rags knelt in front of the gold and silver silk robes. The ceremony was called "Donning Buddha," his mother explained. The more expensive the robe, the more devoted the pilgrim. Buddha would then produce miracles in accordance with the donor's devotion. Following his mother's example, he lit a stick of incense and made three wishes. These wishes he had long since forgotten, but not the puzzlement he had experienced.

Believe, and anything's possible. Chief Inspector Chen did not know whether Liu believed in these statues' powers or kept them merely for decoration, but Liu seemed to be convinced that he was doing the right thing.

"Sorry about my temper," Liu said. "She does not understand how things are in China, that American officer."

"It's not her fault. I learned some details about Wen's life as late as last night. Inspector Rohn does not know about them. That was why I wanted to have a talk between ourselves."

"If you know what a hell of life she had with that bastard of a husband, do you still insist on sending her to him? You cannot imagine how we admired her in high school. She led us in everything, her long plait fluttering on her bosom, and her cheeks rosier than the peach blossom in the spring breeze . . . God, why should I tell you all this?"

"Please tell me as much as you can. So I can write a detailed report to the bureau," Chen said, taking out a notebook.

"Fine, if that's what you want," Liu said in bafflement. "Where shall I start?"

"From the beginning, when you first met Wen."

Liu entered high school in 1967, at a time when his father, an owner of a perfume company before 1949, was being denounced as a class enemy. Liu himself was a despicable "black puppy" to his schoolmates, among whom he saw Wen for the first time. They were in the same class. Like others, he was smitten by her beauty, but he never thought of approaching her. A boy from a black family was not considered worthy to be a Red Guard. That Wen was a Red Guard cadre magnified his inferiority. Wen led the class in singing revolutionary songs, in shouting the political slogans, and in reading *Quotations from Chairman Mao*, their only textbook at the time. So she was really more like the rising sun to him, and he was content to admire her from afar.

That year his father was admitted to a hospital for eye surgery. Even there, among the wards, Red Guards or Red Rebels swarmed like raging wasps. His father was ordered to stand to say his confession, blindfolded, in front of Chairman Mao's picture. It was an impossible task for an invalid who was unable to see or move. So it was up to Liu to help, and first, to write the confession speech on behalf of the old man. It was a tough job for a thirteen-year-old boy, and after spending an hour with a splitting headache, he produced only two or three lines. In desperation, clutching his pen, he ran out to the street, where he saw Wen Liping walking with her father. Smiling, she greeted him, and her fingertips brushed against the pen. The golden top of the pen suddenly began to shine in the sunlight. He went back home and finished the speech with his one glittering possession in the world. Afterward, he supported his father in the hospital, standing with him like a wooden prop, not yielding to humiliation, reading for him like a robot. It was a day that contained his brightest and blackest moment.

Their three years in high school flowed away like water, ending in the flood of the educated youth movement. He went to Heilongjiang Province with a group of his schoolmates. She went to Fujian by herself. It was on the day of their departure, at the Shanghai railway station, that he experienced the miracle of his life, as he held the red paper heart with her in the loyal character dance. Her fingers lifted up not only the red paper heart, but also raised him from the black puppy status to an equal footing with her.

Life in Heilongjiang was hard. The memory of that loyal character dance proved to be an unfailing light in that endless tunnel. Then the news of her marriage came, and he was devastated. Ironically, it was then that he first thought seriously about his own future, a future in which he imagined he would be able to help her. And he started to study hard.

Like others, Liu came back to Shanghai in 1978. As a result of the self-study he had done in Heilongjiang, he passed the college entrance examination and became a student at East China Normal University the same year. Though overwhelmed with his studies, he made several inquiries about her. She seemed to have withdrawn. There was no information about her. During his four years at college, never once did she return to Shanghai. After graduation, he got a job at *Wenhui Daily*, as a reporter covering Shanghai industry news, and he started writing poems. One day, he heard that *Wenhui* would run a special story about a commune factory in Fujian Province. He approached the chief editor for the job. He did not know the name of Wen's village. Nor did he really intend to look for her. Just the idea of being somewhere close to her was enough. Indeed, *there's no story without coincidences*. He was shocked when he stepped into the workshop of the factory.

After the visit, he had a long talk with the manager. The manager must have guessed something, telling him that Feng was notoriously jealous, and violent. He thought a lot that night. After all those years, he still cared for her with unabated passion. There seemed to be a voice in his mind urging: *Go to her. Tell her everything. It may not be too late.*

But the following morning, waking up to reality, he left the village in a hurry. He was a successful reporter, with published poems and younger girlfriends. To choose a married woman with somebody else's child, one who was no longer young and beautiful—he did not have the guts to face what others might think.

Back in Shanghai, he turned in the story. It was his assignment. His boss called it poetic. "The revolutionary grinder polishing up the spirit of our society." The metaphor was often quoted. The story must have been reprinted in the Fujian local newspapers. He wondered if she had read it. He thought about writing to her, but what could he say? That was when he started to conceive the poem, which was published in *Star* magazine, selected as one of the best of the year.

In a way, the incident was like a grinder rasping at his illusions about a career in journalism and contributed to his decision to quit. His timing could not have been better. In the early eighties, few made up their minds to let go of an iron rice bowl—a job in a state-run company. That gave him a good start, and the *guanxi* he had accumulated as the *Wenhui* reporter helped a lot, too. He made tons of money. Then he met Zhenzhen, a college student. She fell in love with him. They got married, had a daughter the following year, and his business further expanded. He had no time for poetry by the time the anthology came out. On impulse, he sent Wen a copy with his business card enclosed. There was no response. He was not surprised.

On one occasion, he asked a Fujian businessman to take to her three thousand Yuan anonymously. She would not accept the money. Engaged in one business battle after another, he had no time for sentiment. He thought he had forgotten about her.

He was astonished when, several days earlier, she suddenly walked into his office. She had changed a lot; she was hardly different from an ordinary peasant now. In his mind's eyes, however, she remained what she had been at sixteen, the same oval face, the same infinite tenderness in her eyes, and the same slender fingers that had held up the red paper heart. It did not take him a minute to make up his mind. She had helped him at the darkest moment of his life. Now it was his turn to help her.

Liu paused to take a drink of his tea.

"So to you," Chen said, "she has become an idea—a symbol of your lost youth. It does not matter that she is no longer young or beautiful."

"The difference in her appearance makes it all the more touching."

"All the more romantic, too." Chen nodded. "What did she tell you about herself?"

"That she had to stay away from the village for a few days."

"Did you ask her why?"

"She said that she did not want to join Feng in the United States, but she was afraid she had no choice."

"What did that mean?" Chen inquired. "If she had no choice, why should she have come all the way to you?"

"I did not press her. She broke down a couple of times during our talk. I think it's about her pregnancy."

"So she never really explained."

"She must have her reasons. Perhaps she had to think about her future, and she could not do so in the village."

"Has she spoken to you about her plans?"

"No, she hasn't. She does not seem in a hurry to leave." Liu added reflectively, "Married to such a bastard as Feng, her change of mind would not be surprising to me."

"Well—" Chen guessed that it would be probably useless to push Liu any more in that direction. She could have stayed here without having to make any explanation. "Let me tell you something she has not told you. She fled from the village because she got a phone call from Feng, saying her life was in danger from gangsters."

"She did not tell me that. I did not ask her, and she did not have to."

"It's understandable that she did not tell you everything, but we know she came to you with the intention of staying for a few days—not to think, but to hide from the local triad."

"I'm glad she thought of me in her need." Liu lit a cigarette.

"According to our information, she was supposed to call Feng, her husband, as soon as she found a safe place. So far she has not done so. Now she won't join him even if we guarantee her safety. So she must have made her decision."

"She can stay as long as she likes," Liu said. "Do you suppose she will have a good life there?"

"A lot of people think so. Look at the long line waiting for visas at the American Consulate in Shanghai. Not to mention those people like her husband who sneak out."

"A good life with that bastard?"

"But he is still her husband, isn't he? And if she remains here—with you, what will others think?"

"What matters is what she thinks," Liu said. "When she came to me in need, the least I could do was to shelter her."

"You have done a lot for her. I've seen her passport picture. She looks so different today. Almost like another woman."

"Yes, she's been resurrected. Too romantic a word, you will say."

"No. It is the very word, except that we are not living in a romantic age."

"Romance is not something out there, Chief Inspector Chen. It is in your mind," Liu said, shaking his head. "I've told you what I know, as you have requested. What do you want to tell me?"

"Let me level with you, Liu," Chen said, despite the knowledge that he could not. "I admire your intention to help her, so I would like to say something personal."

"Please, go ahead."

"You're playing with fire."

"What do you mean?"

"She is aware of your feelings for her, isn't she?"

"I liked her—as early as in high school. It was such a long time ago. I do not have to erase the past."

"But your feelings are the same, whether for the queen in high school, or a middle-aged woman pregnant with another man's child," Chen said. "You are Mr. Big Bucks and a lot of women would fall for you head over heels. Let alone after what

you have done for her. She cannot help returning your affec-
tion."

"I'm afraid I do not see your point, Chief Inspector Chen."

"No, you do not see it. As long as you can indulge yourself
in reliving your high-school dream, treating her as part of your
memory, and as long as she is content with being your insub-
stantial dream stuff, existing only in your remembrance of the
past, things may work out between you two. But in time, she
will have recovered enough to be a real woman. Flesh and
blood. So on a romantic evening, she may throw herself into
your arms. What shall you do?" Chen grew sarcastic in spite of
himself. "Will you say no? That will be most cruel. If you say
yes, what about your family?"

"Wen knows I'm married. I don't think she will do that."

"You don't think so? So you'll let her stay as an ex-
schoolmate for months, for years. Yes, you are happy to help.
But will she be happy when she has to suppress her feelings all
the time?"

"Then what the hell am I supposed to do? Turn her away?
Send her to the husband who abused her?" Liu retorted angrily.
"Or let some gang chase her around like a rabbit?"

"That is what I want to discuss with you."

"What?"

"The threat from the gangsters. They are frantically searching
for her at this very moment. Whatever the police bureau's reaction to my report, and I have to make a report, you know
that, I'm sure the gang will soon learn that she's staying here
with you."

"How?" Liu demanded "Will the police pass the information
to the gangsters?"

"No. But the triads have inside connections. Just as they have
learned about Feng's deal, they will get wind of Wen's

whereabouts. During the last few days, Inspector Rohn and I have been followed everywhere"

"Really, Chief Inspector Chen!"

"On the first day, Inspector Rohn was nearly run down by a motorcycle. On the second, a staircase broke down as we were leaving. On the third, a few hours after our visit to a pregnant Guangxi woman, a gang abducted her, mistaking her for Wen. Detective Yu was almost poisoned in a Fujian hotel. Finally, the day before we came to Suzhou, we were almost caught in a police raid set up to entrap us at the Huating Market."

"Are you sure theses incidents were all attributable to gangsters?"

"These were no coincidences. They have ears inside the police both in Shanghai and Fujian. The situation is serious."

Liu nodded. "They are infiltrating the business world, too. Several companies here have hired gangsters to collect their debts."

"You see the point, Liu. According to the latest information I've got, the gangsters will not let her alone even after the trial, whether Feng cooperates or not."

"Why? I'm confused."

"Don't ask me why. All I know is that they will do whatever it takes to ferret her out. To make an example of her. And they'll succeed. It's a matter of time. She simply deludes herself thinking things will work out if she stays with you here."

"As a chief inspector, can't you try to do anything for her, a pregnant woman?"

"I wish I could, Liu. Do you think it's easy for me to admit how helpless I am—a pathetic example of a policeman? Nothing would make me happier than if I could do something for her."

All his frustration came out in his voice. For a cop, it was

more than a simple matter of loss of face to concede his help-
lessness, but he could see the response in Liu's eyes.

"So if you are going to take this into consideration," Chen
continued earnestly, "you can see that it is really in her interest
for her to leave. There is no way you can protect her here for
much longer."

"But how I can let her go to him, only to be abused for the
rest of her life."

"No, I don't think that she will let Feng go on abusing her.
The last few days have made a difference. Resurrected—that's
your word. She has gotten on a new footing, I believe." Chen
added, "Besides, Inspector Rohn will be in charge there. She is
going to act in Wen's interests. I will make sure of it."

"So we are coming back to where we started. Wen has to
leave."

"No. We have a better understanding of the situation. So I'll
try to explain to Wen, and she can decide for herself."

"All right, Chief Inspector Chen," Liu said. "You talk to
her."

Chapter 30

Chief Inspector Chen and Liu Qing emerged from the study
and entered the living room, where Inspector Rohn and Wen
were sitting, waiting in silence.

On the dining room table, however, Chen noticed a difference. There was an impressive array of dishes, among which a

gigantic soy-sauce-braised carp lay with its head and tail sticking out of a willow-patterned platter. Possibly it was the very one dangling from Liu's hand not too long ago. It could not have been easy to prepare a live carp of this size. The other dishes looked tantalizing too. One of them, the pinkish river shrimp stir-fried with green tea leaves, seemed to be still steaming.

There was a plastic apron on the chair by Inspector Rohn. She had probably helped in the kitchen.

"Sorry to keep you waiting so long," Liu said to Wen. "Chief Inspector Chen wants to have a talk with you."

"Haven't you spoken to him?"

"Yes, but it's up to you to decide. He says you should have a full picture of the situation. It may be very important," Liu said. "He also has to hear the decision in your own words."

That was not what Wen had expected to hear. Her shoulders shook uncontrollably, then she said without raising her head. "If you think that it is important."

"Then I'll be waiting for you in the study upstairs."

"What about your carp? The fish will get cold. It's your favorite."

It was something small, yet enormous, Chen observed. Wen actually thought about Liu's favorite dish at such a moment. Did she realize that this could be the last meal she was going to cook for him?

"Don't worry, Wen. We will warm it up afterward," Liu said. "Chief Inspector Chen has promised that he will not force you to make any decision. If you decide to stay, you will always be welcome here."

"So let's have a talk, Wen," Chen said.

As soon as Liu left them, Wen broke down. "What has he said to you?" Her voice was barely above a whisper as she took in deep breaths.

"The same as he has said to you."

"I've nothing to add," Wen said stubbornly, her face covered in her hands. "You can say whatever you want."

"As a cop, I cannot say whatever I want to the police bureau. I have to explain why you refuse to leave, or people will not let the matter drop."

"That's right, Wen. We need to know your reason." Catherine joined in, handing Wen a paper napkin for her tears.

"The fact of your staying with Liu here also calls for some explanation," Chen continued. "If people don't understand, they will come down hard on Liu. You do not want anything to happen to him, do you?"

"How can they blame him? It's my own decision." Wen choked, burying her tear-streaked face in her hands again.

"They can. As a chief inspector, I know how unpleasant things can get for him. This is a joint investigation by China and America. It is not just in your interest, but also in Liu's, for you to talk to us."

"What should I say?"

"Well, start from the time when you graduated from high school," he said, "so that I'll have a comprehensive picture."

"Do you really want to know what I have suffered all these years—" Wen could hardly go on with tears trembling in her eyes, "with that monster?"

"It may be painful for you to talk about it, we understand, but it is important." Catherine poured a cup of water for Wen, who nodded her thanks.

The two of them seemed to be on better terms, Chen observed. He did not know what they had talked about. Wen's earlier hostility toward Catherine was largely gone. There was a fresh Band-Aid on Catherine's finger. She had certainly been helping in the kitchen.

So Wen started to narrate in a mechanical voice, as if she were telling a story about somebody else, her face expressionless, her eye vacant, her body occasionally racked with silent sobs.

In 1970, when the educated youth movement swept all over the country, Wen was only fifteen. Upon her arrival at Changle Village in Fujian, however, she found it impossible to squeeze into the small hut with her relative's three-generation family. As she was the only educated youth in the village, the Revolutionary Committee of the Changle People's Commune, headed by Feng, assigned to her an unused tool room adjacent to the village barn. There was no electricity or water, nor any furniture except a bed in the room, but she believed in Mao's call to young people to reform themselves through hardship. Feng turned out not to be, however, the poor-and-lower-middle-class-peasant of Mao's theory.

Feng started by asking her to talk in his office. As the number-one Party cadre, he was in the position to give political talks, supposedly in an effort to reeducate young people. She had to meet him three or four times a week, with the door locked, Feng sitting like a monkey in human clothes, his hands pawing at her over the red-covered copy of *Quotations from Chairman Mao*. And what she had dreaded happened one night. Feng broke into her room from the barn. She struggled, but he overpowered her. Afterward, he came almost every night. No one dared to say anything about it in the village. He had not thought about marrying her, but upon learning that she was pregnant, he changed his mind. He had no child from his first wife. Wen was desperate. She thought about abortion. The commune clinic was under his control. She thought about running away. There was no bus transportation at the time. Villagers had to ride a commune tractor for miles to the nearest bus stop. She thought about committing suicide, but she could not bring herself to do so when she felt the baby kicking inside her.

So they got married under a portrait of Chairman Mao. "A

revolutionary marriage," as reported by a local radio station. Feng did not bother to have a marriage certificate. For the first few months, she was tempting, young, educated, from the big city—something for his sexual satisfaction. Soon he lost interest. After the baby was born, he became abusive toward her.

She realized there was no use struggling. Feng was so powerful in those years. At first, occasionally, she still dreamed of somebody coming to her rescue. Soon she gave up. In the cracked mirror she saw she was no longer what she had been. Who would take pity on peasant woman with a sallow, wrinkled face, and a baby bundled on her back as she plowed with an ox in the rice paddy. She came to terms with her fate by cutting herself off from the people in Shanghai.

In 1977, after the end of the Cultural Revolution, Feng was removed from his position. Spoiled by the power he had enjoyed, he would not work like a peasant. She had to support the family. What's worse, the perverted monster now had all his time and energy free for abusing her. And a reason, too. Among other things, he had been accused of dumping his first wife and seducing an educated youth. He attributed his downfall to that and wreaked his fury on her. When he became aware of her intention to divorce him, he threatened to kill her and her son. He was capable of anything, she knew. So things went on as before. In the early eighties, he started to stay away from home frequently—on "business," though she never knew what he was really up to. He earned little. The only things he brought home were toys for his son. After the death of their child, things went from bad to worse. He had other women and came home only when he was broke.

She was not surprised that Feng announced he was leaving for the United States. If anything, it was rather surprising that he had not gone earlier. He did not talk to her about his plans. She was a worn-out rag he was going to discard anyway. Last

November, he stayed at home for two weeks. She found herself pregnant. He had her take a test. When it showed that she was carrying a boy, he was a changed man. He told her about his trip and promised that he would send for her when he was settled in the United States. He wanted her to start a new life there with him.

She understood this sudden change. Feng was no longer young. It might be his last chance to have a child. Hers, too. So she asked him to postpone the trip. He would not. He did make a phone call home shortly after his arrival in New York. After several weeks' unexplained silence, he called again to tell her that he was trying to get her out. He wanted her to apply for a passport. She was confounded. Wives left behind usually had to wait for years. Sometimes they, too, had to be smuggled illegally. While waiting for a passport, she got a telephone call that alarmed her and she fled to Suzhou.

It was a long narrative, and difficult to follow, as from time to time, Wen was choked by emotion. Still, she went on resolutely, sparing them no painful details. Chen understood. Wen was catching at her last shred of hope: that the cops would let her stay after hearing a detailed account of her miserable life with Feng. Chen grew more and more uncomfortable. He could write his report to the bureau, describing her misery as he had promised, but he knew that it would be useless.

Inspector Rohn was more visibly disturbed. She rose to make another cup of tea for Wen. Several times she seemed on the verge of saying something, but she swallowed her words.

"Thank you, Wen, but I still need to ask you a couple of questions," Chen said. "So it was in January that he asked you to apply for a passport."

"Yes, January."

"You did not ask how things were with him in the United States, did you?"

"No, I did not."

"I see," he said. "Because you did not want to go there."

"How do you know?" Wen stared at him.

"He wanted you to leave in January, but according to our record, you did not start applying for your passport until mid-February. Why did you change your mind?"

"Oh, I hesitated at first, then I thought of my baby," Wen said with a slight catch in her voice. "It would be too hard for him to grow up without a father, so I changed my mind and started the application process—in February. Then I got that call from him."

"Did he make any further explanation in that last call?"

"No. He just said that somebody was after me."

"Did you know who that 'somebody' was?"

"No, I did not. But I guess he must have had some quarrel about money with the gang. The boat people have to pay a large sum to those thugs. It's an open secret in the village. Our neighbor Xiong failed to mail money back due to a car accident in New York, and his wife went into hiding because she was unable to pay his debts. The gangsters got hold of her in no time. They forced her into prostitution to pay them back."

"The Fujian police did not do anything?" Catherine asked.

"The local police wear the same pants as the Flying Axes. So I had to run far, far away. But where? I did not want to go back to Shanghai. The gang might be able to trace me there. I should not bring trouble to my people."

"How did you decide to come to Suzhou?"

"At first I did not have any specific place in mind. While trying to pack a few things, I came across the anthology with Liu's business card in it. There seemed to be no possibility of tracing me to him. No contact between us since high school. No one could have guessed that I would turn to him for help."

"Yes, that made sense," Catherine said. "The first time you saw him again was on his visit to the factory?"

"I did not even recognize him during his visit. I had not much of an impression of him in high school. He was very quiet. I did not remember him talking to me at all. Nor the loyal character dance described in the poem. But for the poem he sent me, I would not have imagined that it had meant so much to him."

"It did." Chen said. "You must have realized the visitor's identity when you got the anthology."

"Yes. All those years came rushing back. In the biographical sketch, I learned that he had become a poet and reporter. I was happy for him, but I did not have any illusions about myself. Nothing but a pathetic object for his poetic imagination, I knew. I kept the book, and his card hidden in it, as a souvenir of my lost years. I never thought about contacting him," she said, wringing her fingers. "I would rather die than go begging to anybody but for the sake of the baby."

" 'Folk east of the river,' " he murmured.

"I had never expected he would help me so much. He's a very busy man, but he took a day off to accompany me to the hospital. He insisted on shopping for things for me, including baby clothes. And he also promised I could stay here as long as I like."

"I understand." Chen repeated after a pause, "I understand the relationship between you, but what will other people think?"

"Liu says that he does not care what other people think," Wen said with her head hung so low, it looked as if her neck were broken. "Why should I care?"

"So you have decided to stay on here with Liu?"

"What do you mean, Chief Inspector Chen?"

"Well, what's your plan for the future?"

"I want to raise my son by myself."

"Where? Liu's wife has not yet learned about your presence here, has she? It is so close to Shanghai. She may drop in any day. What will she make of this arrangement?"

"No, I will not stay here for long. Liu will rent an apartment for me for the next few months. As soon as my baby is born, I'm planning to leave."

"As long as the gangsters are still lurking about, I don't see how you can be safe anywhere. Any move you make, whether back to Fujian or to Shanghai, may bring them down on you."

"I won't go far away. I'll stay in the area. Liu may find a job for me," Wen said. "Liu has a lot of friends in Suzhou. It will work out, Chief Inspector Chen."

"The gang will find you." He lit a cigarette, then stubbed it out after one puff. "It's a matter of time."

"No one knows anything about me. Not even my real name. Liu has made up a story about me, saying I am his cousin."

Chen said, "This is a matter of national interests. I have to make a report to the police bureau. Sooner or later, the gang will have a copy of that report."

"I don't understand, Chief Inspector Chen."

"There may well be a connection between the gang and the Fujian police, as you are aware."

He noticed the astonishment on Catherine Rohn's face. Party Secretary Li had insisted on his holding the Americans responsible for the leaks. Chen would worry about Li's reaction—and hers—later.

"So you cannot do anything for me?"

"To be honest, I have to say we cannot guarantee your safety. You know only too well how powerful those gangsters are. In fact, Liu agrees with my analysis of the situation. What's more, once they find you, it will surely get Liu into trouble, too. You know what they are capable of."

"Do you think I should leave because of Liu, Chief Inspector Chen?" Wen said slowly, looking up at him.

"As a cop, my answer is yes. Not only the Flying Axes, but the government will bring pressure to bear upon him."

"It's a decision," Catherine said, "in the interests of the two countries."

"Liu cannot win with both the government and the triads against him," Chen said. "And his wife would never forgive him for giving up everything for another woman."

"You don't have to go on." Wen stood up with resolve in her eyes.

"Liu does not want you to leave, because he is concerned about you." Chen continued. "I am too. I'll keep in close touch with Inspector Rohn. Feng will not be able to bully you like before. If there is anything Inspector Rohn can do for you, I'll make sure she does it."

"Yes, I will do my best to help you," Catherine said, grasping Wen's hand. "Trust me."

"All right. I'll leave," Wen said hoarsely. "But I want you, Chief Inspector Chen, to guarantee that nothing will happen to Liu."

"Yes, I guarantee it," he said. "Comrade Liu has done a great service by protecting you. Nothing will happen to him."

"There is one thing I can do," Catherine said. "I will assign you a special post office box number. You cannot write to anyone directly, but you can write to this number, and your letters will be forwarded to Liu or anyone else. And you will receive his, too."

"One more thing, Inspector Rohn and Chief Inspector Chen. I must go back to Fujian before I leave China."

"Why?"

"I left some papers behind in my hurry. And the poetry collection."

"We'll have Detective Yu bring them to Shanghai," Chen said.

"I have to go to my son's grave," Wen said in a voice that seemed to leave no room for further argument. "For a last look."

Chen hesitated. "We may not have enough time, Wen."

"She wants to say good-bye to her son," Catherine intervened. "It's only human nature for a mother to want to bid farewell to her son."

He did not want to appear cold-blooded, though this seemed excessively sentimental to him. He refrained from saying anything more. The very unreasonableness of Wen's request made it intriguing.

Chapter 31

"Where are we going now?" Catherine Rohn asked Chen in the taxi.

"The Suzhou Police Bureau. I called their director. If Wen had decided to stay, Liu could have whisked her away. I had to call on the local cops for help, to put some men outside his place." He added, "And for their protection, too."

"So you're not that trusting even of a fellow poet?"

He did not respond to her question. "We'd better leave Suzhou as soon as possible. Have you heard of the proverb 'There can be many dreams in a long night.' "

"No."

"It's like an English one—'There's many a slip betwixt the cup and the lip.' If we must go to Fujian, I want to take Wen there today. Anything is possible with those gangsters. To get the earliest train or airplane tickets, we need the help of the local police."

"She told me a lot about her life while you were with Liu upstairs. I feel terribly sorry for Wen. That's why I supported her request, Chief Inspector Chen."

"I understand," he said. Suddenly he felt exhausted, and he spoke little the rest of the way.

The moment they entered the reception room of the Suzhou Police Bureau, Director Fan Baohong burst in. "You should have informed us earlier of your visit, Chief Inspector Chen."

"We arrived only yesterday, Director Fan. This is Inspector Catherine Rohn, of the U. S. Marshals Service."

"Welcome to Suzhou, Inspector Rohn. It's a great honor to meet you."

"I'm so happy to meet you, Director Fan."

"It must take an important investigation to bring both of you to Suzhou. We'll do whatever we can do here to assist you."

"It's a sensitive international case, so I cannot give you the details," Chen said. "Are your people still stationed outside Liu's residence?"

"Yes, Chief Inspector Chen."

"Keep them there. I have to ask you another favor. We need three tickets to Fujian as soon as possible, by air or by train."

"Honghua," Fan shouted to a young woman officer sitting at the front desk outside. "Check on the earliest available tickets to Fujian."

"We appreciate your help, Director Fan," Catherine said.

"Now let's move into my office. It is more comfortable there," Fan said.

"No, please don't bother," Chen said. "We have to leave soon. The fewer people know about this, the better."

"I understand, Chief Inspector Chen. I will not say a single word to anyone—"

"Excuse me, Director Fan." The young woman officer appeared in the doorway. "I've got the information for you. There's no direct flight from Suzhou to Fujian. Our guests have to go back to Shanghai first. There will be a flight from Shanghai at three thirty in the afternoon. On the other hand, there is an express train from Suzhou to Fujian this evening, leaving at eleven thirty. The trip takes about fourteen hours."

"We'll take the train." Chen said.

"But all the soft sleepers are sold out. We can get only hard sleepers."

"Go and tell the railway bureau: We must have soft sleepers," Fan said. "If necessary, they can put on an additional car."

"You don't have to do that, Director Fan." Catherine said. "Hard sleeper will be great for me. In fact, I prefer it."

"Inspector Rohn wants to see the real China," Chen explained. "Traveling in hard sleeper like an ordinary Chinese traveler will be an experience for her. It's settled. Three tickets."

"Fine, if Inspector Rohn insists."

"Tell this to your people outside Liu's residence," Chen said. "Liu will accompany a woman to the train station this evening. If they are heading in that direction, follow them at a distance. If not, stop them. In the meantime, watch out for any suspicious people."

"Don't worry. That is their job." Fan took a glance at his watch. "Now, we have several hours before us. For Inspector Rohn's first visit, let's have a typical Suzhou dinner. What about the Pine and Crane Restaurant?"

"I have to take a rain check for dinner, Director Fan," Chen said, standing up.

"Well, we will see you at the station then," Fan said, accompanying them to the doorway, where Honghua handed over two bamboo containers. "Suzhou souvenirs. A pound of tea for each of you. First-class Cloud and Mist, a special product for the emperors in ancient China."

It might have cost five hundred Yuan at Shanghai First Department Store, though probably it would have cost Fan much less—from tea plantations patrolled by Fan's men. Still, it was a valuable present.

"Thank you, Director Fan. I'm overwhelmed." It would be a good gift for his mother, a connoisseur of fine tea. Chen felt bad for not having phoned her before he left Shanghai.

It took ten minutes for them to get back to the hotel, and less than five minutes for him to pack. He went to her room, where he called Liu, informing him of the travel arrangements. Liu agreed to accompany Wen to the station.

The next call was to Detective Yu. "We've found Wen Liping, Detective Yu."

"Where, Chief Inspector Chen?"

"In Suzhou. Staying with Liu Qing, a high-school classmate. A poet in that anthology. It's a long story. I'll tell you more about it back in Shanghai. We are taking tonight's train to Fujian, to pick up a few things at Wen's place."

"Great. I'll meet you at the Fujian railway station."

"No, don't. Peiqin will be waiting for you at home. Return by air today. We have a special budget. Don't tell the locals about our plan."

"I see. Thanks, Chief."

Finally Chen phoned the Fujian Police Bureau. A junior officer, surnamed Dai, said Superintendent Hong was not in the office.

"I want your people to meet me at the railway station with a car at one tomorrow afternoon. Preferably a van." Chen did not mention that Catherine Rohn and Wen Liping would be with him.

"No problem, Chief Inspector Chen. It's an internationally important case, we all know."

"Thanks." Chen put down the phone, wondering how all of them could have known that.

Catherine called her headquarters in Washington, where it was early morning. She left a message, saying she would be bringing Wen back in a couple of days.

It was a few minutes past five. They still had several hours to spend in Suzhou. She started taking her things out of the closet to pack. He felt time weighing heavily on him. Staring out the window, he realized for the first time that they were surrounded by dilapidated buildings. Perhaps the hotel was too close to the railway station.

"What does the phrase *folk east of the river* mean?" Catherine asked, as she put her cosmetics into a small bag.

"It means the people at home who have high hopes for you. Lord Chu was defeated in a battle around 200 B.C. and declared that he was unable to face his folk east of the river. So by the Wu River, he committed suicide."

"I've seen a tape of a Beijing Opera called *Farewell to His Imperial Concubine*. It is about the proud Lord of Chu, isn't it?"

"Yes, that's him." Chen was not in the mood to talk more.

He was increasingly uneasy about this trip back to Fujian. Wen had appeared so determined, yet every delay increased her risk.

He excused himself and went to smoke a cigarette. There were people at one end of the corridor, holding plastic basins filled with clothes. They were carrying their laundry to the public laundry room the hotel manager had shown him—a long concrete groove with a number of faucets. There was no such thing as a washing machine around here. He walked to a window at the other end. Next to it was a door opening to a flight of steps, which led to a small concrete platform, a part of the flat roof. There a young woman was busy hanging her wet clothes on the clothesline. Wearing a slip with thin straps, bare legged and bare of foot, she looked like a gymnast ready to perform. A young man emerged from behind the clothes and embraced her in spite of the beads of water glistening on her shoulders. A couple on their honeymoon trip, Chen guessed, his eyes squinting from the cigarette smoke.

Most of the people here were not affluent and had to endure the inconveniences of a cheap hotel, but they were contented.

He wondered whether he had done the right thing for Wen.

Was Wen going to have a good life with Feng in that far-away country? She knew the answer. That's why she had chosen to stay in Suzhou. With the best years of her life already wasted in the Cultural Revolution and its aftermath, Wen was trying to hang on to the last remnant of her dreams by staying here with Liu.

What had he done? A cop was not paid to be compassionate.

Some unexpected lines came to him as he stared out of the window . . .

"What are you thinking about?" Inspector Rohn came to his side by the window.

"Nothing." He was upset. But for their interference, Wen might have stayed on with Liu, though he knew it was not fair to blame Inspector Rohn. "We have done our job."

"We've done our job," she repeated. "To be exact, you have done it. A wonderful job, I have to say."

"A wonderful job indeed." He ground out the cigarette on the windowsill.

"What did you say to Liu in his study?" she asked, touching his hand lightly. She must have sensed the change in his mood. "It couldn't have been easy for you to bring him around."

"There are so many perspectives from which we can look at one and the same thing. I merely provided another perspective for him."

"A political perspective?"

"No, Inspector Rohn. Not everything is political here." He noticed the young couple staring at them from the roof. From their perspective, what would they think of the two of them, a Chinese man and an American woman standing by the window? He changed the subject. "Oh, sorry about turning down the dinner invitation. It would have been a sumptuous dinner, I imagine. Loads of toasts to friendship between China and the United States. I was not in the mood."

"You made the right choice. Now we have a chance to take a walk in a Suzhou garden."

"You want to go to a garden?"

"I have not visited a single one yet," she said. "If we have to wait, let us wait in a garden."

"Good idea. Let me make one more phone call."

"Fine, I'll take a few pictures of the hotel out front."

He dialed Gu's number. Now that they were about to leave Suzhou, it should be safe for him to make a call to Gu in Shanghai.

"Where are you, Chief Inspector Chen?" Gu sounded genuinely anxious. "I've been looking everywhere for you."

"I'm on my way to another city, Gu. Is there anything you want to tell me?"

"Some people are after you. You have to take care."

"Who are those people?" Chen said.

"An international organization."

"Tell me about them."

"Their base is Hong Kong. I have not yet found out everything. It's not convenient for me to talk at the moment, Chief Inspector Chen. Let's discuss it when you come back, okay?"

"Okay." At least it was not Internal Security.

Catherine was waiting for him in front of the hotel. She wanted to take a picture of him standing by the burnished bronze lion, his hand on its back. It did not feel like bronze. He examined it more closely, and found it was made of plastic, covered with gold paint.

Chapter 32

Chen was still in a dark mood, which soon proved to be infectious. Catherine was also subdued as they entered the Qing-style landscape of the Yi Garden.

There was something on his mind, she knew. A number of unanswered questions were on hers, too. Nevertheless, they had found Wen.

She did not want to raise those questions for the moment. And she felt uncomfortable for a different reason as she walked beside him in the garden. In the past few days, Chen had played the role of the cop in charge, always having something to say—about modernism, Confucianism, or communism. That afternoon, however, their roles had become reversed. She had taken the initiative. She wondered whether he resented her.

The garden was quiet. There were hardly any other visitors. Their footsteps made the only sound.

"Such a beautiful garden," she said, "but it's almost deserted."

"It's the time of the day."

Dusk was beginning to envelop the garden path; the sun

hung above the tilted eaves of the ancient stone pavilion like a stamp. They strolled through a gourd-shaped stone gate to a bamboo bridge where they saw several golden carp swimming in the clear, tranquil water.

"Your heart's not in sightseeing, Chief Inspector Chen."

"No. I'm enjoying every minute of it—in your company."

"You don't have to say that."

"You're not a fish," he said. "How do you know what a fish feels?"

They came to another small bridge, across which they saw a teahouse with vermilion posts, and with a large black Chinese character for "Tea" embroidered on a yellow silk pennant streaming in the breeze. There was an arrangement of strange-shaped rocks in front of the teahouse.

"Shall we go there?" she suggested.

The teahouse might have served as an official reception hall in the original architect's design, spacious, elegant, yet gloomy. The light filtered through the stained-glass windows. High on the wall was a horizontal board inscribed with Chinese characters: *Return of Spring*. By a lacquer screen in the corner, an old woman standing at a glass counter gave them a bamboo-covered thermos bottle, two cups with green tea leaves, a box of dried tofu braised in soy sauce, and a box of greenish cakes. "If you need more water, you can refill the bottle here."

There were no other customers. Nor any service after they seated themselves at a mahogany table. The old woman disappeared behind the screen.

The tea was excellent. Perhaps because of the tea leaves, perhaps because of the water, or perhaps because of the peaceful atmosphere. The dried tofu, rich in a spicy brown sauce, also tasted good, but the green cake was more palatable, sweet with an unusual flavor she had never tasted before.

"This is a wonderful dinner for me," she said, a tiny tea leaf between her lips.

"For me too," he said, adding water into her cup. "In the Chinese way of drinking tea, the first cup is not supposed to be the best. Its taste comes out in a natural way in the second or the third cup. That's why the teahouse gives you the thermos bottle, so you can enjoy the tea at your leisure while you view the garden."

"Yes, the view is fantastic."

"The Hui Emperor of the Song dynasty liked oddly shaped rocks. He ordered a national rock search—*Huashigang*—but he was captured by the Jin invaders before the chosen rocks were transported to the capital. Some of them are said to have been left in Suzhou," Chen said. "Look at this one. It is called Heaven's Gate."

"Really! I don't see the resemblance." Its name seemed a misnomer to her. The rock was shaped more like a spring bamboo shoot, angular, and sharp-pointed. It was in no way suggestive of a magnificent gate to the heavens.

"You have to see it from the right perspective," he said. "It may resemble a lot of things—a cone swaying in the wind, or an old man fishing in the snow, or a dog barking at the moon, or a deserted woman waiting for her lover's return. It all depends on your perspective."

"Yes, it all depends on your point of view," she said, failing to see any of those resemblances. She was pleased that he had recovered enough to play the guide again, though at the same time irritated by her enforced return to the role of tourist.

The sight of the rocks also served as a reminder of reality. Despite all her Chinese studies, a American marshal would never see things exactly the same way as her Chinese partner. That was a sobering realization. "I have some questions for you, Chief Inspector Chen."

"Go ahead, Inspector Rohn."

"Since you phoned the Suzhou Police Bureau from Liu's place, why not call in the local cops to do the job? They could have forced Liu to cooperate."

"They could, but I did not like that idea. Liu was not holding her against her will," Chen said. "Besides, I had a number of unanswered questions. So I wanted to talk to them first."

"Have you got your answers?"

"Some," Chen said, piercing a cube of tofu with a toothpick. "I was also worried about Liu's possible reaction. He's such a romantic. According to Bertrand Russell, romantic passion reaches its height when lovers are fighting against the whole world."

"You have made a study of it, Chief Inspector Chen. What if you had failed to persuade them?"

"As a police officer, I would have to make an objective report to the bureau."

"Then the bureau would make them cooperate, right?"

"Yes, so you see, my effort is just pathetic, isn't it?"

"Well, you succeeded in convincing them. She's willing to leave," she said. "Now for the relationship between Liu and Wen. Can you tell me more about it? It's still hazy to me. You may have given your word to Liu—promised confidentiality perhaps. Tell me what you can."

She was sipping at her tea as he began, but soon she was so absorbed that the tea turned cold in the cup. He included what he considered to be the important details. In addition, he added things from Yu's interview tapes, which focused more on the miseries Wen had suffered with Feng.

Catherine had gathered some of the information but now the various pieces were forming a whole. At the end of his account, she gazed into her cup for several minutes. When she raised her head again, the hall appeared to be even more gloomy. She saw why he had been so depressed.

"One more question, Chief Inspector Chen," she said. "About the connection between the Fujian police and the Flying Axes—is that true?"

"It's very probable. I had to tell her that," Chen said evasively. "I might be able to shield her for a week or two, but more than that, I doubt. She has no choice but to go to the United States."

"You should have discussed this with me earlier."

"It's not pleasant, you know, for a Chinese cop to admit this."

She grasped his hand.

The moment of silence was broken by the sound of the old woman cracking water melon seeds behind the screen.

"Let's go outside," Chen said.

They stepped out, carrying their tea and cakes. Walking across the bridge, they entered the pavilion with the yellow glazed tile roof and vermilion posts. The posts were set into a surrounding bench with a flat marble top and lattice railings. They placed the thermos bottle on the ground and sat with the cups and cakes between them. Small birds chirped in the grotto behind them.

"The Suzhou garden landscape was designed," he said, "to inspire people to feel poetic."

She did not feel so, though she relished the moment. Someday in the future, she knew she would look back on this early evening in Suzhou as special. Leaning sideways against the post, she went through a sudden shift of mood, as if they had undergone another role reversal. Chen was almost his usual self again. And she was becoming sentimental.

What were Wen and Liu doing at this moment?

"Soon Liu and Wen are going to part," she said wistfully.

"Liu may go to the United States someday—"

"No, he will never be able to find her." She shook her head. "That's the way our program works."

"Wen may come back—for a visit—" he cut himself short. "No, that would be too risky for her."

"It's out of the question."

"It's difficult to meet, and to part, too. / The east wind languid, the flowers fallen," he murmured, "Sorry, I'm quoting poetry again."

"What's wrong with that, Chief Inspector Chen?"

"It's sentimental."

"So you have turned into a hermit crab retreating into a rationalist shell."

Instantaneously she knew she had gone too far. Why had she burst out with this? Was it because she was upset with the outcome of the investigation, because neither he nor she could possibly do anything that would really help Wen? Or was it because of a subconscious parallel rising to the surface of her mind? Soon she, too, would be leaving China.

He made no response.

She bent over to rub her aching ankle.

"Finish the last piece," he said, handing the cake to her.

"It's a strange name, Bamboo Leaf Green Cake," she said, studying the box.

"Bamboo leaves may have been used in the cake. Bamboo used to be a very important part of traditional Chinese culture. There must be a bamboo grove in a Chinese garden landscape, and a bamboo shoot dish in a Chinese banquet."

"Interesting," she said. "Even Chinese gangsters use the word *bamboo* in the name of their organizations."

"What are you referring to, Inspector Rohn?"

"Remember the fax I got at the hotel last Sunday? It contained some background information about international triads involved in human smuggling. One of them is called Green Bamboo."

"Do you have the fax with you?"

"No, I left it at the Peace Hotel.

"But you're sure?"

"Yes, I remember the name," she said.

She changed her position. Turning toward him, she reclined against the post. He removed the cups. She slipped off her shoes and put her feet on the bench, her knees doubled against her chin, her bare soles resting on the cold marble bench top.

"Your ankle has not completely recovered," he said. "The bench top is too cold."

And she felt her feet being placed in his lap, the arch of her sole cradled in his hand, which warmed it before rubbing her ankle.

"Thank you," she said, her toes curling against his fingers involuntarily.

"Let me recite a poem for you, Inspector Rohn. It came in fragments to me during the last few days."

"Your own poem?"

"Not really. More like an imitation of MacNeice's 'The Sunlight on the Garden.' It is a poem about people being grateful for the time they share, even though the moment is fleeting."

He started to speak, his hand on her ankle.

"The sunlight burning gold, / we cannot collect the day / from the ancient garden / into an album of old. / Let's pick our play, / or time will not pardon."

"The sunlight on the garden," she said.

"Actually, the central image of the first stanza came to me in Moscow Suburb.

"Then after I got Liu's poem about the loyal character dance, especially after we met Wen and Liu, some more lines appeared," he explained. *"When all is told, / we cannot tell / the question from the answer. / Which is to hold / us under a spell, / the dance or the dancer?"*

"The dance and the dancer, I understand," she said, nodding, "For Liu, it's Wen that turned the loyal character dance into a miracle."

"MacNeice's poem is about how helpless people are."

"Yes, MacNeice is another of your favorite modernist poets."

"How do you know?"

"I have done some research on you, Chief Inspector Chen. In a recent interview, you talked about his melancholy because his job did not allow him to write as much as he wanted, but you felt sorry for yourself, for missing your chance as a poet. People say in poetry what is impossible for them to say in life."

"I don't know what to say—"

"You don't have to say anything, Chief Inspector Chen. I'm going back in a couple of days. Our mission is finished."

A mist enveloped the garden.

"Let me recite the last stanza for you," he said. *"Sad it's no longer sad, / the heart hardened anew, / not expecting pardon / but grateful and glad / to have been with you, / the sunlight lost on the garden."*

She thought she knew why he had chosen to recite the poem.

Not just for Wen and Liu.

They sat there, quietly, the last rays of the sunlight silhouetting them against the garden, but she experienced, indelibly, a moment of gratitude.

The evening spread out like the scroll of a traditional Chinese landscape painting: A changing yet unchanging panorama against the horizon, cool and fresh, a light haze softening hills in the distance.

The same poetic garden, the same creaking Ming dynasty bridge, the same dying Qing dynasty sun.

Hundreds of years earlier.

Hundreds of years later.

It was so tranquil that they were able to hear the bursting bubbles of wrigglers in the green water.

Chapter 33

The train arrived at the Fuzhou Station at 11:32 A.M., on time.

The station was alive with waiting people, some waving their hands, some running alongside the train, and some holding up cardboard placards bearing the passengers' names. However, there was no one from the Fujian Police Bureau waiting for them on the crowded platform.

Chen did not say a single word about this. Some acts of negligence on the part of the local police might be understandable, but not in this case. It did not make sense. A premonition gripped him.

"Let's wait here," Catherine suggested. "They may have been delayed."

Wen looked on in silence, her expression unchanged, as if their arrival meant nothing to her. Throughout the train ride, she had said little.

"No, we are too pressed for time," he said, unwilling to voice his fears. "I'll rent a car."

"Do you have the directions?"

"Detective Yu made a map for me. The directions are marked on it. Wait here with Wen."

When he drove back in a Dazhong van, only the two women were still standing there.

Opening the door for Wen, he said, "Sit in the front with me, Wen. You may be able to help with the directions."

"I'll try." Wen spoke to him for the first time. "Sorry for this trouble."

Catherine tried to comfort her from the backseat. "This is not your fault."

Consulting Wen and the map, Chen was able to find the right road. "Now the map is serving a purpose Detective Yu did not expect."

"I've only spoken to Detective Yu on the phone." Catherine said. "I'm looking forward to meeting him."

"He must be on his way back to Shanghai already. You will meet him there. Both Yu and his wife Peiqin are wonderful people. She is also a marvelous cook."

"She must be some cook to earn a compliment from a gourmet like you."

"We may go to his home for a genuine Chinese meal," he said. "My place is too messy."

"I will look forward to it."

They chose not to talk about work with Wen sitting in the car, clasping her hands over her belly.

It was a long drive. He stopped only once at a village market, where he bought a bag of lichee.

"Good nutrition. Now you have this fruit in big cities, too. It's shipped by air," he said, "but still it's not as good as in the countryside."

"It tastes wonderful," Catherine said, nibbling at a transparent white lichee.

"Freshness makes all the difference," he said, peeling one for himself.

Before they finished half of the lichee in the paper bag, Changle Village came into view. For the first time he noticed a change in Wen. She rubbed her eyes, as if dust had blown into them.

Inside the village, the road became a lane, wide enough only for a light tractor. "Do you have a lot to pack, Wen?"

"No, not a lot."

"Then let's park here."

So they got out of the car. Wen led the way.

It was nearly one o'clock. Most of the villagers were at home having lunch. Several white geese sauntered about near a rain water puddle, stretching out their necks at the strangers. A woman carrying a basket of deep green shepherd's purse recognized Wen, but she scurried away at the sight of the strangers walking behind her.

Wen's house was located in a cul de sac, next to a dilapidated, abandoned barn. Chen's first impression was that the house was a good size. There was a front yard as well as a back one on a steep slope over a creek overgrown with nameless bushes. But its cracked walls, unpainted door, and boarded-up windows made it an eyesore.

They entered the front room. What impressed Chen there was a large, discolored portrait of Chairman Mao hung on the wall above a decrepit wooden table. Flanking the portrait were two strips of dog-eared red paper slogans declaring, despite the change of times: "Listen to Chairman Mao!" "Follow the Communist Party."

There was a spider resting contentedly, like another mole, on Mao's chin.

The expression flashing across Wen's face was unreadable. Instead of beginning to pack, she stood staring at the portrait of Mao, her lips trembling, as if murmuring a pledge to him—like a loyal Red Guard.

Several packages with Chinese or English labels were stored in a bucket under the table. Wen picked up a tiny package and put it in her purse.

"Are those for the precision parts, Wen?" he asked.

"It's the abrasive. I want to take one with me as a reminder of my life here. As a souvenir."

"A souvenir," Chen echoed. The emerald snail climbing up the wall in Liu's poem. He, too, picked up a package whose label bore a heavy cross over a schematic drawing of fire. There was something odd in the way Wen offered her explanation. What was there here she would like to be reminded of? But he decided not to touch on the topic of her life in the village. He did not want to reopen her wounds.

The living room led into a dining room, from which Wen headed into another through a bamboo-bead curtain hung in the doorway. Catherine followed her. Chen saw Wen taking out some child's clothes. There was nothing he could do to help there. So he crossed to a walled back courtyard. Originally, the back door must have opened out onto the slope, but it had been boarded up.

He walked around to the front courtyard. The rattan chair by the door was broken, dust-covered. It seemed to be telling a tale of its owner's indifference. He also saw empty bottles in bamboo baskets, mostly beer bottles, providing a footnote to the general desolation.

Outside, an old dog jumped up from a patch of shade in the village lane and shambled away silently. A puff of wind blew the weeping willow tree into a question mark. Lighting a cigarette, he leaned against the door frame, waiting.

There was a train leaving for Shanghai late in the evening. He decided not to contact the local police, not just because of their failure to appear at the railway station. He could not shake off the ominous feeling he'd had since Wen had demanded they undertake this trip.

He felt worn out. He had hardly slept in the train. The hard sleeper had presented an unforeseen problem during the night. Of the three bunks, the bottom one went to Wen. It was out of the question for a pregnant woman to climb the ladder. The upper bunks across the aisle were left for Catherine and him. It was important to keep a watch on Wen. "Sometimes a cooked duck can fly away." So he lay on his side most of the night, watching. Every time Wen stepped away from her berth, he had to climb down, following her as inconspicuously as possible. He had to resist the temptation to glance at Catherine across the aisle. She, too, lay on her side most of the time, wearing only the black slip they had bought at the Huating Market. The soft light played across the sensuous curves of her body, the skimpy blanket hardly covering her shoulders and legs. She was in no position to look at the bunk directly beneath her. So more often than not, she faced in his direction. It did not help when the lights were turned out at midnight. He felt her nearness in the darkness, turning and tossing, amid the train's irregular whistles in the night . . .

As a result, standing in the doorway now, he had a stiff neck, and had to roll his head like a circus clown.

It was then he heard heavy, hurried footsteps drawing close from the village entrance. Not one or two men. A large group of them.

Startled, he looked out. There were a dozen men coming in his direction, each of them masked with black cloth, carrying something that shone in the sunlight—axes. At the sight of him, they broke into a charge, swinging their axes, yelling over the sound of the chickens screeching and dogs barking.

"The Flying Axes!" he shouted to the two women who were just emerging from the house. "Get back inside. Quick!"

He whipped out his revolver, aimed in haste, and pulled the trigger. One of the masked men spun like a broken robot, tried in vain to raise his ax, and crumpled to his knees. The others seemed to be stunned.

"He has a gun!"

"He's killed the Old Third."

The gangsters did not run away. Instead, they broke into two groups, several taking cover behind the house across the lane, and the others dashing into the barn. As he took a step toward them, a small ax was hurled at him. It missed, but he had to retreat.

Each of them had several axes, large and small, tucked into the front and backs of their belts in addition to those they held in their hands. They threw the small ones like darts.

To his surprise, none of the gangsters seemed to have a gun, even though weapon smuggling was not unheard of in a coastal province like Fujian. This was not the moment for him to find fault with his luck.

What did he have? A revolver with five bullets left. If he did not miss a single shot, he might be able to cut down five of them. Once he fired his last shot, there was nothing else he could do.

The Flying Axes would have surrounded the house. Once they began to attack from all directions, they would overwhelm it. Nor could he hope for timely rescue by the local police. Only the local police had known of their arrival in Fujian.

"Fujian Police, Fujian Police . . ."

He heard Inspector Rohn shouting into her cellular phone.

Another ax came flying through the air. Before he could react, it stuck trembling in the door frame, missing Catherine by only two or three inches.

If anything happened to her—

He felt the blood rushing to his face. He had made a huge

mistake in coming here with the two women. There was no professional justification for it—he had followed a hunch, but he had been wrong to take such a risk.

Cringing besides Catherine, Wen clutched the poetry anthology like a shield.

Poetry makes nothing happen.

It was a line he had read years ago. However, he had hoped that poetry could make some things happen. Here he was, ironically, because of that poetry anthology. It was absurd that he should be thinking of such things in the midst of a desperate fight.

"Do you have any gasoline here, Wen?" Catherine said.

"No."

"Why do you ask, Inspector Rohn?" he said.

"The bottles—Molotov cocktails."

"The abrasive! The chemicals are flammable, aren't they?"

"Yes. They must be as good as gasoline!"

"You know how to make them—Molotov cocktails?"

"Oh yes." She was already running to the bucket of chemicals in the house.

Several gangsters were moving out of hiding. He raised his revolver as one of them charged, chanting loudly as if under a spell, "Flying Axes kill all the evil," like someone out of the Boxer Uprising. Chen fired twice. One bullet slammed into the man's chest, but the momentum carried him sprawling across a few more yards, to fall, still clutching his ax. Sheer luck. Chen remembered how poorly he had scored at the firing range. He had only three bullets left.

Four or five axes came whirring through the air. Aware of Catherine returning with the bottles, Chen instinctively flung up the rattan chair in front of him. The axes crashed into it so heavily he took a step back, involuntarily.

Behind him, Catherine squatted, filling bottles with chemicals, Wen stuffing the bottle tops with rags.

"Have you a light, Catherine?" he asked.

She searched her pockets. "The hotel matchbook—a souvenir of Suzhou." She struck a match.

Grabbing the bottle from her, he hurled it toward the house where the gangsters had taken shelter. There was a blast. Flames shot up with dazzling colors. She lit the second bottle for him. He tossed it toward the barn. It exploded more loudly, and the acrid smell of the burning chemicals filled his nostrils.

It was a moment Chen could not afford to waste. In the confusion brought on by the explosions, they might stand a chance.

He turned to Wen, "Is there a shortcut out of the village across the creek?"

"Yes, there's hardly any water in the creek now."

"There's a door to the backyard, Catherine. Break it down, run out with Wen, and cut across the creek to the car." He handed the gun to her. "Take the gun. There are only three bullets left. I'll cover you."

"How are you going to do that?"

"With Molotov cocktails. I'll throw out several bottles." He plucked the ax out of the door frame. Soon, perhaps, he would have to use it. A kung fu miracle was possible only on the screen. "I will catch up with you."

"No. I can't leave you here like this. The local police must have heard about the fighting. They should arrive any minute."

"Listen, Catherine," Chen said, his throat dry. "We cannot hold out for long. If they start attacking us from both front and back, it will be too late. You have to go now."

So saying, he started to throw the bottles, one after another, in quick succession. The path was engulfed in smoke and flames. Amidst the explosions, he heard Catherine and Wen pounding at the back door. He had no time to look over his shoulder. A gangster was rushing at him, axes flashing through the smoke. Chen hurled a bottle at him, and then the ax.

Nobody came through the fading smoke.

Great, he thought, clutching one of the remaining bottles, when he heard a loud gun shot at the back of the house. There was a thud.

Spinning around, he saw Catherine pulling Wen back into the house. A masked face was rising over the backyard wall, then two hands, and then shoulders. She shot again. The Flying Ax toppled backward.

"The bitch has a gun!" someone shouted outside.

With Chen in front, and Catherine in back, the gangsters were temporarily stopped, but it would only be a few minutes before they resumed their attack.

There was only one bullet left in the gun.

That couple of minutes proved, however, to be more crucial than he had imagined.

He heard a siren coming from a distance, then a car screeching into the village. Hurried footsteps. Blurred shouting. Frantic barking.

He charged out, clutching the last two Molotov cocktails amidst an outburst of gunfire. A volley of bullets was directed at the gangsters sheltered by the house across the lane. Another fusillade of bullets rained onto the barn, which at once burst into new flames. The triad men scrambled out and fled.

"Cops!"

In a matter of a few seconds, only bodies scattered on the ground remained. Armed policemen were chasing the running men, guns held high.

To his amazement, Chen saw Yu coming toward them, waving a pistol.

The battle was over.

Chapter 34

"Detective Yu!" Chen grasped Yu's hand.

"It's good to see you, Chief." Yu was too excited to say more.

Catherine clasped Yu's other hand, her face smudged, her blouse torn at the shoulder. "I'm so glad to see you here, Detective Yu."

"Me too, Inspector Rohn. I am happy to meet you."

"I thought you were on your way back to Shanghai," Chen said.

"My plane was delayed. So I checked my phone one more time before boarding. I got the message left by Inspector Rohn that no one had picked you up at the station."

"When did you place that call, Inspector Rohn?"

"While we were waiting for you to rent a car."

"The absence of the local police at the station did not make sense," Yu said. "The more I thought about it, the more suspicious it appeared to me. After all those accidents, you know—"

"Yes, I do." Chen had to cut Yu short. It was more than suspicious, he knew. Inspector Rohn knew, too. The fact that she had mentioned the absence of the local cops in her message spoke for itself. Still, they did not have to discuss this problem in front of her.

"So I approached the airport police and got a jeep from them. Some of them rode back with me. I had a hunch."

"A good hunch."

As they were talking, Chen heard more cars and people arriving. Looking up, he was not too surprised to see Superintendent Hong, the head of the Fuzhou Police Bureau, leading a group of armed policemen.

"I'm so sorry, Chief Inspector Chen," Hong said in a voice full of apologies. "We missed you at the station. My assistant made a mistake about the arrival time. On our way back to the bureau, we heard about the fight and rushed over."

"Don't worry, Superintendent Hong. It's all over now."

The belated appearance of Hong and his men was intended to be a footnote to a finished chapter.

Was it possible for Chen to attempt to remedy the situation here and now? The answer was no. As an outsider, he had to congratulate himself on being lucky as it was. Their mission was completed, none of them had been seriously hurt, and a handful of gangsters had been punished. He simply said, "The Flying Axes are well-informed. We hardly reached the village when they came upon us."

"Some village folks must have spotted Wen and informed them."

"So they got the news faster than the local police." Chen found it hard not to be sarcastic.

"Now you know how difficult things can be here, Chief Inspector Chen," Hong said, shaking his head before he turned to Inspector Rohn. "I'm sorry about meeting you like this, Inspector Rohn. I apologize on behalf of my colleagues in Fujian."

"You don't have to apologize to me, Superintendent Hong," Inspector Rohn said. "I thank you for your cooperation on behalf of the U.S. Marshals Service."

More policemen appeared to clean up the battlefield. There were several wounded gangsters lying on the ground. One of them might be dead. Chen was about to interrogate another who was muttering something to a local cop, when Hong made a request.

"Can you explain a Chinese proverb for me, Chief Inspector Chen—*Mogao yice, daogao yizhang?*"

"The literal translation is this: The devil is ten inches tall, and the way, or justice, is a hundred inches tall. In other words, powerful as evil is, justice will prevail." The original proverb actually read the other way around. The ancient Chinese sage had been more pessimistic about the power of the evil.

"The Chinese government is determined," Hong declared pompously, "to deal a crushing blow to all evil forces."

Chen nodded as he observed a policeman kicking a wounded gangster viciously and cursing, "Damn it! Shut up with your damned Mandarin."

The gangster uttered a blood-chilling scream that cut into their conversation like another flying ax.

"I apologize, Inspector Rohn," Hong said. "Those gangsters are the worst scum under the sun."

"I have had my fill of apologies every day I've spent here," Detective Yu remarked bitterly, crossing his arms. "What a Fujian experience!"

But Chief Inspector Chen knew better than to push the matter further. On the surface, everything could be attributed to coincidence. There was no point going on with Inspector Rohn and Wen waiting.

"We local police can do little," Hong said, looking Chen in the eye. "You know that, Chief Inspector Chen."

Could that be a hint about the higher-level politics?

The doubts Chen had harbored at the beginning of the investigation were resurfacing. Wen's disappearance might not have been orchestrated from above, but whether the authorities had been so eager to deliver her to the Americans, he was not sure. What was left for Chen to do was perhaps no more than a performance in an ancient shadow play, full of sound and fury, but no substance. In his eagerness to serve as a model Chinese chief inspector of police, however, he had stepped beyond the boundaries of the stage.

If this was so, the battle in the village might truly have been beyond the scope of the local police, as Superintendent Hong intimated.

Maybe "the order of the acts had been schemed and plotted," at the highest level.

He did not really want to believe this.

Perhaps he would never know the truth. Perhaps it would be best if he could be content to be one of those brainless Chinese cops in the Hollywood movies, and to let Inspector Rohn think of him that way.

Whatever his suspicions, he was in no position to confide in her. Or another report by Internal Security would travel to Party Secretary Li's desk even before he got back to Shanghai.

"Now the case has been concluded." Superintendent Hong changed the topic with a ready smile. "You have found Wen. All is well. We should celebrate. The best Fujian cuisine, a banquet of a hundred fishes from the southern sea."

"No thanks, Superintendent Hong," Chen declined. "But I need to ask a favor of you."

"We will do anything we can, Chief Inspector Chen."

"We have to return to Shanghai right now. We are pressed for time."

"That's no problem. Let's go to the airport directly. There are several flights to Shanghai every day. You can take the next one. It's not the high season. I believe there should still be some seats available."

Hong and the others drove off in their jeep, taking the lead. Yu followed with Wen in the car that had brought them from the airport. Chen rode with Catherine in the Dazhong.

The half bag of lichee still lay on the seat. The fruit no longer looked so fresh. Several appeared black rather than red. Or if the color remained the same, his mood had changed.

"I'm sorry," she said.

"For what?"

"I should not have supported Wen's wish to take this trip."

"I was not opposed to the idea, either," he said. "I'm sorry, Inspector Rohn."

"For what?"

"Everything."

"How could the gang have found us so quickly?"

"That's a good question." That's all he said. It was a question Superintendent Hong should have answered.

"You called the Fujian Police Bureau from Suzhou," she said quietly. The tai chi term was: *It is enough to touch the spot.* She did not have to push.

"That was my mistake. But I did not mention Wen." He was puzzled. Only the Suzhou police were aware that Wen was with them, but he went on, "Maybe some villager notified the gangsters as soon as we arrived. That's Superintendent Hong's story."

"Maybe."

"I do not know much about the local situation." He caught himself talking to her in the same evasive way as Superintendent Hong had spoken to him. Still, what else could he say? "Maybe the gangsters were waiting for Wen. Just like 'the old farmer waiting for the rabbit to knock itself out.' "

"Old farmers or not, the Flying Axes were here and the local police were not."

"There's another proverb, 'A powerful dragon cannot fight local snakes.' "

"I have another question, Chief Inspector Chen. Why did these local snakes come with nothing but axes?"

"Perhaps they came at a moment's notice, so they carried whatever weapons they happened to lay their hands on."

"At a moment's notice? I don't think so. Not so many of them, and masked."

"You have a point," he said. In fact, her question led to another one. Why had they bothered to wear masks? Their axes gave them away. Like the ax wounds on the body in Bund Park. A signed crime.

"Now that our mission is completed, we don't have to worry about those questions," he said.

"Or answers." She sensed his reluctance to talk further.

It sounded like a sarcastic reference to the poem read in the Suzhou garden.

He felt her sitting so close, but so far away at the same time.

Chen turned on the car radio. The broadcast was in the local dialect, of which he did not understand a single word.

Presently, the Fujian airport came in view.

As they neared the domestic flights gate, they saw a peddler in Taoist costume displaying his wares on a piece of white cloth spread on the ground. It exhibited an impressive array of herb samples, along with a number of open books, magazines, and pictures, all of them illustrating the beneficial effects of local herbs. The ingenious entrepreneur wore a white beard, an image associated with the legends of a Taoist recluse cultivating herbs in the clouds of the mountains, meditating above the vexing hubbub of the world, and enjoying longevity in harmony with nature.

He spoke a few words to them but neither Catherine nor Chen could understand him. Seeing their puzzlement, he addressed them in Mandarin.

"Look! Fulin cake, the well-known product of Fujian, beneficent to your body system," the peddler declared. "It contains natural energy, and a lot of ingredients essential to health."

The Taoist peddler reminded Chen of the Taoist fortuneteller in the Suzhou temple. Ironically, the cryptic poem's prediction had turned out to be true.

As they walked through the gate, flight information was being broadcast, first in Mandarin, then in Fujian, and finally in English.

Finally, Chen realized something.

Something was terribly wrong.

"Damn!" he cursed, glancing at his watch. It was too late.

"What, Chief Inspector Chen?"

"Nothing," he said.

Chapter 35

The dinner invitation was Detective Yu's idea. To be exact, however, it was an idea he had gotten from Chief Inspector Chen. Chen had mentioned Inspector Rohn's interest in visiting a Chinese home, adding it would not be convenient to invite her to a bachelor's place like his. Chen did not have to say more to his assistant.

The moment he returned, Yu broached the dinner plan to Peiqin. "Inspector Rohn is leaving tomorrow afternoon. So she is available only this evening."

"You have just come back." Peiqin handed him a hot towel from a green plastic basin. "It's such short notice. I don't have any time to prepare. Especially for an American."

"But I have invited them already."

"You could have called me first." Peiqin poured a cup of jasmine tea for him. "Our room is so small. An American will hardly be able to turn around."

Yu's room was on the southern end of the eastern wing, in an apartment which had been assigned to his father, Old Hunter, in the early fifties. Now, forty years later, the four rooms accommodated four families. As a result, each room functioned as a bedroom, dining room, living room, and bathroom. Yu's room, which had once been a dining room, proved particularly inconvenient for entertaining guests. The room next to it, Old Hunter's, was originally the living room, and had the only door opening into the hall. A visitor had to walk through Old Hunter's room to reach theirs.

Yu said, "Well, it may not matter that much. She's studied Chinese. And you know, there may be something between Inspector Rohn and Chief Inspector Chen."

"Really!" Peiqin's voice registered instant interest. "But Chen has an HCC girlfriend in Beijing, hasn't he?"

"I'm not so sure about it—not after Baoshen's case. Remember Chen's trip to the Yellow Mountains?"

"You haven't told me about it. Is it finished between them?"

"It's complicated. Politics. The conclusion of that case was not pleasant for her father. Chen's relationship with her is strained, so I've heard. Not to mention the fact they live in two different cities."

"That's not good. You have been away for a week, and it's been so hard for me. I don't see how they can remain in a relationship, separated like that." Peiqin took the towel from him and touched his unshaved chin. "Why hasn't Chen been transferred to Beijing?"

"He can be stubborn. About the HCC influence, you know."

"I don't know what to say about your boss, but an HCC

connection, and all that goes with it, may not be good for him," she said quietly. "Do you think Inspector Rohn has a soft spot for him? It's time for him to settle down."

"Come on, Peiqin. An American? It's like in the Hollywood movies. A week's fling in China. No, Chief Inspector Chen can settle down with anybody but her."

"You never know, Guangming. So what shall we have for tonight?"

"An ordinary Chinese meal will be great," Yu said. "According to Chen, Inspector Rohn has a passion for everything Chinese. What about a dumpling dinner?"

"A good idea. It's the season for spring bamboo shoots. We will have dumplings with three fresh stuffings: fresh bamboo shoots, fresh meat, and fresh shrimp. I'll fry some dumplings, steam some, and serve the rest in an old duck soup with black tree ears. I'll leave work early and bring some special dishes from the restaurant. Our room may be as small as a piece of dried tofu, but we cannot lose face before an American guest."

Yu stretched. "I don't have to go to the office today," he said. "So I'll go to the market to buy a basket of really fresh bamboo shoots."

"Choose the tender ones. Not thicker than two fingers. We'd better mince the meat ourselves; the ground pork you can buy is not fresh. When will they arrive?"

"Around four thirty."

"Let's start right now. It takes time to make the dumpling skin."

Chen and Catherine arrived more than an hour early. Chen was dressed in a gray suit. Catherine, wearing a red sleeveless cheongsam with high slits, looked like an actress in a Shanghai movie of the thirties. Chen held a bottle of wine, and Catherine carried a large plastic bag.

"You have finally brought a girl here, Chief Inspector Chen," Peiqin smiled.

"Finally," Catherine said, taking Chen's arm with mock seriousness.

Peiqin was intrigued by Catherine's reaction, for as soon as she had made the offhand joke she had regretted it. Apparently, Catherine was not displeased.

"This is Inspector Rohn, of the United States Marshals Service," Chen introduced her formally. "She's also very interested in Chinese culture. Since her arrival, she has been talking about visiting a Shanghai family."

"Nice to meet you, Inspector Rohn." Peiqin wiped her flour-covered hand before taking Catherine's.

"Good to meet you, Peiqin. Chief Inspector Chen has spoken frequently about your excellent cooking."

"A poetic exaggeration," Peiqin said.

Yu tried to speak more formally, like a host, apologizing, "Sorry about the mess. May I introduce our son to you? He is called Qinqin."

The room had space only for one table. The early arrival of the guests put the hosts in an embarrassing situation. The table was still littered with dumpling skins, minced meat, and vegetables. There was no room on the surface for even a teacup. Catherine had to put her bag down on the bed.

"The chief inspector is always busy. He has to go back to the bureau later." Catherine took a couple of boxes out of the bag. "They are just some small things I've chosen at the hotel. I hope you like them."

One was a food processor, and the other, a coffee maker.

"How wonderful, Inspector Rohn," Peiqin exclaimed. "It is

so thoughtful of you. For his next visit, we can serve Chief Inspector Chen fresh coffee."

"You can also use it to make hot water for tea," Chen said. "For this visit, we can use the food processor to mince and mix the meat and vegetable."

"And bamboo shoots too," Yu said proudly, beginning to experiment with the machine.

"I have something for you, too." Chen produced several glass-and-brocade boxes of ink sticks—fantastically shaped as turtles, tigers, dragons. A special product of the Tai Mountains, made of the pine resin, they were supposedly inspirational.

But impractical, Peiqin thought, compared with Catherine's choice.

Chen busied himself with translating the English directions on the box for Yu. Catherine insisted on doing something, too. "Don't treat me as an outsider, Peiqin. That's not why I am here today."

"So she can boast about her Shanghai experience afterward," Chen said.

Peiqin handed Catherine a plastic apron to put on over her dress. Soon Catherine's hands were covered with the flour, and her face was speckled too. She did not give up. A couple of dumplings jumped out of her hands, large and irregular in shape.

"Marvelous!" Yu applauded.

"Great big dumplings for the chief inspector." Catherine had a playful twinkle in her blue eyes. "The big guy in your bureau."

Then it was time to cook. Peiqin made for the kitchen. Catherine followed her. Peiqin felt embarrassed. It was not exactly a kitchen, merely a common cooking and storage area of the original hallway, now crowded with the coal stoves of the seven families on the first floor. The dish she had brought back from the restaurant had to be steamed on a neighbor's stove. Catherine seemed to be cheerful, however, moving about in the cramped area, watching Peiqin put dumplings into water, arrange some in the bamboo steamer, fry some in the wok, and add various seasonings to the duck soup.

"When will Old Hunter come home?" Chen asked Yu as they started to clear the table.

"I don't know. He left early this morning. I have not had a chance to speak to him. Do you have to return to the bureau?"

"Yes, there's something—"

Their talk was interrupted by the appearance of the various dumplings on the table. Catherine carried bowls in both hands. Yu mixed dishes of red pepper sauce with peeled garlic. Chen opened a small urn of Shaoxing yellow wine. Yu also moved the table a few inches toward the bed. Chen sat on one side, Catherine on the other, and Yu and his son, on the edge of the bed. The side close to the kitchen was left for Peiqin, who had to cook fresh dumplings from time to time.

"Fantastic," Catherine said between bites, "I have never tasted anything like this in Chinatown in New York."

"You have to make the dumpling skin yourself," Peiqin explained.

"Thank you, Peiqin," Chen said with half a dumpling in his mouth. "You always give your guests a special treat."

"I've never had fresh bamboo shoots before," Catherine said.

"Fresh bamboo shoots make a world of difference," Chen said. "Su Dongpo once said, *It's more important to have fresh bamboo shoots than to have meat.* It's a delicacy for a highly civilized taste."

"Was he the same Su Dongpo you mentioned at the crab meal, Uncle Chen?" Qinqin asked.

"Qinqin has a very good memory," Chen said.

"Qinqin has a great interest in history," Yu said, "but Peiqin wants him to study computers. Easier to find a job in the future, she thinks."

"It's the same in the United States," Catherine commented.

They finished all the dumplings.

"Let's wait a few more minutes for the duck soup." Peiqin said, holding a small cup of yellow wine in her hand. "It takes time. So please recite a poem for us, Chief Inspector Chen."

"A good idea," Yu seconded. "Like in *The Dream of the Red Chamber*. You promised last time, Chief."

"But I haven't had much time for poetry."

The duck soup arrived. Peiqin ladled out a small bowl for Catherine. The black tree ears floated in the broth. She also brought an unusual dish to the table. "Our restaurant's speciality, called Buddha's Head."

It was a semblance of Buddha's head—carved out of a white gourd, steamed in a bamboo steamer, covered with a huge green lotus leaf. Yu sawed a piece off the "skull" skillfully with a bamboo knife, put the chopsticks into the "brains," and came up with a fried sparrow—inside a grilled quail—inside a braised pigeon.

"So many brains in one head," Catherine said. "No wonder it's called Buddha."

"The flavors of those birds are supposed to mingle together in the steaming process. You can enjoy the different tastes in one bite."

"It's delicious." Chief Inspector Chen sighed with satisfaction, stood up, clanked a chopstick on the rim of the cup, "Now, with Buddha's blessing, I have an announcement to make. It's about our hosts."

"About us?" the Yus asked.

"I went to the bureau this morning. Among other things, I attended a housing committee meeting. The committee has decided to assign Detective Yu a two-bedroom apartment on Tianling Road. Congratulations!"

"A two-bedroom for us!" Peiqin exclaimed. "You are kidding."

"No, I'm not. It's the final decision of the committee."

"You must have put up a fight for us, Chief!" Yu said.

"You deserve it, Yu."

"Congratulations!" Catherine grasped Peiqin's hand, "It's great news, but why was there a fight?"

"There are more than seventy people on the waiting list but how many apartments did the bureau get this time, Chief Inspector Chen?"

"Four."

" 'The watery rice porridge is not enough for all the waiting monks.' The housing committee has to have many meetings before reaching a decision. Chen is a leading member of the committee."

"You are exaggerating again, Peiqin. Your husband was at the top of the list." Chen produced a small envelope. "I did only one thing. When the meeting was over, I took the apartment key. It's officially yours. You may move in as early as next month."

"Thank you so much, Chief Inspector Chen," Peiqin grasped the envelope with both hands. "That's the most important thing, the key. 'There are so many dreams in a long night.' "

"I know that Chinese proverb," Catherine said.

"So cheers." Chen raised his cup.

"Cheers." Catherine leaned over to whisper in his ear, yet loudly enough for others to hear, "Now I see why you like your bureau position so much."

"Now that you've mentioned it, I think I need to return to the bureau."

Catherine said, "And I need to go to the hotel to pack."

* * *

Twenty minutes later, Old Hunter burst into Yu's room as Pei-qin was clearing the dishes.

"Was Chief Inspector Chen here?"

"Yes, he and his American partner were both here," Yu said. "They have just left."

"Where did they go?"

"They went their separate ways, I think. She went back to the hotel, and he, to the bureau."

"Give him a call," Old Hunter said, still slightly out of breath. "To make sure of it."

Yu did. Chen was not at in the bureau, however. Nor at the hotel. Yu finally got hold of him on his cell phone.

"I'm on the road. Give my regards to Old Hunter." Chen added, "It may be difficult for you to reach me tonight. I'll call you."

"What's up, Father?" Yu said, putting down the phone.

Peiqin came back with a bowl of dumplings.

"Thank Heaven and Earth. At least he's not at the hotel," Old Hunter said, taking the bowl. "Your boss has an old head on his young shoulders."

"What do you mean, Father?" Peiqin added a pinch of black pepper to the old man's soup.

"Yu is Chief Inspector Chen's man. People all know that, both in and out of the bureau. So they chose to tell me a thing or two."

"What did they say?" Yu asked.

"Some guys are white-eyed chickens, with the tiniest black guts, only good for back-pecking. Now they are catching the wind and shadow between Chief Inspector Chen and the American woman. Internal Security may have been sent into the hotel."

"Those good-for-nothing bastards."

"Don't worry too much. Chief Inspector Chen is a cautious man," Peiqin said quietly, wiping her hands on the apron. "That's why he wanted to bring her to our place, rather than to his."

"He asked me when you would come back, Father," Yu said.

"I had a talk with him this morning. About Gu Haiguang."

"Who is Gu Haiguang?"

"The owner of the Dynasty Karaoke Club. A Mr. Big Bucks connected to those gangsters. Hasn't your boss spoken to you about him?"

"No. We didn't talk on our flight."

"He said that he would call me about meeting Gu later to-night. I tried to reach him at the bureau, but he was not there." Old Hunter said between bites, "I don't know what Gu's involved in. The case of the victim in the park or that of the woman on the run. But what I gave your boss should be enough to lock Gu up for a couple of years."

"So where is he going now?" Yu said. "That's strange. Wen's case is concluded. I don't know what else he is up to."

"He cannot be too careful," Old Hunter repeated.

"Have some more dumplings, Father," Peiqin said, coming back with another steaming bowl. "He'll call."

Several hours later, Chief Inspector Chen had still not been heard from.

With Qinqin asleep on the convertible sofa, and Old Hunter in his own room, Yu and Peiqin lay quietly on their bed, waiting. There was nothing else Yu could do. Holding her hand, he talked about their guests. "Chief Inspector Chen may have his peach blossom luck, but it will never bear fruit."

"What do you mean?" Peiqin said. "You must have noticed the way she looked at him."

"That makes no difference, Peiqin. Their relationship is impossible."

"Why? Chen is not immune to her attraction. There are so many stories about cross-cultural marriages nowadays."

"Not in his position," he said. "In fact, he could not discuss everything in the investigation with her."

"Did he tell you that?"

"Yes, the line between the insider and outsider, Party Secretary Li's line." Yu had not told Peiqin everything either, like about the food poisoning incident in Fujian.

"He can go to the United States, can't he?"

"Even if he wants to, do you think he will go far there—with his political background here? Politics are everywhere. He will never be a chief inspector there."

"She can come here and make a good wife for him. She enjoyed doing things even in our cramped kitchen."

"To carry out the chamber pot early in the morning, to ride the old bike in the rain and snow, to put out the fire in the coal stove in the evening, day in and day out. No, I don't think so, my wife."

"Haven't I been doing all those things? I am a happy, contented wife."

"It would not work for Chief Inspector Chen. With an American woman in his life, his career would be practically finished." He added somberly. "Besides, we don't know how things stand between Chen and his HCC girlfriend. Whatever their problems, she helped him before, in his time of trouble."

"You may be right." Peiqin softened. "I don't want to argue with you tonight."

"Why?"

"We are moving into a new apartment. In a month. I still

cannot believe it. This may be the last time we will receive your boss or any other guest here."

"Remember Chen's first visit?"

"Of course. During the National Model Worker case. We had a crab meal that night."

"That night, I lay awake for a long time in the dark, listening to the bubbles of crab froth as they moistened each other."

"Why?"

"We're so pathetic, compared with those HCC, partying all night in their mansions. We had to hold our breath in bed, with Qinqin sleeping in the same room."

"Oh that, Guangming. I would love to hold my breath to-night, one more time," she said, touching his chest.

But the telephone rang.

It was Inspector Rohn. She could not reach Chief Inspector Chen. The automated message from his cell phone said it was out of range. She was worried. So was Yu, who promised to call her as soon as he heard anything.

He thought he had lost the mood, but Peiqin's caresses eventually worked.

Chapter 36

The airplane was delayed again.

Inspector Rohn, Wen, Detective Yu, and Party Secretary Li, Sergeant Qian, everyone except Chief Inspector Chen, was at Shanghai's Hongqiao International Airport, standing by the arrival/departure monitor, which as yet showed no departure time scheduled for the United Airlines flight to Washington, D.C.

According to Detective Yu, Chief Inspector Chen was on his way to the airport. Yu had heard from him an hour earlier. That was not like the punctual chief inspector. Inspector Rohn was concerned. Since their meal last night at the Yus', she had not heard from him. In spite of the "successful conclusion" of her mission, as Party Secretary Li had put it, some of the questions they had had during the investigation remained unanswered. And the flight would take off, if not further delayed, in only one and a half hours.

The afternoon sunlight sifted through the tall window. Wen stood alone, her face pallid, lifeless, like an alabaster mask except for the bluish smudges of stress under her eyes. Yu was busy making inquiries about the weather in Tokyo. Qian, whom Catherine met for the first time, seemed a dapper young man who spoke in a pleasing manner and offered to fetch drinks for them. Secretary Li once more harped on the friendship between the Chinese and American peoples. Catherine excused herself and went to Wen's side.

She found it hard to offer comfort in Chinese. "Don't worry, Wen," she said, repeating what she had said in Suzhou. "If there is anything I can do for you in the United States, I will do it."

"Don't worry, Inspector Rohn," Wen echoed. "Your work here is successfully completed."

She did not feel "successful." As she tried to find something else to say, she saw Chen and Liu enter the airport carrying several plastic shopping bags.

"Oh, Liu Qing's has come with Chief Inspector Chen to see you off!" Catherine exclaimed.

"What?" Party Secretary Li hurried over to them. Yu and Qian followed. Wen took a step backward in disbelief.

"I have brought Comrade Liu from Suzhou, Party Secretary Li," Chen said. "I did not have time to ask for your approval."

"Liu has cooperated with us," Catherine said. "We could not have succeeded in persuading Wen without his help. They should have the chance to say good-bye."

"Not just that, Inspector Rohn. There is something further I need to discuss with Comrade Wen Liping," Chen said. "Let's move to the airport meeting room over there. We have to talk."

It was an oblong meeting room, elegantly furnished with a marble table and two rows of leather-covered chairs, where city officials met distinguished foreign guests during their brief, temporary stays in Shanghai. Catherine seated herself with Wen and Liu on one side of the table, Chen with his colleagues on the other. At the end of the meeting room, there was a small anteroom, in which the travelers could relax on the sectional sofas.

"Inspector Rohn, Party Secretary Li, Detective Yu, I apologize for having not discussed a new development with you," Chen said.

Catherine looked at Yu, and then at Li, and they both looked back at her in puzzlement. She noticed that Chen did not address Qian, who seemed to be fidgeting with his drink. Was it because Qian was just one of his low-level subordinates?

"Where were you last night?" Yu was the first to ask. "I waited for your call for hours."

"Well, my original plan was to bring Old Hunter with me to a meeting with Gu Haiguang, but Gu called me first and wanted to meet me alone, earlier. So I came to your dumpling feast early and then met with Gu."

"You did not tell me about this appointment," Catherine said.

"I had no clue as to what Gu was going to say. Then there

was no time to fill you in. I had Little Zhou drive me to Suzhou immediately. Liu had a late business meeting. I waited until he came home, spoke with him, and we started back before dawn. That's why we have just made it to the airport." Chen paused to take a breath, saying in a suddenly official tone. "Inspector Rohn, can you promise us one thing on behalf of the U.S. Marshals?"

"What's that, Chief Inspector Chen?"

"As soon as you arrive in the United States, relocate Wen and Feng. At once."

"That's what we planned, but why the urgency, Chief Inspector Chen?"

"Because the gangsters will make every attempt to harm Wen even after she joins Feng."

"Why?" Yu took out a cigarette.

"It's a long story. The Flying Axes learned about Feng's deal in the States early in January, weeks before Wen started to make her passport application. She preferred to stay in Fujian rather than go to live with him. But they coerced her into a conspiracy: she was to join Feng and then to poison him. They promised to get her out of trouble afterward. She agreed. Not because she hated Feng so much that she wanted to kill him, but because she knew what the gangsters would do to her if she refused.

"Now the situation is even more complicated," Chen went on, heedless of the effect of his revelation upon his audience. "Once she gets there, she will be in danger not only from the Flying Axes, but from the Green Bamboo as well. The latter have a branch in the United States. They present a very serious threat to her."

"What are you talking about?" Yu asked again. "What do these Green Bamboo have to do with anything?"

"The Green Bamboo is an international gang, far larger and more powerful than the Fujian-based Flying Axes. In their effort to extend their operations, and to take over the human smuggling operation in the Fujian area, they planned to extort crucial information from Feng by holding Wen as a hostage. In fact, it was the Green Bamboo, not the Flying Axes, that approached Feng in the United States. And they were the masked men who attacked us in Changle Village."

"How did you learn all this, Chief Inspector Chen?" Li said.

"I will explain everything in due course, Party Secretary Li," Chen said, turning to Wen. "Comrade Wen, I now understand why you changed your mind about the passport application, why you wanted to stay with Liu, and why you insisted on going back to Fujian. If you were going to the United States, you needed to bring with you the poison the Flying Axes had given you. You had left it behind when you fled on April fifth."

Wen did not utter a word but as Liu touched her shoulder lightly, she dropped her face into her hands and began to sob.

"Feng ruined your life. The gangsters gave you no choice. The local police did a poor job protecting you. You had to think of your baby," Chen continued. "Any woman in your position would have considered doing the same thing."

"But you cannot, Wen," Liu said in an emotional voice. "You must start a new life for yourself."

"Liu has done such a lot for you, Wen," Catherine interjected. "If you do something stupid, what will happen to him?"

Chen said, "I am not saying this to scare you, but you have stayed with him for a couple of weeks. People will suspect that you two planned it together. And Liu will be held responsible."

"I cannot see how Liu can keep out of trouble if anything happens to Feng." Yu added, "People must find somebody to punish."

"Nor can I see how the Flying Axes will be able to get you out of trouble afterward," Li joined in.

"They won't be able to," Qian said, speaking up the first time, like an echo.

"I'm sorry, Liu," Wen sobbed, clutching Liu's hand. "I did not think. I would rather die than get you into trouble."

"Let me tell you something about my Heilongjiang years," Liu said. "My life was a long tunnel without any light at the end. Thinking of you made the only difference. Thinking of you holding the red loyal character with me on the railway platform. A miracle. If that was possible, anything might be possible. So I hung on. And everything changed for me in 1976, at the end of the Cultural Revolution. Believe me: Things will change for you, too."

"As I promised you in Suzhou," Chen said, "nothing will happen to Liu as long as you cooperate with the Americans. Now, in the presence of Comrade Party Secretary Li, I'm making the same promise."

"Chief Inspector Chen is right," Li said with all sincerity. "As an old Bolshevik with forty years in the Party, I, too, give you my word. If you act properly, nothing will happen to Liu."

"Here is an English dictionary." Yu took out of his pants pocket a dog-eared book. "My wife and I were both educated youths. In Yunnan, I never dreamed that some day I would become a Shanghai cop speaking English with an American officer. Things change. Liu is right. Take the dictionary. You will have to speak English there."

"Thank you, Detective Yu." Liu accepted it for Wen. "It will be most helpful."

"Here is something else." Chen produced an envelope, which contained the picture of Wen leaving Shanghai as an educated youth, the picture used in the *Wenhui Daily*.

Catherine took it for Wen, who still had her face buried in her hands, sobbing inconsolably.

Twenty years earlier, at the railway station, a turning point in her life . . . Catherine gazed at the picture, and then at Wen. Now at the airport, another turning point in her life, but Wen was no longer the young, spirited Red Guard loyal character dancer looking forward to her future.

"One thing about the witness protection program," Catherine said quietly. "People can leave at their own risk. We do not recommend it. Still, things may change. In several years, when the triads have been wiped out. I may be able to discuss a new arrangement with Chief Inspector Chen."

Wen looked up through her tears, but she did not say anything. Instead, she reached into her purse, produced a small package, and handed it over to her. "Here is the stuff the Flying Axes gave me. You don't have to say more, Inspector Rohn."

"Thank you," Chen and Yu said, in chorus.

"Now that she has promised full cooperation with you," Liu said, casting a glance at the adjoining small room, "can we have some time for ourselves?"

"Of course." Catherine said promptly. "We'll wait here."

Chapter 37

After Wen and Liu had retired, Catherine Rohn turned to Chen, who made an apologetic gesture to the remaining people.

"Now, it's story time, Chief Inspector Chen," she said dryly. The latest development had surprised her, though probably less than his Chinese colleagues. During the last few days, she had more than once sensed something going on with the enigmatic chief inspector.

"This has been an extraordinary investigation, Party Secretary Li," Chen said. "I had to make decisions without being able to consult you or my colleagues, to act on my own responsibility. And I withheld some information because I was not sure of its relevance. So if you hear something you've not heard before, please be patient and let me explain."

Li said expansively. "You had to make such decisions under the circumstances. We all understand."

"Yes, we all understand," Catherine felt obliged to echo, but she decided to take the questioning into her own hands before it turned into a political lecture. "When did you become suspicious of Wen's intentions, Chief Inspector Chen?"

"I did not think about her motives at first. I assumed she was going to the United States because Feng wanted her to, it was obvious. But I was disturbed by a question you raised, the question about the delay in her passport application. So I looked into the process. It was slow, but there was also an inconsistency about the dates. In spite of Feng's claim that she started in early January, Wen did not do anything until mid-February."

"Yes, we discussed that briefly," she said.

"From Detective Yu's detailed report, I came to see a picture of her terrible life with Feng. From those interview tapes, I also learned that Feng called her quite a number of times in early January, and that on one occasion Wen was not willing to come to the phone. So I assumed that Wen was refusing to leave at that point."

"But Feng said she was most eager to join him."

"Feng did not tell you the truth. Too much loss of face for a man to admit his wife's reluctance," he said. "What caused her change of her mind? I checked with the Fujian police. They said they did not put any pressure on her. That I believed, considering their indifference throughout the investigation. And then I found something else in Detective Yu's report."

"What's that, Chief?" Detective Yu did not try to conceal the bafflement in his voice.

"Some of the villagers seemed to be aware of Feng's problem in the United States. Since the word they used—'problem'— could refer to anything, at first I thought that they might have gotten wind of Feng's fight in New York, for which he was arrested. But then Manager Pan used another word, saying he had heard of Feng's 'deal' with the Americans before her disappearance. 'Deal,' that's unmistakable. If that information was available to the villagers, I did not see why the gangsters would have waited so patiently until Inspector Rohn was on her way here. They could have abducted Wen earlier."

"And much more easily," Yu added. "Yes, I overlooked that."

"The gangsters had reasons for trying to beat us in the race for Wen. But as those accidents kept happening in Fujian and Shanghai, I started wondering. Why were they so desperate, all of a sudden? A lot of resources must have been tapped. And cops involved, too. After what happened in the Huating Market last Sunday, I became really suspicious."

"Last Sunday," Li said. "I suggested you take a day off, right?"

"Yes, we did," Catherine replied. "Chief Inspector Chen and I went shopping. There was a raid on the street market. Nothing happened to us." She equivocated, mindful of the fact that Party Secretary Li seemed surprised. "So you knew something then, Chief Inspector Chen?"

"No. I guessed, but things were not clear to me. To be honest, there are one or two things I do not grasp even today."

"Chief Inspector Chen did not want to make a false alarm, Inspector Rohn," Yu intervened hastily.

"I understand." She did not think it necessary for Yu to rush to defend his boss, who had raised valid alarms—not false ones. "Still—"

"The investigation has been full of twists and turns, Inspector Rohn. I'd better try to recapitulate chronologically. We each had our suspicions at various stages of the investigation, and discussed them. It was your observations that more than once threw light on the situation."

"You are being very diplomatic, Chief Inspector Chen."

"No, I am not. Do you remember our talk in the Verdant Willow Village? You called my attention to a fact: Despite Feng's request in his last phone call to Wen, she did not try to contact him when she reached an apparently safe place."

"Yes, that puzzled me, but I was not so sure then that she was in a safe place. That was the seventh or eighth day of her disappearance, I think, the day we had that discussion in the restaurant."

"Then in Deda Café, you convinced me that Gu knew something more than what he had told us. That prompted me to explore further in that direction."

"Oh no, I cannot take credit for that. At the club, you had already told Gu about your connection with the Traffic Control Office—" She stopped herself at a glance from Chen. Had he told Party Secretary Li about the parking lot deal? Or even the visit to the club?

"You did an excellent job in dealing with a man like Gu, Chief Inspector Chen," Li commented. " 'You have to fish for a golden turtle with a sweet-smelling bait.' "

"Thank you, Party Secretary Li," Chen said with surprise. "And then in the evening after the Beijing Opera, following your instruction, I walked Inspector Rohn back to the hotel. On our way, we had some drinks in Bund Park. There I mentioned the two cases I had been assigned to on the same day—the park victim case, and the search for Wen. She touched on the possible connection between the two. I had never thought about such a possibility until that evening. More importantly, she discussed the ax wounds on the body in connection with a Mafia novel, in which a murder was committed in such a way as to direct suspicion onto to a rival gang—"

"The ax wounds suggested a triad killing. It was a signature," Li cut in, "as Detective Yu pointed out at the outset."

"Yes, it's called the death by Eighteen Axes," Yu observed. "The highest form of punishment inflicted by the Flying Axes."

"That's true, and that's exactly what made me suspicious. Wasn't such a signature too obvious? So Inspector Rohn's comment started me thinking of another possibility. The victim in Bund Park could have been killed by somebody in deliberate imitation of the Flying Axes to cast the blame on them. As a result, the Flying Axes had to look into the matter and lose their focus on the search for Wen. Besides, muddying the water diverted the attention of the police, too. Under that hypothesis, who benefited? Someone with an even higher stake in the race to find Wen."

"I'm beginning to see, Chief Inspector Chen," Yu said.

"So you deserve the credit, Inspector Rohn. In spite of my suspicions, I was as puzzled as anybody else, unable to put the pieces together into a comprehensible whole. Your comments really helped."

"Thank you, Inspector Rohn. It's a marvelous example of the fruitful collaboration between the police forces of our two countries. Almost like the tai chi symbol, yin in perfect match with yang—" Li stopped abruptly, coughing with a hand against his mouth.

She understood. As a high-ranking Party official, Li had to be careful in his speech, even in using a seemingly harmless metaphor, which nevertheless crossed the line, due to the male and female elements suggested by the ancient symbol.

"I also got a call from Old Hunter that evening," Chen went on. "He told me that Gu had called to ask for information about a missing Fujianese. That was a surprise. Gu had told us about a mysterious visitor from Hong Kong. Why was Gu looking for a Fujianese? So that evening in Bund Park put me on the right track for the first time."

"The park is a lucky place for you," she said, "in accordance with the five-element theory. Little wonder, Chief Inspector Chen."

"Explain, Chief Inspector Chen?" Li asked.

Apparently Li did not know so much about Chen's life as she did, though the Party Secretary had hand-picked Chen as his successor.

"It's a joke made by my father, Party Secretary Li," Chen said. "Actually I had another idea that evening. Inspector Rohn happened to ask me about the two lines on my folding fan. Daifu's couplet. My thoughts flowed to the mysterious death of Daifu, and then back to the body in the park. It further supported the supposition that the body had been placed there to distract attention or to shift the blame, as I had suspected in Daifu's case."

"But you did not mention that to me, Chief Inspector Chen," she said.

"Well, these ideas did not coalesce until I got back home late that night. I dug out the poem in an attempt to recollect all the possibilities I had studied before writing it. As an unexpected result. I was able to recite those lines in Moscow Suburb the following day," he said with a smile. "No, it's not my favorite poem, Inspector Rohn, though it might have put me in a poetic mood at the Huating Market."

Party Secretary Li looked at Chen, and then at Catherine, before he broke into a broad smile. "That's how Chief Inspector Chen moves in his investigation—by leaps and bounds."

"As for what happened at the market, let me say a word about contingency. There's no better way to describe it. I happened to be there, together with Inspector Rohn. As she put it, it's a chain of seemingly irrelevant links. Daifu's couplet, a light green cellular phone, the rain, the line of Oriole's wet footprints, Su Dongpu's lines. So I thought of the poetry anthology left at Wen's home. If one link had been missing, we would not be sitting here at this moment."

She wondered whether his colleagues could follow this cryptic explanation. She happened to be there, but even she did not understand all his references. The light green cellular phone, for instance. He had never mentioned that before.

Yu made an obvious effort to refrain from asking questions. Qian remained respectfully self-effacing throughout. But Li appeared eager to season the discussion with political clichés.

"You have performed brilliant work in the glorious tradition of the Chinese police force, Chief Inspector Chen," Li declared, though perhaps he was still largely in the dark.

"I could not have made progress without the collaboration of Inspector Rohn, or the work of Detective Yu," Chen said earnestly. "In his interview with Zheng, for example, Detective Yu pushed for the clarification of a gangster's phrase—*She changed her mind*. What did he mean—changed her mind? That was a question I had in my mind while talking with Wen the following day."

"You kept a lot of questions to yourself, Chief Inspector Chen," Catherine said.

"I was not sure whether they were worth exploring, Inspector Rohn. After our visit to Wen, you asked me why I insisted on talking to Wen and Liu instead of bringing in the local police. For one thing, Wen's cup is full. I did not want to put too much pressure on her. But there's another reason. I tried to find some answers from my conversation with them."

"Did you find any?"

"Not from Liu, except that Wen had not told him anything. Then we both talked to Wen. What she said about her life in Fujian was true, but she did not say a single word about the gang's contact with her. Nor did she really answer my question about the delay in making her passport application. But what made me most suspicious was her insistence on going back to Fujian."

"Was that so suspicious?" Li asked. "A mother wanted to see her son's grave for the last time."

"Did she go to visit his grave when we were there? No. She did not even mention it. Back home, the first thing she did was to take a small package of chemicals from under the table. To keep as a souvenir, she explained to me. That might make sense, but the fact that she explained her action to me did not. It was her home. She could have taken anything she wanted without comment. On the way, she had said little, and now she was volunteering explanations."

"That's true," she said, "Wen hardly said anything during the trip."

"After the battle in the village, she could have paid a visit to the grave, but she still didn't. It no longer seemed important to her. Then I happened to hear one of the local policeman silence a wounded gangster speaking Mandarin. That was strange. Before I had time to inquire, however, Superintendent Hong's request for elucidation of a proverb diverted my attention."

"The Chinese proverb about justice eventually overcoming evil," she said.

"Exactly. So it was not until we reached the airport, and heard the flight announcement in both Mandarin and Fujian dialects, that I realized what I had overlooked. The Flying Axes is a local gang. How come the wounded gangster spoke Mandarin? I decided not to stop to investigate because my top priority was to get Wen and you safely back to Shanghai."

"That was the right decision, Chief Inspector Chen." Li nodded.

"The moment I got back to Shanghai, I talked to Old Hunter, who had gathered information on Gu. I also had a discussion with Meiling. The parking lot could legally be granted to the club, according to her research. Then I went to meet Gu. At first Gu did not put much on the table, so I laid out my cards and Gu turned cooperative."

Catherine stole a glance at Li, wondering whether Chen had discussed everything with his boss.

"Yes, you had to open the door to the mountain," Li said.

"According to Gu, the victim in Bund Park was a liaison head of the Flying Axes, surnamed Ai. Ai came to Shanghai to look for Wen. He paid a formal visit to the Eldest Brother of the Blue, who was against a chicken-flying-and-dog-barking search in the city. As long as Wen was not in police hands, the Eldest Brother saw no danger for Jia Xinzhi. So Ai had no choice but to disclose the real plan of the Flying Axes—the plan to have Wen poison her husband once she had joined him. With a stinking rat like Feng, the Fujian gang considered it in their best interests to get rid of him once for all. The Green Bamboo learned of the plan. They need Feng alive; they want Jia eliminated. And they murdered Ai."

"How did Gu get all this information?" Yu asked.

"The Eldest Brother of the Blue was upset that without his permission, Ai had brought Fujian problems to Shanghai. But then what the Green Bamboo did—planting Ai's body in Bund Park—was even worse. So Gu learned from the Eldest Brother not only about the Green Bamboo, but about the Flying Axes as well. The moment I had all this from Gu, I decided to go to

Suzhou. Wen was determined that if she had to go to the United States, she would kill Feng. I did not think I could change her mind. If there was anyone capable of doing that, it would be Liu. Liu agreed to accompany me here. That was early this morning."

"You made the right decision, Chief Inspector Chen," Li said, loud with official approval. "As one of our old sayings goes, 'When a general fights on the borders, he does not have to listen to the emperor all the time.' "

It was then that a phone started ringing in the meeting room. Qian produced his cell phone in embarrassment. With his hand cupped over the receiver he hurriedly said, "I'll call you later."

"A light green cell phone. Almost bamboo-colored. It's a rarity," Chen said deliberately. "The only other one of the same color I have ever seen was in the Huating Market."

"It's a coincidence." Qian seemed to be flustered.

"That could explain all suspicious incidents," Chen said.

There had been many coincidences during the course of the investigation, Catherine reflected, but she did not know what Chen was hinting at.

"There's no telling what people are capable of—" Chen paused emphatically, looking directly at Qian.

"Indeed, there's no telling what people are capable of doing." Li quickly joined in and shook his head sadly. "Imagine Wen getting involved in such a murderous scheme!"

"I want to say something on behalf of Wen—in the light of the revelation made by Chief Inspector Chen." Catherine spoke with a passion surprising to herself. "The Flying Axes had left her no choice. So she started applying for her passport, but I don't think she was necessarily going to carry out their plan. When she arrived in the United States, she might have tried to seek help from the American police."

"That's what I think, too," Yu said, nodding.

"But when Feng telephoned to warn her to run for her life, she was panic-stricken. Who were the 'people' referred to in the message? The Flying Axes? If so, had Feng discovered the plot? She fled, but after ten days in Liu's company, she was resurrected—as a woman."

"Resurrected! That's the very word Liu used," Chen said.

Catherine said, "After all those wasted years, she suddenly had hopes. She looked so changed from the woman in that passport picture. Alive, I mean. I could hardly recognize her in Suzhou. When she realized that she had to leave Liu, she could not bear the thought of living with Feng anymore. The realization of how Feng had ruined her life filled her with hatred. And a desire for vengeance, too. That was why she insisted on going back to Changle Village. She wanted to get the poison she had left there. This time she was determined."

"I agree," Yu said. "This also proves that she did not want to carry out the gang's plan at first. She did not take the poison with her when she left the village on April fifth. Thank you, Inspector Rohn."

"Inspector Rohn has summed up that part well. And the rest of it," Chen said, taking a drink of his water, "you learned when Wen was in the room."

"A wonderful job, Chief Inspector Chen!" Li clapped his hands. "The American Consul has called the city government, expressing thanks, but he did not know what a great job you have done."

"I could have done nothing without your firm support throughout the investigation, Party Secretary Li."

She could see Chen was more than willing to let Li share the laurels. After conducting such an unorthodox investigation, the chief inspector had to be diplomatic.

"If we were not already at the airport, we would have a grand banquet to celebrate this successful conclusion," Li said with warmth. "Indeed, all's well that ends well."

"I'll make a report to our government, Party Secretary Li, about the outstanding work of the Shanghai Police Bureau," she said before turning to Chen. "In the meantime, I would like to ask you a few more questions, Chief Inspector Chen, over a cup of coffee. Last night, I worked quite late writing up my case summary. You must also be worn out after spending the night traveling."

"Now that you mention it," Chen said.

"Yes, you two go to the airport café. It's the bureau's farewell treat." Li was all smiles. "We will keep an eye on Wen."

Chapter 38

It was not exactly a café, but a corner partitioned off from the waiting area by metal posts and plastic cords. There were several tables and chairs, and a counter sporting an array of imported coffees. A waitress stood near the tall window framing the airplanes on the runway.

"Black coffee?" Catherine asked.

"Tea for me today," Chen said.

"Can we have tea?" she said in Chinese to the waitress.

"Lipton?" The waitress said in English.

"No. Chinese green tea. With the tea leaves in the cup."

"Sure." The waitress gave them a stainless thermos bottle with two cups and a small bag of tea leaves.

As they moved toward a table, Chen cast a glance in the direction of the meeting room. His colleagues sat behind the glass door, watching over Wen and Liu. There were a number of plainclothes men stationed around the area. He was not concerned with the airport's security.

He experienced a deflation of mood as he seated himself at the table. In the meeting room, he had had to persuade Wen, and then to explain his decisions to others. He'd had to worry about the reaction of Party Secretary Li—with Internal Security prowling in the background. To his relief, Li had reacted positively, though Chen knew that this reaction in the presence of Inspector Rohn was not something to be relied upon.

Now, sitting with her, he did not feel the satisfaction of a detective in a mystery story at the successful conclusion of a case. He might have done his job—a "wonderful job"—according to Party Secretary Li. Yet was it wonderful for Wen? Her life in China was coming to an end, a chapter closing with a tragic climax. And her life in the United States was nothing to look forward to.

What role had he played in bringing about this result? Chief Inspector Chen could make all the convenient excuses for himself, of course, that 'Eight or nine out of ten times, things go wrong in this world,' or that 'It's nothing but the ironic causality of misplaced yin and yang.' There was no denying the fact, however, that he had done his part in sending a helpless woman to live with the rogue who had ruined her life.

And what could he do about the gangs? Any major move against an international organization like the Green Bamboo had to be decided upon, in Party Secretary Li's words, after careful review of political considerations. The body in the park had been identified, but what then? The information from Gu about the power of the triads and their operation would be easily dismissed. Li had said that they should celebrate the successful conclusion of the matter. 'All's well that ends well.' The message was clear: there would be no further investigation of the gangs. Chen was in no position to do anything about it.

Nor was Chen in a position to be elated about his remaining work.

There was something never to be done, like a probe into corruption in the Fujian police or an inquiry into the source of Qian's cell phone. There was something to be done, but never mentioned, like the parking lot deal for the karaoke club. And there was something perhaps never to be thought of, like the higher authorities' possible involvement.

And he wondered whether Internal Security would choose to disappear at the conclusion of the case.

Inspector Rohn was carefully putting green tea leaves into the white cups, pinchful by pinchful, like a Chinese, as if concentrating on something far more important than the questions she was going to ask.

As on the day when she first arrived, sitting in the car, so on the day she was going to leave, sitting in the café, he did not know what she was thinking.

She picked up the thermos bottle, poured an arc of water into a cup for him, and then prepared another cup for herself.

"I like the Chinese way of drinking tea, watching the leaves leisurely unfolding, so green, so tender in the white cup."

He gazed at her as she sipped her tea. For a second, she was merging into another woman, one who had accompanied him in another teahouse, in Beijing. She, too, had looked pale, with black circles under her eyes revealed in a flood of sunlight, with a green tea leaf in her white teeth.

The tenderness of the tea leaf between her lips. / Everything's possible, but not pardonable . . .

"Li is not behaving like a Party Secretary today," she said, meeting his gaze. "To encourage his hand-picked successor to have a tête-à-tête with an American officer!"

"I don't know how you get your information, but that is just like Party Secretary Li—politically correct, but not to a fault."

"So you will be like him one of those days?"

"No one can tell, you know that."

"I know. What will happen to you, Chief Inspector Chen?" She gazed into her cup. "I mean, when will your next promotion be?"

"That depends on a lot of unforseeable factors, factors beyond my control."

"You're a political rising star, you cannot help yourself."

"Do we have to talk about politics until you take off?"

"No, we don't, but we live in politics, like it or not. That's one of the modernist theories you have lectured me on, Chief Inspector Chen. I'm learning the Chinese way fast."

"You are being sarcastic, Catherine," he said, trying to change the subject. "Ten days here will be enough. I hope, to keep up your interest in Chinese studies."

"Yes, I'll go on with my Chinese studies. Perhaps I'll take some evening courses this year."

He had expected she would ask more questions about the investigation. She was entitled to, but she did not.

Actually, there were some things he had chosen not to disclose in the meeting room. For one, he had learned from Gu that the gangsters had been instructed not to carry guns while following the chief inspector and his American partner. According to Gu, because of Chen's connections at the highest level, the gangsters did not want to make an enemy of him. Then, too, the Beijing government would never let the matter drop if an American marshal was killed in China. This might also explain a common aspect of the earlier accidents, which, though serious, had not been intended to be fatal. Not even the shot fired at Yu.

Putting down her cup, she took a picture out of her purse. "I have something for you."

It showed a young girl sitting at a table in a sidewalk café, playing a guitar, her shoulder-length hair shining in the sunlight, her sandals dangling over a brass plaque on the sidewalk.

He recognized her. "It's you, Catherine."

"Yes, five or six years ago, at a café on Delmar. Do you see the brass plaque? There are more than a dozen there, like in Hollywood, except that these honor celebrities associated with St. Louis. Including T. S. Eliot, of course."

"Is that one of the celebrity plaques?"

"Eliot's," she said. "Sorry, I did not mean any disrespect to your favorite poet."

"No, he would have liked it—a beautiful girl weaving the sunlight in her hair, singing, dangling her sandals over his memorial."

"I asked my mother to dig out the picture and send it to me. It's the only one connecting me to him."

"What a lovely picture!"

"Someday you may be sitting there, talking about Eliot, stirring memories with a coffee spoon, when the evening is spread out against the sky."

"I would like that."

"That's a promise, Chief Inspector Chen. You are on the invitation list of the U. S. News Agency, aren't you?" she said. "Keep the picture. When you think of T. S. Eliot, you may think of me, too—occasionally."

"I will not think of Eliot as often as—" he stopped short. He would be crossing the line. It was forbidden. Abruptly he envisioned himself, as Eliot put it, *hearing the mermaids singing, each to each, but not to him,* as he walked in Bund Park.

"And I look forward to reading more of your poems, in English or in Chinese."

"I tried to work out some lines last night, but sitting beside Liu in the car, I realized what a lousy poet I am—And a lousy cop too."

"Why are you so hard on yourself?" She took his hand across the table. "You are doing your best in a difficult situation. I understand."

But there was a lot she might not understand. He did not make an immediate response.

She continued, "Did you tell Party Secretary Li about the parking lot deal with Gu?"

"No, I didn't." He had anticipated this question. Li had shown no surprise at his dealing with Gu. It appeared as if Li had known about it.

How deeply was Li connected with the Blue? As the number-one police official responsible for the security of the city, Party Secretary Li might have had to maintain some sort of working relationship with the local triad. In the Party's newspapers, the slogan, "political stability," was still emphasized as the highest priority after the eventful summer of 1989. But he seemed to be more deeply involved.

"What about Qian's light green cell phone?" she said. "I did not remember seeing one in the market."

"When you were behind the fitting room curtain, I saw someone dialing a cell phone of the same unusual color."

A melody was being played in the bar. It was another song that had been popular during the Cultural Revolution. Chen failed to remember its words except for one refrain—"*We shall be beholden to Chairman Mao, generation after generation.*" He shook his head.

"What is it?"

"Just the song." He was relieved at the change of topic.

"There is a revival of those popular songs from the time of the Cultural Revolution. This one's a Red Guard song. Wen could have danced the loyal character dance to it."

"Do people miss those songs?"

"They appeal to people, I think, not because of their contents, but they were part of people's lives—for ten years."

"Which holds meaning for them, the melody or their memories?" she said, subtly echoing the line he had recited for her in the Suzhou garden.

"I don't have the answer," he said, thinking of another question that had just come up in their conversation.

Was he himself a loyal character dancer, in a different time and place?

He'd better turn in a report to Minister Huang now. He was not yet sure what exactly to say. At this stage of his career, it might be best for him to show his loyalty directly to the Beijing ministry, circumventing Party Secretary Li.

"What are you thinking about, Chief Inspector Chen?"

"Nothing."

They heard Party Secretary Li calling to them from a distance, "Comrade Chief Inspector Chen, boarding in ten minutes."

Li was walking toward the café, pointing at the new information displayed on the screen above the gate.

"I'm coming," he responded before he turned back to her. "I have something for you too, Inspector Rohn. When Liu did his shopping for Wen on the way to the airport, I chose a fan and copied several lines on it."

Long, long I lament
there is not a self for me to claim,
oh, when can I forget
all the cares of the world?
The night deep, the wind still, no ripples on the river.

"Your lines?"

"No, Su Dongpu's."

"Can you recite the poem for me?"

"No, I cannot remember the rest of the poem. These few lines alone came to me."

"I'll find the poem in a library. Thank you, Chief Inspector Chen." She stood up, folding the fan.

"Hurry up. Please. It's time," Party Secretary Li urged.

The line of passengers started moving through the gate.

"Hurry up." Qian was now at Li's side, holding that light green cell phone in his hand.

Wen and Liu stood at the end of the newly formed line, holding each other's hand.

It would be Chief Inspector Chen's responsibility to separate the two, and to send Wen through the gate.

And Inspector Rohn, too.

Along with a part of himself, he thought, though he might have lost it long ago, perhaps as early as those mornings on the dew-decked green bench in Bund Park.